Irwin Shaw

TWO WEEKS IN ANOTHER TOWN

Random House
New York

First Printing

© Copyright, 1960, by Irwin Shaw

All rights reserved under International and Pan-American Copyright
Conventions. Published in New York by Random House, Inc., and
simultaneously in Toronto, Canada, by Random House of Canada, Limited.

Library of Congress Catalog Card Number: 60–5560

Manufactured in the United States of America
by H. Wolff Book Mfg. Co., Inc.

The great elephant has by nature qualities which are rarely found in man, namely honesty, prudence, a sense of justice, and of religious observance. Consequently, when the moon is new they go down to the rivers and there solemnly cleansing themselves bathe, and after having thus saluted the planet they return to the woods.

*

They fear shame and only pair at night and secretly, nor do they then rejoin the herd but first bathe in the river.

Leonardo da Vinci,
after Pliny.

TWO WEEKS
IN ANOTHER
TOWN

1

It was a gray, cold day, without wind. By nightfall, it would rain. Above the airport, in the wintry cover of cloud, there was the spasmodic engine-whine of unseen planes. Although it was early afternoon all the lights in the restaurant were on. The plane from New York had been delayed and the echoing voice had announced in French and English over the public-address system that the flight for Rome had been put back by a half-hour.

The usual gloom of airports, that mixture of haste and apprehension which has become the atmosphere of travel, because nobody waits comfortably for the take-off of an airplane, was intensified by the weather. The neon light made everyone look poor and unwell and suffering from lack of sleep. There was a feeling in the room that if each traveler there had the choice to make over again he would cancel his passage and go by boat or train or automobile.

In a corner of the restaurant, whose tables were decked with the sad little banners of the companies that flew out of Orly, a man and woman waited, drinking coffee, watching the two small children, a boy and a girl, who were plastered against the big window that overlooked the field. The man was big, with a long bony face. He had rough dark hair neatly brushed back, in a style that was somewhat longer than crew-cut, and there was a little sprinkle of gray that could be seen only from close up. His eyes were deep-set and blue under heavy eyebrows, and his eyelids were heavy and guarded, making him seem reserved and observant and giving him an air of cool, emotionless judgment as he looked out at the world. He moved slowly and carefully, like a man who would be more comfortable out of doors, in old clothes, and who had been constrained for many years to live in enclosed places that were just a little too narrow for him. His skin was incongruously pale, the result of winter living in a gray city. The air of patience and good humor that his face wore seemed to have been applied that day under considerable pressure. From a little distance, these small modifications were not evident, and he looked bold, healthy, and easygoing. The woman was in her early thirties, with a pretty figure pleasantly displayed by a modest gray suit. She had short black hair swept back in the latest fashion, and her large gray eyes in the white triangle of her face were accented cleverly by make-up. There was a secret elegance in her manner, a way of sitting very erect, of moving definitely and cleanly, without flourishes, a sense of crispness about her clothes, the tone of crispness in her voice. She was French and looked it, Parisienne and looked it, with a composed, reasonable sensuality constantly at play in her face, mixed with decision and a conscious ability to handle the people surrounding her with skill and tact. The two children were mannerly and neat, and if the family were not examined too closely, they made the sort of group that advertising men like to use, all subjects smiling widely, in color, on a sunny field, to demonstrate the safety and pleasure of travel by air. But the sun hadn't shone on Paris in six days, the neon restaurant light debased every surface it touched, and, at the moment, no one was smiling.

The children tried to clear away a part of the window, which was streaked and steamy. Through it the planes looked blurred and aquatic on the apron and runways.

"That's a Vee-count," the boy said to his sister. "It's a turbo-prop."

"Viscount," the man said. "That's the way it's pronounced in

English, Charlie." He had a voice, low and reverberating, that went with his size.

"Viscount," the boy said obediently. He was five years old. He was grave and dressed with formality for the departure of his father.

The woman smiled. "Don't worry," she said. "By the time he's twenty-one, he'll learn to stick to one language at a time." She spoke English swiftly, with a trace of a French accent.

The man smiled absently at her. He had tried to come to the airport alone. He didn't like the prolonged ceremonies of leave-taking. But his wife had insisted upon driving him out and bringing the children. "They love to see the planes," she had said, supporting her action. But the man suspected that she had come with the hope that at the last moment, in the presence of them all, he would change his mind and call the trip off. Or, at the worst, with the sentimental view of the three of them, the pretty mother and the two handsome small children at her side to tug at his memory, he would hurry his trip and cut it as short as possible.

He drank his bitter coffee and looked impatiently at his watch. "I hate airports," he said.

"I do, too," the woman said. "Half the time. I love arrivals." She reached out and touched his hand. Feeling obscurely blackmailed, he took her hand in his and squeezed it. God, he thought, I'm in a filthy mood.

"It's only for a little while," he said. "I'll be back soon enough."

"Not soon enough," she said. "Never soon enough."

"When I grow up," Charlie was saying, "I am only going to travel in *avions à réaction*."

"Jets, Charlie," the man said automatically.

"Jets," the boy said, without turning away from the window.

I must be careful, the man thought. He'll grow up with the idea that I nag him continually. It's not his fault he speaks half in French all the time.

"I can't blame you," his wife said, "for being so eager to leave Paris in this weather."

"I'm not so eager," said the man. "It's just that I have to go."

"Of course," said his wife. He had been married to her long enough to know that when she said Of course like that, she did not mean of course.

"It's a lot of money, Hélène," he said.

"Yes, Jack," she said.

"I don't like airplanes," the little girl said. "They take people away."

"Of course," said the little boy. "That's what they're for. Silly."

"I don't like airplanes," the little girl said.

"It's more than four months' salary," Jack said. "We'll be able to get a new car, finally. And go to a decent place for once this summer."

"Of course," she said.

He drank some of his coffee and looked once more at his watch.

"It's just unfortunate," she said, "that it had to come just at this time."

"This is the time he needs me," Jack said.

"Well, you're a better judge of that than I am."

"What do you mean by that?"

"I don't mean anything. All I meant was that you know better than I do. I don't even know the man. I've heard you talk about him from time to time, but that's all. Only . . ."

"Only what?"

"Only if you're as close as you say you are . . ."

"Were."

"Were. It's funny that all these years, he's never bothered to see you."

"This is the first time he's ever been in Europe. I told you . . ."

"I know you told me," she said. "But he's been in Europe more than six months. And he didn't even bother to write you till last week . . ."

"It goes too far back for me to try to explain," Jack said.

"Daddy"—the boy turned away from the window toward his father—"were you ever in a plane that caught fire?"

"Yes," Jack said.

"What happened?"

"They put the fire out."

"That was lucky," the boy said.

"Yes."

The boy turned back to his sister. "Daddy was in a plane that caught fire," he said, "but he didn't die."

"Anne called just this morning," Hélène said, "and said Joe was in an ugly mood about your taking off just now."

Joe Morrison was Jack's boss and Anne was his wife. Anne Morrison and Hélène were close friends.

"I told Joe last week I wanted some time off. I have a lot coming to me. He said it was okay with him."

"But then this conference came up, and he said he needed you," Hélène said, "and Anne said you were very stiff with Joe about it."

"I'd promised I'd go to Rome. They're depending on me."

"Joe depends on you, too," Hélène said.

"He'll have to get on without me for a couple of weeks."

"You know how Joe is about loyalty," Hélène said.

Jack sighed. "I know how Joe is about loyalty," he said.

"He's had men transferred for less than this," Hélène said. "We're liable to find ourselves in Ankara or Iraq or Washington next September."

"Washington," Jack said, in mock horror. "Heavens."

"Would you want to live in Washington?"

"No," Jack said.

"When I am eighteen," the boy said, "I am going to traverse *la barrière de son.*"

"I'm going to tell you something," Hélène said. "You're not sorry to be going. I've watched you the last three days. You're *eager* to go."

"I'm eager to make the money," Jack said.

"It's more than that."

"I'm also eager to help Delaney," Jack said, "if I *can* help him."

"It's more than that, too," she said. Her face was sad. Resigned, beautiful and sad, he thought. "You're eager to leave me, too. Us." With a gloved hand, she indicated the children.

"Now, Hélène . . ."

"Not for good. I don't mean that," she said. "But now. For a while. Even at the risk of getting Joe Morrison angry with you."

"I won't comment on that," he said wearily.

"You know," she said, "you haven't made love to me for more than two weeks."

"This is why I don't like people to come to see me off at airports. Conversations like this."

"People," she said.

"You."

"In the old days," she went on, her voice sweet and sober and without criticism, "before you went off on a trip, you'd make love to me the last half-hour before you left. After the bags were packed and all. Do you remember that?"

"I remember that."

"I like Air France better," the boy said. "Blue is a faster color."

"Do you still love me?" Hélène asked in a low voice, leaning over the table toward him and looking searchingly into his face.

He stared at her. Objectively, without emotion, he realized that she was very beautiful, with her wide gray eyes and the high bones of her cheeks and the rich dark hair cut short and girlishly on her neat head. But at the moment, he didn't love her. At the moment, he thought, I don't love anybody. Except for the two children. And that was almost automatic. Although not completely automatic. He had three children and of those he loved only these two. Two out of three. A respectable average.

"Of course I love you," he said.

She smiled a little. She had a charming, young girl's smile, trusting and expectant. "Come back in better shape," she said.

Then the voice in French and English announced that the passengers were begged to pass through Customs, the plane for Rome, flight number 804, was ready and was loading. Gratefully, Jack paid the bill, kissed the children, kissed his wife, and started off.

"Enjoy yourself, *chéri*," Hélène said, standing there, flanked by the little boy and the blond, slender girl in her red coat. At the last moment, he thought, she has managed to make it sound as though I am going on a holiday.

Jack hurried past the customs, and out on the wet tarmac toward the waiting plane. The other passengers were already climbing the ramp in a flurry of boarding cards, magazines, coats, and canvas hand baggage marked with the name of the air line.

As the plane taxied off toward the starting point on the runway, he saw his wife and children, outside the restaurant now, waving, their coats bright swabs of color in the gray afternoon.

He waved through the window, then settled back in his seat, relieved. It could have been worse, he thought, as the plane gathered speed for the take-off.

*

"It's time for tea," the stewardess said, her voice decorated with air-line charm.

"What kind of cake do you have, my dear?" asked the little old lady on her way to Damascus.

"Cherry tart," said the stewardess.

"We are now passing over Mont Blanc," the public-address system announced in the tones of Texas. "If you look through the windows on the raght you will see the ee-ternal snows."

"I'll have a cherry tart and a bourbon on the rocks," said the little old lady. She was on the left side of the plane and she didn't get up to see Mont Blanc. "That makes a nice little tea." She giggled, on her way to Damascus from Portland, Oregon, daring to do things at an altitude of twenty-five thousand feet that she would never do in Portland, Oregon.

"Would you like something, Mr. Andrus?" The stewardess tilted her smile in the direction of Mont Blanc.

"No, thank you," Jack said. He had wanted a whisky, but when he heard the little old lady ask for bourbon he had had a small ascetic flicker of revulsion against the continual senseless ingestion of air travel.

He looked down at the white slab of Mont Blanc, couched on cloud, surrounded by the stone teeth of the lesser peaks. He put on his dark glasses and peered at the sunlit snow, looking for the broken helicopter in which the two climbers had been left to die when the storm had risen and the guides and the crashed airman who had come to their rescue had had to make their way to the refuge hut to save themselves. He couldn't see the helicopter. The Alps moved slowly below him, peaks shifting behind peaks, deep blue shadows and a huge round, thin sun, like an afternoon in the Ice Age, with no dead visible.

He pulled the curtains and sat back and reflected on the events that had so surprisingly put him on this plane. He had known that Maurice Delaney was in Rome, from reading the papers, but he hadn't heard from him for five or six years and it was with a sense of disbelief that he had heard the voice of Delaney's wife, Clara, on the crackling connection a week before, from Rome.

"Maurice can't get to the phone just now," Clara had said, after the preliminary explanations were over, "but he's writing you a letter telling just what the situation is. He wants you to come down here right away, Jack. You're the only man who can help him, he says. He's desperate. These people down here are driving him crazy. He's got them to agree to give you five thousand dollars for the two weeks— Is that enough?"

Jack laughed.

"Why're you laughing?"

"Private joke, Clara."

"He's depending upon you, Jack. What'll I tell him?"

"Tell him I'll do everything I can to come. I'll send a wire tomorrow."

The next day Morrison had said he could spare Jack for two weeks and Jack had sent the wire.

The letter that had come from Delaney had outlined what Delaney wanted Jack to do for him. It was so little, and in Jack's eyes so comparatively unimportant, that it was inconceivable to him that anyone would pay him five thousand dollars just for that. Delaney, he was sure, had other reasons for asking Jack to come to Rome, reasons that Delaney would divulge in his own time.

Meanwhile, Jack leaned back luxuriously in the first-class seat that was being paid for by the company, and thought with satisfaction of being away from the routine of his job and the routine of his marriage for two weeks.

He looked forward to seeing Delaney, who, long ago, had been his best friend, and whom he had loved. Whom I still love, he corrected himself. Aside from everything else, Jack thought, trouble or not, anything involved with Maurice Delaney won't be routine.

He loosened his collar, to make himself more comfortable. In doing so his hand touched the bulk of the letter in his inside pocket. He made a grimace of distaste. I'd better do it now, he thought. In Rome I probably won't have the time.

He reached into the inside pocket of his jacket and took out the letter that he had read three times in the last two days. Before rereading it again, he stared gloomily at the envelope, addressed to him in the artificially elegant finishing-school orthography of his first wife. Three wives, he thought, and two of them are giving me trouble. Two out of three. Today's recurring ratio. He sighed and took the letter out of the envelope and began to read it.

"Dear Jack," he read, "I imagine you are surprised to hear from me after all this time, but it's a question that involves you or should involve you as much as it does me, since Steve is your son as well as mine, even though you haven't taken much interest in him all these years, and what he does with his life should be of *some* concern to you." Jack sighed again when he came to the ironic underlining. The years had not improved his first wife's prose style. "I have done everything humanly possible to influence Steve and have nearly brought myself to the edge of a nervous breakdown in the process, and William, who at all times has been most loving and correct and tolerant with Steve, more so than most real fathers I have seen, has also done his best to make him change his mind. But Steve, since the earliest days, has exhibited only the utmost, iciest scorn for William's opinions, and no amount of reasoning on my part has been able to improve his behavior." Jack grinned malevolently as he read this passage, then went on. "When Steve came back after visiting you in Europe last summer, he spoke of you more favorably, or, anyway, less unfavorably than of most people he knows . . ." Jack smiled again, wryly this time. ". . . and it occurred to me that at this moment of crisis, maybe you are the one to write to him and try to put him straight.

"I don't like to burden you, but the problem has become too much for me. In the last few months, in Chicago, Steve has fallen under the spell of a terrible girl by the name of McCarthy, and now he says he is going to marry her. The girl is twenty years old, a nobody, from an absolutely nondescript family, without a penny to their name. As you can tell from the name, she is Irish, and I suppose was born a Catholic, although like Steve, and all his other friends, she just laughs ironically when the subject of religion comes up. Steve, as you know, is completely dependent upon the goodness of William for whatever money he gets, outside the bare minimum you send for his tuition and board and lodging at the University. I just can't see William handing over enough money to a boy, who is, after all not his son, and who has openly showed his scorn of him since he was five years old, to set up housekeeping with a silly little coed he picked up at a dance somewhere, and I must say, I don't blame him."

Once more Jack found himself puzzling over the rich confusion of his first wife's syntax, although the general idea was all too clear.

"What's worse," the letter went on, "the girl is one of those rabid little intellectuals of the kind we both knew in the thirties, full of half-baked provocative ideas and rebellious opposition to authority. She has infected Steve and has led him into some very dangerous activities. He is the president of some sort of group which is constantly agitating against H-bomb experiments and signing all sorts of petitions all the time and generally making himself very unpopular with the authorities. Until this came up, Steve was doing marvelously, as you know, at the University, and was practically assured a research fellowship after he had taken his Ph.D. Now, I understand, they are beginning to have doubts about him and he has been warned once or twice by older men in the department, although you can guess how he responded to that, especially with that girl egging him on. What's more, as a straight A student, he's been deferred from the draft until now, as a matter of course, but he's threatening to list himself as a Conscientious Objector. You can just about imagine what that will do to him. He's at a crucial point in his life now and if he persists in marrying this girl and in his idiotic political activities, it will mean absolute ruin for him.

"I don't know what you can do, but if you have any love left for your son or any desire to see him happy, you will at least try to do *some*thing. Even a letter might help, coming from you.

"I'm sorry that the first communication from me in so many years is such a disturbing one, but I don't know where else to turn.

As ever,

Julia."

Jack held the letter in his hand, watching the pages vibrate gently with the throbbing of the plane. *As ever,* he thought. What does she mean by that? As ever false, as ever foolish, as ever incompetent, as ever pretentious? If the "as ever" was an accurate description of herself, it was no wonder Steve didn't listen to her.

Jack asked the stewardess for some stationery and, when it came, set about composing a letter to his son. "Dear Steve," he wrote, then hesitated, as a vision of his son's cold, narrow, intelligent young face interposed between him and the paper on his knees. Steve had visited him and Hélène the summer before, handsome, aloof, taciturn, observant. He had spoken surprisingly good French for a boy who had never been in France before, he had been polite with them all, had drunk, Jack noticed gratefully, very little, had explained in simple terms what his thesis was going to be about, had made Jack vaguely uncomfortable, and then had disappeared toward Italy with two friends from Chicago. It had been an edgy time, although there had been no incidents, and Jack had been relieved when Steve had suddenly announced his departure. Jack had not been able to love the boy, as, rather foolishly, he had hoped he might, and Steve himself had been merely proper, not loving. He had gone off toward Italy leaving Jack with an uneasy sense of guilt, of opportunities lost, of dissatisfaction with his son and himself and with the course his life had taken.

Now, here he was, high over the bony white spine of Europe, committed to writing a letter that must be loving and tactful, and helpful and instructive, to that taciturn cold young man who was, as his mother pointed out, ruining his life in Chicago.

"Dear Steve," he wrote, "I've just received a disturbing letter from your mother. She's worried about you, and from what I can tell from here, justifiably so. There isn't much sense in my going through all the reasons why a young man of 22, without any money, and with all his way to make in the world, should not marry. I, myself, married early, and you should know better than anyone how disastrously it turned out. There is a Greek saying, 'Only a foolish man marries young and only a foolish woman marries old,' and from my experience, I would say that the first half, at least, of the adage is all too correct. I would wait if I were you, at least until you're through with your studies and established somewhere. Marriage has crippled more young men than alcohol. If you're ambitious, as I think you are, you will finally be grateful to me if you heed this advice."

Jack looked up from the letter. He was suddenly conscious that the little old lady across the aisle was staring intently at him. He turned his head and smiled at her. Embarrassed, she looked quickly out the window on her side.

"Your mother also writes," Jack continued, "that you are endangering your future by certain political activities in the University. Perhaps you are justified in your opinions and probably you feel very strongly that you have to express them, but you must realize that for a young man today who intends to pursue a career as a nuclear physicist, either as an experimenter or teacher, or both, open opposition to the government's policies can only be dangerous. The government of the United States today is under a continuing strain and the men who run the government (which, as you know as well as anyone, is now involved in a great deal of the research and financing of the work in your chosen field) are fretful and suspicious. The government also has a long memory and is not hesitant about using its powers to put pressure on organizations, or people, who might be inclined to hire a man who attacked its position at such a vulnerable and controversial point. Here again, as in the idea of marriage, it might be wise to wait quietly for a while, until you are less dangerously exposed, before taking any irrevocable steps. Just from the viewpoint of practical accomplishment, you might consider whether your protest now, the protest of an untried young man, would serve any real purpose, or merely expose you to the punishments which the system is perfectly prepared and willing to hand out. It is not necessary, Steve, as young people are likely to believe, to say everything that comes to your mind, openly and with complete disregard for the consequences. Strategy and tact need not be taken for submission. It is only recently that reticence has come to be thought of as a flaw of character . . ."

He reread what he had written. Lord Chesterfield to his son, he thought with disgust. I have been writing too many speeches for generals. If I really loved him, this letter would be entirely different.

"Let me try to express what I feel more completely," he wrote. "It is not that I do not understand why you are aghast at the prospect of more nuclear explosions, another war. I, too, am aghast, and would like to see the experiments halted, the war avoided. I realize that it is because men on both sides are bankrupt of fruitful ideas that the experiments continue, the threat of war is not laid. But even bankrupts have the right to try to survive, under whatever terms are open to them. What we Americans are doing is perhaps dictated by a bankrupt's policy of survival, but who has offered us a better policy? I am involved with our present policy, and while I am not satisfied with it, I am not satisfied with any alternative that has been put forward until now. Your half-brother Charlie has expressed my feeling about what I am doing better than I have done to date. When asked by a classmate what his father did in life (a French way of saying what a man's work is), he answered, 'My father works at keeping the world from having another war.'"

Jack smiled to himself, thinking of the little boy at the airport, frail against the steamed glass, saying, "I like Air France better. Blue is a faster color." Then he looked down once more at the letter, frowning, wondering if it wouldn't be better to tear it up, try to get Steven to fly over to Rome so that they could have it out at length, man-to-man. It would cost at least a thousand dollars, and if the events of the last summer were any way of judging, not much good would come of it. So he continued to write.

"I am dissatisfied with this letter," he wrote, "but my motives for writing it are pure. I want to save you from dangers that I see perhaps more clearly than you and that you do not necessarily have to run. Please do not be rash." He hesitated. Then he wrote, swiftly, "Your loving father," and folded the pages and put them into an envelope and addressed the envelope. One lie more, he thought, to fly the ocean at four hundred miles an hour.

He put the letter in his pocket, to be mailed later, and sat back with the feeling of an unpleasant duty respectably but not brilliantly performed. He closed his eyes and tried to sleep, tried to forget all the irritations and nerve-grinding of the last few months, which had culminated in Hélène's attack on him, in Joe Morrison's chilly attitude toward him when he had insisted upon holding Morrison to his promise to give him time off for Rome. The hell with it, he thought, all his problems mingling in distasteful confusion in his head. I don't care if he sends me to Washington or Outer Mongolia or the South Pole, I don't mind if my son marries a bearded lady from the circus and defects to Russia with the latest secrets of chemical warfare, I don't care if I don't make love to my wife from now till the end of the century, I don't care, I don't care . . .

Then he slept, the fitful, twitching sleep of overburdened, swiftly traveling modern man, the restless, unrefreshing, upright sleep of air liners.

The little old lady peered over her bourbon at the sleeping man. Ever since he had boarded the plane at Orly, she had stolen glances at him when she thought he was not looking in her direction. "Ssst," she said to the hostess, who was walking down the aisle with a pillow.

"Who is the gentleman, my dear?" the little old lady whispered, holding onto the hostess's arm. "I've seen him somewhere before."

"His name is Andrus, Mrs. Willoughby," said the hostess. "He's getting off at Rome."

The little old lady regarded the sleeping face. "No." She shook her head. "I know I've seen him before, but I can't place him. You're sure his name is Andrus?"

"Oh, yes, Mrs. Willoughby." The hostess smiled politely.

"He has brutal hands," said Mrs. Willoughby. "But he has a copious face. It'll come back to me. From the depths of the past."

"I'm sure it will," said the hostess, thinking, Thank God I get off at Istanbul.

"I'm sure you're too young to remember," Mrs. Willoughby said obscurely, dismissing her.

The hostess passed forward with her pillow and Mrs. Willoughby took a small sip at her bourbon, staring accusingly at the brutal hands and the almost remembered copious face across the aisle.

Jack slept uneasily, moving fitfully against the cushion, a large man with a long, heavy head, the jaw on the side toward Mrs. Willoughby thickened and irregular and marked by a scar that curved down from his wiry, gray-flecked dark hair. Thirty-seven, thirty-eight, Mrs. Willoughby decided, making the usual mistake of the old, judging people to be younger than they actually were. She approved of his size. She liked Americans to be big when they traveled in other countries. She approved of his clothes, too, a neutral gray suit, cut in the loose and comfortable manner which makes Europeans say that Americans don't know how to dress, and a soft dark tie. But his identity eluded her. The name she was searching for was on the tip of her tongue, tantalizingly, and she knew it wasn't Andrus. The gap in her memory made her feel insecure and old.

*

When Jack awoke, he pulled back the curtains and saw that they were losing altitude on the approach to Rome. Turning away from the window, he was conscious that the old lady across the aisle from him was staring at him intently, frowning. As he straightened in his seat and buckled the safety belt, he had the feeling that he must have spoken in his sleep and uttered a word of which the old lady hadn't approved.

In the dusk, the runways were gleaming from a shower that had come in from the Alban Hills, and scraps of cloud, lit by the last dull red of the setting sun, raced across the streaked sky. Looking out of the window as the plane tilted and the flaps came down, Jack remembered the soft thick pewter color of the winter sky over Paris and was pleased with the contrast. Arriving almost anyplace in Italy, he thought, by any means of transportation, was calculated to lift the spirit and renew one's appreciation of such simple things as color, rain, and the shapes the wind created in the sky.

2

Mrs. Willoughby made a last, furrowed examination of him as she turned off toward the restaurant, where the passengers in transit were to wait while the plane was refueled. Jack tipped his hat politely at her, and as he moved toward the passport-control desk he heard her say, with severe satisfaction, "James Royal." She said it to a Syrian gentleman who was walking beside her. The Syrian gentleman, who understood Arabic and French, spoke the only two words he knew in English. "Very good," he said, sweating with the effort of international amity.

"I thought he was dead," Mrs. Willoughby said, walking energetically toward the restaurant. "I'm sure somebody told me he was dead."

Jack was almost through customs, across the counter from the official in a baggy striped suit who was marking his bags with a piece of chalk, when he saw Delaney. Delaney was standing beyond the glass doors that separated the customs enclosure from the waiting room. He was wearing a little tweed cap, like an Irish race-track tout, and a bright tweed coat, and his face shone, sun-burned, near-sighted, welcoming on the other side of the glass. To Jack's eyes, he didn't look like a man who was in trouble. By the strength of his relief at seeing Delaney standing there looking so much as he had remembered him, Jack realized how fearful he had been of the first sight of his friend, fearful of the marks that the years might have made on him.

When Jack came through the door, Delaney shook his hand roughly, beaming, saying in his thick, hoarse voice, "I told them the hell with it, they could all go home, I wasn't going to let you arrive with only a driver to meet you." He grabbed the small brief case that Jack was carrying. "Here, let me," he said. "Unless it's all Top Secret and you'll be broken to a pulp if you let it out of your hands."

Jack smiled, walking beside the robust, fierce-looking little man toward the parking lot. "Actually, it's the line of battle for Northern Europe," he said. "But I have six other copies at home, if I lose this one."

While the porter and the driver were putting Jack's bags in the trunk of the car, Delaney stepped back and frowned thoughtfully at Jack. "You don't look like a boy any more, Jack," he said.

"I didn't look like a boy the last time you saw me," Jack said, remembering the day he had gone to Delaney's house to say good-bye.

"Yes you did," Delaney said, shaking his head. "It was against nature, but you did. A damaged boy. But a boy. I didn't think I'd ever live to see the gray hairs and the lines. Christ," he said, "I won't ask you for any comments on how I look. I weep when I happen to see myself when I'm shaving. *Ecco!*" he said to the porter, stuffing hundred-lire coins into his hand. "Let's go."

They sped toward Rome in the rattly green Fiat. The driver was an olive-skinned young man with beautifully combed, gleaming hair and sad, black-fringed dark eyes. He swung the car in and out among the trucks and the motorcycles and Vespas like a racing driver, blinking his headlights impatiently when he was blocked momentarily on the narrow, bumpy road past the racecourse and the walls of the movie studio that Mussolini had built, in his big years, to challenge Hollywood.

18

"You can have the car and the driver," Delaney said. "Whenever you want. For the whole two weeks. I insisted."

"Thanks," Jack said. "But if it's any trouble, I can walk. I like walking around Rome."

"Nonsense." Delaney waved his hand in an imperial gesture. He had small, soft, surprising hands, like a child pianist's, incongruous on his rough, short-coupled, broad body. "You have to make these people feel you're important. Otherwise they have no use for you and they piss on your work. Be snotty enough and they'll wreathe themselves in smiles when they give you the five thousand bucks."

"Seriously," Jack said, "I want to thank you for . . ."

"Forget it, forget it." Delaney waved his hand again. "You're doing me a favor."

"That's a lot of money for me, you know," Jack said.

"I believe in throwing a little backsheesh in the way of our loyal public servants." Delaney's ice-blue, clear little monkey eyes glittered with amusement. "Keep them contented with their sorry lot. Tell me, what's the inside dope? Are we going to have a war in the next ten minutes?"

"I don't think so," Jack said.

"Good. I'll be able to finish the picture."

"How's it going?" Jack asked.

"The usual," Delaney said. "Some mornings I want to kiss everyone on the set. Some mornings I want to put a bullet through my brain. I've gone through it fifty times. The only difference is that this time we have the addition of a little Italian chaos, to make it more amusing. I have the script here." He patted a bulky pile of paper on the seat beside him, stapled together in flimsy pink cardboard. "You can look it over tomorrow morning."

"Don't expect much," Jack said. "You know, I haven't read a line of dialogue for more than ten years."

"Three days after they bury you," Delaney said, "you'll be a better actor than the boy I have in there now."

"What's the matter with him?" Jack asked. "I always thought he was pretty good."

"The bottle," Delaney said. "Six fathoms deep in Scotch. He *looks* all right, although that'll go in another year or two, but you can't understand a word he says. All I want you to do is put in the sound track—simple, clear, sexy, and comprehensible to the twelve-year-old mind." He grinned. Then he spoke more seriously. "You've got to be good, kid," he said. "You've got to be like the old days, Jack . . ."

"I'll try," Jack said uneasily. For a moment he was disturbed by the intensity of the expression in the cold blue eyes. There was a desperate, veiled signal there, a fierce appeal, that was out of all proportion with the actual job that Delaney wanted him to perform. For the first time in his life, Jack had the feeling that Maurice Delaney might one day break down.

"You've got to do more than try, Jack boy," Delaney said quietly. "What you do will make or break the whole thing. It's the keystone of the picture. That's why I hunted all over the place to find you, because you're the only one who can do it. You'll see when you read it and when you run the stuff we've shot so far tomorrow."

"Maurice," Jack said, trying to lighten the sudden tension that had sprung up in the car, "you're still taking movies too seriously."

"Don't say that," Delaney said harshly.

"But after all these years," Jack protested, "you could let up a little . . ."

"The day I let up a little," Delaney said, "they can come for me and pack me away. With my permission."

"They'll never pack you away," Jack said.

"That's what you say." Delaney grunted savagely. "Have you read some of the reviews of my last few pictures? Have you seen the financial reports?"

"No," Jack said. He had read some reviews, but he had decided on tact. And he had not seen the financial reports. That, at least, was true.

"There's a good friend." Delaney smiled widely, with monkey-cynicism and mischief. "One more thing." He looked around him as though afraid that he was being overheard. "I'd be grateful if you kept this to yourself."

"What do you mean?"

"Well," Delaney said, "we've still got more than a week's shooting to do and if Stiles catches on we're not using his own famous golden voice he may turn sullen."

"Can you keep something like that quiet in Rome?"

"For one week," Delaney said. "With luck. Yes. After that, let him scream. We don't get onto the set until eleven thirty in the morning, and you and I'll do our dirty work before then. Do you mind getting up at dawn?"

"You forget, I work for the government," Jack said.

"Does the government get up early these days?" Delaney said. "It never occurred to me. God, what a life you must lead."

"It's not too bad," Jack said, vaguely defending the last ten years.

"Anyway, it's good of them to let you off for me. Tell them I'll pay an extra hundred thousand bucks in taxes next year to show my appreciation."

"Don't bother." Jack smiled. Delaney's troubles with the Internal Revenue Department had been widely recounted in the newspapers, and someone had figured out that if he lived until the age of ninety, giving all his salary to the department, he would still be in debt for over two hundred thousand dollars at the end. "They owe me months of back leave," Jack said. "And I was getting so nasty everybody in Paris cheered when I took off." He had no intention of burdening Delaney with the story of the dangers he was running with Morrison by his insistence on coming to Rome.

"Working hard protecting civilization as we know it, kid?" Delaney asked.

"Only day and night," Jack said.

"Do you think the Russians're working day and night, too?"

"That's what the man tells me," Jack said.

"God," Delaney said, "maybe we ought to blow the whole thing up and get it over with. Do you think when it blows they'll get the income-tax records?"

"No," Jack said, "it's all on microfilm in underground vaults."

"Ah," Delaney said, "not even that hope. There's no escape. Say," he said, "just what do you do with all those soldiers in Paris?"

"A little bit of everything," Jack said. "I brief visiting congressmen when my boss is busy, I draw up reports, I lie to newspapermen, I escort newsreel photographers and keep them away from secret installations, I write speeches for generals . . ."

"Since when have you learned how to write?"

"I haven't," Jack said. "But anybody who knows enough to spell deterrent with two *r*'s can write a speech for a general."

Delaney laughed hoarsely. "How the hell did you ever get mixed up in anything like that?"

"By accident," Jack said. Just the way I've gotten mixed up with everything else in my life, he thought. With Delaney, too. "I was playing tennis at St.-Germain one Sunday," Jack said, "and my partner turned out to be an Air Force colonel. We won. He wanted to keep me as a partner, so he offered me a job."

"Come on now," Delaney said. "Even the Air Force can't be as sloppy as that. He must have known *some*thing about you."

"Of course," Jack said. "He knew that I'd been mixed up with the movies at one time or another and there was a project on foot to make a documentary about the NATO forces, and one thing led to another . . ."

"Guido!" Delaney shouted at the driver, who had just missed a taxi, "you'll never forgive yourself if you get me killed. Remember that!"

The driver turned his head and smiled widely, his teeth perfect and gleaming and happy, his eyes changelessly dark and full of sorrow.

"Does he understand English?" Jack asked.

"No. But he's Italian. He's sensitive to emotional intonations. Tell me," Delaney asked, "how's your family? How many kids you got now? Three?"

"Out of how many marriages?" Jack said.

Delaney grinned. "Out of the current one. I know how many you have by the previous ones."

"Two," Jack said. "A boy and a girl."

"Happy?" Delaney eyed him inquisitively.

"Uh-huh," Jack said. Except at airports, he thought, and certain other places, at certain other times.

"Maybe I should have married a Frenchwoman," Delaney said. He had been married four times and his third wife had once shot at him in a parking lot with a hunting rifle.

"Try it some day," Jack said.

"When I finish the picture maybe I'll visit you in Paris," Delaney said. "I could use a little Paris. And a short vision of domestic bliss. *If* I ever finish the picture."

"What's it about?" Jack touched the pink cardboard cover on the seat beside him.

"The usual." Delaney made a face. "Ex-G.I. comes back to Rome, his life all fouled up, and meets the girl he loved on the way up from Salerno. Mediterranean passion and Anglo-Saxon guilt. God, stories are getting wearier and wearier these days." He fell silent and stared moodily out the window at the bustling evening traffic.

Jack looked out the window on his side. They were passing the church of Santa Maria Maggiore, massive and forbidding.

"Some day," Jack said, "I'm going to stop off on the way in from the airport and actually see what's inside that building."

"This is the one town," Delaney said, "I'm never tempted to go into a church." He chuckled drily. "Believe it or not," he said, "I went to confession in 1942. But that was in California. A heart man told me I was going to die in six months."

They rode in silence for a moment, the church disappearing behind them.

"Ah," Delaney said, "we had a hot run together for a few years, you and me."

"Yes," Jack said.

"God, we were lucky for each other," Delaney said. "For a little while it looked as though there was a federal law prohibiting us from doing anything wrong." He chuckled a little sadly. "Then the godamn war had to happen." He shook his head. "Maybe we can still be lucky for each other. Again. It's possible, isn't it?"

"It's possible," Jack said.

"Jesus," Delaney said, "you were a marvelous boy in those days." He sighed. "The godamn war," he repeated softly. Then he looked around him more brightly. "Well, anyway, we're both alive," he said. "This isn't a bad place to be alive, Rome. You ever been here before?"

"Two or three times," Jack said. "Just for a few days at a time."

"Listen," Delaney said, "have you got anything on for tonight?"

"No," Jack said.

"No full-breasted little Italian starlet notified to be on the alert for the Big Night?"

"I have to keep reminding you," Jack said mildly, "that I work for the government now. All that is behind me."

"Okay," Delaney said. "I'll call for you in an hour. Give you a chance to take a bath and wipe the dust of travel off your face. I've got a surprise for you."

"What is it?" Jack asked as they drove up to the hotel and the doorman opened the door of the car.

"You'll see," Delaney said mysteriously, as Jack got out. "Be prepared for a funny evening. I'll see you in the bar in about an hour."

The driver already had Jack's bags out and the doorman was putting them to one side, under the *portico,* as the car drove off.

23

Jack waved at the rear window and turned and started up the steps of the hotel. Two women and a man were coming out through the revolving door and Jack waited for a moment, as they stood abreast, blocking the entrance. The two women were holding the man solicitously, each by an elbow, as though he were ill, and the taller of the women had her arm around the man's waist. When Jack started to move past them, the man suddenly broke away from the women and rolled uncertainly across to Jack. He looked at Jack for an instant, smiling loosely, bareheaded, his hair uncombed, his eyes bloodshot. Then he swung and hit Jack on the nose.

"Sanford!" one of the women wailed, and the other woman said, "Oh, God!"

Jack stumbled back, the tears starting in his eyes from the blow. He would have fallen if it hadn't been for a pillar of the *portico* behind him. He shook his head once, clearing his eyes, and straightened himself, raising his fists instinctively and taking a step toward the man who had hit him. But it was too late. The man had slid down in front of the revolving door, and was sitting there, his legs sprawled under him, smiling foolishly up at Jack, his hands waving languorously in the air, like a bandleader conducting a waltz.

"What the hell do you think you're doing?" Jack stood over the man, touching him with the point of his shoe, wanting him to get up so he could hit him.

"*Arrivederci, Roma,*" the man said.

The women fluttered around him, pulling limply at his armpits, making little murmurs of disapproval, not budging him. They were all Americans, the women in their forties and dressed like matrons at a flower show, the man about thirty-five, stocky and rumpled.

"Oh, Sanford," the taller of the women said, near tears, "why do you do things like that?" She was wearing a hat with two artificial gardenias sewed on it, flat across her head.

"Should I call a policeman, sahr?" It was the doorman, looking grave, standing at Jack's shoulder. "There's one on the corner."

"Oh, please . . ." the woman with the gardenias cried.

"Just let the sonofabitch stand up," Jack said. He felt his nose and his hand came away bloody.

The man sprawled on the steps looked up at Jack, his head rocking, the cunning and triumphant smile on his lips. " '*Arrivederci, Roma,*' " he sang.

"He's drunk," the short woman said. "Please don't hit him." She and the other woman managed to haul the man to his feet and fussed around him protectively, straightening his clothes, supporting him, whispering to him, pleading with Jack and the doorman, standing between Jack and the drunk. "He's been drinking ever since we got to Europe. Oh, Sanford, you ought to be ashamed of yourself." The woman with the hat spoke rapidly, in all directions. "My dear man, you're bleeding horribly. I do hope you have a handkerchief, you're ruining that nice gray suit."

Before Jack could break in, the woman had whipped out a handkerchief and thrust it into his hand. As Jack put it to his nose, the shorter woman pushed the drunk back a little farther away from danger, murmuring, "Oh, Sanford, you promised you'd be good."

Jack could feel the handkerchief, which was soft and fragrant, soaking quickly in his hand. Even through the blood the perfume on it smelled familiar and he puzzled about it as he stood there, snuffing uncertainly.

A taxi drew up under the *portico* and the man and the woman who dismounted from it stared curiously, first at Jack and then at the two women and the drunk, as the man paid the fare. Their disapproving cool eyes made Jack feel, stupidly, that, out of a sense of social responsibility, he owed it to them to explain what had happened.

The woman with the hat fumbled once more in her bag, talking all the while. "Prudence," she said in a loud Bostonian whisper, "put that bad boy right in that cab. This is becoming a scene." She took a ten-thousand-lire note from her bag and crumpled it into Jack's pocket. "There's no need to call the police, is there now? I'm frightfully sorry. That's for cleaning the suit, of course."

"Now, see here," Jack said, taking the note out of his pocket and trying to give it back to her. "I don't want . . ."

"I wouldn't dream of it," the woman said, recoiling. She produced a thousand-lire note and gave it to the doorman, while the new arrivals went slowly past them, into the hotel, staring. "For being so kind," she said grandly. "Now you get into that taxi, Sanford. And apologize to the man."

"That's what they sang," the drunk said, nodding and grinning, "when the *Doria* went down."

"There's just nothing to be done with him when he drinks," the woman said. With athletic dexterity she bundled the drunk into the cab and slammed the door behind them.

" '*Arrivederci, Roma,*' " the man's voice floated back as the cab drove off. "Italian navigation. While the crew went off in the life-boats. The bastard had it coming to him. Did you see his face when I gave it to him? Did you see it?"

Surprisingly, from the open windows of the taxi, came the sound of women's laughter, high, shrill, uncontrollable, over the coughing of the old engine and the whining tires.

"Are you hurt badly, sahr?" the doorman asked.

"No," Jack said, shaking his head, watching the cab as it turned into the street and vanished. "It's nothing."

"Is the gentleman a friend of yours?" The doorman gently held Jack's elbow as Jack went toward the entrance, almost as though he were afraid that Jack, reacting slowly, might finally drop at his feet.

"No, I never saw him before in my life. Do you know who he is?"

"This is the first time I saw the gentleman," said the doorman. "Or the ladies. I'm terribly sorry it happened, sahr." His long, military face over the smart flared coat grew anxious. "I trust there will be no results, sahr?"

"What's that?" Jack turned at the revolving door, not understanding. "What do you mean, results?"

"I mean complaints to the management, sahr, inquiries into how it happened, and so on, sahr," the doorman said.

"No," Jack said. "Don't worry. There won't be any results."

"You understand, sahr," the doorman said delicately, "they were not Italian."

Jack smiled. "I know. Forget it."

The doorman, relieved at this national absolution, bowed stiffly. "I am very grateful, sahr, for your attitude. I trust your nose suffers no permanent damage."

He started the door revolving, and Jack went into the hotel lobby, holding the bloody handkerchief to his nose, sniffing the perfume. As he crossed to the desk, he recognized it. It was the same perfume his wife used. Femme, he said to himself, Femme.

When he gave his name at the desk, and his passport, the clerk bowed and smiled warmly at him. "Yes, Mr. Andrus, there's a suite reserved for you." He rang for a porter and, while waiting, stared sympathetically at Jack. "Have you hurt yourself, sir?" he asked, earning his money, gravely solicitous for the welfare of guests who had suites reserved for them.

"No," Jack said, tentatively taking the handkerchief away from his nose. "I have a tendency to nosebleeds. It's a family weakness."

"Ah," said the clerk, sympathetic for Jack's entire family.

The blood was still dripping, so Jack had to go up in the elevator holding the stained handkerchief in front of his face. He stared grimly at the porter's back, pretending he didn't notice the two young women who were in the elevator with him and who were looking at him curiously and whispering to each other in Spanish.

There were flowers in the salon of the suite and Renaissance drawings of Rome on the high walls, and Jack, remembering the children-cluttered small apartment with the stained ceilings in Paris, smiled with pleasure at the severe, empty, elegant room. He had been home for so long that he had forgotten the bachelor joy of being alone in a hotel room. He tipped the porter and gave him the letter to his son and inspected the bedroom and the huge marble bathroom, with the two basins. One for me, he thought idly, and one for whoever. He looked at himself in the mirror and saw that his nose was beginning to swell. He pushed it experimentally. A little jet of blood spurted out into the white bowl of the basin, staining it dramatically. But the nose didn't feel broken and it didn't look as though he was going to get a black eye.

"The sonofabitch," he said, remembering the drunk sprawling in front of the revolving doors, out of the reach of punishment. He stuffed some toilet paper into his nostrils to clot the blood and rang for the maid and the waiter. He opened his bags and took out a bottle of whisky and a suit and a bathrobe. He looked at the suit critically. The valise was advertised in America as being capable of carrying three suits without creasing them. According to the advertising, it was possible to take a suit out of the case and put it on, impeccably preserved, immediately. Somehow, every time Jack took a suit out of the case it looked as though it had been used for weeks as a nest for a litter of puppies. He grimaced at the thought of what the case had cost him. The suit he was wearing was out of the question. There were long brownish wet stains down the front of it and he looked like the first person the police would arrest ten minutes after a murder had been committed.

The waiter and the maid came in together, the waiter young and dapper and on the way to greater things in large dining rooms and fancy restaurants, the woman gray and old and shapeless, with a toothless, whining smile, and a history of back stairs, childbearing, privation, widowhood, minor theft, printed in every line of her body.

Jack ordered some ice from the waiter and gave the maid the crumpled suit to be pressed and the jacket he was wearing. *"Per pulire, per favore,"* he said, pleased with himself for remembering the word for cleaning.

The maid looked down doubtfully at the jacket over her arm and touched one of the soggy brownish spots. She looked questioningly at Jack.

"Blood," he said. He tried to remember the word in Italian, but he couldn't. "Blood," he said more loudly.

The maid smiled anxiously, wanting to please, not understanding. *"Va bene,"* she said.

"Sangue," the young waiter said from the door, his voice superior, impatient. *"Sangue."*

"Ah, si, si, sangue." The maid nodded her frizzled, sad head, as though she should have known all along, as though all guests in this excellent hotel always arrived in bloodstained jackets. *"Subito, subito."* She trotted through the door, following the waiter.

Jack unpacked while waiting for the waiter to come back with the ice. He hung up the other suits, hoping the creases would disappear by themselves by morning, and put the leather-framed photograph of his wife and his two children on the dresser in the bedroom. There was a little balcony outside the bedroom window and he stepped out on it, but the suite was at the rear of the hotel and all he could see were the windows of the buildings across the narrow street, rain-washed and gray against the night sky, which reflected the multicolored neon of Rome. From below came the sound of a radio playing, loudly, a brassy, insistent tune with a rock-and-roll beat. It was cold on the balcony and there was still rain in the air, and with the nondescript silhouette of the buildings across the street, and the neon and the rough, unpleasant beat of the music, it might have been almost any city on a wintry night in the American Age. There was no reminder on the hotel balcony that at one time Caesar had ruled the ground below or that Michelangelo had argued with a Pope in the city or that kings had traveled across Europe to be crowned two miles away.

Chilled, Jack went back into the room, closing the long glass doors against the sound of the radio below. On the dresser, he saw the crumpled ten-thousand-lire note that the woman had forced on him. He smiled as he looked at it, thinking, I've shed blood for less. He decided to get a present for his children with it before he left Rome. He smoothed it out and folded it carefully and put it in his wallet, not in the money section, but next to his driver's license, so he wouldn't mix it up with his other money.

When the waiter came in with the ice, Jack poured himself a whisky and water. He took his shoes off and sat on the edge of the bed, sipping the whisky, feeling tired from his trip and uncomfortable from his puffy nose.

Sitting like that, his eyes half-closed, tasting blood, an image began to form hazily in his mind, the faint memory of another moment long ago when he had sat bent over like that, only it was on a wooden bench, with the flavor of blood in his throat. He closed his eyes completely, to concentrate, and it became clearer. It was on a spring afternoon and there was the smell of damp grass and he was ten years old and he was on the school baseball field and a ground ball had taken a bad hop and hit him squarely between the eyes and the bleeding hadn't stopped for three hours, until his father had come home and held ice to the back of his neck and made him lie with his head down over the edge of the bed. "Next time," his father had said cheerfully, while his mother hovered over him, worrying, "you won't try to field ground balls with your nose."

"It took a bad hop, Pa," Jack had said, thickly.

"The world is full of bad hops," his father had said, undisturbed. "It's a law of nature. Learn to expect them."

Jack smiled, remembering, and felt better. The taste of blood, linking him now with his childhood, made him feel younger. He put the whisky down half-finished and got a piece of ice out of the bucket and lay down on the bed, holding the ice behind his head, at the base of his skull. He was glad he had thought of his father, on a spring evening, when his father had been a young man.

He drowsed a little, not minding the thin cold trickle going down into his collar. *"Sangue, sangue,"* he said sleepily to himself. "Why couldn't I remember a simple word like that?"

3

Delaney was not in the bar when Jack arrived there. He had show-
ered and his hair was wet and neatly brushed, and he was wearing
the newly pressed suit. His nose was still puffy, but the bleeding had
stopped and the shower had made him feel fresh and wide-awake
and ready to enjoy the night in the city. The bar was crowded, with
many Americans, solid and middle-aged, who had earned their
cocktails with long hours in front of statues and altarpieces, visiting
ruins and triumphal arches and arranging for audiences with the
Pope. All the bar stools were taken and Jack had to stand and reach
between a man and woman who were sitting there to get his martini.

"He said he didn't understand German," the woman was saying,
in a thick German accent, "but I knew he was lying. All Jews understand German."

"Where're you from?" the man asked.

"Hamburg," the woman said. She was red-headed and dressed **in** a tight black dress, cut low between her breasts. She was a plump, curved woman with a shrewd, perverse face and reddish, big, farm-girl hands. Jack had been in the bar at the cocktail hour three or four times during the past few years and each time he had seen her there, and her profession was plain. It was a polite bar and she waited to be asked, but it was obvious that she had an arrangement with the chief bartender.

The Germans, Jack thought, looking at her with distaste, ready to supply all the needs of post-war Europe. At least the whores in Paris don't look so satisfied with themselves.

He turned his back on the couple at the bar, holding his glass in his hand, looking around the room, his view of the near corner obscured by a group of young Italians, marvelously barbered, with spreading, immaculate collars and pale neckties and narrow-waisted short jackets, who were standing close to him, talking des-ultorily, handsome, predatory, their eyes candidly appraising each new woman who entered the room, ready for money or vice or love or travel. Looking at them, Jack had a momentary sharp pang of envy, for their good looks, for their assurance, for their youth, but most of all for their openness. Like most Americans, Jack had the feeling that he had spent most of his life submerging almost every-thing that he felt, and this unattainable Italian overtness, this adver-tised zest and shameless availability made him feel unpracticed and foolishly innocent.

Jack moved a little, so as to be able to see beyond the group of young men. Carefully, he looked at the faces of the other drinkers. After a moment, he realized he was looking for the man who had hit him and the two women with him. They were not in the bar. An-noyed with himself, Jack shrugged. What would I do with him if I found him? he thought.

He finished his drink and was about to order another when he saw Delaney come striding into the bar, still in the same coat, but with his cap jammed in his pocket, his pale, childish hair rumpled over the red face, marked by the lines of power and temper.

"We're late," Delaney said, without a greeting. "Let's get out of here. I hate this joint anyway. It's full of bloodsuckers." He stared angrily at the group of Italians, at the German whore, at the monu-ment-worn Americans.

Jack paid for his drink and started out with Delaney.

"What're we late for?" he asked.

"You'll see, you'll see," Delaney said, enjoying the suspense. Suddenly he stopped and squinted curiously at Jack. "What happened to your nose?" he asked.

"A drunk hit me outside the hotel," Jack said, feeling embarrassed.

"When?"

"A minute after you left."

"Did you know him?"

"Never saw him before."

Delaney grinned. "It didn't take you long to enter into the thrilling life of the Eternal City, did it? I've been here five months and I haven't been hit yet."

"But you've been here long enough to get lipstick on your collar," Jack said as they started toward the exit.

Delaney's hand moved guiltily toward his throat. "Now where in hell could that have come from?"

"Is Clara eating with us?" Jack asked, as they got to the door.

"No." Delaney didn't volunteer anything more.

They got into the green Fiat, assisted by the military doorman, who stared mournfully at Jack's nose, as though it reminded him of a sin of his youth.

Delaney sat erect in his corner, glaring at the cars darting wildly past the street corners. "God," he said, "the way Italians drive. Like kids out to make a new record in the soapbox derby."

"Well," Jack said, "it's better than the way Frenchmen drive. As though they're all trying to get to the bank to get their savings out before the bank fails. I once asked a Frenchman why they drove that way and he thought for a moment and said, 'Well, we lost the war.' "

Delaney chuckled. "I guess by now you're an expert on the French," he said.

"Nobody's an expert on the French," Jack said. "Now, Maurice, tell me—where're we going?"

"If ye have tears, prepare to shed them now. Old Roman quotation," Delaney said. "You'll see soon enough." He began to hum a song, smiling mysteriously. It was an old popular song, and Delaney had a croaking, almost tuneless way of hitting the notes, and Jack didn't recognize it, although he had the feeling he should and that it carried some special significance for him.

The car drove up to the front of a movie theatre and stopped. "Here we are," Delaney said. He got out and held the door for

Jack. "I hope you don't mind waiting for dinner." He watched Jack closely as Jack looked up at the poster in front of the theatre.

"Oh, Christ," Jack said softly, standing in front of the poster, which advertised a picture called *The Stolen Midnight,* directed by Maurice Delaney. In the list of actors on the poster was the name James Royal and in the small stills pasted up near the entrance there was a close-up of himself, twenty years younger, before the wound and the thickening of the jaw, thin, laughing, handsomer than he ever remembered himself.

"What an idea," Jack said.

"I thought it might interest you," Delaney said innocently.

"So would a hanging." Now Jack understood why Delaney had hummed the song in the car. It was a song of the thirties, "Walkin' My Baby Back Home," and it was played several times in the picture and had been used as a theme behind several of the key scenes by the composer of the incidental music.

"The publicity department arranged it," Maurice said. "Famous director doing picture in Rome, let the public see what he perpetrated when he was young."

"Have you seen it yet?" Jack kept staring at the photograph of himself on the glossy, brilliantly illuminated paper.

"No," Delaney said. "And anyway, I thought it would be a friendly idea to sit next to you while they were running it."

"Friendly," Jack said. "There's the word. When was the last time you saw it?"

"Ten, fifteen years ago." Delaney looked at his watch. "The hell with it," he said. "The bastard's late again. Let's not wait for him. He'll find us after the picture."

"Who's that?" Jack asked, following Delaney to the ticket booth.

"A French newspaperman who's writing a piece on me for a Paris magazine," Delaney said, shoveling money through the wicket. He handled Italian money as though it irritated the skin of his hands. "He says he's an old friend of yours. Jean-Baptiste Despière."

"Yes, he's a friend of mine," Jack said, pleased. He had known Despière for ten or eleven years, and they played tennis together in Paris, whenever Despière came back from his wanderings, and Jack knew that Rome would be made much more enjoyable by his presence. Despière had met him the first night he arrived in Rome, in 1949, and had made him drive around the Colosseum in the moonlight, in a fiacre, with two pretty nineteen-year-old American girls, because, he said, everybody on his first night in Rome had to see the Colosseum under the moon in the company of two nineteen-year-old American girls.

"Gay little bugger, isn't he?" Delaney said as they entered the theatre.

"Some of the time," said Jack, remembering times when Despière hadn't been so gay.

"You might tell him," Delaney said, in a hoarse whisper, following the usher through the darkness, speaking over the roar of the newsreel, "that in the United States newspapermen come early for appointments."

They sat down close to the screen, because Delaney was astigmatic. He put on a pair of thick, horn-rimmed glasses, which he wore defiantly and, being vain, only when absolutely necessary. The newsreel, over which bubbled an excited Italian voice, was the usual mixture of disasters, processions, pronouncements by politicians—wounded Arabs being rounded up in Algeria by French troops, a riot in Northern Italy, the Queen of England visiting somewhere, the wreckage of a crashed airplane being inspected by men in uniform. While it was on, Delaney grunted disapprovingly. He had stuck a piece of chewing gum in his mouth, and Jack could tell, by the loudness and the wetness of Delaney's chomping, the comparative scale of his distaste for the events and persons flickering across the screen. "What a prelude to a work of art," Delaney said loudly, as the newsreel came to an end. "Bloodshed and the faces of politicians. I'd like to see them do it at Carnegie Hall. Put on a man being broken on the rack, followed by a speech by a senator from Mississippi on the offshore-oil question, then play the Seventh Symphony. The movies . . ." He shook his head despairingly, contemplating the art to which he had given thirty years of his life.

There was a rhetorical fanfare of music from the screen and the title of the picture came on. Jack had an uncomfortable feeling of immodesty when he saw the card with the name James Royal printed on it, a feeling that he had had each time that he had seen this false, highly advertised, empty name in print or in electric lights, a feeling that he had almost forgotten in the years since the time when, in every town in America, that name had burned on the marquees of movie houses.

The head of the studio in Hollywood had given him the name, although Jack had already played on the stage in New York under his own name.

"John Andrus," Kutzer, the studio head, had said, shaking his head. "It won't do. I mean no offense, but it doesn't sound American."

"My family came here in 1848, you know," Jack had said mildly.

"Nobody is impugning anything," the head of the studio had said. "It is merely a matter of practical business, how it will look in lights, how it will strike the native ear. We are experts in these things, Mr. Andrus, trust yourself in our hands."

"I trust myself in your hands," Jack had said, with a little smile. He was young and he was excited by the idea of fame, even under an invented name, and he had been poor as an actor in New York and was hungry for the money that this man could offer him.

"Offhand," the head of the studio had said, "I have no ideas. Come back tomorrow—" He looked at the appointment pad on his desk. "At ten fifteen A.M., and I will have a name for you."

At ten fifteen A.M. the next day, Jack was James Royal. He hadn't liked the name then and he had never grown to like it, but it had seemed innocuous enough, and the head of the studio had kept his promise and had put the name up in lights in all the major cities, as he had phrased it, and on enormous billboards along all the major arteries of travel. The head of the studio had also kept his promise about the money, and for a few years Jack had been richer than he had ever thought he could possibly be. He had never changed his name legally and when he went into the Army, he enlisted, with a sense of relief and homecoming, as John Andrus.

The other names on the list of credits and in the cast of characters swam up out of the past, names he hadn't thought of for many years. Walter Bushell, Otis Carrington, Genevieve Carr, Harry Davies, Charles McKnight, Lawrence Myers, Frederick Swift, Boris Ilenski (not very American, that, but he was a musician and a musician did not have to have his name in lights or strike the native ear), Carlotta Lee, a dozen others, the names of people who had died or who had failed or who had become famous or disappeared from sight, and the name of the woman he had married and divorced. Sitting there in the darkness, he had an almost irrepressible desire to flee. If he had been alone, he knew he would have gotten up and run out of the theatre, but he looked over at Delaney, slumped in the seat beside him, loudly chewing his gum, squinting coldly through his glasses at the screen, and he thought, If he can take it, so can I.

Then the picture started and he didn't look over at Delaney again.

The story was about a young boy in a small town who fell in love with an older woman who ran a bookshop. In the third reel, after the stolen midnight which gave the movie its title, and the discreet fade-out for the censors in the dark backroom of the bookshop, their sin was discovered and the scandal started, and the woman was attacked and there was some foolish melodrama about a crime that the boy committed to get money to help her stay in town and there was a kindly and philosophic judge who set the boy to rights and showed him where his duty lay, and a sorrowful parting between the boy and the older woman, and a standard ending in which the boy returned to the wholesome girl who had remained true to him through all his troubles. But the foolishness of the story and the familiarity of the ingredients didn't make any difference. Jack was swept up in it, not because it was himself as a boy of twenty-two that he was watching (the boy seemed as strange to him and as remote as any of the other people on the screen), and not because he saw again, in the slightly comic clothes of another period, the beautiful woman who had been his wife and whom he had once loved and later hated, but because of the swiftness, the assurance, the sense of vigor and reality that Delaney had brought to every scene, the silly ones as well as the good ones, the quiet, true scenes between the boy and the older woman and the scenes of melodrama and sentimentality that the industry had imposed on them all. The picture had a clipped, tumbling style that carried everything along with it, and even now Jack could see why it had been so successful, could see how Delaney had made a star of him, even if that hadn't lasted very long, could see why the picture had survived and had been played again and again, all over the world, for so many years.

Watching himself, he was surprised that he had been so good. He was a little old for the part (he was supposed to be a boy of nineteen in the picture, just out of high school), but somehow he had caught the slippery movements of a complicated adolescent emerging, in fits and starts, into maturity. He was funny when he had to be and pitiable when he had to be and he seemed to be looking within himself at all times and dragging out of himself, with pain and with laughter, the accurate report on himself.

He hadn't remembered that he had been that good. After that he had been as good again only in the two other pictures he had made with Delaney, and his memory of himself from that time was overlaid with recollections of worse performances under other directors. This was Delaney's best picture, too, made when he was in his prime, confident of his luck and savagely scornful of everything in the world but his own talent, before he had begun to repeat himself, before the many wives, before the big money and the interviews and the troubles with the income tax.

When the climax of the picture came, the scene at night at the railroad station, shadowy and deserted in a lonely drizzle, when the boy appeared out of the murk to wait with the woman he had loved for the train which was to take her away and out of his life, Jack forgot that he was in a foreign city, five thousand miles and more than twenty years away from the buried innocent America of small-town railroad stations, of distant whistles across plowed farm lands, of lighted diner windows, Negro baggage handlers, old taxis waiting, dripping in the rain, with their drivers smoking cigarettes in the darkness and speaking in flat, desultory, unlovely voices of baseball scores and women and hard times.

Caught in the sorrow of the fictional moment on the screen, watching the scratched old print, listening to the uneven sound track as the two lovers walked slowly down the platform, appearing and reappearing in the dim patches of light of the spaced station lamps, hearing the half-sentences of heartbreak and farewell, he was no longer conscious that it was himself he was watching, doing an actor's job, no longer conscious that it was a woman he had lived with and who had been false to him who walked brokenly, for a last, despairing two minutes, beside the boyish shadow on the screen. For that moment, he was that age again, and he knew what it was like to be young and bereft in a place like that. And he felt, all over again, with all its old trouble, the powerful and endless desire for the body of the woman whose image, full and youthful and untouched by time, appeared and reappeared under the station lamps, the desire that he had thought had vanished forever in betrayal and recriminations and divorce courts.

When the lights came up, he sat silently for a moment. Then he shook his head, to clear away the past. He turned to Delaney, who was slumped in his seat, his hand up to the earpiece of his glasses, looking tough and bitter, like an old catcher who had just lost a close game.

"Maurice," he said gently, loving him, and meaning what he said, "you're a great man."

Delaney sat without stirring, almost as if he hadn't heard Jack. He took off the heavy, thick-rimmed glasses and stared down at them, symbol of pride outraged, vanity at bay, of vision clouded and distorted by age.

"I *was* a great man," he said harshly. "Let's get out of here."

*

Despière was waiting on the sidewalk outside the theatre. When he saw Jack and Delaney coming out with the last stragglers from the audience, he hurried over to them, beaming. "I saw it, *Maestro*," he said. *"Jolissimo.* The tears still flow from my eyes." He threw his arms around Delaney and kissed him on both cheeks. Sometimes it amused Despière to behave like a Frenchman on the stage. Two or three of the people who had been in the theatre stared curiously at the three men, and Jack heard a girl say, "I bet it's him," and knew, as usual, that he had been half recognized. "You must tell me just how it felt to be sitting there," Despière was saying, "after all this time, watching reel after marvelous reel pass by."

"I won't tell you a godamn thing," Delaney said, pulling away. "I don't want to talk about it. I want to eat. I'm hungry." He peered out into the street, looking for the car and the driver.

"Delaney," said Despière, "you must learn to be more charming to your admirers among the journalists." He turned to Jack and held him affectionately by the arms. *"Dottore,"* he said, "I had no idea you were so beautiful when you were young. My God, *Dottore,* how the girls must have dropped." Despière spoke Italian, English, German, and Spanish, aside from French, and when he was with Jack in Italy, he paid tribute to the manners of the country by calling Jack *Dottore*. In France, it was *Monsieur le Ministre,* in ironic recognition of Jack's diplomatic status. "Weren't you overflowing with pride of yourself in there tonight?" Despière gestured toward the theatre.

"Overflowing," Jack said.

"You don't want to talk about it?" Despière said, surprised.

"No."

"Imagine that," Despière said. "If I'd made that picture, I'd walk up and down the streets of Rome with sandwich boards on my back, announcing, I, Jean-Baptiste Despière, am totally responsible."

Despière was a nimble, slender man, his narrow, rectangular shape disguised by nipped-in suits with padded shoulders that had clearly been made for him in Rome. His face was sallow and brilliantly alive, with a cynical, narrow French mouth and large, luminous gray eyes. His hair was black and cut short and worn brushed forward in a style that came from the cafés of St.-Germain-des-Prés. It was hard to judge his age. Jack had known him for more than ten years and he hadn't seemed to have grown a day older in that time, but Jack guessed he was somewhere in his late thirties. He had lived in America, and while his accent was unmistakably French, he had soaked up a good deal of American slang, which he used knowingly and without affectation. He had been in the Free French Air Force during the war, after escaping to London at the time of the surrender, and had served as a navigator in a Halifax, in a squadron that had been sent to Russia. He had come back from Russia with a ruined stomach, and he was constantly inquiring, especially of Americans, for a cure for ulcers which would not interfere with his drinking. He was a successful journalist and worked for one of the best magazines in France, but was always in debt, partly because of his carelessness with money and his easy generosity, but also because for long periods at a time he refused to work. He knew where all the restaurants were, and who was in what town at what time, and the first names of all the pretty girls of the crop of the current year. He was invited everywhere and given inside information by cabinet ministers and staff officers and movie stars and he paid his way with his wit and high energy and he had a surprising number of enemies.

The car drove up and they all got in. Delaney didn't ask them where they would like to eat, but growled out the name of a restaurant and then subsided in his corner. He was silent and didn't seem to be listening to either Despière or Jack all the way to the restaurant.

*

"Chaos begins at the top," Despière was saying, across the table, in the quiet restaurant. "In the big, official buildings, with the

39

statues of Reason and Justice and ancient heroes in the halls. Where would you find a private citizen foolish enough to attack the Suez Canal without any reserve of oil?" He chuckled happily. "One day's fighting and they had to ration gasoline for a year. You have to be carefully selected by your fellow citizens to run a government to be able to be that splendidly idiotic. The most inept of kings, let us say Louis the Sixteenth, would never have pulled off a master stroke like that. Or maybe it is only France . . ." He shrugged. He looked around him with pleasure at the other diners. "Ah," he said, "you have no idea how enjoyable it is to sit in a restaurant and be reasonably sure nobody will throw a bomb through the front door."

"What do you mean by that?" Delaney asked. He had been sullen and untalkative, drinking his wine and picking lightly at the plate of *pasta* in front of him and crumbling breadsticks absently on the tablecloth.

"In the last five years," Despière said, eating with relish, "I've been in Korea, Indochina, Cyprus, Morocco, Algeria, Tunisia, Israel, Egypt. I am like a doctor in an ambulance. I run to all emergencies."

"You're going to get yourself killed one of these days," Delaney said.

"*Maestro,*" said Despière, "brutality is your chief charm." He smiled benignly, his teeth strong, squarish, tobacco-stained, behind the thin lips. "The last time was in Philippeville about six months ago. Three Arabs drove past in an open taxi and machine-gunned a fashion show."

"A what?" Jack asked, incredulously.

"A fashion show." Despière poured himself another glass of wine. "Eight beautiful girls showing the latest French dresses. That is how one liberates one's country these days."

"What the hell were they doing in Philippeville?" Delaney asked.

"Bringing the Paris message to our overseas possessions," Despière said. "Chic for all occasions. Teas, sieges, Communist rallies, ambushes, state dinners, parades by the Foreign Legion, receptions for visiting American statesmen . . . They just drove past the front of the hotel and sprayed away. Imagine the corruption of the mind of a man who would shoot eight beautiful girls."

"Did they hit any of them?" Jack asked.

"No. But they killed six people sitting in a café next door."

"How about you?" Delaney asked. "Were you really there?"

"I was there. On the floor, behind a table," Despière said, smiling. "I am getting very quick at dropping behind tables. It would not surprise me if I was told I held the world's record. I was also present in Casablanca when the crowd poured gasoline over two gentlemen they didn't like and set them on fire. I am highly paid," he said, "because I have a knack of being on the spot at those moments when modern civilization expresses itself in a typical manner." He held his glass up and looked at it critically. "I do like Italian wine. It's simple. It is what it is. It does not pretend to be velvet like French wine. I also like Italian colors. When I saw the color of the walls of Rome for the first time on a summer morning, I knew I had been longing for the city all my life, although I was only seventeen at the time. I recognized the city from the beginning. The first time I came to Rome, with my father, when I was a boy, I entered the city through the Flaminia Gate, into the Piazza del Popolo. There were hundreds of people all over the piazza. My father stopped the car and took me to a café on a corner for coffee. The prettiest girl in the world was behind the cashier's counter, selling those little tickets you give to the man who works the *espresso* machine. I sat there, in love with the girl behind the counter, and I said to myself, immediately, 'What a wonderful place to live, surrounded by Italians. I will come here to drink coffee for the rest of my life. I have found the city for me.' There are cities that your soul recognizes at first glance. Am I right, *Dottore?*" He turned to Jack.

"Yes," Jack said. He thought of himself and the first time he had seen Paris, during the war, and the pull that the city had exerted upon him, so that, finally, much later, he had come to live there.

"There are some men," Despière said, "who can only live fully in the capitals of countries not their own. I am one of them. You, *Dottore*, I suspect, are another. The happy exiles. The *Maestro*, now." He squinted at Delaney, whose mood had improved somewhat during Despière's recitation. "The *Maestro* is a different animal. He is invincibly American. That means he is brusque, careless, constantly worried, and uneasy when he finds himself living among people who are not constantly worried."

"Balls," Delaney said, but he was smiling.

"He has given us a typically charming response," Despière said. "On the subject of cities. New York. I could live happily in New York, too. Although I think any American who manages to live there must end up with a crippled soul. What we need," he declaimed with a wide sweep of his hand, "is an interchange of cities. A city should be regarded as a university—open to qualified and serious students, to be lived in for four or five years for the knowledge to be gained from it—and then to be left for other places— and to be revisited from time to time for brushing up on certain subjects and for sentimental reunions. In Paris," he said, grinning, "I brush up on comedy and intrigue and camouflage and despair. In Rome on wine and love and architecture and atheism. When I am an old man, I intend to settle on a farm near Frascati, drinking the white wine, and each time I feel the approach of death, come into the city and have a coffee on the Piazza del Popolo . . ." He stopped and looked across, puzzled, at Jack. "What's the matter, *Dottore?*"

Jack was sitting with his head bent over his plate, his handkerchief up to his nose. He was rocking a little on his chair and the handkerchief was slowly turning red. "Nothing. I'll see you tomorrow." He stood up, blinking his eyes because he couldn't see very well. He tried to smile. "Sorry. I think I'd better go home."

Despière jumped up. "I'll go with you," he said.

Jack waved him back. "I'd rather you wouldn't," he said. He started out of the restaurant, gagging, trying not to throw up, walking uncertainly, feeling the sweat come out on his face, not answering the headwaiter when the headwaiter said something to him on the way to the door. Outside, he leaned against the building, breathing deeply of the night air, tasting blood.

I'm never sick, he thought, with an edge of panic, I'm never sick, what's happening? He had an ominous feeling of change, of crossing over from one season to another, of a cold current suddenly flowing through him, of being exposed and vulnerable to accident. Standing there shakily, feeling the blood wet on his lip, his head tilted back against the cold stone, he had a dreamlike sense of events, words, people being translated into numbers and being put down in a long row of figures and the figures being added up mysteriously, endlessly, by an invisible, noiseless, unstoppable machine. If only I were drunk, he thought, I'd know I'd get over this in the morning. But he had only had half a glass of thin wine. Not velvet, he thought. Chaos begins at the top. Where is the man who hit me? *"Arrivederci, Roma,"* he heard the man's voice singing, drunken and mocking. When the *Doria* went down.

He shook his head and the bleeding stopped, as suddenly as it had begun. Now he felt the cold night air reviving him. He wasn't dizzy or nauseated any more, just weary and hazily apprehensive, and he had to open his eyes very wide and take deep, conscious breaths to reassure himself that he was not on a station platform on a wet night, saying good-bye.

He started walking back toward the hotel, pacing slowly, forcing himself to think about taking one step after another and making serious decisions about such things as curbstones and keeping from being run over and whether or not to buy a newspaper at the lighted kiosk on the street corner.

He heard high heels coming up behind him and a woman passed him on the sidewalk and he saw that it was the German whore from the bar. Hamburg, he remembered, and the large reddened hands. Lewdly, he reflected on the nature of the business the red hands had been involved in that night. The woman was wearing red shoes. She was walking fast and she gave the impression of being angry, as though the night had disappointed her. Another number in the addition.

He went into his hotel. From the bar downstairs came the sound of a radio playing a song he had never heard before. Upstairs, the corridors of the hotel were long and silent and dimly lit and the travelers' shoes outside the doors were like the last personal effects of people who had been executed that afternoon at cocktail time.

He passed twenty doors. There was not a sound coming from behind any of them. The guests, locked in, safe with their unchanging names and undivided lives, slept secretly, not divulging their positions. There were no red shoes before any of the twenty doors. He made sure of that.

He forgot the number of his room and for a moment stood stupidly in the middle of the hushed corridor, overcome with the feeling that he would never find it again. Look for the room with a bloodstained jacket hanging in the wardrobe. No, he remembered, the old lady is cleaning it. *Per pulire, per favore, Dottore.*

Then he had a brilliant idea. He looked at his key. There was a big plastic tag to which the key was attached and on the tag there was a number. 654. He was favorably impressed with his wisdom and the cold and logical precision of his thinking processes. He traveled cleverly down the corridor, avoiding both walls, and stopped in front of 654. He had the feeling that he had never been there before, but that he had been at another door, marked with the same number, and that significant transactions had taken place there. Night clerks, making their nighttime errors. Where had the other door been? In what city? New York, Los Angeles, London? There was the smell of laurel and eucalyptus, tropic and medicinal, about 654. Beverly Hills, he remembered, Delaney's town, Delaney's punishment, with the fog coming in from the Pacific, and a girl in a convertible late at night and a dog in the back seat that kept barking, the bared, carnivorous, California fangs of love.

He put the key into the lock and went into the room, bachelor-like, without children, that he was sure he had never visited before, smelling the eucalyptus and the laurel. The glass on the etchings of Rome reflected the light from the glass chandelier coldly, cutting medieval Rome into chaotic fragments, rhomboid battlements, polygonal towers, unrecognizable to the dead men who had built it.

He went into the bathroom and stared at his face, first over one basin, then over the other. One for me and one for whoever. He almost recognized himself, like the ghost watchers coming out of theatres year after year, and his name was on the tip of his tongue. I bet it's him, he said, in a girl's voice.

He went into the bedroom and looked at the picture of his wife and his son and his daughter. The picture had been taken in the Alps, on a skiing holiday, and a whole family was smiling there in the mountain sunshine, the sunny claims of memory. The helicopter was down, in a swirl of snow, on the ledge at three thousand meters, with the dead men in it, in polite attitudes, waiting to be photographed. He sat on the bed and looked at the telephone and thought of himself picking the instrument up and saying, "I will take the midnight plane, or the dawn plane, or the unscheduled plane." But he didn't touch the telephone.

He undressed, hanging his clothes up carefully (the liars who advertised valises that did not crease three suits). He lay naked in the darkness between the sheets, saying to himself, Morning, morning.

He thought of the red shoes and the red German hands, handling lire and flesh. Then he slept.

4

*The bull roars in his pen, but the president, in a black mask, and
wearing a Berber headdress, comes into the ring and declares the
bull unsuitable. The crowd attempts to pour gasoline over him. It is
imperative, for a reason that is not clear, to get the bull out of his
pen without permitting him to enter the arena. Two attendants,
dressed in white, goad a white cow, theoretically in heat, into the
passageway, lit by a glass chandelier, before the entrance to the
bull's pen. The cow is frightened and makes difficulties and wedges
herself across the passageway. The white-clothed attendants strug-
gle with the white cow to straighten her out and present her most appetizing, or bull-baiting, view to the pen entrance. The bull roars
underground. The cow lows, tenor, then contralto, tosses her head
from side to side, supplicating the chandelier. The president, still
dressed in black, appears, unharmed, legally elected, and raises the
iron door to the bull's pen. The bull comes out, black, humped,*

wide-horned, like a wave going over sand. The froth, the spume, the wrack, the curl of the breaker, the suck of the tide, is Attendant Number One, impaled, then trampled, no longer white.

After humanity, the animal kingdom. The bull regards the white, supplicating cow, theoretically in heat, opts for death as against procreation, bunches his legs delicately, drives the horns into the white, frantic flank, so appetizing on other occasions. The white cow is no longer white, no longer standing, her flank no longer frantic, her supplication finished. The bull stands beside her, dreaming under the glass chandelier.

Humanity's turn again. Attendant Number Two, dressed in white, races down the corridor, past the box stall where I am hidden, crouched behind the bolted iron door, next to a man whose face is averted and whose name is on the tip of my tongue.

The attendant's feet on the corridor make a sandy, dragging noise, like the sound of the wire brush on a drummer's traps. From his throat comes a noise. Water glugging down a tin rain pipe. Attendant Number Two flees into the stall next to mine and bolts the door, breathing rainily. The bull trots up to the door and surveys it without malice. Then he breaks it down. From the next stall come the sounds one might expect to hear, loud, explicit, intermingled with calls on Christ, as the bull does the work he has been bred to do.

Then Attendant Number Two is as silent as Attendant Number One, as silent as the white cow.

The bull reappears in the corridor, in a dim light, and snuffs intelligently at the door to the stall in which I crouch, next to the man whose face is averted. I hunch against the iron, not breathing, seeing both sides of every question, every door. The other man remains rigid and motionless. The bull decides that the shoes outside the door are data of no importance and turns to seek more interesting diversions. But the man with the averted face has passed his limit of silence and immobility. He moves, he makes a noise, he sighs, he bubbles, he moans. I jab him sharply in reproof, my index finger going in up to the knuckle, between the fourth and fifth ribs. The bull stops, comes back to the door, discovers humanity on the other side of the iron, Columbus off the coast of Hispaniola, land birds, the smell of flowers, sweet water. The bull charges the door. It clangs, but it holds. The bull charges again and again, the horns splintering, sparks flying, the door groaning, the rhythm increasing, becoming intolerable, the dust like rain, the noise like the scream of

46

*a jet in close support. I throw my weight against the door, flesh
against iron, shuddering with each assault, howling wordlessly. The
other man sits on the yellow straw of the stall, his face averted.*

The door holds.

The bull backs off, considering.

*Then he begins to leap, a lion with horns, athletic, ambitious, an
iron gazelle, his hooves reaching higher with each leap, his horns
like torches in the open space above the door. Finally, he gets his
front legs over the top of the door. He hangs there, filling the space
between the door and the ceiling beams. He looks down at me and
the other man, who has turned his back and sits regarding the rear
wall of the stall.*

*The bull stares down reflectively, with mild, fatal eyes, and I
know that now is the time for distraction, for song and dance and
laughter. I go to stage center, squarely in the middle of the stall, and
looking winningly at the bull, who has paid his entrance fee and
deserves the best, I begin to dance and sing: tap, soft-shoe, buck
and wing, modern, classic,* Petrouchka, *entrechats,* Swan Lake,
Fancy Free, *my head lolling from side to side, the sweat all over,
the music wailing from my throat, drums, violins, French horn, triangle, as the bull watches with intelligent interest, bemused, hung
by his horns to the rafters, his front legs neatly slung over the top
of the door, front row in the balcony.*

*I am singing the chorus of "Walkin' My Baby Back Home" for
the third time when I sense that the man behind me has turned and
no longer has his face averted. I have to see the man's face, I have
to say, "Oh, friend, don't die with your head averted—" and for a
hundredth of a dream I look away from the appreciative, placid
eyes of the bull, to know the face of my partner.*

Then the bull moves, the door trembles . . .

*

These are the dreams of the Roman night.

He awoke.

The room was dark and quiet and no light came in through the
cracks in the shutters or through the split between the curtains. The
curtains rustled softly in a light breeze.

He lay tight between the sheets, cold with the sweat of the dream, on the lip of death. He had the feeling that if the dream had gone on a moment more he would have seen the man's face and that the face would have been that of the drunk who had hit him earlier that night. In another room in Rome the drunk was snoring, smiling in his sleep, content with the night's work.

Why bulls? Jack thought. I haven't been in Spain for three years.

He sat up and turned on the light and looked at the clock on the table beside the bed. It was four fifteen. He reached for a cigarette and lit it. He rarely smoked and he hadn't smoked in the middle of the night for many years, but he had to have something to do with his hands. He was surprised that his hands did not shake as he held the match.

He sat on the edge of the bed, his bare feet touching the hotel carpet, thinking about his dream, still in the presence of death. It missed me that time, he thought. It will get me the next.

The horned lion, he remembered, the white cow.

The Presence in the room. It was no good, being alone with it, at four fifteen in the morning, and a cigarette was no weapon against it. He looked at the telephone and thought of calling his wife in Paris. Only what could he say to her? *I have had a bad dream. Mother, Mother, I have had a bad dream in my Roman crib, and next time the horns will get me.*

He thought of the oceanic confusion of the Italian telephone system and the high irritated voices of the operators in the Paris central and the erratic ringing in the apartment on the quai and his wife getting out of bed and going out into the hall where the telephone was, frightened, with the dead light of dawn at the windows. He gave up the idea of telephoning.

He looked at the rumpled bed and thought of sleeping. Then he gave up the idea of sleeping.

Walter Bushell, he remembered, Carrington, Carr, McKnight, Myers, Davies, Swift, Ilenski, Carlotta Lee. The movie that night had called the roster of the past and he was confronted by names that had sunk away in his memory, confronted by the shapes and voices of people who had died or failed or become famous or who had disappeared from sight.

The Night Watchman will whisper the roll call, on a scratched sound track.

The dead, the missing, the wounded, the replacements, the fit for duty, appropriately dressed, wearing all decorations. Star with bar, the celluloid cross, the canceled check, the toupee, the pancake, the iron wreath of immortelles. Andrus' First Corps (or was it the Second or Third or Ninth?), sometimes called Royal's Foot, the survivors of the crossing of the Los Angeles River, drawn up on the sound stage, at parade rest.

All present and unaccounted for.

The heroes first, those Who Had Made the Supreme . . .

Carrington. Dressed in a black suit and a black tie, philosophic, judgelike. Dead in Berlin, several years ago, on location, working on a picture (in all the papers—it had meant eighteen days of re-shooting, an extra cost of $750,000). A tall, soft-spoken, ambassa-dorial-looking man, white-haired, beak-nosed, Roman in linea-ment, who had been a matinée idol and who had had to fight the drink all his life and who had been the lover of great beauties for thirty years and who had died in the arms of an assistant cutter in a hotel room, among the rebuilt ruins ("Kiss me, Hardy," in the bloody surgery off Trafalgar), sitting up in bed and calling out the name of a girl he had known when he was twenty years old, a hun-dred women away.

McKnight, small, hypochondriacal, violent in drawing rooms and on the edges of swimming pools. Killed in the war, run over by a tank. At the time they were making *Stolen Midnight* he had been a bit-part actor, trying to act like Cary Grant, whom he resembled faintly. "I have the gift of the comic spirit," McKnight said, re-peated, insisted, pleaded. "I would have been great in the twenties, when people still really knew how to laugh." He was too short to be a star and he had nearly been killed when he had been thrown from a horse during the shooting of a Western picture at Universal, but he had been reserved for the tank in the Atlas Mountains, dislo-cated in time, the comic spirit.

Lawrence Myers was dead, too. Sallow, dome-headed, in need of a haircut, with the shaky hands of a man of eighty. He had writ-ten the script and had fought bitterly with Delaney, who changed every line. He was married to a woman who was crazily jealous and who cut off the sleeves of the jackets of his suits with a knife when he failed to get home at seven o'clock in the evening. Myers was gaunt and sickly-looking and had tuberculosis. He squandered all his money and he died at the age of thirty-three, when he got up out of bed, leaving an oxygen tent, to go to a story conference at MGM for a musical comedy.

Those were the dead, or at least the known dead, the remem-bered dead, and did not include grips, secretaries, cutters, publicity

men, studio policemen, script girls, waitresses in the studio com-
missary, all of whom were alive, pushing, hopeful, with plans for
the future, at the time the picture was made, and who might also
be expected to have succumbed in a predictable ratio to the wear
and tear of twenty years, in accordance with Jack's mortality tables.

To say nothing of the living . . .

First among the living, Carlotta . . .

Hell, Jack thought, sitting on the edge of the bed, with the cigarette between his lips, I'm not going to go through *that* again. He
stood up briskly, like a man who knew what he was doing, and went,
barefooted, dragging a blanket, to get away from the bedroom, the
dream, the unleashed dead. He put on all the lights in the living
room, the glass chandelier, the desk lamps, the wall brackets, and
picked up the pink-covered script Delaney had asked him to read.

He made himself comfortable on the couch, shivering a little under the blanket, and opened the script.

FADE IN, AFTER CREDITS

A four-motor plane landing at the Ciampino Airport, Rome. It
has been raining and the runways are still wet.

THE AIRPLANE taxis toward the point of disembarkation and the
workmen run out with the ramp.

THE DOOR OPENS and the passengers begin to come out. Among
the passengers is ROBERT JOHNSON.

HE walks a little apart from the other passengers. HE seems to be
searching for something. HE approaches the camera and we see
that he is a man of about thirty-five, very handsome, with pierc-
ing, intelligent eyes.

Jack sighed as he read the stale, familiar words, and thought again,
in recurrent pain, of his dream, trying to sort out the symbols. The
bull, dealing death, appeased momentarily by song and dance,
deterred from his sinister intention by clowning and vaudeville
tricks. What was that? The public? Unreasonable, brutelike, deadly
—kept at bay only so long as you could jig and caper and howl
amusingly? Jack remembered how he had felt before the curtain
went up on opening nights and how shaky he had been, seated
among the audiences at the previews of films in which he had acted
—dry-mouthed, sweating, with electric-like little shivers in his elbows and knees. Was it because, after so many years, he was coming back to all that, even if it was only for two weeks and as the

anonymous, paid voice of a shadow on the screen, that he had had the dream?

And what about the man with the averted face, the enemy locked in the same place, confronted with the same danger, paralyzed by terror? And when you turned to know the face of the enemy, the face of fear, just at the moment of knowledge, of recognition, the doors broke down . . .

He shook his head wearily. I will buy a dream book tomorrow, he told himself mockingly, in Italian. I will find out that I am to avoid traveling by water or by air or by land and that an uncle of whom I have never heard is on the verge of leaving me a large ranch in the Argentine.

Maybe what it all means, he thought, is merely to get the hell out of here, leave the five thousand dollars, leave Delaney, leave my youth, leave the buried life buried. Maybe it's as simple as that.

But he read on dutifully, feeling pity and a little shame for all the souls, himself included, searching for fame or money or escape or amusement in this sad enterprise. He read through to the end, rapidly, in an impatient shuffle of pages, then dropped the script onto the floor and stood up, feeling bruised by the night, and went over to the windows. He threw the windows open and looked, without pleasure, at the dawn breaking cold and green over the narrow, yellowish Roman street. God, he thought, nagged by memories and premonitions, I wish these two weeks were over.

5

They sat in the darkened projection room, Delaney, Jack, and Delaney's secretary, watching the running of the film. Delaney had called for Jack at seven thirty in the morning. He had asked how Jack was feeling and had peered shrewdly and a little worriedly into Jack's bloodshot eyes, but had grunted in satisfaction when Jack told him, falsely, that he was feeling all right.

"Good," Delaney had said. "We can get right to work."

Because Delaney wanted to keep Stiles, the actor whose voice Jack was dubbing, from finding out what was being done, they had gone to another studio than the one where Delaney was shooting the picture. Delaney had put on dark glasses and pulled his cap down low in a conspiratorial attempt to remain incognito, although everyone he passed on the lot said, loudly, *"Buon giorno,* Signor Delaney." He hadn't introduced Jack to anyone, not even to the slender middle-aged woman in flat shoes who was working as his secretary and who sat just behind Jack in the projection room.

As the roughly cut sequences flickered past on the screen, Jack could see that, despite Delaney's complaints the night before, he was enjoying himself watching what he had shot. He grunted approvingly, he laughed aloud two or three times, short, harsh bursts, he nodded, half-unconsciously, at the climax of two scenes. Only when the image of Stiles appeared on the screen, did Delaney seem to be suffering. He wriggled in his seat, he lowered his head and glared up at the screen from beneath his brows, as though he were protecting his eyes from a blow. "The son of a bitch," he kept muttering, "the swilling son of a bitch."

Jack found the picture very little better than the script he had read. There were felicitous inventions here and there on the part of Delaney, and happy moments in the performances of some of the actors, especially that of Barzelli, the girl who played the leading part, but the general effect was heavy and lifeless and there was a leaden feeling that everybody concerned had done the same thing many times before. Stiles, as Delaney had said, looked all right, but his speech, when it wasn't slippery and almost incomprehensible from drink, was stilted and wooden and even the rudimentary indications of passion and intelligence which the script had offered were wiped out in his performance.

"The godamn Italians," Delaney said. "They can't resist a bargain. They got him for half his usual salary, so they didn't ask any questions and they signed him. Why don't you shut up?" he growled at the screen, where Stiles was telling the girl that he loved her but that he felt he had to leave her for her own good.

The showing ended abruptly, in the middle of a sequence which Jack remembered, from reading the script, was somewhere in the last third of the story. The lights went on and Delaney turned to Jack. "Well, what you think?" he asked.

"I can see why you want somebody else's voice for Stiles," Jack said.

"The sonofabitch," Delaney said, almost automatically. "Cirrhosis of the liver is too good for him. What about the rest of it?"

"Well." Jack hesitated. After all, he hadn't seen Delaney for more than ten years and he wasn't sure how frank he could be after the interruption in their friendship. In the old days, Delaney had used Jack as critic and sounding board for everything he did. In the world of sycophants and money-hunters in which Delaney lived, Jack had performed a great service for his friend. His standards had been youthfully strict, his taste astringent, his nose for falseness and pretension sharp, and he had been mercilessly candid with Delaney, who from time to time called him a supercilious young snot, but who listened, and more often than not redid the work of which Jack disapproved. Delaney did as much for Jack, never sparing him for a moment when he felt Jack was not doing his best. They had made three pictures together in three years, in this loose, informal, candid arrangement. The pictures had been among the best of their time and they had created the Delaney legend, on which, in a fashion, he still lived. Delaney had never approached that level again. He and Jack had had a sardonic, symbolic phrase that they used with each other, both for their own work or the work of others, when they detected the sugariness or false violence or pseudo-profundity that was so easy to get away with in the booming Hollywood of those days. "It's terribly original," they would say to each other, drawling the words out affectedly. Or if the offense was greater, "It's terribly, *terribly* original, my dear boy. . . ."

Now, after seeing the film that Delaney had run for him in the projection room, Jack wanted to say, "It's terribly, *terribly* original, my dear boy. . . ." But remembering the tension in Delaney's voice in the car the night before and the fierce appeal that had lain under the surface of his words, Jack sensed that it would be better to feel his way before he ventured any real criticism. "The script is pretty weak," he started.

"The script!" Delaney said bitterly. "You can say that again."

"Who wrote it?" Jack asked.

"Sugarman," Delaney said, spitting out the name as though it left a bad taste in his mouth. "The crook."

"That's surprising," said Jack. Sugarman had written three or four good plays in the past fifteen years, but there was no hint in what Jack had read the night before or seen that morning of any of the talent of his other work.

"He came here for three months," Delaney said, accusingly, "and went to all the museums and sat in the cafés with all the crappy, unwashed painters and writers that this town is lousy with, and he told everybody I was a stupid sonofabitch, and he wouldn't write a line the way I could shoot it and I wound up rewriting the whole godamn thing. Writers! The same old story. You can have Sugarman."

54

"I see," Jack said noncommitally. From the time he had begun to be successful, Delaney had fought with all the writers he had worked with and had finally taken to rewriting his scripts himself. He had the reputation around Hollywood of a director who had written himself into failure, and producers who were tempted to hire him were apt to say to his agent, "I'd take him, if I could tear the pencil out of his hand." Until now, nobody had managed to tear the pencil out of his hand.

"It's still rough," Delaney said, waving at the screen, "but I'll whip it into shape yet. If I don't die from Italian exasperation first." He stood up. "Look, Jack, you stay here and run it a couple of times and get familiar with it. Maybe you might even read the script again this afternoon. Then, tomorrow at seven thirty, we start dubbing."

"Okay."

"I made a date for you with Despière," Delaney said, shoving his dark glasses onto his face. "At Doney's. Ten to one. He wants to get some dope from you for his piece. About my early triumphs." Delaney smiled thinly. "Lie to him a little, like a good friend."

"Have no fear," Jack said. "I'll make you sound like a combination of Stanislavski and Michelangelo."

"Use your own judgment." Delaney laughed and patted Jack's shoulder. "Guido's waiting for you outside with the car. And there's a cocktail party tonight at eight o'clock. He's got the address. Anything else I can do for you?"

"Not at the moment."

Delaney patted his shoulder again, paternal, friendly. "See you at eight," he said. "All right, Hilda," he said to the secretary, and the woman stood up, docile and plain in a frayed cloth coat, and followed him out the projection-room door.

Jack took a deep breath, then looked at the screen with distaste, envying Sugarman his three months in the museums and cafés and his escape to America. Then Jack pressed the button and the room went dark and once more the unconvincing images started passing across the screen, pretending at tragedy.

As he watched the man whose voice he would eventually simulate, Jack thought about Delaney and the appointment he had made for Jack with Despière, and smiled to himself. It hadn't been only chance, Jack realized now, or a desire to do Jack a good turn, or even a desire to make the picture better, that had made Delaney call Jack down to Rome, although all these considerations had gone into it. Delaney knew Jack was a friend and loyal, and that he re-membered Delaney from his good days, and he wanted all that in the article that Despière was writing. For all his exterior bluffness, Delaney had always been a clever and devious man. It was clear that he hadn't changed. He maneuvered people subtly to his advantage and, as much as he could, controlled the working of chance. But even recognizing the maneuver, Jack could only feel pity for Delaney be-cause he believed in its necessity. When Jack first knew Delaney, a newspaperman could write that he was the Antichrist and raped choirboys and Delaney wouldn't as much as cross the street to get the man to change a line. Age, Jack thought, failure . . .

Five thousand dollars, Jack thought, watching the silly, handsome face on the screen. Five thousand dollars.

*

Despière was sitting at one of the small tables outside Doney's when Jack pushed through the slowly moving lunchtime crowd of tourists, clerks, movie people, and buxom girls on the Via Veneto. The noonday sun was warm and for an hour or two it made every-body feel that Rome was a wonderful place to be in the winter and you could see it on the faces going by and hear it in the pleased tones of the voices speaking a dozen different languages on all sides.

"Sit down," Despière said, touching the chair next to his, "and enjoy the sunshine of Italy." Jack settled in the chair and ordered a vermouth from one of the white-jacketed waiters who fought their way irritably through the passers-by with their trays, carrying tiny cups of coffee and thin individual bottles of Campari and ver-mouth. *"Dottore,"* Despière said, "I was afraid for you last night. You looked like a man who was preparing to come down with something serious."

"No," Jack said, lying, remembering the night he had passed, "it wasn't anything. I was a little tired, that's all."

"Are you a healthy man, *Dottore?"* Despière asked.

"Of course," Jack said.

"You look like a rock," said Despière. "It would be too deceiving if a man who looked like you turned out to be riddled with disease. Myself, now, that's a different story." He chuckled. "When scientists

56

look at me, they rush back to their laboratories and work night and day in the search for a serum, before it's too late to save me. Do you know that I've taken injections made from the placenta of women who have just given birth and from the secret cells of young men who have died in accidents?"

"What do you do that for?" Jack asked, half believing him.

"To prolong my life," Despière said lightly, waving at a man and a blond woman who were walking past the table. "Don't you think I ought to be interested in prolonging my life?"

"Does it work?" Jack asked.

Despière shrugged. "I'm alive," he said.

The waiter put down Jack's glass and poured the vermouth into it. Despière waved to two girls with long hair and pale faces devoid of make-up or lipstick who were parading past, on leave for the lunch hour from a movie set. He seemed to know half the people who passed the table and he greeted them all with the same languid wave of his hand and the same warm, brilliant, mocking smile.

"Tell me, *Dottore*," Despière said, slouching down in his seat, talking without taking his cigarette from his mouth, so that he had to squint a bit because of the smoke that continually blew into his eyes, "tell me, how was Delaney's masterpiece this morning?"

"Well," Jack said cautiously, "it's all in bits and pieces so far. It's a little early to tell."

"You mean it's lousy." Despière looked amused.

"Not at all," Jack said. Despière was his friend, but so was Delaney, and there was no need to sacrifice one for the other just for a magazine article. "I think it's liable to turn out to be a pretty good picture."

"It better be," Despière said.

"What do you mean by that?" This morning, Despière was making Jack uncomfortable.

"You know as well as I do, *Dottore*," Despière said, "that our friend Delaney is staggering against the ropes. One more stinker and he won't be able to make a picture anyplace. Not in Hollywood, not in Rome, not in Peru . . ."

"I don't know anything about that," Jack said shortly. "I haven't kept up with the fan magazines."

"Oh," Despière said ironically, "if I had his gift of commanding loyalty from my friends."

"Listen, Jean-Baptiste," Jack said, "what's this piece going to be like, anyway? Are you going to cut him up?"

"Me?" Despière touched his chest in elaborate surprise. "Am I known as a man who would do things like that?"

"You're known as a man who would do a lot of things," Jack said. "What're you going to say about him?"

"I haven't made up my mind yet." Despière grinned teasingly. "I am just a poor, honest newspaperman, serving the interests of truth, like poor, honest newspapermen everywhere."

"What's it going to be like?"

Despière shrugged. "I'm not going to cover him with roses, if that's what you mean. He hasn't made a decent picture in ten years, you know, even though he still behaves as though he's the man who invented the motion-picture camera. Let me ask you something. Was he always like that?"

"Always like what?" Jack asked, purposely not understanding.

"You know what I mean. Lordly, impatient of the small, mean minds he's forced to work with, gluttonous for flattery, deaf to criticism, turning out crap and thinking it's great, not giving credit to anyone else for anything, jealous of anybody else's work, splurging other people's dough like Nero with his violin, grabbing other people's women as though he had a license from the Irish National Stud to screw every pretty dame in sight . . ."

"You can stop now," Jack said. "I get the idea." He had a swift bleak vision of what Delaney's face was going to look like when the article came out and he got somebody to translate it from the French for him. He would have to warn Delaney to stay away from Despière or try to handle him differently. He wondered what Delaney had done to Despière to unleash this venom and wondered, too, what he himself could do to repair the damage.

Despière was grinning at him, squinting over the cigarette burning down small in his long, thin lips, rubbing his St.-Germain-des-Prés hair forward on his forehead, enjoying the glimpse of destruction and rage he was giving Jack, looking, with all that, like a sallow, unhealthy, handsome small boy, successfully baiting the grown-up world.

"Tell me, *Dottore*," he said, "am I a dirty, untrustworthy Frenchman?"

"You don't know him, really," Jack said. "He's not like what you think, at all. Or at least, if he is, that's only part of it. The worst part."

"All right, Jack," Despière said, "I'm open. Tell me about the bastard's good parts."

Jack hesitated. He was tired and his mind felt dull and heavy from the night's wakefulness and he was conscious that people were looking strangely at his bruised nose and the small dark swelling under one eye and he wasn't in the mood to defend anyone today. He felt like telling Despière that he didn't like the breezy, quick malice with which newspapermen served up victims to the public. Then he remembered Delaney in the theatre the night before, after the picture, saying harshly, "I *was* a great man," and his hollow, shaky confidence in himself that morning in the projection room, when he had said, "Lie to him a little, like a good friend."

"I met him," Jack began, "before the war, in 1937, when I was in a play that was being tried out in Philadelphia . . ."

He stopped. Despière was smiling up at two girls who were standing in front of the table. With his deliberate absence of manners, Despière did not stand, but talked across the table in Italian, looking up at the girls. The sun was behind them and Jack couldn't get a clear impression of what they looked like. He was annoyed that Despière talked to them at such length, purposely, Jack thought, to postpone the anecdote about Delaney. Jack stood up abruptly.

"Look, Jean-Baptiste," he said, breaking in, "I'll talk to you some other time. You're busy now and I . . ."

"Now, now," Despière put his hand out and gripped Jack's arm. "Don't be so impatient. You're in Rome now, remember, not New York. *Dolce far niente.* Anyway, the girls want to meet you. They saw your picture and they're overflowing with admiration. Aren't you, girls?"

"Which picture?" Jack asked stupidly.

"Stolen Midnight," Despière said. "Miss Henken. Signorina Rienzi."

"How do you do?" Jack said, with minimum politeness. He changed his position slightly, to get the sun out of his eyes, and saw the girls clearly for the first time. Unpatriotically, he assumed that the plainer of the two girls was the American. She had sandy hair, and a dry, streaked complexion and a half-bitter smile on her thin lips, as though she had tried many cities and all kinds of men in her thirty years and was resigned to the fact that she had been treated badly by all of them. The other girl was Italian, younger, with liquid dark eyes and long black hair and olive skin. She was a tall girl and she had a beige wool coat thrown back from her shoulders because of the heat of the sun and she stood dramatically before the table, conscious, Jack was sure, of the striking effect her long hair and full figure were making on the men passing by. She smiled often, her eyes darting back and forth, noting and evaluating the other people sipping their drinks at the tables, and she had a little trick of tipping her head that let her hair swing loose and which Jack was sure some man had told her was provocative and pretty. He also felt that there was something self-satisfied and stupid in the long, healthy face and the soft, deep body. A glossy female brute, he decided, displeased with her, on the everlasting, profitable prowl. Her voice was rapid and musical, and there was a note in it that reminded Jack of a trumpeter playing, low and muted, in a night club. She had a habit, too, of wetting the corner of her mouth often with the tip of her tongue. Jack was sure she practiced this particular bit of business cold-bloodedly before a mirror at home, conscious of the little hint and promise of sensuality that it evoked.

Despière pulled a chair over from the vacant table next to theirs and the waiter got a chair for the sandy girl and they sat down brightly and there was nothing for Jack to do but sit down, too.

"You ought to have a lot to talk about with Felice, Jack," said Despière. "You're in the same line of business."

"Which one is Felice?" Jack asked ungraciously.

"Me," said the sandy girl. "An unpleasant surprise, isn't it?" She smiled painfully.

"She does dubbing for the movies, too," Despière said. "English versions."

"Oh." Jack wondered momentarily if Despière knew that his job in Rome was supposed to be kept secret. Then he decided that Despière knew it and was spreading the word around to start trouble because he was mean that day, and anti-Delaney. "This is my first and last time," Jack said, with a feeling that he was being misrepresented by Despière for some reason of his own. "Actually, I forge checks for a living."

"Don't be stuffy with the girls, *Dottore*," Despière said. "They adore you. Don't you adore him, girls?"

"Mr. Royal," the Italian girl said, in English, "I've seen your picture three times already this week. I weep like a baby." Her English was slower than her Italian, harsher, not as musical, not so much like a trumpet playing muted late at night, and from her accent it was clear that she had been around many Americans.

"My name isn't Royal," Jack said, wondering how he could get out of there. "It's Andrus."

"He leads a double life," Despière said. "In his spare time, he selects sites for hydrogen-bomb launchers."

The girls smiled, politely confused.

"I search for the other pictures of yours," the Italian girl said, tilting her head, her hair flipping down to one shoulder, "but nobody seems to know where they are playing."

"They're not playing anywhere," Jack said. "I haven't acted for more than ten years."

"What a pity," the girl said. She said it as though she meant it. "There are so few people who have anything at all, the ones who do must not stop."

"I outgrew the sport," Jack said. "Look, Jean-Baptiste, give me a ring later in the afternoon and we'll . . ."

"I'm busy later," Despière said. "Jack was telling me about Mr. Delaney." He turned toward the two girls. "About the days a hundred years ago when he was a younger man. Go ahead, Jack. I'm sure the girls'd love to hear."

"When he was young," the Italian girl said, "when he made that picture, Mr. Delaney must have been full of excitement."

"And now?" Jack asked.

"I have seen some of his other pictures." The girl shrugged apologetically. "Not so full of excitement. More full of Hollywood, now. Am I wrong?"

"I don't know," said Jack, thinking, I'm going to have a busy time here, I'm going to have to defend Maurice Delaney against everybody I meet in Rome. "I don't go to the movies much any more." Still, he looked at the girl with new interest. She wasn't as senseless as she looked.

"It was in Philadelphia before the war, in 1937," Despière prompted him. "You were in a play . . ."

Jack hesitated, annoyed at the way Despière made a social event out of his work, the way he liked to conduct his life before a constant feminine audience. "I don't think the girls'd be interested," he began.

"Sure they would," Despière said. "Wouldn't you, girls?"

"I'd love to hear about Philadelphia in 1937," the sandy American girl said. "I was ten years old then. It was the best year of my life." She smiled with dry, sad, unpleasant self-disgust.

"And how old were you, *cara mia?*" Despière asked the Italian girl. "And where were you in 1937?"

"Two," she said, looking surprisingly shy. "And I was in San

Sebastián, in Spain. If Mr. Royal—excuse me, Mr. Andrus—doesn't want to tell us, it is impolite to push."

"I am a newspaperman, remember, Veronica," Despière said. "For a newspaperman, to breathe is to push."

That's no lie, Jack thought sourly. Veronica. That's her name. Veronica. That's the basic pass with the cape in a bullfight. San Sebastián, in Spain. He had a slippery, uncomfortable flicker of memory of the dream last night, and the link disturbed him.

"I have a great idea, *mes enfants,*" Despière said, unwinding languidly from his chair and standing up. "We will all have lunch and exchange the secrets of our lives."

They all stood up, uncertainly. "If Mr. Andrus doesn't object . . ." Veronica said, looking seriously, again with that unexpected youthful shyness, at Jack.

"Of course not," Jack said, giving in, thinking, Well, I have to eat lunch *someplace.*

"Follow me," Despière said, taking Veronica's arm and starting off up the street. "I will take you to a place where there hasn't been a tourist since the twelfth century."

Jack stayed behind to pay the bill. It was 1100 lire. With Miss Henken walking beside him, he followed Despière and Veronica, thinking, Well, the bastard's figured out a way to get somebody else to buy his girl lunch, too.

Miss Henken had a pleased, doubtful look on her face, the look of a girl who gets invited out to lunch only by accident.

Jack watched the couple in front of him, Despière's hand possessively on the girl's arm, their laughter floating back across their shoulders, intimate, linked. The girl had marvelous legs, too, long and rosy in her high-heeled shoes, under the swinging beige coat, and, unreasonably, it made Jack more morose than ever. I bet they find an excuse to duck us after the coffee, he thought, savagely. For the afternoon session.

"My God," Miss Henken said flatly, gazing at the girl in front of her, "why couldn't I have been born Italian?"

Jack glanced at her with pity and revulsion. "She'll be blowzy by the time she's thirty," he said, to support Miss Henken in the waste of her self-understanding.

Miss Henken laughed drily and patted her poor flat breast. "Well, I'm thirty. I'd settle for that."

I have not come to Rome to comfort the rejects, Jack thought, hardening his heart, and kept quiet. But one thing he was sure of—

he was going to make Despière pay for his own and Veronica's lunch. If it was the only thing he accomplished all that day.

It turned out that Despière was wrong about there having been no tourists since the twelfth century in the restaurant that he led them to. Sitting across the room from Jack and Despière and the two girls was a young couple, very clean and polite and quiet and American, who looked as though they were on their honeymoon. They were studying the menu very seriously and the bride looked up at the waiter standing in front of her and said, "I want something particularly Italian. Is an omelet particularly Italian?" and Jack would have liked to go over and kiss her pure, polite, earnest, beautiful American forehead.

The restaurant was one of the standard ugly Roman restaurants, with the bay of Naples painted garishly on the walls and hideous modernistic lighting fixtures and high ceilings that played tricks with the voices of the diners and made it necessary to shout just to be heard across the table. Despière ordered *spaghetti alle vongole* for them all, because it was a specialty of the house, and the waiter put an open wide-lipped carafe of wine on the table and Despière said, "According to Jack, there are hidden beauties in Maurice Delaney's character, and now he's going to reveal them to us, so I can give a rounded picture of the great man to the world."

Jack began slowly, trying to remember the night more than twenty years ago, when he had met Delaney for the first time in the dressing room where Lawrence Myers and his girl, who was later to become his wife, were sitting in the harsh make-up light. It was after a performance during the tryout week in Philadelphia, and Myers and his girl were sitting side by side on a broken, mud-colored sofa while Jack wiped his face with cold cream and a stained towel at the mirror.

"It was Myers' first play," Jack said, "and he was all excited, because the reviews'd been good and the audiences seemed to like it all right, and everybody kept saying that Harry Davies— he was playing the leading part—was going to be a star. He's dead now, Davies," Jack said. "Myers, too." He stopped, wondering why he had felt he had to say that, what stones he was piling on the forlorn graves of those lost Americans by announcing their death on another continent. Myers seemed very alive to Jack that moment, as he spoke of him, the sallow, nervous boy in the shabby suit, sitting there next to the uneasy girl who looked like a governess on her day off and who loved Myers so ferociously that she made his life a cascade of hideous scenes of jealousy right up until the day he left the oxygen tent to die.

"Myers had gotten friendly somewhere with Delaney and everybody knew Delaney was in the audience to see the show," Jack went on. "Delaney had just made his first big, successful picture as a director, and he was back East on a holiday and he took the trouble to come down to Philadelphia to see the show and give Myers his opinion."

The waiter came with the food and while the fuss of service was being made at the table, Jack half closed his eyes and remembered what Delaney had looked like, gusting into the dressing room, twenty years younger, rough and confident, hoarse-voiced, carelessly dressed, but with an expensive camel's-hair overcoat, and a floating cashmere scarf, like a banner, his face flushed and furious, his movements jerky with excessive vitality, as though nothing he could find to do in his life could tire him enough so that he could move at the rhythm of the people around him.

"What he said was this," Jack said, when the waiter had gone and they had begun to eat, " 'Forget the reviews, Myers, you're a dead man. What do they know in Philadelphia? You're going to get murdered in New York. Murdered!' "

"That sounds like him." Despière chuckled drily, his fork poised over his plate. "That sounds like my boy."

"He was being merciful," Jack said, remembering how pale Myers had gone in the flat light of the dressing room and how the tears had started in his girl's eyes. "Better know right off, better be prepared, than to go into New York hoping and have the hopes crash."

Jack saw Veronica nodding, understanding about false hopes, lying dreams.

Miss Henken ate swiftly, secretly, as though she rarely got enough to eat, as though she were afraid that at any moment people would discover that there had been some mistake, that she had been invited by accident and she would be asked to leave.

"What other charming things did he say?" Despière asked.

"Well, the producer and the director came in," Jack went on, "because they wanted to hear what Delaney had to say, too, and Delaney turned on them and yelled, 'You bringing this show to New York? What's happening to the theatre? Haven't the people in the theatre any honor any more? Haven't they any respect, taste, decency, love for their bread and butter?' " Even now, Jack could hear the harsh, rasping, outraged voice in the crowded dressing room, could remember his own feeling, sitting there at the mirror, unnoticed in the riot of denunciation, admiring Delaney, because he, too, understood the failings of the play and despised the people around him who deceived themselves, out of weakness and sentimentality, about it. " 'When I first came to New York,' Delaney shouted, and he was shaking his fist under the nose of the producer, and I thought he was going to hit him, 'when I first came to New York, if a play wasn't any better than this, we would take one look at it and flee to the mountains and leave the scenery to be burnt by the street-cleaning department. And now, today, Holy God, you have the indecency to stand there and tell me you're going to bring it in! Shame! Shame!' "

"What did the producer say?" Despière asked.

"The producer said, 'Mr. Delaney, I believe you're drunk,' and he ran out of the dressing room, with the director after him." Jack chuckled, remembering that panicky flight so long ago.

"See," Veronica said, "I told you in those days he was full of excitement—Mr. Delaney." She had been so interested in what Jack had been saying that she had forgotten to eat, and Jack was conscious all the time of her eyes fixed intently on his face as he spoke.

"And what about that poor bastard of a writer?" Despière asked. "What did he do? Go out and jump into the river?"

"No," Jack said. "Delaney told him to forget this play. It was his first one, anyway, Delaney said, and most of the time, it was a good thing for a man if his first play failed. And Delaney told him how he'd hung around the theatre for seven years before he had any recognition at all and how he was kicked off his first two pictures right in the beginning of shooting. And he said, 'Listen, kid, this one's no good, but you're a talented man, and you're going to be all right, in the long run.' "

Jack hesitated. Myers had been talented all right, but in the long run he had been unhappy and taken to the bottle and he had died at the age of thirty-three, but how was Delaney to know that that night in Philadelphia?

"Then he asked Myers if he had any money and Myers laughed a little and said, 'Sixty-five dollars,' and Delaney told him he'd take him out to Hollywood with him right after the play opened, to write Delaney's next picture, so that he'd have enough money to write another play. And he told him to avoid his friends and relatives on opening night in New York and to come and visit him in his hotel, so Myers wouldn't have to talk about the play. And that's what Myers and his girl did. The opening night was a disaster, with people walking out, starting in the middle of the first act, and Myers' girl weeping in the back row. It was her birthday besides, and she'd got leave from her job in Stamford to celebrate with Myers, because, naturally, she didn't believe Delaney, she thought the play was the greatest play since *Hamlet,* and everything was going so wrong. So Myers and his girl went over to Delaney's hotel on Central Park South and they went up to his suite and he was alone, waiting for them, with a birthday cake with candles for the girl, and he took them down to the bar and got them a little drunk and told them not to read the reviews the next morning, because they could cripple a man forever, he said. Then he asked them where they planned to spend the night. Myers was living in a cold-water flat with two actors, and he couldn't take his girl there, and she was supposed to stay the night with an uncle and aunt on Morningside Heights, and Delaney told them this was not a night for them to spend apart and he took them to the front desk and he told the clerk, 'Listen, these're two friends of mine. They're not married and I want them to have a great room overlooking the park, high up, where it's quiet and the breeze is fresh and where they can see the George Washington Bridge and Jersey from the window. And I want them to have everything this hotel has to offer. Let them send down for champagne and caviar and roast pheasant and put it all on my bill.' Then he kissed them good night and told them they would have tickets for California on the Chief two days later and he left them alone."

Jack stopped, caught in the memory of those distant days which his own voice had evoked, those forgotten catastrophes, lost hopes, spent tears, that vigorous honesty, that rough, effective, human doctoring, that youthful belief. He hadn't told them about himself at that time, either, about Delaney's hiring him, too, almost casually, without compliments or duplicity, and he hadn't told them about his own wife, his first wife, either, and how she hated Delaney and hated what Delaney meant to Jack. Well, that wasn't part of the story and it wouldn't fit into an article in a French magazine. "So," Jack said, looking down at his plate, and beginning to eat again, "that's what it was like in New York a hundred years ago, when I was young."

"If I was writing the article," Veronica said, and Jack was conscious that she hadn't moved her eyes from his face, "I would put it all in like that, every word, just the way he said it."

"What does it prove?" Despière shrugged. "That we were all better when we were young? Everybody knows that."

"Maybe," Veronica said, surprisingly, "that wouldn't be such a bad thing to put in an article. Not such a bad thing at all."

"He was terrific with the ladies," Miss Henken said, chewing away like a grazing spinster horse at her spaghetti and clams. "I heard. It was common gossip. He had them all. Put that in. That's what people like to read."

"Listen to Felice," Despière said gravely. "She has her finger on the public pulse."

"I bet," Miss Henken said, looking with sandy-eyebrowed archness at Jack, "that when you were young, when you looked the way you did in the picture, I bet you had them all, too."

"I will draw up a list for you, Miss Henken," Jack said, with distaste, "before I leave Rome."

"He's a married man now," Despière said, grinning, "and a pillar of government. Don't disturb him with lascivious memories."

"I was just paying him a compliment," Miss Henken said, aggrieved. "Can't you even pay a man a compliment any more?"

Jack caught Veronica's eye, across the table, and Veronica smiled at him, swiftly, secretly, tilting her head. Why, Jack thought, surprised, she doesn't think I look so bad even now.

Despière, who missed nothing, caught the almost imperceptible interchange, and he leaned back in his chair, regarding them both, his heavy eyelids almost closed, deciding, Jack realized, how he was going to make the girl and Jack pay for the moment. "Be careful what you say to the man," he said lazily. "His wife is famously jealous. Aside from being beautiful. She is so beautiful," Despière went on, "that when Jack leaves town she becomes the most popular lady in Paris. By the way, Jack," he said, "did I tell you? I got a call from Paris this morning from a lady and she said she saw your wife last night. Did I tell you?"

"No," said Jack, "you didn't tell me."

"She was at L'Eléphant Blanc at three in the morning," Despière said. "Dancing with a Greek. The lady didn't know who he was, but he was very light of foot, she said. She said Hélène looked beautiful."

"I'm sure she did," Jack said shortly.

"They're the happiest married couple I know," Despière said to the girls, his revenge completed. "Aren't you, Jack?"

"I don't know," Jack said. "I don't know all your other married friends."

"If there was any chance of success," Despière said, "Hélène is just the sort of girl I would apply myself to. She herself is beautiful, and"—he nodded graciously at Jack—"her husband is amusing. It is too boring to have an affair with a woman who has a dull husband. No matter how attractive she is, it never makes up for the hours you have to spend with him, pretending to be his friend."

Miss Henken laughed nervously, impressed by this *boulevardier* glimpse into a world where she would never be welcome, and Despière attacked his food happily, his triumph secure behind him.

Before the coffee came, he looked at his watch and jumped up, saying, "I've got to leave you, children, I've got a date. We must have lunch together every day." With a wave, he was away from the table. The proprietor came bustling over toward him and Despière put his arm around the man's shoulders and walked to the door with him and the proprietor went outside with him to speed him on his way, while Jack sat glaring at their disappearing backs, annoyed with himself for being so slow and letting Despière get away without paying the bill, or at least his share of the bill. He looked suddenly at Veronica, to see how she was taking being left like that by Despière, but she was eating a pear happily, unmoved.

Somewhere, Jack thought, I've gotten something all wrong.

And then, a few minutes later, when they had finished their coffee, and Jack called, with bad grace, for the bill, the proprietor came over and said, smiling widely, that it had already been paid, that Signor Despière had said this lunch was on him, they were all his friends that afternoon.

6

Outside the restaurant, Miss Henken said she had to go to Cinecittà to ask about a job and they found a taxi for her and she went off with the expression on her face of a woman who always leaves every place alone.

"Which way do you go?" Veronica asked, standing there, with her coat thrown back from her shoulders, in what Jack now recognized as a habitual attitude of self-display.

"I'm walking back to my hotel. It's not far from here." Jack prepared to say good-bye and wondered if, out of politeness, he ought to ask for her telephone number. The hell with it, he decided, I wouldn't use it.

"May I walk with you?" she asked. Tip of the tongue again, he noticed.

"Of course," Jack said, and they started walking, side by side, not touching. "I'd be delighted. If you're not in a hurry."

"I have nothing to do until five," she said.

"What do you have to do then?" Jack asked.

"I work," she said. "In a travel bureau. I send people off to places I would rather go myself."

The sun was behind the clouds and the clouds were piling up ominously, slate black, in the north, and coming over Rome in invading formations and the wind was making torn poster edges flap against the ocher walls of the buildings with snapping, whiplike reports. It was going to rain soon.

They passed a doorway where a ragged, bent woman with a dirty child in her arms was begging. Holding her child with one arm, the woman ran after Jack, saying, *"Americano, americano,"* holding out her other hand, clawlike and filthy, for charity.

Jack stopped and gave her a hundred-lire piece and the woman turned, without a word of thanks, and went back to her doorway, where she crouched once more against the stone. Jack felt the woman staring after him, ungrateful, unappeased, and he had the feeling that the hundred lire he had given her did not make up for the warmth of the meal he had just eaten, for the pretty girl by his side, for the luxury of the hotel rooms he was approaching.

"It is to remind us," Veronica said soberly. "Women like that."

"Remind us of what?"

"Remind us of how close we are to Africa here in Italy," she said, "and how we pay for it."

"There're beggars in America, too," Jack said.

"Not the same kind," the girl said. She was walking quickly, as though to get away from the woman and her child.

"Have you been in America?" Jack asked.

"No," Veronica said. "But I know."

They walked in silence for a moment, and crossed a street and turned a corner, passing a grocery window heaped with cheeses, sausages, and flasks of Chianti wrapped in straw.

"Do you mind," Veronica asked, abruptly, her voice low, "that your wife was dancing at three o'clock this morning in Paris with another man?"

"No," Jack said, thinking, That is not quite true.

"Americans marry better than Italians," Veronica said. She said it flatly, but with bitterness.

Well, Jack thought, smiling inwardly, I could find you an argument on that subject.

"Anyway," he said, "there's a good chance she wasn't dancing at three o'clock this morning."

"You mean maybe Jean-Baptiste was lying?"

"Inventing," Jack said.

"There's a bad man there," Veronica said. "Mixed up with a very good man."

Then Jack felt the wetness on his lip and he knew he was bleeding again. Embarrassed, he stopped and got out his handkerchief and put it to his nose.

"What is it?" Veronica looked at him, alarmed.

"Nothing," he said, his voice muffled a little. "A nosebleed." He tried to make a joke of it. "The Royal disease."

"Does it do it like this all the time? For no reason?" Veronica asked.

"Only in Rome," he said. "Somebody hit me last night."

"Somebody hit you?" She sounded incredulous. "Why?"

"I don't know." Jack shook his head, annoyed at the scene, at the blood, which was flowing heavily now. "As a warning." He stood there, depressed and shaken, weighed down, all over again, on the busy daytime street, by the dreams, the premonitions, the images of the dead, the nearness of danger, the loneliness and fear of the night. "We'd better get you to your hotel quickly," Veronica said. She hailed a taxi and helped him in, like an invalid. Her hand was firm and gentle on his arm and he was glad that he wasn't alone this time.

At the hotel, she insisted upon paying for the taxi, and got the key from the desk and stood close to him in the elevator, watching carefully, ready to hold him, as though she were afraid he was going to fall. The blood kept coming.

In the elevator, trying to look polite, unbloody, ordinary, for the sake of the tall boy in livery who pushed the buttons with his white-gloved hand, Jack had a curious, clear after-image. He was sure that while he had been waiting in the middle of the lobby for Veronica to get the key, he had seen Despière and a woman in a blue suit, seated close together, talking earnestly, in the long, empty lounge that stretched away from the lobby. And now, rising in the gilt cage from floor to floor, he was sure that at one point Despière had looked up, recognized him, smiled, then ducked his head.

"Did you see them?" he asked Veronica standing protectively next to him.

"See whom?"

"Despière and a woman," Jack said. "In the lounge."

"No," Veronica said, looking at him strangely. "I didn't see anybody."

"No matter," Jack said thickly. "No matter at all." Now the living are haunting me, too, he thought, in broad daylight.

In the hotel bedroom, he took off his jacket and opened his collar and pulled down his tie and lay back on the bed. Veronica hung up his jacket neatly in the wardrobe, like a meticulous housewife, and found a clean handkerchief in the bureau drawer and gave it to him. Then she stood over him for a moment, her outlines vague in the dimness of the curtained room, with the sound of the new rain lashing at the windows. Then she lay down beside him, without a word, and took him comfortingly in her arms. They lay there together in silence, listening to the rain, in the warm, wavy, watery obscurity of the dark afternoon. After a while he dropped the handkerchief away from his face because he didn't need it any more, and he turned his head and kissed her throat, pressing his lips hard against the firm, warm skin, shutting out everything that was not that room, that moment, that bed, shutting out omens and premonitions, wounds and blood, memories and loyalties.

*

He turned and lay on his back, her head on his shoulder, the long hair a dark blur against the dull, hidden gleam of his skin. Slowly, he returned to himself, slowly he became the visitor in apartment 654, husband, father, sane, deliberate, aloof, reasonable. He looked at Veronica's shadowy face beside him, the face of a stranger, the face of a girl who, no more than two hours before, he had thought, looked stupid and self-satisfied. She was lying with her eyes wide-open, staring at the ceiling, a small, placid, public smile on her lips. Yes, he thought reasonably, there *is* something stupid about her face. He remembered his first judgment of her at the table on the street in front of the café—a glossy female brute. He smiled, thinking, What marvelous uses there are for glossy female brutes.

They lay together in the secret rain, with the noise of Rome outside the walls muffled by curtains and shutters and windows.

He chuckled softly to himself.

"Why do you laugh?" she asked, without moving, speaking next to his ear in her soft, trumpet voice.

"I was laughing because I'm so clever," he said.

"What is so clever?"

"I had it all figured out," he said. "At lunch. That you were going to go off, finally, with Jean-Baptiste."

"You thought I was his girl?"

"Yes. Aren't you?"

"No," she said. "I am not his girl." She took Jack's hand and kissed it, on the palm. "I am your girl."

"When did you decide that?" he asked, pleased and surprised by the swift declaration, thinking, How long it has been since anything like this has happened to me.

Then it was her turn to chuckle. "I decided two nights ago," she said.

"You hadn't even met me two nights ago," he said. "You didn't know I existed."

"I hadn't met you," she said. "But I knew you existed. I knew very well you existed. I saw your film, you see. You were so beautiful, so capable of love, I became your girl in a half-hour, sitting alone in a movie house."

Maybe, later, Jack thought sorrowfully, I will laugh at this when I remember it, but I don't feel like laughing now. "But, baby," he said, "I was twenty years younger then. I was younger than you are now."

"I know," she said.

"I'm not the same man now," he said, regretfully, feeling that this lovely, simple-minded, slightly foolish girl was being cheated, cheated by time and the tricky durability of celluloid, and that somehow he was taking advantage unfairly of that trick. "Not the same man at all."

"When I was sitting there in the movie house," she said, "I knew what it would be like if you made love to me."

Jack laughed harshly. "I guess I ought to give you your money back," he said.

"What does that mean?"

"It means that you were paying for something you didn't get," he said, withdrawing his arm from under her head, letting her head fall back on the pillow. "You were paying for a twenty-two-year-old boy who vanished a long time ago."

"No," Veronica said slowly, "I wasn't paying for anything. And he didn't vanish as you say, the twenty-two-year-old boy. When I sat in the restaurant, listening to you tell about Mr. Delaney and that poor friend of yours with the play, I saw that boy was still there." Then she chuckled and moved closer to him, turning her head and whispering into his ear. "No, I am not telling the whole truth. It is not exactly the same as I imagined in the movie house. It is better, much better."

Then they laughed together. Thank God for fans, Jack thought basely. He put his arm around her again, his hand caught in the rough, dark hair. Well, he thought, delighted, and I thought I had received my salary for that picture long ago. Now it turns out that I have what the Screen Actors Guild calls residual rights. Rich residual rights.

He turned toward her and put his hand on her.

"What do you want?" she whispered.

"Something particularly Italian," he said. "Is this particularly Italian?"

7

He was aware of a knocking. He opened his eyes reluctantly. The room was dark and for a moment he was floating in time, not knowing where he was, what hour of the day or night it was, and not caring, happy in soft, clockless depths. Then the knocking came again, timidly, and he saw the door from the living room open a crack and a thin shaft of yellow light slant into the bedroom, and he knew he was in his bed in apartment 654 in the hotel in Rome and he knew he was alone.

"Come in," he said, pulling the covers up around his neck, because he was naked under the twisted sheets and blankets.

The door opened wider and he saw it was the chambermaid, the old lady, with his jacket. She stood there, smiling, gap-toothed, holding the jacket up on its hanger like a trophy of the chase, *See what I have caught today in the Roman jungle: one American jacket, stained with American blood.*

"La giacca," she said, in a happy whine. *"La giacca del signore. È pulita."*

She shuffled across the carpet, in a thin aroma of old-lady sweat, and hung the suit up in the wardrobe, stroking and fondling it as though it were her dearest pet. Jack would have liked to give her a tip, but he couldn't get out of bed naked in front of the old lady. It wouldn't shock the old lady, he was sure (what scenes she must have come upon, walking into the hotel bedrooms of Rome for thirty years, with a towel over her arm, what surprised nakedness of body and soul), but she would have to wait for another time for her hundred lire.

"Grazie," Jack said, hunching under the covers, conscious of the slight perfume of Veronica's body that clung to the sheets. *"Grazie tanto."*

"Prego, prego," she whined, her eyes roving around the room, taking it all in, cognizant of everything, no clues ever lost on her, Holmes with dugs, in a blue apron, compiling her endless backstairs thunderous dossier in this Christian city. She backed out of the room, deprived of her hundred lire, her face an accusation of the everlasting meanness of the rich, poverty once more, and not unexpectedly, further impoverished. She didn't close the door, and Jack heard her going out through the living room grumbling to herself, the dying sound of her passage a grandmother's echo of the roar the crowd must have made outside the Kremlin walls in 1917. He heard the salon door close behind her and he stretched luxuriously in the warm bed, listening to the chug of the steam in the radiators, allowing the memory of the afternoon to flood deliciously over him. Well, now, he thought lazily, it wasn't such a bad thing that the nose began to bleed, or else what excuse would she have been able to make to come up to the room? The next time I see the drunk who hit me, maybe I'll shake the bastard's hand.

He reached out and turned on the bedside lamp, and looked at his watch. Seven o'clock. Insomnia, there are cures available. There was no sign that Veronica had been there, unless you accepted the frail, close fragrance that clung to the sheets as a sign. He wondered when she had left. He remembered hearing a Frenchwoman say once that it was rude for a man to fall asleep after making love. Oh, you rude, uncultivated American, he thought comfortably, oh you Comanche.

He thought of his wife and tested himself for guilt. He felt a lot of things, lying there in the warm tumbled bed, but he didn't feel guilty. In the eight years that he had been married to Hélène, he had had nothing to do with other women. He had thought of it often enough, of course, and approached it once or twice, but had always pulled back at the last moment. Not from a sense of morality —his moral sense was involved in other ways, and he had been through too much marriage and seen too much of other marriages to be able to believe that physical fidelity was the rule rather than the exception, in the age and in the places in which he lived. He had been faithful until that afternoon to Hélène because— Because he loved her? There were times, like the afternoon at the airport, when he didn't love her at all. Because he felt guilty at not being able to love her enough, and scrupulously kept to the form of the marriage, hoping that one day the substance would materialize? Because he was grateful to her for her goodness and her beauty and her love for him? Because he had been married too often and had suffered and had made others suffer too much? Because, after all the riot, he was satisfying himself with comfort and routine and cannily renouncing passion? Well, he thought, this afternoon, comfort and routine had been forgotten, and well forgotten. Still, if there had been any danger of his falling in love with Veronica, he told himself, he would not have let her come up to the room. But this way—he moved lazily in the bed, turning toward the place where Veronica's head had lain and where two long dark hairs webbed the pillow—this way (O, benevolent accident) no harm would come to anyone, and maybe a great deal of good. What the hell, he thought, it's only two weeks.

As for Hélène (dancing—one reported, one invented, one telephoned, one lied or didn't lie—in a night club at three in the morning)—he wasn't sure what she did, at all. She was Parisienne, her religion was fashionable French, in other words, almost nonoperative on questions like this—she was beautiful and attractive to men, she had had several affairs he knew of, before marrying him, and probably others he didn't know of, she was out of the house almost every afternoon on the hazy and flexible errands women invent for themselves in Paris, and he made no investigation of how she used her time. He knew that if he were to come into a Paris drawing room and see her for the first time, he would take it for granted that she was a woman who took lovers. Well, if she does, he thought, with the tolerance of recent pleasure warm in his veins, and if she doesn't tell me about it, and if it makes her feel as good as I do now, more power to her.

He threw back the covers and got out of bed, whistling tunelessly under his breath. He flipped on the switch for the chandelier and looked at the bureau for a note from Veronica. There was nothing there. He was certain she wouldn't have gone without leaving her address and telephone number and he padded, barefooted and naked, into the salon to search for it. But there was nothing there, either. He shrugged, undisturbed. Maybe it's better that way, he thought, love and farewell, maybe she's smarter than I give her credit for being.

He went back through the bedroom, still whistling. Then he recognized what he was whistling. Walkin' My Baby Back Home. He stopped whistling and went into the bathroom to turn the water on for a bath. When he switched on the light he saw, scrawled in lipstick on the mirror over one of the basins, a large crimson V. He grinned, looking at it. No, he thought, that doesn't mean farewell. The phone will ring eventually.

Happily, he turned on the water for the bath. There was a wide full-length mirror in the bathroom and he stopped in front of it and regarded himself thoughtfully, standing there naked, with the steam of the bath rising in clouds behind him. When he was young, he had spent considerable time looking at his body in the mirror. He had played football in high school and part of his freshman year in college, until he had torn a cartilage in his knee and the doctors had told him he had to quit or risk being lame for life. He had had the body of an athlete then, and he had stared into the glass with almost embarrassed pride in the sloping powerful shoulders, the flat ridges of muscle across the stomach, the long, heavy legs so finely conditioned that with each move you would see the small play of the tendons under the smooth skin. And when he had gone into the theatre he worked out in the gymnasium four times a week, on the bags, sparring, on the bars, so that no matter what claims any role might make on him, his body would be able to respond completely and with grace. But after the war, after the time in the hospital, with all the muscles gone slack and soft from the morphia months, and the scars from the grafting still red on his skin, and the curious, thick disarrangement of his jaw, he had avoided looking at himself, to spare himself pain. And since then, when a mirror happened to surprise him, in a locker room or in a strange bedroom, he had observed himself with distaste, noting critically the growing heaviness, the thickening of the years. He had recovered completely—the invalid's flabbiness had disappeared, and his body looked powerful and healthy—but the grace and suppleness had gone, he felt. The body of the boy who had raced down the field under punts and leaped high into the air for passes was only a memory, submerged in the grossness of time.

But now he found himself regarding his body with approval. Remembering how well it had served him that afternoon, he looked at his naked reflection with new eyes. Not so bad, he thought, with an inner smile for his vanity, the monopoly of youth is not complete—after all, a body is made to wear for a long time and not all the changes of maturity are for the worse. Take off ten pounds, he thought, staring critically at his waist, and it wouldn't be too bad at all. Anyway, there's no paunch yet, and the important lines are still flat.

He got into the deep old-fashioned bathtub and lay there for a long time, luxuriously adding hot water every two or three minutes, feeling the cleansing sweat run down his forehead. Lying there, he saw the big lipstick V on the mirror above the basin, now misted over with steam, and he wondered how he could prevail upon the maid to leave it there, for the whole two weeks of his stay.

Later, getting dressed, he decided that he felt too good to go to a cocktail party. He went downstairs and told the doorman to tell his driver he wouldn't need him that night. Then he went into the bar and ordered a martini, pleased at being alone and at the prospect of solitude for the evening. The same group of young Italians who had been in the bar the night before were there again, but this time Jack suffered them benignly, without jealousy.

He finished his drink and left the hotel and strolled slowly down the tree-lined avenue, looking in at the windows, his coat thrown open, despite the dark nip in the air. Half by accident, he found himself walking toward the theatre where *The Stolen Midnight* was playing. When he reached the theatre he stood in front of it and looked at the stills of himself curiously, but without emotion, without regret. He looked at the pictures of Carlotta and wondered where she was now and what she was like after all the years and how he would feel if she were to come into a room in which he happened to be. For a moment, he was tempted to go in and see the picture again, to study his ancient self in the covering darkness and try to find out just what it was about him twenty years before that had captured Veronica. But he decided against it, feeling he had indulged himself in enough narcissism for one day.

He had dinner quietly, in a small, deserted restaurant. Remembering the ten pounds, he ate no bread or *pasta*. After dinner, he walked down toward the Forum, stopping in for an *espresso* and a glass of sweet Italian brandy. The Forum, locked for the night behind its gates, was deserted and shadowy in the pale light of a quarter moon, and a freshening wind made him button the collar of his coat tight around his neck.

Standing there bareheaded in the winter wind, he had a happy feeling of being disconnected, private to himself. At that moment, nobody in the whole world knew where he was. No matter what claims anybody might have on him, no matter how much anyone might want or need him, he was, for the time he stood there, unreachable, his own man. I am in the heart of Europe, at the roots of the continent, alone, he thought, secret among the ruins.

He remembered a few lines of one of Cicero's orations that had been spoken in this place, reverberating among these stones. *O tempora, o mores! Senatus haec intellegit, consul videt; hic tamen vivit. Vivit? Immo vero etiam in senatum venit, fit publici consili particeps, notat et designat oculis ad caedem unum quemque nostrum.* High-school Latin and the scrawled-in pony on his desk at home when he was fifteen years old. *What an age! What morals! The senate knows these things, the consul sees them. Yet this man lives. Lives, did I say? Nay, more, he walks into the senate, he takes part in the public counsel. He singles out and marks with his glance each one of us for murder.* Then they strangled Cicero, far from the scene of his triumphs, after the applause had died down. Poor old man, how he must have regretted his gifted tongue when they came to get him.

I am a Roman, he thought, playing a game he had indulged in when he was a child, when he would close his eyes in bed at night and say to himself, I am an Eskimo, my igloo is warm, the seals are barking across the ice, or, I am Nathan Hale, they are coming to hang me in the morning, or, I am Jubal Early, on a black horse, riding around the Union lines. I am a Roman, he thought, and Christ has just been born and just been crucified, although in my lifetime I will not hear of either event. I have had my dinner, and the wind from the Apennines is heavy with winter and I have drunk a little too much wine and heard a man from Athens play on the flute, accompanied by a boy on the lyre. The silence and the darkness in front of the Senate steps is doubly welcome now because of all this. Tomorrow, they say, Augustus will make an appearance, and there will be games, and the gladiator with the net and trident will be matched against an African lion. You can hear the roars of the beasts even now, locked in their stone pens beneath the Colosseum floor. The man with the net and trident, you imagine, is quiet for the moment, mending his net, making sure of the knots, sharpening his long fork, contemplating the next morning.

Roman, you stroll alone in the cold midnight air, surrounded by the tall marble pillars, thinking of the violent, merciless men, the astute voluptuaries in togas who throng the place in daylight and you feel how permanent and indestructible it all is, how this stone seed grows and flourishes, days without end, on these low, central hills.

He heard steps in the distance and he saw, outlined against the light of a lamppost, the figures of two policemen. The policemen stopped and looked at him and Jack could guess at the everlasting policemen's suspicion in their eyes as they surveyed him, waiting for him to make one false move, scale a wall, bend for one marble fragment, pocket one crumbling shard of history.

The policemen Americanized him, took away his ghostly Roman citizenship. Eyes were upon him; he was no longer unreachable; the world once more put its claims upon him; he was subject to search and seizure and could be forced to announce his identity. The noise of chariot wheels drummed away to a whisper in the distance, the lions fell silent and their pens were open to the moon in the stripped arena; the music heard far off came from a bar and it was a record playing "Trumpet Rag." No pipes, no lyres under the policemen's eyes, and the Vespas coughed in the streets under their control. Christ and Cicero were dead a round two thousand years and only the night wind coming from the mountains to the north was the same.

Jack made his way along the wall, looking down at the uneven paving below (blood, sandals, bronze wheels). The policemen watched him, thinking, If necessary, we will get him another night.

He'd walked enough and he found a cab and rode back toward the hotel. He went across the street from the hotel to the newspaper kiosk, lurid with plump movie beauties on the covers of magazines. He bought the Paris *Tribune* and looked at the stacks of bright, paper-covered books in English that were banked all along one side of the kiosk. One book caught his eye because of the sobriety of its cover among the shiny reclining ladies and the gentlemen with pistols who advertised the literature being offered for sale in English that year in Rome. He picked up the dark book and saw that it was the poems of Catullus, translated by an English poet. After the revery in the Forum, Jack felt Catullus was a fitting discovery, and he paid for the book and crossed the street and entered his hotel.

When he got his key from the concierge, he felt a flicker of disappointment because there was no message for him in his box. Well, he thought, getting into the elevator, tonight I'll make do with Catullus.

*

He was sitting in the salon, with his jacket and shoes off and his collar unbuttoned, reading, *Look, where the youths are coming, Lightly up they spring, and not for nothing, hark! it's good to hear them sing. Hymen O Hymenaeus Hymen hither O Hymenaeus,* when the phone rang. He let it ring twice, pleasantly anticipating the sound of the voice he would hear when he picked up the receiver. Then he reached over for the phone and said, "Hello."

"Mr. Andrus," a man's voice said.

"Yes."

"You don't know me," the voice said. "My name is Robert Bresach. I wonder if I could see you for a moment, Mr. Andrus." The voice was polite, educated American, and sounded young.

Jack looked at his watch. It was after midnight. "Couldn't it wait until morning?" he said.

"I'm a friend of Mr. Despière's," the man said. "It really is rather urgent."

Jack sighed. "All right," he said. "Room six fifty-four."

He hung up the phone, annoyed. It was just like Despière to have friends who insisted upon seeing you in your hotel room at twelve o'clock at night.

Jack put Catullus in the bedroom. He felt a little embarrassed about leaving it lying open on a table, the only book in the room, aside from a 1928 Baedeker he had found on a bookstall along the Seine and had brought with him on the chance he might have some time for sightseeing. If the man were observant and reported the presence of Catullus to Despière, Despière would be sure to think Jack had stage-managed it that way, to impress visitors.

There was a knock on the salon door and Jack crossed the room and opened the door. A tall figure in a khaki duffel coat stood there.

"Come in," Jack said and stood to one side to allow the man to go through the small foyer into the salon. Jack closed the door and followed him. In the living room, the man turned around and faced Jack. He was young and had dark blond hair, cut short and he was very handsome, with the same kind of knifelike, intense, bony good looks as Jack's son, Steven. He stood there, staring curiously at Jack, through rimless glasses, his face grave, his blue eyes intent and serious.

"I'm going to kill you, Andrus," he said.

8

He said something else, Jack thought, standing there, smiling puzzledly at the blond boy in the duffel coat, but it sounded like, I'm going to kill you.

"What did you say?" Jack asked.

The boy had his hands in the deep pockets of the coat. Now he took his hands out of the pockets. In his right hand there was a clasp knife. There was a click and Jack saw the long ugly blade, heavy, dull steel, reflecting the light off the chandelier. The boy's hand was shaking and the reflection on the steel kept changing and trembling. He didn't say anything, but merely stood there in the middle of the room, tall and bulky in the big coat, his face rigid, his eyes fixed on Jack's face, with an expression that was somehow appealing and touched with beggary.

This is it, Jack thought, this is what it was all about—the blow, the blood, the dream, the premonition, the sense of being warned, the recapitulation of the dead. The knife was behind it all.

"Put that godamn thing away," Jack said roughly. The door behind him that led to the corridor was closed and no matter how quickly he could turn and run, the boy would have him before he could wrench the door half-open. And the door opened inward, into the room, to make it worse.

The boy remained still, only the minute trembling of the knife in his hand showing what pressure he was under. His mouth was opened slightly, and he took in air with a small, regular sighing noise. He was making a conscious effort to breathe calmly. There was no other sound. The closed windows, the drawn drapes, the heavy doors and thick walls of the old hotel cut off all noises of any life outside the room. If he called for help, Jack thought, even if he could keep the boy from his throat for a minute or two, there was almost no chance that anyone would hear him.

In two or three of the movies in which he had played, long ago, there had been scenes like this—Jack, unarmed, facing a man with a knife who was out to kill him. In the movies, Jack had always escaped, making a sudden lunge at the murderer's wrist, cleverly throwing a lamp and disconcerting the attacker, knocking over a table with a kick and plunging the room into darkness. In seeing the scenes later, on film, the action had always seemed quite reasonable. But what was going to happen here, tonight, was not going to be on film later and the knife, with its quivering reflections, was steel and not prop rubber, and was not going to be pushed aside with the flick of a scenario writer's wrist.

"Where is she?" Bresach asked. "Is she in there?" He motioned toward the bedroom, with a stiff, spasmodic gesture of the knife.

"Where is who?" Jack asked.

"Don't kid me," Bresach said. "I didn't come here to have anyone kid me." His voice was deep, baritone, with a pleasant, clear timbre, not made for threats. "Veronica."

"No," Jack said, "she's not in there."

"Are you lying to me?"

"Go in and see for yourself," Jack said, carelessly. He knew that he couldn't afford to show the boy that he was afraid.

The boy looked uncertainly at the doorway to the bedroom. His mouth twisted and Jack saw a muscle working in his jaw. His face was thin and the bones were prominent and sharp, making triangular shadows in his cheeks.

"All right," Bresach said. He took a step nearer Jack. "You go in ahead of me."

Jack hesitated for a moment. Here, in the living room, with only space between him and Bresach, he was at the mercy of the knife. In the bedroom, with a little luck, he could get the bed between them, move innocently near a lamp, perhaps even pick up the heavy leather bag that was on a stand there, to use as a shield or weapon. He turned and walked quickly into the bedroom, with Bresach close behind him.

Only the bed-table lamp was on and the room was in shadow, the shadow slashed by the white light from the bathroom that poured in past the half-opened door. As Jack went into the room, he saw one diagonal of the crimson V Veronica had scrawled on the mirror over the basin. Jack moved away from the bathroom door, toward the giant wardrobe that filled one side of the room. Bresach followed him closely.

"Stop moving," Bresach said.

Jack stopped. He didn't have the bed between him and Bresach, but the leather bag was only two feet away now, and if Bresach started toward him, there was a chance he could grab the bag in time. Bresach was standing next to the big double bed, now made up for the night, with the blankets and the sheet folded down in a neat triangle on one side. There were two pillows, side by side, neatly plumped out.

"So, this is where it happened," Bresach said. He touched the bed with his knee. He wavered a little and his head rolled slightly from side to side as he spoke, and for the first time Jack realized that he had been drinking. "Did you have an enjoyable afternoon, Mr. Andrus?" he asked, harshly, his mouth twisting down to one side again in what looked like a habitual, disfiguring tic. "She's a great lay, isn't she, our little Veronica?" With an abrupt movement, he tore back the covers of the bed with the knife. "Right here, in this bed," he repeated. "In this bed." His eyes filled with tears, and the tears, instead of reassuring Jack, made the boy seem more dangerous than before. "Not a bad sight for a man to see in his bed, is it?" Bresach demanded, "Veronica, with her legs apart."

"Stop that," Jack said, but without hope that his words would have any effect on the weeping boy. "What good does it do to talk like that?"

"A lot of good," Bresach said. Now he waved the knife aimlessly, in a stiff oratorical gesture. "I want to get the picture, see? The exact picture. I'm interested in the girl and I like to know exactly what's happening to her. When you put it in her, did she whisper 'Oh, God'? Did she? Am I being a cad when I tell you, she always does it with me?" He grinned crookedly, weeping. "It's her strict Catholic upbringing. Sanctifying the union." The grin, the tears, broke into a tortured laugh. "Did she? Did she say, 'Oh, God'?"

"I'm not going to talk to you," Jack said, steadily, "until you put that damn knife away."

"I'll put the knife away when I'm good and ready." Bresach waved it again, crazily. "And I know where I'll put it." He leaned down and ran his left hand caressingly over the creased sheet of the bed. "Right here," he whispered, "right here." He raised his head, fixing the swamped blue eyes on Jack. "Did she put her tongue in your ear while you were doing it to her? Do you know the word for fuck in Italian? Where is she?" Now he was shouting. "She's left me, where is she now?"

He moved closer toward Jack, the handsome bony face wet with tears, and Jack took a half step backward and put his hand on the handle of the leather valise, prepared to grab it and swing it.

"You must have been awful good in there this afternoon," Bresach said. "You must be a godamn wonder, because she couldn't wait to get her clothes on and come home and start packing her bags to leave me. She couldn't wait . . ." he whispered. "What are you, you bastard, a bull, a stallion? You pick up a girl at lunch and you give her a casual roll because you have an hour to waste in the afternoon, and it changes her whole life. Love, she says, love, love, love. What've you got in there?" The knife suddenly dropped below belt level and Jack could feel his testicles pulling up in tight, electrical spasms. "It must be a wonder, the godamned eighth wonder of the world. Open your pants; I want to see it, I want to pay homage to the eighth wonder of the world." Bresach was gasping for breath now and his lips were pulled away from his teeth in an animal-like snarl and his whole arm was shaking and he kept half opening his hand and then closing it convulsively, so that the knife jumped erratically.

Jack tightened his hand on the grip of the valise. He kept his right arm crooked in front of him protectively and his eyes on the knife. If the boy moved, he was going to go into him, swinging the bag and trying for the wrist of the knife hand with his own right hand.

"Listen," Jack said soothingly, "you're all upset now, you don't know what you're doing. Give yourself a little time to think about it, and then . . ."

"Where is she? Where're you hiding her?" Bresach looked

around him wildly. With a violent movement, he threw open the door of the big wardrobe, as though a sudden conviction had hit him that the girl was secreted there. Jack's suits swung on their hangers. "Come on, Andrus," Bresach said, pleading. "Tell me where she is. I've got to know where she is."

"I don't know where she is," Jack said. "And I wouldn't tell you if I knew. Not while you're waving that knife at me."

"There's no sense in talking to you," Bresach said, thickly. He took off his glasses and wiped his wet eyes with the sleeve of his coat. The stiff cloth made a grating noise against his forehead. "I don't know why I bothered this long. Why do I waste my time? I should've jabbed you the minute I came through the door. Well, it's never too late." He smiled convulsively. "Never too late for a good deed."

Here it comes, Jack thought. His hand on the grip of the valise was slippery with sweat. He waited tensely, waiting for the boy to start his move.

Then the telephone rang.

They both stood there, motionless, the sound freezing them.

The phone rang again. The boy looked uncertainly at it. He's had no practice at murder, Jack thought, inconsequentially. Like me. We're two novices. This is no job for amateurs.

"Answer it," Bresach said finally, his voice trembling. "It's probably her. Tell her to come up. ANSWER IT!"

Jack moved over toward the bed table, past Bresach. He picked up the phone, holding it close to his ear, so that Bresach wouldn't be able to hear the voice on the other end. "Hello," Jack said. He was surprised at the calmness of his voice.

"Delaney," Maurice's voice said. "Where the hell have you been all night? I thought you were coming to the party."

"I couldn't make it," Jack said, conscious of the boy's eyes ranging him suspiciously. "I'm sorry."

"Is it her?" Bresach whispered.

Jack hesitated. Then he nodded.

"Tell her to come up. Right away," Bresach whispered.

"Listen," Delaney was saying, "there're some people I want you to meet. We're down in the lobby. You got anything to drink up there?"

"Sure," Jack said. "Come on up . . ." He looked across at Bresach. "Darling."

"What? What did you say?" Delaney asked irritably and Jack

was afraid that the loud voice could be heard in the room, even though he was pressing the instrument tight against his ear.

"I said come on up. You remember the number of the room," Jack said clearly. "Six fifty-four." He hung up and turned to face Bresach.

"Now," he said calmly, sounding much more confident than he felt, "now, maybe we can settle this like sensible human beings." He brushed past Bresach, standing irresolutely next to the bed, the knife dangling loosely in his hand, and walked collectedly into the salon. Bresach jumped after him and ran toward the door leading to the corridor, blocking it. "No tricks," he said.

"Oh, shut up," Jack said wearily. He sat down in the easy chair next to which his shoes were lying. He put on his shoes slowly, having difficulty because they fitted snugly and he didn't have a shoehorn. The back of the right shoe kept bending over and it took him almost a minute, scraping his finger, to get the shoe on. He tied the bows neatly, tight, and stretched low in the chair, regarding the shoes, which were heavy, with double soles, and which might prove useful later on. A well-placed kick with those thick shoes would take the fight out of any man.

"Take a drink," Jack said, carelessly waving to the table near the window, where there was a bottle of Scotch and a bottle of bourbon. "It might help your nerves."

"Don't worry about my nerves," Bresach said, sounding like a belligerent and uncertain schoolboy. "There's nothing wrong with my nerves."

"You're crazy," Jack said. "You know—if you go around behaving like this, they're going to come for you and take you away and lock you up as a certifiable lunatic. Even in Italy," Jack said, beginning, surprisingly, to enjoy himself, "even in Italy, there're limits."

The boy sighed. He looked tired and drained and the stiff coat seemed too big for him, as though it had been designed for a larger man. "Ah, Christ," he said in a low voice, "ah, Christ." He looked down at the knife in his hand, uncertainly. Then he closed it slowly and put it in his pocket. "Give her back to me," he whispered. "Please give her back to me."

There was a knock on the door and before either of them could make a move toward it, the door was pushed open and there was a confused rumble of voices and Delaney came into the room with two women in fur coats and three other men. One of the other men was wearing a pale gray sombrero with a narrow tan band.

"Put on your coat," Delaney was saying. "In the elevator the girls decided they wanted to go dancing." He stopped and stared at Bresach. Bresach stood facing the group, his hands away from his body, the fingers spread, as if bracing himself against the possibility that they were going to tackle him en masse. His mouth was twitching again and he looked disappointed and pitiful, and he kept peering near-sightedly over the women's shoulders into the hall, as if somehow there must have been some mistake, and one more visitor, the one he expected, was even then making her appearance in the doorway. Delaney was still looking curiously at Bresach, as Jack stood up and smiled at the group. "Say, Jack," Delaney said, still looking at Bresach, "did you call me darling over the phone?"

"Yes, I guess I did," Jack said. "At the moment I was feeling very affectionate toward you."

Bresach twisted his head bitterly in Jack's direction. "You bastard," he muttered. Then he plunged toward the door through the mink. Jack could hear the sound of his steps fading away as he ran down the hall.

"Say, who the hell is that?" Delaney asked.

"An old friend," Jack said. "I'll be right with you. I just want to freshen up a bit. There're the bottles." He waved toward the table near the window and went into the bedroom, closing the door behind him, leaving his visitors under the living-room chandelier.

He went into the bathroom and looked at his face in the mirror. His forehead was covered with beads of sweat and his cheeks were drawn with fatigue, as though he had just run a mile uphill. His hands trembled as he turned the faucets of the basin, and he doused his face and hair with icy water, again and again, coughing into his wet hands in nervous spasms. He dried himself roughly, rubbing color back into his cheeks, then combed his hair carefully, adjusted his tie, his face framed in the mirror by the two wings of the rouged V. In the bedroom he put on his jacket, hearing the sound of women's laughter in the next room. Before going into the salon, he pulled the covers up over the bed, noticing that Bresach had ripped the sheet with his knife. That's something for the old lady to figure out tomorrow morning, Jack thought, when she comes in to make up the room. Look for hidden American daggers.

Catullus lay open, face down, on the bureau. *Look where the youths are coming* . . .

He went into the living room to be presented to his guests.

9

The night club was dark and decorated like a Renaissance palace, with tapestries on the walls and candles in gilt sconces throwing a soft glow over the crowded tables. It occupied the top floor of a sixteenth-century building near the Tiber. On the ground floor there was a small bar with a Negro pianist. On the second floor there was a restaurant, with a string trio, and on the top floor, there was another bar through which you had to pass to get to the night club proper. At this bar Jack recognized some of the glossy-haired young men he had seen two nights running at the bar of his hotel, still, so late at night, unwearied, youthful, avid, corrupt, a continuing thread of color through the Roman night.

Jack sat at the table in the corner, in shadow, listening to the music of the band, well into his third whisky and grateful for it, feeling pleasantly remote from the people around him. One of the women in mink was Barzelli, the star of the picture Delaney was shooting. She was sitting next to Delaney at the other end of the table, drinking champagne and gently and methodically stroking his thigh under the table, a look of blank boredom on her noble and beautiful dark face, as though after working hours she could not take the trouble to speak or to understand English. Next to her sat the other woman in mink, a thin blonde of about forty-five, with dyed hair and a girlish, lacy dress, also drinking champagne. Her name was Mrs. Holt and she was a little drunk. From time to time, looking at the dancers swaying in and out of the amber beams of the baby spotlights cleverly concealed around the room, Mrs. Holt would wipe away a tear with an enormous lace handkerchief.

Across from her sat Tucino, the producer of the picture. He was a small Neapolitan-eyed man who would have been handsome enough to play the lead in his own pictures, if he had been four inches taller. He spoke a quick, rough brand of English, and was leaning over the table, speaking violently to Delaney, oblivious of what was going on under the table.

At Jack's end of the table was another Italian, by the name of Tasseti, a squat, square man, with the face of a sad gangster, who was Tucino's bodyguard or attendant or prime minister and who occasionally turned in his chair and scanned the room with a liquid, dangerous eye, on the lookout for assassins, creditors, or unwelcome applicants for roles among the shadowy guests of the night club. He spoke no English, but sat there patiently, not unamused, from time to time saying a few words to Jack in primitive Sicilianized French.

The other man was the one who wore the sombrero. He was the husband of Mrs. Holt and he came from Oklahoma and every once in a while he said, in the friendliest tones possible, "Boy, you can't beat Italy." When he saw his wife wiping away her peculiar tears he would smile widely and lovingly at her and raise his hand to the level of his eyes and signal her gaily with his fingers. He was about fifty years old, wrinkled and weatherbeaten and spare, like a veteran foreman on a dust-bowl ranch. In between the times he said, "Boy, you can't beat Italy," he told Jack that he was investing in Delaney's picture and was thinking of setting up a company to make three more pictures in Europe with Delaney and Tucino. It turned out that Mr. Holt owned an oil company and that he had interests in fields in Texas and on the shores of the Persian Gulf as well as in Oklahoma. He spoke slowly, with an almost shy, farm boy politeness, and whenever the level of Jack's or Tasseti's glass lowered a bit, he insisted upon pouring them more whisky from the bottle the waiter had left for them on the table.

Ordinarily, Jack would have fled from such a gathering, with its mixture of sex, investment, intrigue and drunkenness. But now, after what had happened to him that night, smiling mechanically once a minute at Mr. Holt, saying *"Oui, vous avez raison"* or, *"Non, c'est exacte,"* to Tasseti, enjoying the Etruscan beauty of Barzelli without the necessity of talking to her, vaguely moved by the sight of the beautiful women in floating gowns who drifted darkly over the dance floor, the combination of the people, the place, the hour, was relaxing, reassuring. There was no weeping revengeful boy here, and no bed to be ripped with a knife. On his third whisky, in the melodious Renaissance night, Jack would have been content to sit there, a removed, untouched spectator, until daylight grayed the windows. If he was the prey of pity now, it was only for Delaney's wife Clara, alone in a rented baroque bedroom, her claims on Delaney skillfully being caressed into oblivion by the famous, practiced peasant hand on her husband's leg.

It had been Jack's intention, when he heard Delaney's voice on the hotel phone, to enlist his aid in handling Bresach. Delaney was an expert at scandal, like all men who had ever been powerful in Hollywood, and would be useful as an adviser. But now, lulled by the music and the alcohol, Jack decided he would take care of it alone. Bresach was becoming shadowy, improbable, a grotesque, fleeting apparition, a night figure, who, weeping and foolishly armed, would disappear as suddenly as he had come. It was impossible for Jack to believe, in the glow of whisky and Cuban music, that just one hour ago his life had been at stake. Morning would arrange all. Probably, he thought, tomorrow Veronica would repent her impulsiveness and take her bags back to the apartment she had shared with the boy, beg forgiveness, and so it would end. For the moment, Jack contemplated it without emotion. I'm not twenty-five years old, he thought, I do not die for jealousy. Mine or anyone else's.

"I didn't do this without advice, you understand," Holt was saying to him. "I'm not like some people. I don't pay a high-priced New York lawyer a hundred thousand a year and then say, Go hump yourself. I pay a man and I listen to him. And he showed me, black on white, I could put up a half a million a year for five years, even if I lost it all, and still come out ahead. There's one thing about the government—they pay some poor little feller ten thousand a year to figure out a way of taxing our money away from us, without figuring that we're paying one hundred thousand to some feller to save it for us. Now, it stands to reason—who's gonna do better?—a hundred-thousand-a-year brain or a ten-thousand-a-year brain?"

"Of course," said Jack, thinking, I am paying too high for this whisky.

"You want to live in Europe with your missis, this shyster says," Holt went on, in his flat, agreeable Oklahoma drawl, "the thing to do is find a way to live in Europe where it don't cost you a cent. It stands to reason, don't it?"

"Of course," Jack said.

"Naturally," Holt said, "me and Mother don't want to live all year round here. Six, seven months, in the good weather, you understand. Well, sir, the most important thing in this day and age is to live deductible. Legitimate and deductible. Food, drink, travel, servants, entertainment—all on good old Uncle Sam. Now, you tell me, sir, what's more legitimate than making movies in Rome with an honest to God Italian movie producer like Mr. Tucino, there? A brilliant man, Mr. Tucino." Holt smiled, in a blaze of flawless false teeth, at the back of Mr. Tucino's head, pleased with Tucino for permitting him to have such a high opinion of him. "Do you know that in 1945 he was peddling American Army surplus from a donkey cart on the streets of Naples?"

"No, I didn't know that," Jack said.

"Shoes, blankets, canteen cups, C-rations, a junkman, to be honest about it. But a junkman with vision. I like men with vision," Holt said, in the solemn tones of a board chairman at an annual meeting. "I like men with enterprise, who've made theirselves with their own two hands. I can look them in the eye and they can look me in the eye. Of whatever race, Mr. Andrus, of whatever race. He's an Eyetalian, Mr. Tucino, but look what he's done with himself. Not like these degenerate counts you meet in these parts." Holt surveyed the dance floor coldly, the puritanical American set of his mouth showing that he suspected a high ratio of degenerate counts among the men on the dance floor.

"That's the nice thing about the movie business, sir," Mr. Holt went on gaily. "The type of interesting people you meet."

"There's no doubt about it," Jack said. "The type is interesting."

"Mr. Delaney, for example. Where would you meet a man as interesting as Mr. Delaney?" Holt gave the award of his smile to

94

Delaney, as he had to Tucino. Delaney sat talking to Tucino, unaware of the flood of approval surging in his direction from the other end of the table, his thigh under the ringed, soft hand of his leading lady. Jack looked at Delaney, too, but with less approval. Ten years ago, Delaney wouldn't have sat there, fatuously pleased with that secret, calculated caress. Ten years ago, he would have grabbed the hand angrily and plumped it up on top of the table for everyone to see and he would have told the woman to stop making a fool of herself in public.

"And that beautiful young girl," Holt said, indicating Barzelli with a reverential nod of his head. "You see movie stars on the screen and you never think they could be simple, kindhearted people like her. And grateful." Holt rapped the table sharply with his knuckles for emphasis. Like most men who had many favors to dispense, he ranked gratitude high on the list of virtues. "Why, it's almost pathetic, how grateful that girl is to Mr. Delaney. She has told me in confidence that he is the only director who ever understood her. Why, she's told me she'd appear in his next three pictures for nothing, just for the opportunity of working with him."

I bet, Jack thought, regarding the bored, languid face of Barzelli. For nothing. Wait till her agent comes in with the contract.

"Mother is just crazy about her," Holt said.

"What's that?" Jack asked, feeling he had missed a link somewhere. "Sorry."

"Mother," Holt said. "Mrs. Holt."

"Oh," Jack said, hoping to get off the movies onto another subject, "you have children?"

"No," Holt said. He sighed. Mrs. Holt was dabbing at her eyes again at the same time that she was draining her sixth glass of champagne, and Holt pursed his mouth cooingly, and wiggled his fingers at her, like a nurse amusing a child in a carriage. "No," he said, "we do not have children. This is wonderful for her. I mean living here in Rome. She's in all the museums every day. There isn't a church she hasn't visited. She's a Catholic, but she's very artistic besides that. She was a piano teacher in Tulsa when I married her. Why, back home, we have two grand pianos. We live in a palazzo here—that's a palace in Eyetalian—but the piano doesn't work. The Germans occupied it during the war."

Maybe, Jack thought, I ought to get up from here and go back to the hotel and get hold of Bresach again. The conversation was more amusing, knife or no knife.

"Mother is most anxious for me to set up a company with Mr. Tucino and Mr. Delaney. A three-picture deal," Holt said, savoring the technical language of this magic world. "Aside from living abroad in a palazzo deductible. She has a brother—well you know how brothers sometimes are—" He smiled apologetically. "Younger, you know, not a bad boy, but he's never found just the right spot for his talents. I had him in with me for a couple of years, but finally my partners laid down the law. What we'll do with him here is make him associate producer, that's a feller who—"

"I know," Jack said.

"He costs me twenty, twenty-five thousand a year now, hard money, after taxes," Holt said. "But if he's associate producer he can pull down fifty thousand a year and it won't cost me hardly a penny. It'll make Mother very happy," Holt said gently.

Jack had a sudden new vision of Holt, the tough, capable, hard-working prospector, driller, gambler, boss, coming home from his office in Oklahoma City where gigantic struggles took place and empires shook and changed hands each working day, to find his wispy, dipsomaniac wife fumbling at one of the two grand pianos, with a bottle of whisky on the floor beside her and the ne'er-do-well brother with yet another hard-luck story, yet another request for another ten thousand (*absolutely the last, I swear it . . .*). And the gentle, loving kiss, the absolving, sacrificial checkbook, all hardness and resolution left at the door, and the signature on the check a continuing, unfading declaration of love for the sad, destroyed, lost woman he had married.

Jack forgot all the inanities he had had to listen to up to then and smiled at Holt, seeing the wrinkled rancher's face, the balding skull, the puzzled, friendly eyes, with new compassion.

A curious, reflective expression passed fleetingly across Holt's face, as though he had caught the change in Jack, and he unexpectedly patted the back of Jack's hand in a little quick sympathetic movement. His hand was calloused and confident. I mustn't underrate him, Jack thought, there's a deft, sensitive man behind the ranch-foreman face, behind the banalities. He didn't reach the Persian Gulf by being an idiot.

"I want to say here and now," Holt said solemnly, "how grateful we all are that you consented to come down and help us out like this, Mr. Andrus, in our disgraceful predicament with Mr. Stiles."

"It was a pleasant surprise for me," Jack said honestly.

"Mr. Delaney has told me all about you," Holt went on, "and

I'm mighty glad to get this opportunity to tell you what I think personally. You're in the government, I know, in Paris."

"Well—NATO," Jack said.

"The same thing," said Holt, dismissing airily all niggling little distinctions of function and organization among people who were paid out of the public treasury. He laughed, with his flash of false teeth. "I hope you won't feel that your duty compels you to report back everything I said here tonight on the subject of taxes, etcetera."

"Your views on taxes, Mr. Holt," Jack said gravely, "will go with me to the grave."

Holt laughed spontaneously. "I wish more fellers like you in the government had your sense of humor, Jack." He squinted uncertainly at Jack. "It's all right, isn't it, if I call you Jack? You know, out in Oklahoma, in the oil business . . ."

"Of course," Jack said.

"And everybody calls me Sam," Holt said, almost shyly, as if asking for a favor.

"Sure, Sam."

"*Ecco*," Tasseti said, scowling at the dance floor. "*La pluss grande puttain de Roma. La Principessa.*" He bunched his mouth, as if he were going to spit.

Jack looked at the dance floor. A twenty-year-old girl with a blond pony-tail floating over her bare shoulders and pure white dress was dancing with a short fat man of about thirty.

"What did he say?" Holt asked. "What did the Eyetalian say?"

"He said, There's the biggest whore in Rome," Jack translated. "The Princess."

"Is that so?" Holt said flatly. Politely, he waited a moment before turning around, then took a quick glance at the girl. "She looks very nice," he said. "A nice young girl."

"*Elle fasse tutti,*" Tasseti said. "*Elle couche avec son fratello.*"

"What did he say now?" Holt asked.

Jack hesitated. Well, Sam, he thought, you're in Rome now, learn what the natives are saying. "He said she does everything," Jack said, without inflection. "She sleeps with her brother."

Holt sat absolutely still. A slow flush came up from his collar and blazed on his cheeks and forehead. "I don't think people ought to gossip like that about other people," he said, swallowing hard. "I'm sure it's merely an unbased rumor." He looked worriedly down the table at his wife. "I'm glad Mother didn't hear that," he said. "It would've ruined her evening. Excuse me, Jack." He stood up and went around the table and pulled up a chair from the next table and sat down protectively next to Mrs. Holt, smiling at her and taking her hand in his. A moment later, when the Princess and her escort had left the dance floor, Holt took his wife out onto the floor and they danced. They danced very well, Jack noted with surprise, Holt erect and light on his feet and going through the intricate rhythms of a rumba with practiced efficiency. He must have spent hours taking lessons, Jack thought. Anything to keep her away from the bottle.

"Ecco," Tasseti said heavily, indicating a white-haired man with a cardinal's face who was dancing with a girl in a red dress, *"le pluss grand voleur de Roma."*

There was a burst of laughter from Delaney and Barzelli at the other end of the table, where Tucino had just finished telling a story. Tucino sat back, grinning, and Delaney called down the table, "Come up here, Jack, and listen to this."

Jack stood up, happy to get away from Tasseti and his dark Sicilian judgments on the clientele of the night club. Delaney made room for Jack at the corner of the table and said, "Marco was telling us about his father. Tell Andrus about your father, Marco."

"Allora," Tucino said, smiling happily, as wide-awake and full of energy as a schoolboy, using his hands, speaking in his fluent vaudeville-Italian English, *"allora,* my father, his name is Sebastiano. He is seventy-three, seventy-six year old, he has the hair white like snow, he walk straight like a rifle, all his life he chase after the girl, he is crazy after the girl, he come from the South, you unnerstand, he drive my mother crazy for fifty year, on his last birthday, she tell him, 'This year, Sebastiano, I think I give you up for good, I no longer stand the girls, a man your age.' She made him swear before the priest, no more girls, on his birthday, before we give him the presents, I gave him a Fiat and a Leica camera for his birthday, he go out to St. Peter's and take picture of the dome. But of course, he never give up the girl. He comes into the studio visit me in my office every afternoon, take a cup of coffee with his son, show me the pictures of St. Peter. It's a habit, a tradition, five o'clock, after the *siesta.* Every day the workmen in the studio watch for him to walk through the gate. He come through the gate, each day, he knows they watch him, he puts up a finger, like this, overhead." Tucino raised his arm above his head with the index finger of his right hand pointing toward the ceiling. "You know what it mean?

No? But the workmen know and they laugh each day. Each day I hear the laugh downstairs from my office at the gate and I know in two minute my father come through the door of my office. You know what it mean—it mean that day my father had one girl one time. The workmen love him, they laugh with him, they say, 'Old Sebastiano, he is a green old man, he will live till age hundred.' Then, one day—" Tucino hunched down dramatically in his chair, shoulders drooping, eyes lackluster, senility incarnate, death at the door. "One day, the papa arrive my office, but no warning, no laugh at the gate before. He look gray, like he come from the funeral of his best friend and friend sure to go to Hell. I say nothing. We have coffee like usual. He don't show me any picture. He go out walking slow. Then, one, two month go by, and my father come each afternoon, walking slow, no laughing at gate, the workmen look at him sad now, they say, 'Poor old Sebastiano, he no live age hundred, lucky see the springtime.' I see my mama, she look ten, twenty year younger. She put on weight, she laugh like a young girl, she buy three new hats with flowers, she take up bridge. I am sorry for the papa, he is not straight like a rifle no more, he hardly use the Fiat, he make me think, Ah, it is sad to see the father come to winter. I try to tell him go to doctor, but he tell me, 'Shut your dirty mouth. I don't need children tell me how to live my life.' It is first time in thirty year my father say mean word to me. I shut up. I am sad and I shut up. Then today, this afternoon, at five o'clock, I hear biggest shout of laughing at gate, applause, like returning war hero. I look out the window. My father coming through gate, straight like a rifle, white hair standing up like it just come back starched from the laundry, smile on his face from one ear to other ear, his hand up. He is making the V sign." Tucino smiled gently and lovingly. "Two fingers up today."

Delaney chuckled and Jack chuckled, too. After all, he thought, it isn't *my* father. But Barzelli, even though she had just heard the story five minutes before, leaned back in her chair and rolled out a long peal of coarse peasant laughter, resounding, vulgar, robust, surprising and almost masculine issuing from that slender throat and that perfect, womanly mouth. Arrogant, Italian, beautiful, sure of herself, she was in the male Mediterranean world, sharing its triumphs. The old lady with her three new hats and her afternoon bridge and her extorted pledges had no connection to her.

Jack looked at his watch and stood up. "I'd better be going," he said. "If we're going to start work at seven thirty this morning."

Delaney waved carelessly. "No rush, Jack," he said. "The hell with the morning. We'll start at ten."

"Just the same," Jack said. He noticed the little, cold contraction of Tucino's eyes at Delaney's debonair postponement. The producer's eyes, immediately veiled, announced that it was *his* time, *his* money Delaney was wasting, and that if things went badly between them in the future, Tucino would bring it up and use it as a lever in the argument.

Jack shook hands with Barzelli, who looked at him without interest. He was not a producer, he was not a director, he could not give her extra close-ups or a richer contract, and she had seen from his first greeting in his hotel room that he was never going to make any advances to her. She would remember his name with difficulty.

He went to the other end of the table to say good night to Tasseti. Tasseti was swiveled around in his chair, staring disdainfully past the dancers at a group of men and women on the other side of the room. As he shook hands with Jack, he said, harshly, indicating the host at the distant table, *"Ecco, le pluss grand pederaste de Roma."*

Jack grinned, thinking, Three for three, all sins in Roman order, whoredom, theft, and perversion in precise arrangement. Tasseti's had himself a perfect day, how happy he must be.

Jack skirted the dance floor, waving good night to the Holts, who were now dancing cheek to cheek to the music of "On the Street Where You Live." They stopped dancing and came over to Jack. "I wonder, Jack," Holt said, "if you could spare a minute. I'd like to talk to you."

"Of course," Jack said.

"Good night, Jack," Mrs. Holt said, her voice wispy and soaked in alcohol. She smiled mistily at him. "Sam has been telling me how much he likes you, how sympathetic you are."

"Well, thank you, Mrs. Holt," Jack said.

"Bertha," said Mrs. Holt, pleadingly. "Please do have the kindness to call me Bertha." She made the faintest ghost of a coquettish grimace. "Mrs. Holt makes me feel so old."

"Of course," Jack said. "Uh . . . Bertha."

"Arrivederci, Jack," she said and floated on Holt's arm back to the table, where her husband deposited her in a chair, like a newly excavated treasure frail with the erosion of the years. Then Holt

came back to Jack, lightly, not breathing hard, even after all that dancing.

"I'll accompany you to the door," Holt said formally, "if I may."

As they went out of the room, Jack glanced back, just in time to see Barzelli slide her hand once more under the table.

Jack and Mr. Holt went downstairs, past the closed restaurant on the second floor, past the painting of a nude on the landing, to the street-level floor, where there was a little bar with a Negro pianist playing softly for an American couple who were having a whispered argument in a corner. "I'll tell you what," Holt said, as Jack got his coat from the hat-check girl, "I could use a little air. Would you like to walk a block or two?"

"I'd love to," Jack said. Now that he was actually on his way to his hotel, Jack realized he was in no hurry to face the empty (or perhaps not empty) rooms and the problem of sleep.

They went out into the night, Holt taking his coat and sombrero and placing the sombrero squarely and soberly on his balding head. Outside, taxi drivers and chauffeurs were talking desultorily, huddled into their overcoats, and a shapeless woman with a basket of violets waited for lovers in the darkness. A fiacre, the horse dozing under a blanket in the light of the fiacre's kerosene lamp, stood against the opposite wall.

Jack and Holt turned the corner and walked along the river, the proprietors of sleeping Rome.

"Bertha hates to go home until the band stops playing," Holt said. He chuckled tolerantly. "You'd be surprised how many times a year I see the dawn come up." He peered down at the Tiber. "Not much of a stream, is it? 'The troubled Tiber chafing with her shores,' " he quoted, surprisingly. "Well, you know, I think I could swim it myself, even with armor. I guess Shakespeare never got a look at it." He smiled shyly at this audacious literary reflection. "Funny people, the Italians," he said. "They live in this city just like people anyplace else. As though nothing ever happened here."

Jack walked in silence, looking across the river at the dark bulk of the Palazzo di Giustizia, thinking about his hotel bedroom, waiting for Holt to say what he had followed him to say.

Holt cleared his throat uncomfortably. "We were talking back there"—he gestured toward the building behind them which housed the night club—"about your being in the government."

Jack didn't bother to correct him.

"What I mean is, chances are, you know quite a few people in the Embassy here."

"A few," Jack said.

"I've been in and out of there a dozen times the last month or so," Holt said. "They're very nice to me. Don't get me wrong, they couldn't be more polite and obliging, but—" He shrugged. "It never hurts to know someone who's really in the business, does it?"

"No," Jack said, noncommittally, wondering what trouble Holt could be in with the State Department that he could conceivably help him with.

"You see, what we've been trying to do is adopt a baby, Mother and me." Holt sounded diffident, almost a little guilty, as though he had just confessed that he and his wife were planning a crime. "And you'd be surprised how many difficulties there are in the way."

"Adopt a baby?" Jack said. *"Here?"*

"As I said before, in the night club," Holt said stiffly, embarrassed, "I think I can honestly say I've got over any prejudices about race that I might ever have had. Being born and bred in Oklahoma . . ." He stopped. "I mean"—now his voice was defiant —"what's wrong with Italian babies?"

"Nothing," Jack said hurriedly. "But wouldn't it be easier to adopt a baby back home?"

Holt coughed self-consciously and put both hands to the rim of his sombrero and settled it a quarter of an inch more squarely on the center of his head.

"We have . . . uh . . . a few problems, a few little problems, back home," he said. "Jack, I feel I can talk to you. I got that feeling back there at the table. You're a man with understanding. Mr. Delaney tells me you're the father of two children yourself . . ."

"Three," Jack said automatically.

"Three," Holt said. "I beg your pardon. You know how it is. Women need children. There's something empty about a woman's life if she doesn't . . . Ah, hell, I don't have to tell you. She's liable to look for other things to fill the space . . ." His voice trailed off, and Jack once more had the vision of the bottle beside the piano. "And, for some reason, we haven't been blessed," Holt said. "The doctors say we are perfectly healthy, normal people, but we haven't been blessed. It's not as unusual as you think. You look around and you see the world crawling with kids, poor, starving, neglected"—his voice was hard and bitter as he contemplated the callous, undeserving fecundity of the poor—"and you never have any idea of how many homes're empty and're doomed to stay empty. And with all the scientists, all the vaccines, all the penicillin, all the hydrogen bombs and rockets to the moon, nothing to be done about it. Ah, the things we tried . . ." Holt looked out across the sliding dark river, with its country smell, its odor of winter loam and wet, frozen grass between its concrete banks. "What the hell, you're a grown man," he said harshly, "you've created sons, it's not as though I'm going to shock you. Gas in the tubes, the fertility rhythm, the taking the temperature at six o'clock in the morning and then trying to . . ." He stopped. He seemed to be choking up. Then he continued in his calm, flat, conversational Oklahoma drawl. "We even went so far as to try artificial in—insemination, in a doctor's office. Nothing. Poor Bertha," he said, with twenty year's love and pity, carried from one continent to another, in his voice. "You've only seen her for an hour or two so I don't suppose you've noticed—but—" He hesitated, then plunged on. "She—well, if it was a man, you'd say she was a drinking man. A hard drinking man."

"No," Jack said, "I didn't notice."

"Well, she's a lady, of course," Holt said, "she could drink from morning to night and she'd never say a word that wasn't right and proper, a cruel word, or an off-color word, or a word that couldn't be spoken in the best home in the land, but—there's no getting around it, Jack—it's getting worse, year by year. If she had a family—one child—"

"I still don't see," Jack said, puzzled, "why it should be so hard to find a baby to adopt back home."

Holt took in a deep, loud breath. He walked ten paces in silence. "Bertha's a Catholic," he said at last, "as I think I told you back there."

"Yes."

"And I was born and raised a Baptist and if I'm anything now, I'm still a Baptist," Holt said. "And in America—well, the people who run orphanages put a lot of store in things like that. What I mean is, the system is Catholics give to Catholic families, Protestants give to Protestant families, even Jews—" He stopped, afraid that he had said something that he didn't mean. "Of course, I have nothing against the Jews. I don't have anything against any of them," he said wearily. "In principle, I'm sure they're right. In the majority of cases. Maybe if I turned Catholic . . . Bertha's never asked me, of course," he said quickly. "Don't think she'd ever ask anything like that, and we haven't even ever discussed it, not as much as a hint. But, privately, I must confess, there've been times when I've been tempted to go to Bertha and say to her, 'Mother, take me for instruction to the nearest priest.' "

They were walking past a church, its medieval bronze doors shut against the night, the church dark and closed, not prepared to answer questions or gather in supplicants or absolve sin until daylight. Holt looked thoughtfully at the huge implacable doors and the sculptured saint, in an attitude of benediction in his niche to one side of the portal. "They're powerful," he whispered, "powerful." He shook his head, shaking Romanism out from under the sombrero once and for all. "I'm not much of a Baptist," he said. "I sometimes don't go near a church for years, unless it's to a funeral or a wedding. But I'm not a Catholic. I can't say to anyone I am or I will be. A man can't do that, can he, Jack? No matter what the bribe."

It's a funny question to ask in Rome, Jack thought, contemplating all the gods that had been overturned here, repudiated, installed, altered, swallowed, and for what bribes. "No, I guess not," he said, because he knew that that was what Holt wanted to hear. "Still," he said, "it seems to me that every once in a while I hear of people with different religions adopting children . . ."

"It happens," Holt said. "Occasionally. But not to me."

"Why not?" Jack asked.

"Delaney didn't tell you about me?" Holt asked, suspiciously.

"No."

"I guess it's not so damn interesting." Holt laughed harshly. "Only to me. It's damn interesting to me." He buttoned up his coat, as though he were cold. "I'm a felon, Jack," he said flatly. "I served time. I served six years in Joliet, Illinois, for armed robbery."

"Oh, Christ," Jack said involuntarily.

"That's it. Oh, Christ," Holt said.

"I'm sorry," said Jack.

"You got nothing to be sorry about. I held up a hardware store when I was twenty years old and I got a hundred and eighty bucks out of the till and I walked into an off-duty cop who was coming into the store to buy a hammer and a pound of nails and instead he got me. And it wasn't the first time I pulled something like that," Holt said harshly. "I had two misdemeanors on my sheet before that, and they didn't know the half of it. Well," he said briskly, "now I'm trying to adopt a little boy in Leghorn. Everybody back home told me it would be easy." He chuckled ruefully. "You'd think it would, wouldn't you? Overpopulation, homes broken up by the war, they're always yelling they have five million people too many, that they have to emigrate." He shook his head at his former naïveté. "Why, sir, you would be horrified—and I use the word advisedly—horrified—if I told you what degradation you have to go through just to give a poor little starving wop bastard a home with a swimming pool and seven servants and a Harvard education." He stopped and looked around him, squinting, lost in the sleeping city. "I guess I'd better be getting back," he said. "Bertha'll begin to worry."

"If there's anything I can do," Jack said.

"I don't like to take up your time," Holt said. "I know you're down here to do an important job, and you're a busy man—but if you just happen to drop into the Embassy and there's a friend of yours who happens to be in good with the Italians . . ." He looked at his watch. "It's late, now. Maybe some day this week, we'll have dinner, you and me and Bertha, and I'll tell you what I've done already, what people I've seen . . ."

"Of course," Jack said.

"You're a good boy, Jack," Holt said. "I'm glad I had this talk. I tell you frankly, in the beginning, for the first hour or so, I was afraid I wasn't going to like you. But I like you fine, now," he said heartily. "Fine."

He turned and went down the street toward the night club, the felon-millionaire with his six years in Joliet, Illinois, with his carefully nurtured tolerance of Italians, orphans, Catholics, Jews, Protestants, junkmen, with his sombrero, his oil wells, his deductible living in a Roman palazzo. Upright and helpless, he walked past the shut, implacable church, back to the wife who would be called a drinking man, if she were a man, and who could be wrenched away from the bottle (one thought) only by infant fingers.

Jack watched the tall, square-shouldered figure under the wide hat, the plainsman now committed to tax avoidance and artificial insemination, as he diminished under the foreign lampposts, beside the river he was sure he could swim, despite the testimony of literature, even clad in armor.

Back in Paris, Jack thought wryly, all I worry about are small things, like whether or not the Russians are going to drop the bomb before the end of the year.

Watching Holt until he was a small, anonymous blur in the perspective of stone and concrete of lampposts and dead trees, Jack understood why Delaney had been so insistent upon his meeting the oilman and his wife. Delaney wanted something from Holt—the three-picture deal might restore his prestige and his finances for the next ten years—and in return, he was ready to offer any favors within his powers. If Jack, through Delaney's arrangement, could help steer the Holts through the tangle of Italo-American bureaucracy and get them their Leghorn orphan, Holt's gratitude could be counted upon. Jack chuckled, thinking, it's Despière and the article all over again. Delaney never stops. He maneuvers day and night. Maybe I ought to ask for a raise in pay. Andrus, the all-purpose actor, call in case of emergency, civil, artistic, alcoholic.

Then the chuckle died on his lips. Delaney had always maneuvered, it was true, but on a grand scale and for large stakes. When Jack had known him as a young man, he would never have condescended to this petty trading of favors. Today, with all his bluster, Delaney was fighting for his life, and he knew it, and was clawing around him wildly for anything that would save him. Well, if this is what he needs, or thinks he needs, Jack thought, I shall do my best to deliver. And if he needs more later on, I shall do my best to deliver then.

Even as he understood all this, Jack understood, too, that it was not only for Delaney that he was in this city, at Delaney's bidding. He was there for himself, too. Delaney was a part of the image of the best time of Jack's own life, the bright years before the war, when he had loved Delaney as a son might love a father, a brother a brother, a soldier the soldier who fought at his side, their fates dependent on each other's courage and skill and fortitude. In rescuing Delaney, he was rescuing the purest image of his youth. If Delaney were to be shabby and defeated, Jack, too, would be shabby and defeated. I'm going to save him, Jack thought grimly, if it kills him. I don't know how I'm going to do it, but I'm going to save him.

It's going to be a crowded two weeks, he thought, as he started back toward his hotel, passing shuttered windows, locked churches, fountains playing in dark deserted squares, past broken temples and crumbling bits of walls that had guarded the citizens of the city two thousand years before.

Enjoy yourself, chéri, he remembered his wife's voice at the airport.

When he reached his hotel, he hesitated outside. Two policemen walked soberly up the street, past the entrance, and Jack looked at them speculatively, thinking, How do you say in Italian, "My dear friends, a little earlier this evening, a young man threatened to kill me. Would you be so kind as to come up with me and look under my bed?"

The policemen passed on. For a moment, Jack played with the idea of going to another hotel for the night, where he could get a few hours sleep untroubled by the possibility that Bresach might find him. Then, in the morning, he could decide what should be done about him.

The idea was tempting. But he shook his head irritably, annoyed at the arguments of cowardice. He went into the hotel and got his key. There were no messages.

When he reached his apartment he went in without hesitation. The lights were on, as he had left them. There was no one in the living room. He went through the rest of the suite. No one. He went back into the living room, bolted the door, turned out the light, and started undressing as he crossed the threshold of the bedroom. The bed was cold when he got into it, and he shivered a little. If Delaney hadn't called at just that moment, he wondered, where would I be now?

He lay there, feeling the warmth come back under the covers, on the ripped sheet. *"Hymen O Hymenaeus,"* he said softly in the darkness. He shut his eyes and waited for sleep.

10

It was a bad morning. He awoke late, feeling headachy and hung-over from the liquor of the night before and he had to bathe and dress in a hurry so as not to be late for the dubbing session at the studio. There was no message at the desk from Veronica and when he left the hotel to get into the car that Guido had waiting for him out front, Jack thought he caught a glimpse of Bresach, standing leaning against a store front on the other side of the street, staring at the hotel entrance. At any rate, it was a man in a duffel coat, briefly seen through the traffic, ominous, attendant.

Delaney was waiting for him with his secretary in the projection room, impatient, his eyes bloodshot from lack of sleep. "Christ, Jack," Delaney said as he came into the room, "we haven't got ten years to do this job."

Jack looked at his watch. "I'm only five minutes late, Maurice," he said mildly.

"Five minutes," Delaney said. "Five minutes. Let's get to work."

He signaled and the room faded into darkness and there was Stiles, mumbling once more on the screen.

"I've come back," Stiles said. "It was too strong for me. I have been unhappy since the day I left you."

Jack sighed.

"Save your criticisms," Delaney said. "You just think about how to say the lines without making him sound like a godamn fool."

The tone of his voice was abrupt and harsh, and Jack was grateful that his instinct had warned him the day before against being too candid in his conversation about the picture with Delaney. I will have to play this by ear, Jack thought, and seize the proper moment for honesty, when it comes. If it ever comes.

They worked on the same short scene for an hour, rehearsing, without registering anything. Even to Jack's own ears, the sound of his voice going through the lines was flat and false. Delaney sat there, not helping, not suggesting any changes, merely grunting and signaling the projectionist to run the scene over again, and saying to Jack, "Now let's try it once more."

By the end of the hour nothing he was saying seemed to make any sense to Jack or to have any connection with the language that any living human being might possibly employ in any situation whatever. Abruptly, Delaney said, "All right, now we'll try to put it on the track. And now, Jack, for the love of God, try to *think* of what you're doing. It's a big confession, it's a confession of love, this feller has been dreaming about this girl for ten years, and now he sees her by accident for the first time. He can't sound as though he's saying, 'I'll have noodles for dinner.' "

"Wait a minute, Maurice," Jack said. "Maybe this isn't going to work. Maybe it's been too long and I've lost the gift. If I ever had it."

"You had it, you had it," Delaney said impatiently.

"Anyway," Jack said, "if you want to get somebody else, I'll bow out right now. Before we waste any more of your time and my time. I'll get on the afternoon plane to Paris and maybe everybody'll be a lot happier."

"Don't be in such a godamn hurry to give up," Delaney said. "After one hour. What the hell's wrong with you? Where do you think I'd be today if I quit like that?"

"I just wanted to let you know that you're not stuck with me, if you don't want to be," Jack said.

"Now, Jack . . ." Maurice smiled at him winningly, warmly.

"You're not going to turn sensitive on me, are you? Christ, you're the only actor I ever made a friend of, just because you behaved like a man, not like a miserable . . ." He stopped and grinned at the secretary, sitting in the row behind them. "Excuse me, Hilda," he said, "I was just going to say a dirty word. Derogatory to your sex. Extremely derrrogatorry." He rolled the r's of the last word in a sudden, exaggerated, comic brogue. "It's a word that has been used to describe sensitive and artistic actors for many centuries." He patted Jack's shoulder, companionably. "It's not as bad as all that, Jack. It'll come. It'll come."

"I hope so," Jack said. "But even if it finally comes, will it make that much difference? After all it's only one small part of the whole picture . . ." He stopped. This was still not the time to tell Delaney that he had been studying the script and the film that had already been shot and that there were many other things that offended him, that should be changed or cut altogether, and which were, in Jack's opinion, more important than the mere substitution of his voice for that of Stiles, no matter how well the substitution worked out.

"It's not only one small part of the picture," Delaney said. "I told you before—it's the keystone of the whole thing. And even if it *was* only a small part, it still might be the thing that made the difference between a work of art and a piece of crap. You know as well as I do, Jack, NOTHING IS UNIMPORTANT." He spoke with fanatical emphasis, rooted in his belief. "One frame, the reading of one line, one movement at a crucial time, in a two-hour picture, can blow you to bits. Or it can rake in the whole pot. That's the nature of a movie, Jack. Why do you think I work as hard as I do on every little detail . . . ?"

"I know that theoretically it's true," Jack said, thinking, No wonder he still seems so young. Fanatics do not age. "But this time . . ."

"This time and every time, lad," Delaney said, with finality. "Now let's start all over again."

They worked for half an hour more, Jack conscientiously trying to put some life into the lines, but without success. In the middle of a speech, Delaney held up his hand and the lights went up. "That'll do for the day," he said.

"It's no good," Jack said.

"Not much." Delaney smiled good-naturedly. Then he peered closely at Jack. "You got something on your mind?"

110

Jack hesitated. "No," he said, "I've got nothing on my mind."

"Lucky man," Delaney said. "Lunch?"

Again Jack hesitated. "Let me call my hotel first. I had a tentative appointment."

Jack telephoned the hotel. There was a message for him. Signorina Rienzi was lunching at Ernesto's, Piazza dei Santissimi Apostoli. She would be there at one, and she would be pleased if Signor Andrus could join her.

"Thank you," Jack said over the phone and hung up. "I'm busy for lunch," he told Delaney.

Delaney regarded him shrewdly for a moment and Jack wondered what his face had revealed, what pleasure, what anticipation, what fears, as he had talked on the phone.

Delaney grunted, gathered his papers, and they went out into a light drizzle, where the two cars were waiting, parked alongside the projection-room building. "Jack," Delaney said, "did Holt talk to you last night?"

"A little," Jack said.

"Can you help him?"

"I'll call a couple of people," Jack said.

Delaney nodded, pleased. "He's okay, Holt," Delaney said. "It'd be nice if we could help the poor bastard."

Jack didn't mention the three-picture deal. "I'll do my best," he said. He put the collar of his topcoat up. The drizzle was cold.

"Thanks," Delaney said. "He likes you a lot, he told me. He told me you had a warm heart when he came back to the table last night."

"That's me," Jack said. "Warm-hearted."

"They're giving a cocktail party at their place tonight," said Delaney. "They asked me especially to get you to come."

"I'll be there."

"Not like last night, Jack," Delaney said warningly. "Show up this time."

"Not like last night," said Jack, thinking, I hope not like last night.

"Guido knows the address." Delaney got into the car and he and Hilda drove off.

In the car going toward the Piazza dei Santissimi Apostoli, Jack found out that Guido could speak French and they each had a cigarette to celebrate the discovery that now they could communicate with each other. Their first exchanges were general and noncommittal. Guido said that he'd learned French when he'd been stationed, in the Italian Army, near Toulon, during the war, and Jack used the gift of the common language to explain that the traffic in Paris was worse than in Rome, and the weather in general grayer. Still, a new and gratifying flavor of humanity now permeated the green Fiat, and Jack was happy to notice that when Guido had an opportunity to talk he drove more slowly and risked death less frequently. Finally, Jack thought, it may turn out that the French language has saved my life.

*

She was sitting in the back room, against a white wall, facing the door. She was wearing the same clothes that she had worn the day before and she was staring boldly at a party of three men who were seated across the room from her. As Jack approached her, just before she turned her head to greet him, he thought, Wherever she is, whatever else she is doing, she is in constant communication with the male sex. She smiled at him, and he was disturbed by the overt animal brilliance of her smile. Conscious that the three men were watching him, he experienced some of the same embarrassment he had felt as a young man when he had gone out with girls who were too blond, or too flamboyantly shaped or dressed. At such times, he would think, There's only one reason I'm out with this girl, and everybody here knows it.

He slid into the chair next to hers and touched her hand and said, "I'm crazy about a girl who didn't leave her address or telephone number. Have you any idea where I can find her?"

It was only when they had finished their meal and were sitting over their coffee, now the only guests left in the restaurant, that Jack said, "You moved yesterday. Where to?"

"What's that?" Veronica asked, surprised.

"Yesterday evening," Jack said soberly, "when you left me, when I was sleeping in the hotel, you went back to the place you were liv-

112

ing and you packed your bags and you moved. Where are you now?"

Veronica looked at him, startled. "How do you know all this?" she asked.

Then he told her about Bresach's visit, leaving out nothing, describing the knife, the tears, the raving in the bedroom. As he talked, Veronica's face became harder, pitiless, full of scorn.

"*Il cafone,*" she said.

"What does that mean?"

She shrugged. "Many bad things all mixed up," she said. "Stupid, cowardly . . ."

"How did he know about me?" Jack asked.

"I told him," Veronica said. "Why? Do you object?"

"Well," Jack said, mildly, "at this moment I don't object. But there were a couple of seconds last night, when he was waving that knife around . . ."

"Well, if you must know . . ." There was a hint of a pout in the way she pursed her mouth. "That was the only way he would let me out of the house. Otherwise, he would have made a big scene, he would have followed me. He promised me if I told him whom I'd been with, the name of the man, just the name of the man, he would let me go. And he promised he would not bother whoever it was."

"Maybe he thought putting a knife into a man's ribs in the middle of the night doesn't come under the heading of bothering him," Jack said.

"Don't joke," Veronica said. "He is capable of doing it." She laughed harshly. "And I thought, I am getting a nice American boy, I am getting away from all that crazy Italian jealousy."

"Who is he?" Jack asked. "What's he doing in Rome? What's his connection with you?"

Veronica opened her mouth, then closed it, cutting off speech. She looked down at her hands. The pretty, insensitive face took on a look of slyness, cunning, as she turned over the questions in her mind and decided whether or not to tell the truth. "Why do you have to know all that?" she asked, postponing.

"If a man tried to kill you," Jack said, "wouldn't you like to know as much as possible about him?"

"He has been here in Rome nearly two years," Veronica said. "He has some sort of small pension from the American Army. He

113

tells me his family is very rich, but they don't seem to send him very much money. He says he came here to learn about the movies. He's crazy about the Italian movies. He wants to be a director or a producer or something. It's account of him I went to see that movie you were in." She smiled mischievously. "He said I had to see your performance. Well, I saw your performance, didn't I?"

"Oh, God," Jack said.

"He does translations from the Italian into English," Veronica went on. "He makes some extra money that way."

"Does he have any talent?" Jack asked curiously.

"He thinks so," she said. "According to him he has more talent than anyone else in Rome."

"Does anybody else think he has any talent?"

"Oh, he goes around with a whole group of starving young actors and writers and people like that, that have never been heard of, and they keep telling him he's a genius." She laughed scornfully. "They hate everybody else. The only people they like are other people like themselves that nobody has ever heard of, either. He's written a script that he can't get anybody to buy, but when his friends talk about it, they make it sound as though he's just written *The Divine Comedy*."

"What do *you* think?"

"If that's what geniuses are like," she said, "let them find other women. Not me."

"How long have you known him?"

"About a year," Veronica said.

"How long have you been living with him?"

She hesitated, balancing once more, Jack could see, between truth and falsehood. "Only three months," she said. "He kept after me and after me. He is very handsome," she said, excusing herself.

"Yes, he is," said Jack.

"I told him I did not love him," Veronica said, her voice whining a little, unpleasantly, her eyes shifting uneasily and falsely, as though she weren't talking to Jack now, but to her deserted lover, explaining herself, blaming him. "I told him I insisted on being free, going out with other men when I wanted to. He said, of course, but once he had me—" She shrugged. "Just like an Italian," she said bitterly. "If I as much as said hello to a man on the street. *Tragedia*. No wonder he likes Rome, that one. He is an Italian at heart. And now this with the knife . . ." She made a scornful little hissing sound. "I would like to tell him a thing or two. What does he want me to do—sleep with him if I am in love with another man? And I thought Americans had pride."

"Did you tell him you were in love with me?" Jack asked, disbelievingly.

"Of course I did." Veronica's soft, long, plump hands played erratically with the catch of her bag.

"What did he say to that?" Jack asked.

"The usual." Again she made the scornful hissing sound. "He called me a whore. I'm telling you, they ought to make him an honorary Italian citizen."

"Did he threaten you, too?"

"No. Not yet," Veronica said carelessly. "That will come."

"What're you going to do?" Jack demanded. He had an unpleasant vision of Veronica lying in a pool of blood, and the newspapers, and the testimony at the trial. At least, he thought, with all this, I should be able to tell her I love her. At least a little bit.

"What am I going to do?" She shrugged. "Nothing. I won't tell him where I live and he won't find me."

"He'll go to the place you work," Jack said.

"He's already been there," Veronica said. "This morning. They called me. I have a friend there and he called me. I will take a vacation. I will not work for the next two weeks." She smiled softly at him. "I will devote myself to you. I need a vacation, anyway. It would be nice . . ." She covered his hand with hers and played softly with his fingers. "It would be nice if we could go away someplace for two weeks."

"It would be nice," Jack said, not really meaning it, not enjoying the prospect of two weeks alone with her. "Only I can't take the two weeks. I have to stay here. He knows where I am. Even if I move, he'll be able to find me in ten minutes."

"What I think," Veronica said, "is you should go to the police. Tell them he has threatened you with a knife. They'll lock him up for two weeks and we won't be bothered with him."

Jack took his hand away deliberately. "What did you say your name was, lady?" he asked, "de' Medici? Borgia?"

"What?" Veronica said, puzzled. "What did you say?"

"No," Jack said, "for the time being, let's forget the police."

"I was just trying to be practical," Veronica said, sounding aggrieved.

"Let me ask you another question," Jack said. "What're you going to do when the two weeks're up and I leave?"

"I will worry about that later," she said simply.

Jack sighed. God damn Despière, he thought irrationally. He had to say hello to everybody on the Via Veneto yesterday afternoon. "There's one other thing we could do," Jack said. He swallowed and spoke in a flat voice. "We could quit."

She looked like a punished child. "Do you want to do that?"

Jack hesitated. Whatever he answered would not be the truth. "No," he said.

Veronica smiled, and licked the corner of her mouth with her tongue. Eventually, Jack thought, if I get to know her well enough, I'm going to make her stop that.

"I didn't think you did," she said. "Ah, well"—briskly, she brushed some crumbs from the front of her skirt—"I will write him a letter and tell him to behave like a man. I will write him such a stiff letter. Maybe that will cool him off."

"Maybe," Jack said doubtfully. Suddenly, now that the decision, such as it was, had been made, he wanted her enormously. Sitting there, holding her hand, looking at the smooth olive throat rising from the open V of her sweater, the memory of the afternoon before swelled up in him overpoweringly. "Let's go back to my hotel," he said.

Veronica shook her head. Oh, God, he thought, now she is going to coquette. That's too much.

"No," she said, "he is liable to be there, watching. The pig."

"Well, let's go to your place, then," he said.

Again she shook her head. "We can't. I'm in a little family hotel. They won't let you up. It's full of German priests, they are very moral."

"What do we do, then?" Jack asked. "Wait until it's dark and find a quiet bush in the Borghese Gardens?"

"Tomorrow," Veronica said, "I am moving in with a friend. She goes to work all day and the apartment's empty."

"What do we do until tomorrow?" Jack asked.

Veronica chuckled. "You can't wait?"

"No."

"Neither can I." She looked at her watch. "I am busy another two hours. I will be at your room at five o'clock."

"I thought you said he's liable to be there—at my hotel. Watching," Jack said.

"Not at five o'clock," she said.

"How do you know?"

116

"At five o'clock every day," Veronica said, gathering her things together and rising, "he goes to his analyst. Nothing ever stops him. Don't worry. He will not be there." She leaned over and kissed him. "Let me go out first," she said. "You wait five minutes. Just in case."

He watched her walk toward the door, her long dark hair swung back over one shoulder, her hips swaying a trifle more than usual because Jack was watching her, because two waiters were watching her, her narrow feet in their high-heeled pointed Roman shoes making a rhythmic provocative tapping on the mosaic floor.

My dear God, Jack thought, as the door closed behind her and he settled back to wait the cautionary five minutes, what have I got myself in for? And is it worth it?

*

When he left the restaurant, Jack told Guido to drop him at the Embassy, and then take off until eight o'clock that evening. Curiously, he asked Guido what he would do with his free time. "I will go home," Guido said soberly, "and play with my three children."

"I have three children, too," Jack said.

"It is the meaning of life," said Guido, and drove off sedately.

The marine guard at the door was young and tall and reminded Jack of high-school graduation classes. He wore decorations from the Pacific and from Korea and the Silver Star and the Purple Heart. He had rosy cheeks and smiled warmly and innocently at Jack and looked too young to have been in either war and too healthy ever to have been wounded. There was something about his size and pinkness that made Jack remember Bresach. What betrayals do you suffer off duty, Jack thought, as he passed into the building, what doors do you guard on your own time, when do you visit your analyst?

Jack gave his name to the girl behind the reception desk and told her whom he wished to see and two minutes later he was in the press office, in a rattle of typewriters, seated across the desk from Hanson Moss, a young man who had been in Paris for several years before being transferred to Rome.

Italian food was putting weight on Moss and he looked comfortable, rumpled, and unambitious behind the desk piled high with Italian newspapers. After five minutes of civilities in which they exchanged information about their families, and Jack explained that he was in Rome on a short vacation, and Moss complained that the Italian newspapers attacked American policy every day just the way the French newspapers did, only in worse prose, Jack told him why he had come to visit him. "There's a man I know," Jack said, "name of Holt. From Oklahoma. He owns an oil company. Maybe a couple of oil companies."

"The Foreign Service," Moss said gravely, "will split its last gut for an oil company. Every Italian knows that. What's his problem? Did they catch him changing a five-dollar bill on the black market?"

"He wants to adopt a baby," Jack said.

"What does he want it for?" Moss asked. "A souvenir of his trip to Italy?"

Jack explained, as briefly as he could, some of Holt's problems. He didn't think it necessary to tell Moss about the six years in Joliet. "There must be somebody here who's equipped to handle things like this," Jack said. "I thought you might tell me."

Moss scratched his head. "I guess Kern, over in the Consulate, is the man you want. Do you know him?"

"No, I don't think so," Jack said.

Moss picked up the phone and dialed a number. "Mr. Kern," he said, "this is Moss in the press attaché's office. I have a friend of mine here with a problem. Mr. Andrus. NATO in Paris. He's here on a short visit. Could you see him right away? Thanks." He hung up. "I've greased the wheels," he said. "Tell your friend if he has a little old oil well he doesn't have any use for, I'll be only too happy to look after it for him."

"I will," Jack said. He stood up.

"Say, wait a minute . . ." Moss was ruffling through the papers on his desk and came up with an embossed card. "Samuel Holt," he said. "Is that the feller?"

"Yes."

"I'm invited to a cocktail party at his house tonight." He peered at the card. "Palazzo Pavini. Chic, eh? You going?"

"Yes," Jack said.

"Good," Moss said. "I'll see you later. Be circumspect with Kern. He's a sod."

Kern was a large, mournful man with sparse hair, a big nose, and the complexion of a man who was having trouble with his stomach. His suit was black and diplomatic, his collar starched, his desk rigorously neat, with an In basket and an Out basket in which the papers were geometrically arranged. He had sad, suspicious, yellow-rimmed eyes, and he sat behind his desk with the air of a man who terrorized his secretaries and who gave visas for entrance to the United States only with the greatest reluctance. In Jack's years of dealings with governmental agencies, he had seen faces like Kern's many times, and the owners of the faces had always been people who regarded all foreigners as real or potential enemies of America. He knew the facts behind alliances, Kern's face announced, and they were not savory. He heard the real tones under the honeyed voices of applicants, he saw the duplicity and self-interest in their hearts.

"What is your interest in this affair, Mr. Andrus?" Kern asked, when Jack had finished explaining about who the Holts were and why they wanted to adopt a child. The question, and the tone in which it was put, made the clear insinuation that whatever interest Jack had in it was probably corrupt.

"No interest, really," Jack said. "It's just that Mr. Holt is a friend of mine . . ."

"Ah," Kern said. "A friend. You've known him a long time?"

"No," Jack said. He couldn't say that he had met Holt for the first time that midnight. "I just thought that perhaps a personal word might help—maybe speed things up a bit—"

"A personal word." Kern made the phrase sound like the offer of a bribe. "I see. Actually, while we don't have any set policy, we are not too happy about transactions like this. Children, religious differences . . ." Kern spread his hands carefully and ominously on his shining desk. "There're always liable to be unpleasant repercussions. Still, if he's a friend of yours, and you're a friend of Hanson Moss . . . Between you and me, of course—there are several people on the Italian side I might approach."

"That'd be very kind of you," Jack said, anxious to leave.

Kern looked consideringly across the desk at Jack. "You would be willing to vouch for the character of your—of the applicants, of course?"

Jack hesitated. "Naturally," he said.

"That might weigh in the balance," Kern said sonorously. He opened a drawer and took out a dossier and put it squarely in front of him. "Actually," he said, "the case has already reached my desk. The preliminary papers." He opened the dossier and studied them for a full minute, in silence. "There are certain conditions the applicants must fulfill. First—the medical requirements."

"I'm sure they're perfectly healthy," Jack said hastily.

"The Italian government," Kern said, his eyes lowered, reading from the sheets in front of him, "demands that the husband of the couple making the request for the child must be over fifty years of age and present a certificate from an Italian physician, duly witnessed, that the husband is incapable of having a child of his own. In other words—one-hundred-percent sterile." Kern smiled yellowly across at Jack. "Do you believe your friend is capable of obtaining such a certificate?"

Jack stood up. "If it's all the same to you, Mr. Kern," he said, "I think I'd like to ask Mr. Holt to come in and talk to you himself." He was prepared to do a great deal for Maurice Delaney, but he felt his obligation stopped short of guaranteeing the absolute sterility of millionaires.

"Very well," Kern stood up, too. "You will be hearing from me."

As Jack walked back toward his hotel, he had an absurd feeling of relief at having finished with Kern and having left the man's office behind him. Government offices, he thought, with distaste, remembering his own. They are the real breeding ground for rebellion and anarchy.

11

He was opening the door to his suite, when he heard a noise in the deserted corridor. A door leading to a servant's pantry twenty feet behind him swung open, and as Jack turned, he saw Bresach hurrying out of the pantry, advancing swiftly on him from his ambush among the sinks and coffee pots, his duffel coat open and billowing around him.

"Oh, God," Jack said, angrily, moving toward Bresach, holding the heavy key on its plastic plaque in his fist, like a weapon. "Don't start anything."

Bresach halted. "I've been waiting for you," he said, blinking his eyes nervously behind his glasses. "I'm unarmed. You've got nothing to be afraid of. Honest. I haven't got the knife." His voice was pleading. "I swear to God I haven't got the knife. You can search me. I just want to talk to you. Honest." He put his hands up over his head. "Search me. You'll see."

Jack hesitated. Well, I owe him *that* much, he thought. "All right," he said. "Come on in."

"Don't you want to search me?" Bresach said. He was still standing with his arms in the air, his coat open. He was wearing a pair of creased corduroy trousers and a workman's heavy blue shirt, without a tie, and a thick, raveling, discolored brown tweed jacket. On his feet he had high, scuffed old army shoes.

"No, I don't want to search you," Jack said. Bresach dropped his arms, looking almost disappointed, as Jack opened the door and went in. Bresach followed slowly. Jack took off his coat and threw it over a chair and turned and faced him.

"Now," Jack said briskly, "what do you want?" There was a gilt clock set in the wall over the doorway and Jack saw that it was five minutes past four. If Veronica kept her word and arrived at five o'clock, he would have to work fast to get the boy out of there.

"Do you mind if I sit down?" Bresach asked, his voice tentative.

"Sit down, sit down," Jack said. Bresach looked worn, exhausted, like a student who has stayed up many nights cramming for an examination he fears he is going to fail. It was impossible not to feel a touch of pity for him. "Do you want a whisky?"

"Thank you," Bresach sat down on a straight chair. Self-consciously he crossed his legs and put his hand on the ankle of the upraised foot, like a man posing stiffly for a photograph.

Jack poured him a whisky with some soda from a bottle that had been open since the night before and was now flat. He poured a little whisky for himself and then gave Bresach his drink. Bresach lifted his glass awkwardly. *"Salute,"* he said.

"Salute," Jack said. They drank. Bresach drank thirstily, finishing a quarter of his drink in one long gulp. He put one arm over the back of his chair in what looked like a conscious effort to make himself appear at home.

"You have a nice place here," Bresach said, waving his glass. "You're doing yourself pretty well."

"Did you come up here to admire the room?" Jack said.

"No," Bresach said humbly. "Of course not. It—it was just to break the ice. After last night. I have to tell you something, Mr. Andrus." He peered mildly at Jack, through his glasses, like a student with poor eyes seated at the back of a classroom, trying to make out a scrawled formula chalked on a blackboard. "I don't have my knife with me today. But that doesn't mean I won't bring it another time. And that I won't use it. I just wanted to let you know."

Jack sank into an easy chair, glass in hand, sitting low, facing the boy. "Thanks," he said. "It's nice of you to tell me."

"I don't want you to have any false ideas about me," Bresach said, in his low, pleasant, earnest voice. "I don't want you to think that I've forgiven you or that you can put anything over on me."

Jack put his glass down deliberately on the table next to his chair. Maybe, he thought, this is the moment for me to get up and go over and hit him a couple of times around the head. Hard. Administer what the French call a severe correction. Maybe that would shake some of those damned ideas out of his head. Bresach was tall, but he was skinny under the bulky coat, and the bones of his wrist, sticking out from his frayed tweed sleeves, were slender and not strong-looking. Jack hadn't been in a fistfight since the war, but he was a powerful man, with heavy arms and shoulders and thick hands and he had had more than his share of fights as a boy. He had boxed for pleasure in gymnasiums until his wound and he was sure he hadn't slipped back too far even now. Besides, it wouldn't take a heavyweight champion of the world to teach Bresach a lesson. Three or four sharp blows and it would be over. Jack shook his head, rejecting the idea. If Bresach had been bigger and stronger, he could do it. But even as a boy Jack had avoided hitting anybody who wasn't a match for him. He hated bullies, in all fields, physical and moral, and even the probability that a little violence now might ward off worse violence later couldn't move him to stand up and cross to where Bresach was sitting and hit him.

"Good," Jack said. "If I understand you correctly, you're warning me that you reserve the right to murder me in the future."

"Yes," Bresach said.

"What made you decide to call an armistice today?" Jack asked.

"I wanted to talk to you," Bresach said soberly. "There are some things I have to know."

"What makes you think I'll talk to you?"

"You're here, aren't you?" said Bresach. "You let me in. You're talking to me, aren't you?"

"Look, Bresach," Jack said, "I'm going to deliver some warnings of my own. I may pick up the phone in two minutes and tell the manager I want him to send the police to this room to pick you up. You'd be in an awful lot of trouble if I swore that you'd been threatening to kill me, you know."

"You won't do that," Bresach said.

"I'm not so sure I won't," Jack said.

"It would all come out then," Bresach said calmly. "It would be in the papers. Your wife would find out. The people you work for. How long would you hold your job with the government if it was all over the newspapers that you'd gotten into trouble in Rome because you were sleeping with a young Italian girl?"

Skinny or not skinny, Jack thought, maybe I ought to hit him.

"No," Bresach said, "you're not going to call the police." He drank thirstily. "I figured *that* out." He finished his drink and put the glass down. "Did you see Veronica today?"

"Yes," Jack said. "We had lunch. Do you want the menu?"

"How is she?" Bresach leaned forward, searching Jack's face to see if he was telling the truth.

"She is blooming," Jack said cruelly, avenging himself for Bresach's disquisition about his wife and his job. "She is in the first fine transports of love."

"Don't make fun of me." Bresach tried to make his voice sound threatening, but the effect was hurt and sorrowful. "Where is she now? Where is she staying?"

"I don't know," Jack said, "and if I did I wouldn't tell you."

"What did she say about me?"

Jack hesitated. His moment of cruelty had passed. "She didn't say anything about you," he lied.

"I don't believe you," Bresach said. "Don't lie to me. I'm nervous enough as it is. If you lie to me, I won't be responsible for what I do . . ."

"If you're going to threaten me," Jack said, "I'll kick you out of here right now."

"All right, all right." Bresach spread his hands, like a coach on a baseball field motioning a runner to hold onto his base. "I'm going to be calm. I'm going to make a great effort to be calm. I didn't come up here to fight with you. I have some questions to ask you. Perfectly reasonable questions. All I want is some honest answers. I have some rights," he said, defiantly. "Don't I have some rights? At least the answers to a couple of questions."

"What do you want to know?" Jack asked. The boy was so obviously suffering, was so naked and exposed to pain, that Jack's instinct was to soothe him as much as possible.

"First—the important question." Bresach's chin sank onto his chest and he mumbled almost incomprehensibly into his open collar. "Do you love her?"

Jack hesitated, trying not so much to phrase the truth, which was easy and simple to do, but to say the thing which would cause the least pain to Bresach.

"God damn it, Andrus," Bresach said loudly, "don't sit there making up stories. All you have to say is yes or no."

"Well, then—no," Jack said.

"So," Bresach said, "for you she's just a—an entertainment."

"If it makes you feel any better," Jack said, "having you hanging around like this is making it a lot less entertaining."

"Have you told her?" Bresach persisted.

"Told her what?"

"That you don't love her."

"The question hasn't come up," Jack said.

"I love her," Bresach said, flatly. He peered at Jack as though waiting for Jack's reaction to this. Jack kept quiet. Bresach rubbed his hands together nervously, warming them against each other. "Aren't you going to say something?" Bresach demanded.

"What do you want me to say?" Jack said. "Hallelujah, you love her?"

"I want her to marry me," Bresach whispered. "I've asked her ten times. It's only a technicality that we aren't married now."

"What?" Jack asked, puzzled.

"A technicality. She's a Catholic. Her family's devout. I'm an atheist. Even for her I wouldn't go through that hypocritical crap . . ."

"I see," said Jack, remembering Holt and his wife. Religion, he thought, is more complicated in Rome than anyplace else in the world.

"But she was wavering," Bresach said. "She goes to see her family in Florence every weekend and they gabble at her and drive her to Mass. But it was just a question of time. It's just that one thing. She knows I'd do anything else for her. She knows I can't live without her."

"Nonsense," Jack said, sharply. "Anybody can live without anybody."

"That's disgusting," Bresach said. He jumped up, and began striding erratically around the room. "Disgusting. It's cynical. Heartless. That's one of the things I hate about getting old like you," he said. "I'd kill myself before I let myself get cynical and cold like that. If that's the way I'm going to feel, I'd rather die before I'm thirty. When you were young, when you were my age, I bet you weren't like that. I've seen you. I've seen you in your pictures. Before you became rotten."

Jack watched Bresach carefully, prepared for any sudden, dangerous move, now that Bresach was on his feet and loose from his chair. He felt himself growing angry again. Part of the reason he was angry was that in a way Bresach was right—when he was twenty-five he wouldn't have said anybody could live without anybody. "Be careful of your language," Jack warned the boy. "I'm ready to listen to you—although I don't know quite why—but I'm not going to let you insult me."

"She was a virgin when I met her," Bresach said loudly, the words tumbling over each other. "It was four months before I even tried to kiss her. The day she moved into my room, I felt, Now, finally, my life is worth while. Then she meets you and in a half-hour you take her away from me. Somebody old like you," he sneered at Jack, with his mouth pulled down in the tic that affected him when he was excited, "fat, married . . ." Bresach made the word married sound like the secret name of a loathsome perversion. "Complacent. A clerk in an office. A man who had a big talent, a real talent, and didn't have the guts to stick with it. A man who surrendered. A man who sits in an office all day figuring out ways of blowing up the world . . ."

"I think," Jack said, "you have a slightly lurid notion of what I do in NATO. Maybe you've been reading the communist papers too much."

"And it all shows in your face," Bresach went on wildly, striding up and down the room. "The surrender, the corruption, the tricks, the sensuality. You're ugly!" He shouted. "You're an ugly old man! And she left me for you! I'm going to tell you something," he shouted crazily. "I'm beautiful! Ask her yourself, ask her if she hasn't told me I'm beautiful."

Jack laughed, the sound forced out of him by the surprising description Bresach was giving of himself.

"That's right—laugh," Bresach said, standing threateningly over Jack. "That's what I ought to expect from a man like you. Any real word—any real description of the way things are embarrasses you, so you laugh. That cocktail-party laugh, that barroom laugh, that diplomatic laugh, that worn-out laugh. One day that godamn laugh is going to be stuffed back into everybody's throat."

"You're raving, boy," Jack said quietly. "I think you'd better get out of here."

"What did you promise her?" Bresach demanded. His face was dead white, except for two small, round spots of burning color on his cheekbones, and for a moment Jack wondered if the boy were sick, if the real reason he had come to Rome was because he suffered from tuberculosis. Keats on his deathbed in the room over the Spanish steps, the rouged English ladies, talking too brightly in the tearooms, avoiding the murderous London winters, coughing nervously into their handkerchiefs. He had an impulse to tell the boy he ought to go see a doctor. "What did you offer her at that godamn lunch?" Bresach shouted. "What tricks did you use? What did you do—get her drunk? What did you give her—money, jewels? What lies did you tell her? Did you tell her you would divorce your wife and marry her and take her back with you to America?"

"Let's get this straight," Jack said correctively, standing up. "I didn't tell her anything and I didn't offer her anything. It never even occurred to me that I wanted her. If you're so crazy about the truth, here it is—she put herself in my bed without being asked. If you must know," Jack said astringently, advancing on the boy, wanting to get rid of him once and for all, "she was a volunteer. An enthusiastic volunteer."

Bresach glared at him, then sprang suddenly, swinging. The blow was wild and slow and Jack automatically went inside it and punched Bresach on the side of the head. Even as he swung, Jack pulled back a little, not wishing to hurt Bresach too much. But even the half blow shook the boy. He didn't go down, but wobbled, put out his hands blindly in front of him, low, trying to hold his balance, and staggered backwards, turning. He wound up against the wall, under one of the etchings of medieval Rome, his head tilted sidewise against the wall, his cheek twisted by the pressure.

"Oh, Christ," Jack said, watching him, ashamed of what he had done, the defensive reflex which had made him strike out.

Bresach remained in the strange, twisted position against the wall, bent over, recovering, his back to Jack, gasping painfully.

"I'm sorry," Jack said. He touched the thick material of the duffel coat on Bresach's shoulder. "I didn't mean . . ."

"You're so lucky," Bresach whispered, talking into the wall, not moving his head, pressed against the plaster. "You've got everything. I haven't got anything. She doesn't mean anything to you. You don't even want her. There're ten thousand girls in Rome. Prettier girls. Why don't you give her back to me?"

At the moment, alone in the room with the suffering boy whom he'd hit, Jack felt that he would gladly give Veronica back to him, if he could. Or at least say that he would try to send her back. At that moment, he didn't have the slightest interest in Veronica. It was only when she was there, next to him, with her bold eyes, and her little tricks of swinging her hair, of licking the corner of her mouth, of reaching out and stroking his hand with her soft, long fingers that he wanted her. If he didn't see her again, he thought, he would forget her in two days. At the moment he was more annoyed with her than anything else, for getting him involved in this ludicrous embroilment with Bresach. But of course, he couldn't say that, either to her or to the boy. And he couldn't tell the boy either, no matter how magnanimous he would have liked to be, that he could deliver his girl over to him. After what Veronica had said about Bresach at lunch, it was hard to imagine her going back to him. There are some possessions, he thought sadly, that even the most generous of us can never transform into gifts.

"Do you want another drink?" Jack asked lamely, touching Bresach's shoulder again.

Bresach straightened up, then turned around and faced Jack. The left side of his face was raw and red. "I don't want anything from you," he whispered. "I made a mistake. I made a big mistake today. I should've brought my knife."

He put the collar of his coat up around his ears and walked out of the apartment. Jack sighed and rubbed the knuckles of his right hand. They had stung for a moment, but the blow had been so light that his hand now felt normal. He went to the window and looked down at the narrow Roman street, where an Alfa Romeo was growling like a hunting lion at a red light, and a girl in a waitress's uniform was hurrying along the pavement bearing three small cups of black coffee on a silver tray.

He thought of going out and leaving a note for Veronica saying that he had been called away. Then it occurred to him that perhaps the reason he was weighing this withdrawal was connected to Bresach's last threat, and an almost childish sense of defiance in the face of a dare made him decide to stay and wait for her.

"You ugly old man," he murmured, remembering. Curiously, he went over to the big mirror over the mantelpiece and looked at himself. It was growing dark and the reflection of his face was shadowy and mysterious. His face was sad, thoughtful, lined by experience, and his eyes were clear and alive. No, he thought, I'm not an ugly old man. He searched his face for complacency, cynicism, surrender. No, he thought, the boy's lying. Or anyway, half lying. Or, with bad luck, prophesying a face that might, if care were not taken, emerge in the future. Well, then, he said to himself, we will take care.

12

"After you've been in Italy for three days and looked at these Mediterranean faces," the American composer was saying, "you can't bear to look at American faces any more. They look so unfinished." He was a guest at the Academy for a year, and he had written some pretty good music, Jack remembered. Jack had the feeling that a man who wrote music as well as that should know better than to talk like that.

Glass of whisky in his hand, Jack wandered back toward the bar set up along one end of the huge red silk room of the Palazzo Pavini, now crowded with friends of the Holts, friends of friends, people working on Delaney's movie, a batch of starlets, newspapermen, people from the Embassy, two Irish priests from Boston, a flock of college girls on a guided tour of Europe, some young men from the Embassy, three or four American divorcées who were living in Rome because their alimony went further in Italy, a publicity man from one of the air lines and two pilots, accompanied by French stewardesses, a clump of English and American doctors who were in Rome for a conference on the diseases of the bone, the usual band of young Italians in their beautiful suits who numbered among them a good proportion of titles (Holt's degenerate counts), and who circled the two prettiest of the American college girls, making private jokes, superciliously disregarding the rest of the company, a hearty Chicagoan, growing bald, who said he was an investment counselor for American firms who wished to do business in Europe, and who was reputed to be a member of Central Intelligence, two or three Italian-Americans who represented the big movie companies in Rome and who were experts at currency exchange and making hotel reservations and getting concessions from the police and who could be depended upon to send flowers to the wives of important people when they arrived in Rome. There were also two middle-aged Jewish couples from New York who had just come back from Tel Aviv and an Egyptian cotton planter whose lands had been confiscated by Nasser and two British ladies with thin faces and burning eyes who pretended they never had had tuberculosis and who almost made a living as typists and who drank whatever was offered them. There was also an actor who had been charged with being a Communist in Hollywood six or seven years before and who could no longer find work in America because by the time he confessed and exposed his friends his vogue was over and producers and directors had forgotten him. He had learned enough Italian to play small parts in Italian movies, and after years of dickering, the State Department had finally given him a normal passport.

Tucino was there, too, and his man Tasseti, and Barzelli and Delaney and Delaney's wife, Clara. Stiles stood unsteadily near the bar, a lofty, wooden smile on his face. Jean-Baptiste Despière was in the middle of the room, making a group of three with Moss, Jack's friend from the Embassy, and a young Italian movie director who had won a big prize in Venice the year before. Through it all, the Holts wandered, arm in arm, flushed with hospitality, embarrassed smiles flitting across their faces, pleased because back in Oklahoma City they never would have been able to give a party like this. Mrs. Holt was not yet drunk.

The volume of talk in the ornate room was at third-drink level, a base of masculine laughter swamped and curlicued by the massed choir of the soprano voice, shrilled by alcohol. Hunters and huntresses, excited by the abundance of game, firing at the slightest movement in the confused international foliage of conversation, the guests moved restlessly about, seeking new positions of advantage. When Jack was younger, when he was unmarried or between marriages and on the prowl for women, he had from time to time enjoyed these senseless conglomerations of people who had no connection to each other, who would, in all probability, never see each other again, who responded to no social necessity and composed no coherent social pattern. Or rather, the pattern was made and broken each night between seven and ten, a whole turbulent society, afloat on alcohol, born and buried, arriving and departing, loving, mating, despairing, wounding, flattering, and conspiring evening after evening in the capitals of the world. Tonight, Jack wasn't interested, and he wondered how soon he might be able to slip away without offending the Holts. He had asked Veronica to come with him, but she had refused. "I have a connection with you for two weeks," she had said, when they had parted at the hotel that afternoon, "and I want that it should be private. I do not want to waste it away at one of those parties. I do not even want to *talk* to anyone else these two weeks." He had a date with her for dinner at nine thirty and he nursed his one drink, conscientiously remaining sober for her, thinking, I bet I'm the only one in the room who's been threatened with murder this afternoon.

"Tel Aviv was wonderful," one of the motherly New York ladies was saying, "even the mailmen are Jewish."

"Take me, for example," the young Italian movie director in the same group with Moss and Despière was saying, speaking in French, for Moss's sake. "The two components of the Italian completely mingled. Look at the back of my head." He turned from side to side, exhibiting the back of his head. "Flat. I was born in Venice of a Venetian father. The northern Italian is really Swiss, Alpine, Tyrolian, Bavarian, the flat, severe, nonspeculative, rather unaesthetic line. But my face—my mother was born in Calabria —see the orphan's sad, dark eye, the southern spirit, the wit, the sudden bursts of energy, the long periods of languor. The northern Italian is practical, continuously energetic, and like most people who are too up-to-date, not particularly interesting in himself. The southerners are the dreamers, the philosophers, the abstract thinkers, the non-accomplishers, the residual, intellectual aurochs of Italy, who, if they were left alone would never have erected an electric dynamo or kept a locomotive in repair, who would still be farming with a wooden plow and a team of an ox and an ass. It is the combination of the two elements, the dream and the fingers, that makes the explosive, hopeful Italian mixture, the decadence suddenly exploding into some new and startling idea. Don Quixote and Edison, Henry Ford and Benedetto Croce. At any moment, we are capable of astonishing discoveries. Even now, we can teach Europe many things. For example—see how much faster we recovered than anyone else after the war. Why? Because we admitted immediately that we were beaten. Defeat is as natural as anything else to Italians, it is like the weather, we accept it. That didn't work, we said to ourselves, now let us go on to something else. The French, on the other hand, the rational French"—he looked mockingly at Despière—"keep pretending that they were not defeated. They are constantly standing in a challenging posture, they are listening defiantly for a voice that will say, 'You lost.' The French are so intent on defending the past, on illusory grounds, that they have not yet moved into the present. I will tell you something else about the Italians and the French. The world has forgiven us Italians our sins because we have forgiven ourselves so promptly. The French are unforgiven—listen to the bitterness in the voices of your English and American friends, even to this day—because the French cannot bring themselves to forgive themselves for anything—not for Stavisky, not for Blum, not for the Maginot Line, Pétain, Laval, Doriot, the Milice, not even for de Gaulle, while the Italians gaily forgive themselves not only for their defeats, but for their victories—for Addis Ababa as well as Guernica, for Albania and Greece, for Mussolini and the King, for the invasion of France and the secret surrender after Sicily."

Jack listened to the intelligent accented voice coming from the mobile Roman mouth, thinking, Where were you when Mussolini was on the balcony, how high did you raise your arm, friend?

"As for the Germans," the director went on, waving his hands, chuckling, enjoying himself, his arguments, his audience of ex-enemies, "they, of course, have no need to forgive themselves anything. They were right, they feel, always right—do not events bear them out?—and they bowed only to superior force. They are a lucky people, the Germans, they are upheld by the two most powerful racial forces—self-righteousness and self-pity . . ."

Jack drifted on, away from the flood of half-truths, away from the handsome fluent man with his mane of coal-black hair, his neat, self-satisfied arrangement of categories—North, South, flat heads, round heads, the dreamers, the fingers, the defeated and unde-feated, the forgiven and unforgiven, everything clear and manage-able after the third drink.

Clara Delaney, alone against a brocaded wall, was pretending to smile at the conversation of a group near her who were speaking in Italian. She caught Jack's eye and waved to him. He went over to her and kissed her cheek. She was a plain waxy woman, yellowed, angular and spare, well over forty, who had been Delaney's secre-tary through two of Delaney's other marriages. She had prominent, slightly hyperthyroid, dark eyes, hungry and permanently insulted.

"How are things, Jack?" she asked, her voice dry, unmusical. "How is the family? How do you keep looking so young? Don't you ever come back to America any more?"

Jack answered the questions as best he could, noticing that even as he talked Clara kept peering nervously over his shoulder at De-laney and Barzelli and Tucino, who were speaking together near the bar. It hasn't changed in all the years, Jack thought, Clara's always by herself, making her solitary patrol, suffering her solitary wounds, spying on her husband from afar, like a soldier surveying the actions of enemy forces in the field.

"How do you like Rome?" Jack asked, lapsing immediately into banality, the world's inevitable tribute to Clara Delaney.

"I hate it," Clara said. "They're so insincere. You never hear a sincere word spoken. And it's the same old story with *him*—" She indicated Barzelli and her husband with a bitter twist of her head. "The leading-lady disease. He can't keep his hands off them. If he made a picture with Ubangis, he'd have to crawl into bed with the nigger playing the Cannibal Queen."

"Now, Clara," Jack said soothingly, "I'm sure you're making things up."

"Hah!" Clara snorted briefly, her yellowish eyes fixed on her husband. "Making things up! If I told you where I found lipstick stains."

Clara had never been famous as a woman who kept her troubles to herself, and Jack saw that the years had not made her more discreet. He made a sympathetic, noncommittal noise, anxious to avoid further revelations.

"I'm telling you, Jack," Clara went on, rasping, "if he didn't need me so badly, I'd've left him years ago. I swear I would. By God, if this picture is a success, I think I'll do it. Then let him see who'll hold his hand and baby him and tell him he's still a great man when the reviews come out, no matter what the bastards say. Do you know, when his last picture opened in New York, he sat in his room and cried like an infant for three days. That's when he calls for me," she said, with bleak satisfaction, "that's when he calls me his only love, that's when he says he'd die without me. When he's sore and bleeding and wondering where it all went to. Now, look at him—the money's coming in for a couple of months, everybody's saying, Yes, Signor Delaney, no, Signor Delaney, whatever you say, Signor Delaney, and listening to his stories and laughing at his jokes, and he forgets that he ever cried for three days, he forgets what he owes me, he's so damned cocky he doesn't even bother to wipe the lipstick off when he comes home at night."

"Now, Clara," Jack said, feeling committed, out of friendship, to a healing word, "it isn't as though you didn't know he was a difficult man when you married him. You better than anyone."

"I know, I know," Clara said. "The years I lied for him to all those women. Just the way that Hilda of his is lying to me for him now. But you'd think a man'd give up finally, wouldn't you— you'd think that a man would improve. After all, he's fifty-six years old. How about you?" She peered at Jack harshly. "You don't drive your wife crazy, do you?"

"Well," Jack said carefully, "we have our problems like everybody else."

"Nobody has problems like me," Clara said flatly. "Look at that one." Her mouth curled in distaste as she indicated Barzelli, standing close to Delaney, her shoulder just touching his. "That common fat Italian. I'd like to see what she's going to look like when she's my age. And they're shameless. They let everybody know. The whole damned city. He doesn't care what anybody says about him."

That used to be one of the best things about him, Jack thought, he never cared what anybody said about him.

"It's not as though he has to go out of the house," Clara went on. "He's crazy about me. Ask him, he'll tell you. God knows, I'm no beauty and I never was, but I still have the body of a young girl . . ." She stopped and glared at Jack, waiting for him to contradict her, to tell her that she did not have the body of a young girl. Elaborately, Jack lit a cigarette. "We have a passionate relationship," Clara said loudly. "Like young lovers in the full flush of youth. He can't get enough of me." She hesitated. "Sometimes," she added. "Some months."

Rome, Jack thought uneasily. Everybody confesses in Rome. To me. There must be a particular absolving look on my face these days.

"And it's not only that," Clara continued, chapter one thousand in the endless book of love, self-pity, self-justification, jealousy, longing, possession that she had begun the day she walked, a young, unbeautiful woman, into the office in the studio in Hollywood and said, "Mr. Delaney, they sent me over from the stenographic pool." She dropped her voice, as though she had secret information, for Jack's ears only, and he had to move closer to hear her, above the roar of conversation all around them. "There's the work. Who do you think helps him with the scripts? Who do you think helped him rewrite this picture?"

Ah, Jack thought, criminals everywhere, penciling their nameless conjoined crimes.

"We think like one mind," Clara whispered. "When we work together, we're closer even than when we're in bed. And then he goes on the set and there's another of those fat whores waving her behind and I might as well be dead. He forgets the days and nights of work, he forgets . . ." She sniffled. Then she brightened self-consciously. "I'm not a complainer," she said. "I never complained before and I'm not going to start now. And this time, it's going to be worth it. You've read the script, haven't you? You've seen the picture?"

"Yes," Jack said.

"It's beautiful," Clara said, pleading. "Isn't it beautiful?"

"Yes," Jack said. "Beautiful."

"It's going to make all the difference, this one," Clara said, almost confidently. "This is going to put him right on top. Don't you think so?"

"No doubt about it," said Jack. There was nothing in his relationship with Delaney that committed him to honesty with Delaney's wife.

"You know, they're after him to sign a three-picture deal right here in Rome," Clara said proudly.

"Mr. Holt told me something about it," Jack said.

"I'm looking for an apartment," Clara said, "on a year-round basis. With a good cook. Give him something to come home to at night. If he has security like that, I have an idea he'd settle down more. The last few years've been so—" She stopped, looked thoughtfully across the room at Delaney and Barzelli. "You know

136

what I'm going to do, Jack. I'm going to get out of here. He hates it when he feels I'm being possessive. I'll just slip out. You have to know how to handle a man like that, Jack, you have to know when to stand in his way and when you mustn't. Don't tell anybody I'm leaving." She sidled toward the door through the throng of guests, then vanished, unnoticed. Two hours later Delaney might peer around hazily, wondering where she was, then shrug and go off with Barzelli, relieved that there were no excuses to be made to her for sending her home alone.

Jack sighed. And there was a time, he thought, when I believed people went to parties to enjoy themselves.

He felt a light touch on his arm. It was Mrs. Holt, accompanied, as always, by her husband. "It was so thoughtful of you to come," Mrs. Holt said, in her wispy, apologetic voice. "There must be so many things you have to do in Rome, so many people you must see . . ."

"Not at all," Jack said, shaking hands with Holt. Holt was in a dinner jacket of raw silk, obviously made in Rome, and Mrs. Holt was the only woman in the room in an evening gown. It was a girlish, wispy blue, to go with her voice, and her shoulders were covered with a tulle shawl. Her hands kept wandering upwards as she kept arranging and rearranging the shawl. "I hardly know anybody," Jack said. "By the way, Sam, about that thing we talked about last night . . ."

"Oh, yes," Holt said, with a quick, worried sideways glance at his wife. "If it's too much trouble . . ."

"I talked to someone at the Consulate," Jack said. "A Mr. Kern. You might drop in on him. I think perhaps he can help a bit."

Holt beamed. "Now, that was friendly of you, Jack," he said. "To do it so fast."

"There's some information he has to have," Jack said, not prepared to warn Holt more definitely than that. "I thought it might be better if you talked to him personally."

"Of course, of course," Holt said. "It's about the adoption papers," he explained to Mrs. Holt.

"They have such sad eyes," Mrs. Holt said, her own eyes blurring a little with tears. "They're so polite, it breaks your heart. I couldn't sleep all night, after the last visit, poor little tragic ladies and gentlemen in those horrible black clothes. I would like to take them all to my bosom."

"Jack," Holt said, "I'd like to ask you a question—are you committed to the government for life?"

"Well," Jack said, puzzled, "I hadn't really thought about it, I guess. They don't have chains on me, if that's what you mean . . ."

"What I'm driving at," Holt said, "is, if something—uh—something advantageous, something very advantageous—came up, would you have an open mind on it?"

"I suppose so," Jack said, wondering if Holt was going to offer him a job on the basis of the hour in the night club and the walk along the Tiber the night before. "I guess I'm as open-minded as the next man. I haven't thought about it." He smiled. "Nothing very advantageous has come up for about ten years."

"Good," Holt said crisply, as though Jack had just shaken hands on a deal. "I'm glad to hear that."

"I want to tell you something, Jack," Mrs. Holt said. "When we got home last night, Sam said to me, I like that young man. He's solid. He's not like most of the Americans you meet who've lived abroad for years—light and smart-alecky and cynical." She beamed at Jack, decorating him officially with her husband's approval.

"Well," Jack said gravely, "that *is* nice to hear. Especially the young man part."

"I don't know how old you are, Jack," said Mrs. Holt, "but you leave a young impression."

"Thank you, Bertha," Jack said, thinking, Maybe I ought to get her to talk to Bresach on my behalf.

"Please feel free to drop in here anytime, Jack," Holt said. "Now you know the way. You're always welcome. And"—he looked around him with pride at the assemblage of guests drinking his liquor—"there's no telling who you're likely to meet up with here."

"It's an intellectual experience," said Mrs. Holt. "Since I've come to Rome, I feel my brain expanding. Actually expanding. Would you believe it, until tonight, I never met a real, live modern composer of modern music."

They drifted off, radiant, to greet a Sicilian novelist who had just published a book about the war, the villain of which was a captain in the American Army.

"Jack . . ." It was Despière, touching his arm. "I was hoping you'd come tonight."

"I didn't get a chance to say hello," Jack said, shaking hands. "I was busy trying to figure out whether I was a round-headed aurochs or a flat-headed Henry Ford."

Despière chuckled. "I like him, the Italian. At least he has theories. You'd be surprised how many people I meet these days who refuse to have any theories at all."

"Oh, by the way," Jack said, making himself sound offhand, "I met a boy who says he's a friend of yours. A kid called Bresach."

"Bresach?" Despière wrinkled his eyebrows in an effort of memory and pushed at the short bangs of hair that fell onto his forehead. "A friend of mine?"

"That's what he said."

"Oh, yes. I've seen him a couple of times with Veronica." He looked slyly and mischievously at Jack. "Very handsome boy. Veronica's crazy about him."

"So he told me," Jack said noncommittally.

"What did he want?"

"Nothing," Jack lied. "I just met him by accident."

"Be careful of him," said Despière. "He once tried to commit suicide in somebody's bathroom. He's a very dramatic boy. I've seen him slap Veronica in the face because she smiled at an old friend in a restaurant."

"What did she do?" Jack asked, not believing Despière.

"She stopped smiling at old friends," Despière looked around him and drew Jack into a corner. "Will you do something for me, Jack?" he asked, his voice light and casual, as usual, but his eyes serious, searching Jack's face.

"Of course," Jack said. "What is it?"

Despière reached into his inside breast pocket and drew out a long sealed envelope. "Hold onto this for me for a while." He gave Jack the envelope. "Put it away, put it away."

Jack put the envelope, which was plump and bulging, into his pocket. "Do you want to tell me what to do with it?" he asked.

"Just hold onto it. When I come back, give it to me."

"What do you mean, when you come back?"

"I'm leaving for Algiers tomorrow," Despière said. "They cabled me from the office this morning. There's a story they want me to get. I'll just be gone six or seven days. You'll still be here, won't you?"

"Yes."

"The paper wants a couple of thousand words on how atrocious the Algerian atrocities are," Despière said. "I'm the atrocity editor. No decent up-to-date magazine is without one. Thanks. You're a good boy."

"You want to tell me anything else?"

Despière shrugged. "Well . . ." he drawled, "if I don't come back, open the envelope."

"Now, Jean-Baptiste," Jack began.

Despière laughed. "It's a small war, I know," he said, "but I understand they're using live ammunition. Anyway, atrocity editors have to think of all eventualities. One other thing. Don't tell anybody I'm going to Algiers. Not anybody," he repeated slowly.

"Where're you supposed to be?" Jack said. "If anybody asks."

"St. Moritz. I heard the snow was good. I'm staying with some friends. But you don't know their name."

"What about the piece about Delaney?"

"I'll finish it when I get back," Despière said. "This is the twentieth century—atrocities before art." He looked at his watch. "I'm late," he said. He patted Jack's arm and smiled at him, his smile sweet and boyish and friendly, untouched by malice, and turned and walked off through the drinkers toward his small secret war, a short, swaggering, tough little figure in his sharply cut Roman suit. Jack watched him leave and noticed that he didn't say good-bye to anyone.

Jack touched the bulge in his coat. Its weight disturbed him. *If I don't come back, open the envelope.*

Moved by a sudden impulse, Jack started through the crowd toward the door, to follow Despière. If a man is going to a war, however small, he thought, his friend can leave a cocktail party and accompany him. At least part of the way. At least to the nearest taxicab.

But as he neared the door a new, large group of guests came in, blocking his way, and before he could make his way through them, he felt a hand grasping him, hard, on the elbow, holding him back. Jack turned and saw that it was Stiles, grinning woodenly at him, standing close, the hand firm on his arm.

"Hi, brother," Stiles said. "I've been wanting to say hello to you all night."

"Some other time, if you don't mind." Jack tried to pull away without making it too obvious to the people around him, but Stiles, who was a large man, gripped him more firmly.

"That's no way to treat an old friend, brother," Stiles said. "Don't tell me you don't remember me, Mr. Royal."

"I remember you," Jack said. He jerked his arm suddenly and was free, but Stiles slid, with surprising agility, between him and the door, blocking it. The two men faced each other. Stiles still had

140

the glazed, pugnacious drunkard's grin on his face, happily prepared to make a scene. It's not worth it, Jack thought. I probably
can't catch up with Jean-Baptiste by now, anyway.

"What's on your mind?" Jack asked shortly. He felt uncomfortable in the actor's presence, foolishly guilty.

"I thought maybe you and me could have a nice little talk together," Stiles said. He had a curious, stiff-lipped manner of talking, hardly moving his mouth, the drunkard's evening disguise.
"About art and acting and allied subjects. I'm an old admirer of
yours. When I first started acting, I used to try and sound like you."
He laughed breathily. "And now you're getting paid to sound like
me. Life's little ironies, eh, Jack?" He rocked unevenly, his face
coming close to Jack's, the smell of gin strong on his breath, the
drink in his glass slopping over and staining his trousers, unnoticed. "You're not going to deny it, are you, Jack? The sneaky little dubbing-room sessions. You used to have a reputation as an
honest man, you're not going to deny it, are you?"

"I'm not going to deny anything," Jack said.

"You've seen my performance, in fact, you must be the biggest
godamn expert on my performance alive today," Stiles said loudly.
"Have you got any little hints on what I should do to improve it?"

"Yes," Jack said. "Join Alcoholics Anonymous."

"You're a help," Stiles said flatly. "You're a big help. You
sound like my godamned mother." He sipped noisily at his martini.
"Tell me," he said, "how am I going to sound? Am I going to sound
sincere and troubled? Am I going to sound pathetic and brave?
Will I sound virile and tragic? Will the girls like me, Jack? My
fate is in your hands, Jack. Don't take it lightly."

"I'm not taking anything lightly," Jack said.

"Maybe when the picture comes out, I'll sue you for de-de—
formation of character." Stiles laughed loudly at his pun. "A half
million dollars. I could use a half million dollars. Especially when
the news gets around that they had to bring in a clerk to read the
lines for me in Rome. Boy, that'll raise my price back home, won't
it?"

"Stop whining," Jack said, annoyed with the gin-stained, foul-
breathed actor clutching at him, grimacing close to his face. "You've
got nobody to blame but yourself."

"The saddest words of tongue or pen," Stiles said, grinning
loosely, the spit bubbling on his lips. "You've got nobody to blame
but yourself." He moved his hand clumsily, and brushed Jack's

shoulder with the glass. The glass dropped onto the floor, shattering. Stiles didn't bother to look down at it. "Serves them right," he said, looking around him bellicosely. "The bastards didn't invite me. I'm the stinking pariah of the company. I'm the Leper of Rome. But I came anyway. And they didn't have the guts to say, Blow, bud, this party is for ladies and gentlemen. I came for you, Jack. I'm an old fan, Jack, and I came for you. Aren't you touched?"

"Why don't you go home and get a good night's sleep?" Jack said.

"You don't know anything, Jack." Stiles shook his head sadly. "A big grown man like you and you don't know anything. I'm still a quart away from sleep, boy, a good fat quart . . ."

"Well, have a good time," Jack started to move away, but Stiles held him once more, his hand shaky but tight on Jack's sleeve.

"Wait a minute, Jack," Stiles said. "I got a proposition to make you." His voice sank to a hoarse whisper, and the drunkard's flesh around his mouth quivered loosely. "Go away. Get out of town. Tell that bastard Delaney you reconsidered. Tell him you're too proud. Tell him your wife's dying. Anything. Leave tonight, eh, Jack? I won't ask you what they're paying you, but I'll pay it. For doing nothing. Out of my own pocket," he said desperately, his bloodshot eyes blinking, as though he were trying to hold back tears. "Go have a holiday. On me. If you do that, I swear I won't touch a drop till the picture is finished . . ." He stopped. His hand dropped from Jack's sleeve. He laughed loudly and wiped his mouth. "Ah, I was only kidding. What the hell, I wouldn't give you ten cents. It was a joke, boy, I just wanted to see what you would say. What the hell difference does it make to me? The picture stinks anyway. Maybe I'll hire you as my personal ghost. You can dub me in all my pictures. Probably give me a new lease on life. Have a good time in Rome, boy." He clapped Jack on the shoulder, then walked, straight-backed, toward a window, threw it open, and stood there, staring out at the windy dark street, taking deep breaths of air, smiling widely.

Jack would have left then, even though it was still too early to meet Veronica, but he saw Delaney beckoning him to come over. He made his way through the perfume and conversation, passing two doctors who were drinking grapefruit juice in champagne glasses. "There's a man here," one of the doctors was saying, in the accents of Minnesota, "who claims to have extraordinary cures with colitis. He feeds them mashed potatoes for five days. Every two hours for five days. Nothing else. Four kilos a day."

"What was the bastard telling you?" Delaney asked as Jack came up to him and smiled at Tucino and Barzelli and Tasseti. "Stiles?"

"He complained because he wasn't invited tonight," Jack said.

"That didn't stop the bastard from coming, did it?" Delaney said. "Did he say anything else?"

"He offered to pay me to clear out of town tonight," Jack said. "To stop the dubbing."

"Oh, he knows," Delaney said.

"Maurice," said Tucino, smiling tolerantly. "Whatch'yu want? This is Rome. Nobody has kept a secret in Rome for three thousand years."

"If he gives me any more trouble on the set," Delaney said, lowering at Stiles's distant figure, planted in front of the long window, "I'm going to slug him."

Tucino glanced negligently at Stiles. "The actor will not give trouble," he said. "I am behind a month on his salary. He will starve."

"If I had it to do all over again," said Delaney, "I would vote for Prohibition. Especially for actors and writers. He shrugged, dismissing Stiles. "And Clara," he said belligerently. "I saw her filling your ear. What's on *her* mind?"

"She's thinking of hiring a good cook," Jack said, "so that you'll have something to come home to at night. A nourishing meal."

"Oh, my God," Delaney said, as Barzelli laughed softly. "A cook. I tell you, finally I'm going to retire to a hermit's cell and only come out for the first day's shooting."

"I bet," Jack said.

"Jack, my friend," Tucino said, stroking Jack's sleeve, "I am very 'appy. Maurice tells me you are doing very good with the dubbing, very passionate."

"Maurice is a liar," Jack said.

"We all know that," Tucino said. "Maurice is a liar. Otherwise, what would he be doing in Rome?" He laughed, delighted with his city.

"Hi, Jack." Unobserved, Brutton, the actor who could no longer work in Hollywood, had joined the group. He clapped Jack heartily and nervously on the shoulder and stood there, his hand out-stretched, an uncertain smile on his dark, tense face. "You remember me, don't you, Jack?"

"Of course," Jack said. He shook the proffered hand.

"I heard you were in Rome," Brutton said. His voice was hoarse and rushed and you could tell that he meant it to be hearty and full of easy confidence and that he was fooling nobody, especially himself. Beads of sweat stood out on his forehead. He gave the impression of a man who was trying to get into a sporting event with a forged ticket. "Everybody winds up in Rome these days, don't they, Jack?" Brutton said. He laughed windily and Jack could tell that he regretted the sound he was making. "Hi, Mr. Delaney." He turned toward Maurice, offering his hand. "I've been wondering when you were going to decide you needed a good actor and would call me. I still speak English, you know."

"Hello, Brutton," Maurice said, without inflection. He ignored the proffered hand.

The sweat glittered on Brutton's forehead and he blinked his eyes erratically. "My hand is out, Mr. Delaney," he said.

"I see it," Delaney said.

Tasseti moved in a little closer to Delaney, watching with pleasure and interest. These were the scenes for which Tasseti lived and he smiled gently, ready to protect his masters, administer punishment, fulfill his watchdog destiny.

Brutton dropped his hand. He took in two or three short, whistling breaths. "Jack shook my hand," Brutton said shrilly. "He's not too proud. And he's in the government, besides."

"Jack's a diplomat," Delaney said, staring coldly at Brutton. "He has to shake the hand of any sonofabitch who asks him."

"Now be careful," Brutton said loudly and emptily. "I don't let people talk to me like that."

Delaney turned his back on Brutton and said to Barzelli, touching her arm affectionately, "You look beautiful tonight, *carissima*. I like the new way you're doing your hair."

Brutton moved so that he was facing Delaney again and Jack saw Tasseti's fingers twitching hopefully, waiting for the first moment of violence. "I'll tell you what I think about you," Brutton said hoarsely to Delaney. "I think you're a secret Communist sympathizer. There're still plenty like you left in Hollywood, don't think there aren't. The last time I was there, I was in Chasen's, and I was passing a table, and I had my head turned and somebody threw a drink all over me . . . There were six of them there, big men in the industry, contributors to the Republican party, and when I asked them to tell me who did it, they just laughed . . ."

"Calm down," Jack said, ashamed for Brutton, ashamed for the movie business, for Americans at home and abroad. He put his hand on Brutton's sleeve. The man was trembling. "Delaney wouldn't know how to be a secret anything. And everybody knows he was against the Communists for years while you were going to the meetings every Tuesday night. Why don't you go home?"

"The Committee gave me a clean bill of health," Brutton went on, obsessed. "When I testified, they shook my hand, they said I was a loyal, patriotic American, who had recognized his mistake and had courageously rectified it. I can show you the letter."

"The Committee would give a clean bill of health to a typhus bug," Delaney said, "if he turned in the other typhus bugs, the way you did. If you want to know something, Brutton, I think deep in your heart you're *still* a Communist, if you're anything. You're just stupid enough. You're a loyal, patriotic coward, and you screamed to save your own skin, and you denounced a lot of poor bastards who used to be your best friends and who never did anything worse than sign a paper saying hooray for the Russian Army in 1944. I pity you, but I don't shake hands out of pity. If you're busted and need a handout, come to my office tomorrow and I'll give you a few bucks. Because in principle I think I ought to try to keep all actors alive, even bad ones like you, since I make my living off them. Now get out of here, you've made enough noise."

"I ought to hit you," Brutton whispered, but keeping his hands at his sides.

"Try it," Delaney said flatly. "Some day." He turned to Barzelli. "Let's go get a drink, *carissima,*" he said. He took her arm and walked over toward the bar.

Tasseti smiled gently, observing Brutton with pleasure. Tucino shrugged. "I tell you," he said, "I will never understand America."

Brutton wiped his forehead with a green silk handkerchief, his eyes shifting, near tears, from face to face. "He's an egomaniac," Brutton said loudly. "Wait till it all catches up with him." He smiled, baring his teeth painfully. "What's the sense in taking an egomaniac seriously." He waved, in a hideous attempt to be debonair. "See you around, Jack. I'll invite you to dinner. Show you how the poor people live." For a last time he glanced swiftly, appealingly around him. Nobody said anything. Tasseti put his hands in his pockets, disappointed that there was no need for violence. Brutton turned and walked with a crippled attempt at jauntiness over to a corner of the room where two Italian starlets were speaking to each other, and put his arms possessively around their shoulders as he began to talk to them. His laugh came harshly across the room, high over the noise of conversation.

"What is it?" Tasseti asked in his almost incomprehensible Sicilian French. "Did Delaney take a girl away from the actor?"

"Probably," Jack said. "One time or another." He shook hands with Tucino and Tasseti and made his way to the door. He had had enough of the party.

Out in the hall, waiting for his coat, he saw one of the pretty young American college girls seated on a marble bench against the wall, bent over, sobbing. Her lip was bleeding and she kept dabbing at it with a piece of pink Kleenex. Two of her friends were standing in front of her, looking grave and trying to shield her from the eyes of the guests arriving and departing. Politely, Jack avoided looking at her after the first moment, and it was only the next day that he heard that she'd been in a bedroom with one of the young Italians, Count Something, who had thrown her on the bed and had bit her lip when she tried to keep him from kissing her. It took two stitches to sew the wound.

13

Streaked by a quarter moon, the Mediterranean shushed gently into the beach. Jack and Veronica sat against a dune, protected from the sporadic wind, warm in their coats in the unseasonably balmy air. It was nearly midnight, and only a few lights shone in the winter-deserted colony of houses down the beach. When Veronica had suggested going to Fregene for dinner, the prospect had seemed attractive to Jack, after the heat and confusion of the Holts' party. They had dined in a little country *trattoria,* eating simply and drinking a carafe of raw red wine, and had then driven on the edge of the pine forest along the beach to this lonely stretch of sand. The mingled fragrance of salt and pine enveloped them as they sat, Jack's arm around Veronica's waist, looking out at the mild shimmer of the moon on the water in front of them.

The title of this picture, Jack thought, pleasurably, is Two Lovers by the Side of the Sea. For the moment, Delaney and Barzelli and

Stiles and Brutton, all feuds and problems, seemed distant and inconsequential.

"I have been thinking," Veronica said. "Maybe I should come to Paris."

She waited a moment, her head against Jack's shoulder, and he knew that she was waiting for him to say, Yes, you should come to Paris. But he didn't say it.

"I am getting tired of Rome," she said. "And, anyway, I won't be able to keep out of Robert's way forever. And finally, he will make my life miserable."

"At the party," Jack said, "Despière told me that he saw Bresach hit you once, in a restaurant. Is that true?"

"Yes," Veronica laughed, briefly. "Once."

"What did you do?"

"I told him that if he ever did it again, I would leave him," she said. "He never did it again, but I have left him just the same." She laughed again. "He might as well have given himself the pleasure." She gathered some sand in her free hand and then, hour-glass fashion, let it sift slowly down in a thin stream, back onto the beach. "I speak French," she said. "I could get a job in a travel agency. Millions of French come to Italy every year." She hesitated briefly. "I've always wanted to live in Paris. I could find a little flat and you could come and visit me."

Jack moved a little, uneasily. He had a vision of himself hurrying to get away from his office early, swearing at the wheel of his car in the octopus-clutch of evening Parisian traffic, climbing the rickety steps of a crumbling St.-Germain-des-Prés apartment building, making love to Veronica, trying not to look at his watch, then, too soon for a lover, and not early enough for a husband, taking leave of her (regret and blame, voiced or unvoiced at the half-open door) to rush back home in time to kiss Hélène and say good night to the children before they went to bed, and making the proper, shielded answers when Hélène asked, over the pre-dinner drink, "What sort of a day did you have?" *Cinq à sept,* the French called it and, men and women both, seemed to manage it deftly and with pleasure.

"You prefer it if I do not come to Paris," Veronica said.

"Of course not," Jack said, and he wasn't exactly lying. "Why do you say that?"

"You kept quiet in a funny way," Veronica said.

Oh, God, Jack thought, another woman to weigh my silences.

148

"I'm foolish," Veronica said. "I do not want to accept our limits."

"What do you mean by that?" Jack asked.

"The moment that I take you to Ciampino and put you on the plane, that is our limit." She smiled in the darkness. "What the geography books call a natural boundary. The Rhine, the Alps. Ciampino is our Rhine, our Alps, isn't it?"

"Look, Veronica," Jack said, speaking carefully, "I have a wife in Paris. And I love her." For the purposes of this conversation, Jack thought, the phrase is accurate enough.

Veronica made a disdainful noise. "I am getting tired," she said, "of men who sleep with me and tell me how much they love their wives."

"The rebuke is noted," Jack said. "I will never again tell anybody how much I love my wife."

"Well, at least it's different from Italian men," Veronica said. "They always tell you how much they hate their wives. And the truth is, they usually do. There's no divorce in Italy, so they can afford to tell their mistresses they hate their wives. Americans have to be more careful."

They sat quietly for a moment, uncomfortable and opposed. Then Veronica began to hum, low, gently. " 'Volare,' " Veronica sang, " 'oh, oh! Cantare . . . oh, oh, oh, oh! nel blù, dipinto di blù, felice di stare lassù . . . I'm flying, I'm singing . . .' " She laughed harshly. "Love songs for the tourist trade." She whistled two or three bars derisively, purposely flat, then took her hand out of Jack's, and let the song slide away into silence.

Jack felt himself beginning to get angry with the girl, with her shifting and increasing claims, her quick mockery of both him and herself. "You said something just a minute ago," he said, "that I'd like to ask you about."

"What's that?" Veronica said carelessly.

"You said you were getting tired of men who sleep with you and tell you how much they love their wives."

"That's right," Veronica said. "Does that offend you?"

"No," Jack said. "It's only that Bresach said that you were a virgin when he met you."

Veronica laughed. "Americans," she said, "will believe anything. It's their form of optimism. Why?" she asked challengingly. "Would you have preferred it if I'd been a virgin when I met Robert?"

"I don't see that it has anything to do with me at all," Jack said. "I was just curious. Do you mind that I ask you these questions?"

"Of course not," Veronica said. She picked up his hand and kissed his fingers, lightly.

"Despière," Jack said, "told me that Bresach once tried to commit suicide." He felt Veronica stiffen beside him. "Is that true?"

"In a way," she said. "Yes."

"Was it because of you?"

"Not really," she said. "He was going to a psychiatrist here long before he met me. To get talked out of killing himself. An Austrian from Innsbruck. Dr. Gildermeister." She made her voice heavy and Teutonic to pronounce the name, derisively. "I had to go see him, too, after I moved in with Robert. You know what he said to me —'I must warn you, young lady, Robert is a very finely balanced mechanism.' That was news," she said, sounding suddenly American. "Hot from Innsbruck."

"What else did he say?"

"That Robert was potentially violent—that his violence might turn against himself—or against me. *'Volare—cantare . . .'*" she sang. She turned and put her arms around Jack and pulled, making him fall across the top of her body as she sank back into the sand. "I didn't come out with you tonight," she whispered, "to talk about anybody else." She kissed him and touched his cheek with her fingers. "Do you know what I'd like?" she said. "I'd like you to make love to me. Here. Now."

For a moment, Jack was tempted. Then he thought of lying naked in the cold sand, and the grit in his clothes later and the possibility of being stumbled upon by somebody walking along the beach. No, he thought, that's for the younger trade. He kissed Veronica lightly and sat up. "Some other time, darling," he said. "Some warm night, some summer."

Veronica lay back, motionless, her arms behind her head, staring up at the stars. Then, with a brisk movement, she jumped up. "Some summer," she said, standing over him. "Be careful. There will come a day when I will stop making all the advances." Her tone was flat and angry, and she brushed carelessly at her skirt, flicking the sand off, not looking at Jack, as he stood up, too, irresolutely, already beginning to regret his caution. Without a word, Veronica turned and began to walk swiftly across the dunes to where the car was parked under a tree. Jack followed her more slowly, admiring, despite his irritation with her and himself, the swinging, easy way she moved across the soft sand, barefooted, holding her shoes in her hand.

They got into the car and Jack started the engine. He had given Guido the night off when Veronica had suggested driving out to the sea. The lights tunneling into the darkness ahead of the car made the trees on both sides seem engulfing and menacing. The road was narrow and bumpy and he drove slowly, not talking, conscious of Veronica leaning against the right-hand door, carefully keeping her distance from him.

It was only after he had turned into the main highway to Rome that she spoke. "Tell me," she said, "how many times have you been married?"

"Why do you want to know?"

"You don't have to tell me if you don't want to."

"Three times."

"Good God," she said.

"That's it," Jack said. "Good God."

"Is that normal in America?"

"Not exactly," Jack said.

"What was your first wife like?"

"Why do you want to know?" Jack asked.

"I'd like to know how you're going to talk about me when we are finished," Veronica said. "What was she like? Pretty?"

"Very pretty," Jack said. There was a car howling up behind him, going very fast, its lights blinking, and Jack waited until it was safely past before he continued. "She was also a disaster."

"Is that what you're going to say about me, too, later on?" Veronica asked.

"No," Jack said. "I've never said it about my other women. Just my first wife."

"Why did you marry her?"

"I couldn't get her any other way," Jack said, squinting along the headlight beams, peering down into the dead past, with its incomprehensible decisions, its unprofitable sacrifices, its imperious, dead desires.

"You didn't know she was a disaster then?" Veronica curled her legs under her on the seat, facing him, interested, enjoying the revelations he was making, the gleam of female gossip in her eye.

"I had intimations," Jack said. "But I made myself ignore them. Anyway, I thought after we were married, I could change her."

"Change her from what?"

"From being stupid, narrow, grasping, jealous, untalented . . ."

"Did you?"

"Of course not." Jack chuckled remotely. "She became worse."

"And she really wouldn't sleep with you unless you married her?" Veronica asked incredulously.

"No."

"What was she—Italian?"

Jack laughed aloud and patted Veronica's knee. "You're a funny girl," he said. "You have a feeling that if something is bad enough, it must be Italian."

"I have my reasons," Veronica said. *"Was* she Italian?"

"No."

Veronica shook her head wonderingly. "I had the feeling things like that never happened in America."

"Everything happens in America," Jack said. "Just like every place else."

"Was it worth it—finally?" Veronica asked curiously. "I mean, getting married for it . . . ?"

"No," Jack said. "Of course not."

"What did you do when you fell in love with somebody else?"

"I took the plane—I was in Hollywood and my wife and child were in New York—" Jack began.

"Oh," Veronica said. "There was a child."

"Yes. I took the plane and went to New York and told my wife that I'd found somebody else and that I was about to begin a love affair with her."

"Wait a minute," Veronica said incredulously. "You mean you told your wife *before* it happened?"

"Yes," Jack said.

"Why?"

"I had a peculiar sense of honor," Jack said. "In those days."

"And she gave you a divorce—just like that?"

"Of course not," Jack said. "I told you she was stupid and narrow and grasping. She gave it to me six months later, when she wanted to marry someone else."

"And the child. Is it a boy?"

Jack nodded.

"Where is he now?" Veronica asked.

"The University of Chicago. He's twenty-two years old."

"What is he like?"

Jack didn't answer for a moment. That's a question, he thought—what's your son like? "He's very intelligent," Jack said evasively. "He's taking a Ph.D. in physics."

"Ph.D . . ." Veronica said. "What's that?"

"Doctor of Philosophy."

"Does he love you?"

Jack hesitated again. "No," he said. "Not really. Doctors of Philosophy don't love their fathers these days. Let's talk about something else."

"Why? Does talking about your son give you pain?"

"I suppose so," Jack said.

"What about that woman in the movie?" Veronica asked. "What's her name?"

"Carlotta Lee."

"Weren't you married to her?"

"Yes."

"Did she please you?"

Jack smiled at the way Veronica had asked the question, translating literally from the Italian. "Yes," he said, "she pleased me very much."

"Yet you divorced her, too?" Veronica shook her head, puzzled. "It must be painful to divorce a woman as beautiful as that."

"Not so painful," Jack said. "For one thing, she wasn't as beautiful as all that when we separated. Remember, there'd been a war in between. And she was older than I was to begin with . . ."

"Even so . . ."

"She found ways to make it less painful," Jack said. "Like sleeping with all my friends, all my enemies, all my acquaintances, all *anybody's* acquaintances . . ."

"She must have been very unhappy," Veronica said softly.

"On the contrary," Jack said. "It made her very happy, indeed."

"You hate her now," Veronica said.

"Maybe," Jack said. "Anyway, I remember that I hated her then."

"And your wife now?"

"I thought you didn't want me to talk about her."

"I have changed my mind," Veronica said. "Don't tell me how much you love her. Just tell me what she is like."

"She is small, beautiful, with a soft, musical French voice," Jack said, "and she's hard-headed, tricky, feminine, loving. She takes care of me and maneuvers me and makes the children behave sedately when necessary and when I first met her she seemed to me to combine all the virtues of France and the French character."

"And now?" Veronica asked. "What do you think of her now?"

"I haven't changed my opinion," Jack said, "—too much."

"And yet you sleep with other women," Veronica said challengingly.

"No," said Jack.

"Now, Jack . . ." It was the first time Veronica had called him by name. "Remember to whom you are talking."

"I remember," Jack said. "You're the first."

Veronica shook her head wonderingly. "How long have you been married?"

"Eight years."

"And nothing in all that time?"

"Nothing," Jack said. "Until you."

"And then, with me," she said, "after knowing me only for an hour and a half . . . ?"

"Uh-huh." An old man on a bicycle loomed up on the side of the road and Jack swung around him carefully, slowing down. He didn't try to explain to Veronica, or even to himself, what had happened to him, after the eight years, on the rainy afternoon following the lunch with Despière and Miss Henken. It had seemed inevitable, correct, necessary, it had happened without his willing it or foreseeing it. "After knowing you for only an hour and a half," he repeated. He stopped. Whatever else he was going to do tonight, he was not going to expose the intricacies of his relationship with his wife—his inabilty, from the beginning, to give himself completely, the dragging sense of guilt because he didn't love her enough, the frequent sense of boredom, of being stifled and baffled by the net of domesticity and conjugal routine she cunningly threw around him. He was not going to tell this girl about his surge of relief when he had left Hélène at the airport or about not feeling the least flicker of desire for her for the two weeks before his departure, or about the other similar periods that lay like dead gray patches on his life with Hélène. Vaguely, he felt that these facts discredited him and would discredit him even more, in his own eyes and in the eyes of Veronica, if he was disloyal enough to voice them at a time like this.

"Are you going to tell your wife about me when you go back to Paris?"

"I don't think so," Jack said.

"You are not as peculiarly honorable these days, as you were when you were young." Veronica's voice had taken on an edge of harshness, mockery. "Is that it?"

"That's it," Jack said. "I'm not a lot of things now that I was when I was young."

"Would your wife leave you if she found out?"

"I don't think so," Jack said. He grinned. "Remember, she's French."

Veronica was silent for several moments. "It would have been nice, I think," she said softly, "to know you when you were young."

"Probably not," Jack said. "I was arrogant and opinionated and I was so interested in being honest to myself that I never hesitated to hurt people . . ."

"Robert's like that." Veronica laughed drily. "Just like that. Do you mean you were like him?"

"Probably. In some ways," Jack said. "Except that I never threatened to kill anybody. And I never tried to kill myself."

Veronica leaned closer to him, regarding him closely, seriously, in the flaring brief light of headlights sweeping down toward them on the other side of the road. "What happened to you," she said, "I wonder."

"I wonder, too," Jack said. "Very often."

"Are you disappointed in yourself?" she asked.

"No," he said slowly. "I don't think so."

"Would you do it differently, if you had it to do over again?"

He laughed. "What a question to ask. Of course I would. Wouldn't everybody?"

"Do you think it would come out better?"

"No. Probably not."

"But you changed your life completely," she said. "I mean, you started out as an actor, and now you're something entirely different, a . . . a bureaucrat, a kind of politician . . ."

"A drunken actor tonight," Jack said, remembering Stiles, "called me a clerk."

"Whatever you are," Veronica persisted, "you have given up the thing you were in the beginning, the thing at which you were a success, famous . . ."

"I didn't exactly give it up," Jack said. "It more or less gave me up. When I came back from the war my face was twisted into a knot on one side. At least, the camera made it look twisted. And I'd been gone a long time. People'd just about forgotten me."

"Still," she said, "after a while you could have found parts . . . I'm sure."

"I suppose so. Yes," he said definitely, "I could have hung on if

155

I wanted to. I found I wasn't interested any more. The divine Hollywood fire," he said ironically, "had burned out. After the war and nearly two years in the hospital—after Carlotta . . ." He shrugged at the wheel. "The war turned my interests to other things. Europe—I'd never been in Europe before—and after the war it kept pulling at me— Anyway, it's not so unusual. A lot of people are artists of one kind or another when they're young. Then if they're lucky, and they realize that for them, at least, all it is is part of being young, like being able to run fast and stay up all night seven nights in a row—they close the door on it."

"Without regrets?" Veronica asked.

"There's almost nothing I've ever done in my whole life I don't regret—one way or another," Jack said thoughtfully. "Aren't you like that, too?"

"I don't think so," Veronica said. "No."

"Don't you regret breaking with Robert, for example? Or starting with Robert? Later on, won't you regret me?"

"No. Not the way you mean." She ran the point of her fingernail down his arm from his shoulder to his wrist, scratching the cloth of his sleeve. "Do you regret your first wife?"

"Of course. A hundred different ways."

"Carlotta?"

"Hideously."

"Also a hundred different ways?"

"A thousand."

"And how many others? How many other women?"

Jack laughed. "Hordes," he said.

"You've been a bad boy, haven't you, in your time?" She pouted now, reminding him unpleasantly of his first impression of her the first ten minutes after he met her.

"I've been a very bad boy in my time," he said, "and I'll never tell you about it."

"You're not going to be angry with me now, are you?"

"No, of course not."

"Do you know why I really have asked all these questions?" Veronica said, her voice still very low.

"Why?"

"Because if I know more about you," she said, soberly, "you will fade less slowly when you are gone. You will be more real to me. It will take much longer before it all seems like a dream to me this time we have . . . Is that a bad reason?"

156

"No, darling," Jack said gently. "It's a very good reason."

"I wouldn't be angry if you asked *me* questions," she said. "I'd be very happy. I'd like the dream to last longer for you, too . . . Any questions you want."

Veronica seemed to be waiting; waiting, he felt, to judge the quality of his feeling for her by the kind of questions he would ask. He felt a twinge of guilt because until now he had taken her so matter-of-factly, so much in the present, without any real desire to know more about her than she had reavealed so far, casually, with no probing on his part. To know, he felt, is to be entangled. Subconsciously Veronica understood this, too, he was sure, and was insisting on being known, in a blind, female need for entanglement.

"At lunch the other day," he said, "I wanted to ask you a question."

"Yes?"

"You said that when you were two years old, you were in San Sebastián, in Spain . . ."

"Oh, that." Her voice was flat, disappointed. Obviously, this was not the kind of question she had hoped for.

"I figured out that was during the Spanish Civil War," Jack said.

"It was." Now she was impatient, uninterested.

"What the hell were you doing in Spain during the Civil War?"

"My father was a career soldier," she said carelessly.

"In the Spanish Army?" Jack asked, confused.

Veronica laughed. "Didn't they have newspapers in America in 1937?" she said. "In the Italian Army. My father was nonintervening on the side of Franco. Don't you remember *any* of that?"

"Of course I do," Jack said. "Only it never occurred to me that they made a family affair out of things like that."

"My father was very domestic," Veronica said. "He loved his family. And he was a colonel, so he had us delivered to him in Spain."

"What was it like? Do you remember?"

"It's a funny thing," Veronica said. "All the Americans I meet, when I tell them my father fought in Spain for Franco, get enormously interested. I thought people had forgotten all about that. So many people have been killed since then . . ."

"It was a very interesting war for Americans," Jack said drily. "We're still suffering from it, if you want to know the truth."

"That's funny," she said. "We're not."

"Maybe if you fight a war yourself you get over it faster," Jack said. "Anyway, what was it like?"

Veronica shrugged. "I don't remember much," she said. "I remember the beach. It was a nice beach for children. There's an island out in the middle of the bay that I sailed to. And the melons. The melons were delicious. Often now, when I eat a melon in a restaurant, I suddenly feel like a little girl in Spain again."

She remembers melons from that war, Jack thought, tasting his own bitter memories from that time, remembering the boys who had gone to school with him who had been killed in those years. Perhaps, he thought, killed by Veronica's father, that domestic man.

"Where is your father now?" he asked.

"Dead," she said flatly.

One for our side, Jack thought, without charity. Somehow, the idea of the colonel, cozily fighting his war out of the seaside villa at San Sebastián (*did he dandle you on his knee between firing parties?*) canceled the impulse toward pity that Jack usually felt at the thought of all the dead who had fallen, on all sides, in the wars of his time. "Was he killed in Spain?" he asked.

"No," Veronica said. "He was wounded there, but not too badly. He was wounded in Ethiopia, too. He was always up in front. He was very brave, everybody has told me. Actually, he was one of the first men in the Italian Army to be killed in World War Two. We were in Tripoli with him. His general had just come back from an interview with Mussolini, and Mussolini had sworn to the general that Italy would not go into the war. This was the summer when France was falling. My mother gave a garden party to celebrate because we weren't going to have a war. I was dressed in a pink dress and white gloves and I helped pass little cakes with the drinks. Then, of course, we were in it, and one week later my father was dead. He was in an unarmed plane inspecting the positions facing the British, and he was shot down."

Three wars, Jack thought cynically, three hits. He was obviously in the wrong line of business, Veronica's father. Too many garden parties.

"My father hated Mussolini," Veronica said. "Of course, he never told me or my sister. We were too young. But he kept a diary and I've read it since then . . ."

The disease of colonels, Jack thought. The running diary.

"The reason his general went to Mussolini at that time," Veronica said, "was to tell him that there wasn't enough equipment or enough men in North Africa to hold off the British. He and my father worked out a long report together. It's all in my father's diary. That's the way it always was in the Italian Army," she said bitterly. "There wasn't enough equipment so they used up men instead and they were killed. Not like your army."

"Oh," Jack said, "there were several men killed in our army, too."

"You know what I mean," Veronica said. "In Italy it was all graft and propaganda—pretty uniforms, parades, big speeches —Mussolini roaring and lying and making faces. And then after that, ammunition that didn't fit the guns, or tanks without gasoline, or officers who were out dancing when they should've been learning how to read a map. The English killed my brother, too, in Africa. He was eighteen years old. He was at the garden party my mother gave in Tripoli, too, to celebrate because Mussolini had told my father's commanding officer that there wasn't going to be a war." Veronica took a cigarette out of her bag and lit it. Jack looked over at the scratch of the match and saw that the flame was wavering, that her hand was trembling, belying the flat, even, unemotional tone of Veronica's voice. "I tell you," she said, "one day I will have to live somewhere else than Italy."

*

It was late when they drove up in front of Veronica's hotel, and the little square on which the hotel was located was deserted. The hotel was a small one. The front door was open and the narrow lobby was brilliantly lit. When Jack switched off the car headlights in front of the hotel he saw the night porter sitting in a wooden armchair, his back to the street, staring at himself in a huge mirror that ran along the back wall of the lobby. The night porter was young and very good-looking and it must have taken him a half-hour to comb his hair into such shining black perfection. Thoughtfully admiring himself, grateful for the brilliance and luxuriance of his hair, aesthetically pleased by the smooth olive forehead, the intelligent dark eyes, the rich warm shape of the mouth, the strong jaws, the sculptured, powerful Roman throat, the porter let the hours of the night pass without boredom or annoyance, happy in the bright, unchanging reflection of himself in the polished, rewarding mirror. There were no German priests on view at the moment.

"Look at that," Veronica said harshly. "Where else in the world would you ever see anything like it? And he won't be the least embarrassed when I come in and find him like that. He'll give me the key as though he was giving me two dozen roses and before I'm halfway up the stairs to the first floor he'll be back there in that chair again."

Jack chuckled. "Actually," he said, "it's one of the most appealing sights I've seen in Rome."

"It doesn't appeal to me," Veronica said. She started to open the door to get out. Jack leaned over and held her. He put his arm around her and kissed her. For a moment she was tense, unwilling, then sank into him, held his face between her hands, kissed him hungrily.

"What I'd like to do," he said, "is go in with you."

She shook her head. "He won't let you."

"I'll bribe him."

"He'd lose his job. The priests run around the corridors like mice."

"All right then," Jack said. "Come back to *my* hotel."

"I bet Robert is waiting there this minute," she said. "No."

"I have a brilliant idea," Jack said, "I'll rent a room for tonight. Right now."

Veronica thought for a moment. Then she smiled. "American know-how," she said. "No wonder you won the war. Come on."

They got out of the car and went into the lobby. Slowly, turning away reluctantly from the mirror, the porter stood up and bowed to them, saying, *"Buona sera, signorina,"* and walked lightly, but with dignity, behind the desk to take her key off its hook.

"Tell him I want a nice big room with bath," Jack said.

In Italian, Veronica made the request. The porter looked pained, desperate. He leaned over the plan of the hotel that was tacked on a board, studied it as though it were a map indicating the position of buried treasure. He shook his head. The treasure had been removed by others. In Italian, his voice deep with mourning, he spoke to Veronica.

"It's no use," she said. "The house is all filled up. He will be delighted to reserve a room for tomorrow . . ."

"That's a big help," Jack said sourly. "You're moving into your friend's apartment tomorrow, aren't you?"

"Yes." Veronica was smiling at his frustration, enjoying it, taking it as a compliment to herself.

160

"Never mind," Jack said to the porter. "Never mind anything."

"*Scusi, signore.*" A look of operatic pain wavered across the porter's handsome dark face at the realization that he was the obstacle in Rome that night to international love. "*Desolato.*"

"I'm *desolato,* too," Jack said. "You have no idea how *desolato* I am." He turned to Veronica. "When do I see you again?"

"I'll telephone you tomorrow morning," she said, "when I move into the apartment."

"I won't be in in the morning. Let's meet for lunch."

Veronica nodded.

"The same restaurant," Jack said. "Ernesto's. I'm getting very fond of that restaurant. One fifteen."

"Good," she said. She squeezed his hand, with the porter watching interestedly. "I'm sorry about tonight. I warned you, though, didn't I?"

"You warned me."

She chuckled. "You have only yourself to blame," she said. "You had a fair offer on the beach."

"Go to bed," Jack said. Despite the porter, he kissed her cheek. He and the porter watched her start to climb the staircase, swinging just a little too much, her high heels tapping their tantalizing, promising tattoo on the marble steps. Jack glanced at the porter. The man's face shone with simple, eloquent, childlike lust as he watched Veronica's legs disappear up the staircase.

"Good night, friend," Jack said.

"*Buona notte, signore,*" the man said, sighing.

By the time Jack was in the car and turning on the headlights, the porter was back in his wooden armchair in front of the lobby mirror, staring once more, with gratitude and admiration, at his glorious reflection.

The priests have won again, Jack thought, as he started the motor and swung the car roughly in the direction of his hotel. What do you expect in Rome?

14

I am in a brightly lit room and there is a great deal of smoke. There will be another room, not so brightly lit, also with a great deal of smoke, but that will be later on and more dangerous. Now it is only the smoke of many cigarettes, of five men sitting around a table in rumpled uniforms, playing cards. The room is hot, because the blackout blinds are drawn and the windows closed, and we are playing poker. I lose. Jacks back to back, but I lose. Table stakes. You can only bet what you have in front of you. The man on my right has three tens and he sweeps in the pound notes with a wide, white-toothed grin. I look around at the other four men and I suddenly realize that they are all dead. The winner dead on the beach a few weeks later, the others surviving that, but equally dead in their civilian beds, cancer, suicide, alcoholism. The pound notes rustle, the one-armed elevator boy brings in another bottle of black-market

Scotch, the money changes hands. At the moment, I know I will lose a hundred and twenty pounds before the game is over and all London will stink from the smoke of the fires the German planes will start later that night. Now it is dark again and I am approaching a wooden shack at the end of an alley of pine trees. There is the smell of wet loam, spilled whisky, something medicinal. Through cracks in the shack's clapboarding, light slants out into the night. I go down steps. I watch. Two huge bald men in stained white aprons are working over a table, talking jovially. Then I see what they are working on. It is the body of a man, very white, and they are cutting it into rough sections. The men in aprons under the glaring light pay no attention to me. I want to run away from there but I cannot. The reason I cannot run is because it is myself on the table under the knives. I want to scream but no sound comes forth. I am assailed by sorrow, and then, suddenly, relieved, almost light-hearted. It is over, I think, with a flicker of joy. I have managed it. I have finished. The job is done. Nothing more can happen to me. There is nothing more to be afraid of. The funeral bells are ringing. There is a refreshing wetness on my face . . .

The bells became one bell, the clapboard shack became a hotel room, the dew on his face became blood. He awoke. The telephone was ringing by the side of his bed. In the darkness he fumbled for the lamp switch. When he found it and pressed it and the light came on, he looked automatically at the traveling clock on the dresser and saw that it was nearly half past three. He put his hand to his face. His nose was bleeding. He pushed his handkerchief against it. He picked up the phone, with the usual little thrill of fear, the uneasy premonition of bad news that the ringing of a bell at that hour inevitably brings with it.

It was Paris calling and in a moment he heard his wife's voice, clear, awake, calm. Even as he said hello he could tell from her tone that there wasn't going to be any bad news and he immediately began to resent being awakened by her.

"I tried to call you earlier," she said, "but you weren't in, the operator said. Didn't they tell you I was trying to get you?"

"This is Italy," Jack said. "They don't tell you anything."

She chuckled, a thousand miles away. The middle of the night doesn't mean anything to women, Jack thought resentfully, they can sleep all the next day. "Is anything wrong?" he asked. He took the handkerchief away from his face, experimentally. The bleeding was down to a trickle.

"No," she said. "It's just that I missed you and wanted to hear your voice. Did you just get in?"

Probing, Jack thought, annoyed. "No," he said. "I've been asleep for hours."

"Well, I called at one and they said . . ."

"I got in at five minutes past one. Do you want a signed statement?"

"Now, Jack . . ." Her voice sounded hurt. "You're not angry because I wanted to talk to you, are you?"

"Of course not." Silently, he gave thanks that Veronica's hotel had been full and priest-ridden. If Hélène had called all night without finding him in, there would have been unpleasant explanations to follow.

"Have you been having a good time, *chéri?*" Hélène asked.

"Hilarious."

"Are you alone?" Her voice was turning chilly.

"Why do you ask that?" he said, self-righteousness making him belligerent.

"You sound funny. Not natural."

"You guessed it," he said flatly. "I'm not alone. I have five Cuban musicians up here with me and we're all smoking marijuana together."

"I just asked," Hélène said, with dignity. "You don't have to snap my head off."

"I'm sorry," Jack said. "It's just that waking up in the middle of the night like this . . ."

"All right," Hélène said. "I'll let you go back to sleep. And I won't call you again. You can call me . . ."

"Don't be silly, darling," Jack said, pretending an affection that at the moment he did not feel. "You call me whenever you want."

"How's the work going?"

"All right," Jack said. "I'm awful at it, but I guess they'll pay me just the same."

"I'm sure you're not awful at all," Hélène said.

"Lady," said Jack, "I'm here on the spot and I know."

"Are you unhappy, *chéri?*"

What if I told her, *Yes, I am unhappy,* he thought. *I have dreams of death and my blood flows and I couldn't find a room in*

164

my mistress's hotel tonight. What would she say then? "Not at all," he said. "Why do you ask that?"

"No real reason," Hélène said. "The tone of your voice. Intuition . . ."

"No," he said, "I'm fine. Really."

"How is your friend?" she asked, "Mr. Delaney? Have you cured all his troubles yet?"

"Not exactly," Jack said. "He hasn't told me what all his troubles are so far."

"What's he waiting for?" Hélène sounded impatient.

"I don't know," Jack said. "The psychological moment. The change of the moon. A drop in the Market. A rise in the level of pain. Don't worry—he'll let me know in due time what's hurting him."

"Tell him to do it fast," Hélène said. "I want you to come home." There was a silence on the other end of the wire, as though she were waiting for him to say something. Then she continued, "I'll tell you somebody else who wants you to get home, too. Joe Morrison. Anne tells me he's grumbling more and more about you every day. And when I asked her if she thought that there was any danger of our being transferred someplace after the summer, she was very mysterious."

"Why don't you two ladies mind your own business?" Jack said harshly. "This is between Joe Morrison and me."

"If you get transferred to the jungle someplace," Hélène said, her voice rising," don't you think that's my business, too? Or do you plan to leave me and the children in Paris for three or four years at a time?"

"I'm sorry," Jack said wearily. The mention of Morrison had brought back the feeling of boredom and irritation that he had had with his work for the last few months, and he had been annoyed with Hélène for reminding him of it. At the moment, he didn't care if he ever saw Joe Morrison again, and the thought of being at the mercy of Morrison's moods made him feel confined and resentful. "I'm afraid I'm a little jittery. Do me a favor. When you call again, don't talk about Joe Morrison."

"What do you want me to talk about?" she asked, with hostility.

"Our happy married life," he said flatly. "Our children. By the way, how are they?"

"All right," Hélène said. "Except that Charlie had a scare today."

"What's the matter?" Jack asked quickly, alert for trouble.

"He thought he was pregnant this afternoon," Hélène said.

"WHAT?"

"He thought he was pregnant. He came to me at lunchtime, while I was—it was the maid's day off—and he asked me how babies are born, and I was busy, so I put him off and told him I'd let him know some other time. But he kept pestering me and I got impatient with him—after all, there's a time and place for everything—and I said, 'Oh, they come out of peoples' ears . . .'"

"That sounds like a reasonable thing to tell a child," Jack said, gently making fun of her.

"Well, anyway, he went to school and when he came home he said he wasn't feeling well and he lay down on his bed. I went in an hour later and he was holding his ear. It turns out his ear had been hurting him for the last two days—he got water in it in his bath—and he said to me, 'Now I know why my ear hurts. I'm going to have a baby!'"

Jack laughed helplessly. After a moment, Hélène laughed, too. "I hope you set him straight," Jack said.

"I tried to," Hélène said. "I gave him all the exact information. But I don't think he believed me. He was still holding his ear when he went to sleep tonight."

Jack laughed again. "Tell him I'll explain everything when I get home."

"I wish you were home right now," Hélène said softly.

"Me, too," he said. "Well, it won't be long, dearest . . ."

"Take care of yourself," she whispered. "Sleep well. Have a good time . . . *Sois sage.*"

"Kiss the children for me," he said.

He put the telephone down slowly.

The call, with its reminder of old, continuing claims, responsibilities, worries, disturbed him. Hélène was unlike most women in that she took no pleasure in argument and rarely brought fundamental issues to the surface. Shrewd and intuitive, she preferred to let trouble lie buried, to act obliquely, to set up countercurrents, to permit time to do its healing work. But now the telephone call, with its edge of sharpness and rebuke, made Jack remember the time, a year before, when Hélène, uncharacteristically, had forced them both into a scene from the results of which neither of them had as yet fully recovered.

They had been having dinner with Anne and Joe Morrison in a bistro behind the Théatre Sarah Bernhardt, and Joe Morrison had had too much wine to drink. He didn't drink often, but when he did, it made him louder than usual and harsh in his judgments. He was a tall, thin man who at a distance looked somewhere between thirty-five and forty, but up close his face revealed a network of fine lines that no man under fifty could have acquired.

"Jack," he was saying, leaning over the table, playing with his glass, "you're an enigma. Anne, don't I always tell you Jack's an enigma?"

"Only when you've had too much to drink," Anne Morrison said placidly.

"The enigma is—why does a man like you, with so much on the ball—as smart as you are—stay in one place." Morrison peered shrewdly, almost with hostility, at Jack. "Everywhere around you, you see men on the move, going up, men with half your ability, but punching away, doing the necessary, planning the moves for ten years ahead, getting ahead . . . while you . . ." He shook his head. "You're like a runner that everybody knows has a big burst of speed and never bothers to use it. What is it?"

"I do the necessary," Jack said placatingly.

"Not really," Morrison said. "Or only superficially."

"Don't you think I do my job?" Jack asked.

"Sure you do," Morrison said. "As well as anybody. Maybe better than anybody. But not as well as *you* could. I'll tell you what— you're not—not—" He searched for the word. "You're not *involved*. You're remote. You make the proper play, but you give the impression that it doesn't matter a damn whether it gains ground or not." Morrison had played football when he was young and when he drank, locker room images filled his speech. "Sometimes, for Christ's sake, it's hard to tell whether you're in the game or up in the stands, not even bothering to cheer for the team. What the hell is it, Jack, what the hell is it with you?"

"I'm cool, man, cool," Jack said, hoping to shut Morrison up with his flippancy. He had noticed Hélène nodding, almost imperceptibly, through Morrison's speech, and he wanted to shut that off, too. "All the kids're like that these days. We refuse to flip."

"Ah, Christ," Morrison said angrily. He turned to Hélène. "What about *you?*" He demanded. "You're married to the man. What do *you* think?"

Hélène hesitated for a moment, regarding Jack curiously. Then she laughed. "I think Anne had the last word, Joe," she said. "You've had too much to drink."

"Okay, okay," Morrison said resignedly, leaning back. "You don't want to talk about it. Okay. But one day, you're going to have to face it. Both of you."

They had left the restaurant soon after, and Jack and Hélène had gone home. There was a feeling of tension in the car and, although neither of them spoke, a sense of opposition and dispute.

Jack was lying in bed, in the room on the quai, staring up at the ceiling, wondering if it wouldn't be better to take a pill, to make sure he would sleep, when Hélène came in from the bathroom, in pajamas, combing her hair. Jack didn't look at her, even after she came over to the bed and sat down on the edge, next to him, still running the comb through her short dark hair.

Outside, on the quai, there was the soft intermittent swish of cars swiftly passing along the river, the noise hushed by the shutters and the drapes.

"Jack," she said, "you know, Joe Morrison was right tonight . . ."

"About what?" Jack made himself sound sleepy, uninterested.

"About you." There was the sound of the comb going through her hair. "And not only about your work."

"Was he? Why didn't you tell him you agreed with him when he asked you."

"You know I wouldn't do that," she said softly.

"I know."

"Jack," she said, pulling his head around gently so that he would have to look up at her. "Why did you marry me?"

"To brush up on my French."

"Jack . . ." She ran her fingers lightly under his eyes, touching the lines of sleeplessness, age, trouble. "Don't joke. Why did you marry me?"

"Look in the mirror," he said. "There's a pretty good answer there."

She sighed, took her hand away from his face, and went over to the vanity table and began cleaning her face with cold cream, her back to him. He looked speculatively at her, troubled by her question. It was the first time in seven years of marriage that she had said anything like that. Why *had* he married her? Loneliness, fatigue, boredom with the constant repetitive predictable gambits that a man inevitably ran through when he was unmarried and yet liked women and went out with them? He had desired her. That he knew. He had admired her. That he knew. Among the women he had met she most of all had had a sane, practical, possible, healthy goal for her life. She was undivided. She wanted to love and be loved, she wanted to be loyal and claim loyalty, she had no doubts about the validity of the happiness that could be obtained out of marriage, the care of a husband, the birth of children. And with all that she was merry and quick, a comfortable, amusing companion, a dear lover, an unflurried arranger and manager of domestic crises.

But if he had been forced to say at the time of his marriage that he loved her, he could not honestly have said it. And perhaps he couldn't say it now, either. At least, if he were to judge love by what he had felt in the first years with Carlotta, he could not say it.

From the vanity table, with her back to him, Hélène said, "You're not *involved,* Joe said. And he was right, Jack."

"I saw you nodding," he said.

"I'm sorry," she said. "But it's true. And when he said you're remote, he was right about that, too. Thoughtful and remote. Sometimes I wish you weren't so unfailingly thoughtful. It's as though you're making up for something you feel guilty about. Sometimes, I have the feeling that I'm whispering to you across a big wide open field and we can't cross it to each other and we can't quite hear what we are saying to each other—or on other sides of a big thick wall . . ."

He closed his eyes in pain, shutting out the sight of the slender smooth back, the uplifted lovely arms, the small pretty head . . .

"What is it, Jack?" she asked quietly, echoing Joe Morrison. "Is it my fault? Is there anything I can do?"

He kept his eyes closed, and because it wasn't her fault, and because there was nothing she could do, he said, brutally, "Get me a sleeping pill, please."

"God damn you," she said.

*

He sighed in the Roman bed, considering how he had failed the people he loved. Darkness would be better. As he was reaching to put out the light, he heard steps approaching along the corridor outside his room. Whoever it was seemed to hesitate opposite the door. Bresach, Jack thought, tensing. But then the steps continued on, and all was quiet.

For another moment, Jack left the light on, while he listened. On the bureau he saw the bulky envelope that Despière had left in his care, and he told himself he would have to remember to put it in a safe place the first thing in the morning. He was wide-awake now, and he felt like reading, but the only book in the room was Catullus and Catullus was not to his taste for the time being.

With a decisive gesture he turned out the light. He had to be up by a quarter to seven in the morning and be fresh enough, at least, to try to follow Delaney's directions in the dubbing room. Whatever else he did or was involved in during these two weeks, love, recrimination, murder, he had to try to earn his five thousand dollars. I have a bourgeois sense of commercial honesty, he thought, mocking himself, value given for value received.

He closed his eyes conscientiously, for Delaney's sake. But he had never felt more awake. He remembered Hélène's voice over the phone, the small, unobtrusive, delightful lilt of France embedded in the English language. (*"I'm getting tired of men who sleep with me,"* said the other voice, *"and tell me how much they love their wives."*) In the darkness, he thought of Hélène, still awake in the Continental darkness a thousand miles away, thinking of him, disturbed for him, obscurely informed by love's telepathy that all was not well with him. He pictured her lying neatly in her bed, in her boys' pajamas, small, lovely, warm, with her hair in curlers (she always took advantage of his trips to pay attention to her hair), thinking about him, linked to him by their thousand lines and strands, listening to the sounds from the next room, where the children slept. Solid, competent, and wary, his wife lay at the warm center of the family web, worrying, protecting, loving, enjoying, offering up her secret nighttime prayers against the perils of absence, offering up prayers for his return, for health, safety, normalcy, love . . . If he had been in the bed beside her, he told himself, he would not have played that ghostly poker game, he would not have seen the bald men in aprons at their sinister labors.

Jack pushed the soaked handkerchief gently against his face. The bleeding seemed to be coming to an end. He remembered his dream, thinking, How wise of wives to pray in the uneasy hours after midnight.

Hating to examine the dream, with its dead players who were once his friends, and the hideous meaning of the body on the table, he made himself think of his son, sleeping this moment with his hand to his threatened ear. Jack smiled, death pushed back now by that small hand. He remembered an evening during the winter when he came back from work and went into the bathroom where his son was drying himself after his bath. He kissed the damp head, watched thoughtfully as the boy dabbed inaccurately with the towel at the sturdy, smooth body. Suddenly the boy turned to him with a conspiratorial smile. "Daddy," he said, touching the tip of his penis with one finger, speaking resonantly, proudly, "This is me."

"Yes, indeed," Jack said gravely. "That's you."

At the age of five, we draw wisdom from the air, revelations from the wind, the sages of the race whisper confidently in our ears.

Lying awake in the shadowed, dream-haunted room, Jack touched himself. "This is me," he whispered, smiling, joining his son in the magic male incantation, turning back the powers of darkness, using the secret ceremony that his son, in his wisdom and innocence, had discovered, to put down the foul and cowardly temptations of oblivion.

But the magic was not potent enough. When he closed his eyes he could not sleep and the memories stirred by the dream and by the conversation in the car with Veronica began to crowd in on him . . .

*

"There were several men killed in our army, too . . . "

The farmhouse was burning. It was built of stone, but there were a surprising number of things in it that had started burning when the shell hit. He had been asleep on the kitchen floor and when he woke up he had somehow been blown through a wall and his leg was broken and a blanket was on fire around his head and none of the other men who had been in the farmhouse with him were to be seen. They had been luckier than he. They had escaped, in the darkness. In the confusion they had missed him, and after that it was too late, nobody could get near the house.

It took him five hours to crawl across the room to the window. He passed out again and again, with the stink of his own burning hair and flesh in his nostrils, and his foot twisted completely around and the smoke smothering him. But he was very sure he didn't want to die and he used the fingernails of his good hand to draw himself along the splintered farmhouse floor, and finally, he got to the window and pulled himself up so that he could look out over the sill. The field in front of the house was being sporadically explored by machine-gun fire, but someone saw his head poking above the window sill and came and got him. He didn't remember any of that, because when he was pulled out over the window sill, he passed out again. Then they gave him morphine and the next few weeks were a vague, floating blur, and he never found out who had come to get him and whether he was alive or dead. And then the two years in all the hospitals and the eighteen operations and the young doctor who said, "That hand will never be any good again . . ." And Carlotta, with her huge telegraphed bouquets of flowers, and not much else . . .

*

"Look, where the youths are coming, lightly up they spring, and not for nothing, hark! It's good to hear them sing, Hymen O Hymenaeus Hymen hither O Hymenaeus."

It was a curious wedding reception. Conceivably, weddings like it took place all over the world, but while it was happening you had the feeling that it was special to Hollywood, that only in Hollywood would two hundred and fifty people gather to celebrate the marriage of two people who had divorced each other, married other mates, divorced *them* and then remarried. Anywhere else, you felt, the principals would at least have gone off to some obscure country town and been quietly (and, as it turned out, impermanently) joined by a justice of the peace and two witnesses. But not in Hollywood. Not in 1937. Two hundred and fifty guests, with photographers and newspapermen and heads of studios, and the full casts of the two pictures in which the bride and groom were working at the moment, and the bride in a dazzling white gown that had been made for her as a present by the wardrobe department of the studio.

Delaney was the host. He was married at that time to the wife who was later to shoot at him with a hunting rifle. She did not work in the movies, and to keep herself from being bored she gave parties. She was handsome and frivolous and, luckily, a bad shot. Delaney, who did not like parties, but who paid for them to keep peace in the family, spent most of the evening in the bar, playing gin rummy.

The groom, Otis Carrington, tall, courtly, rich-voiced, smiling, was sitting between two of his ex-wives on the sweeping Colonial staircase. He was sipping black coffee out of a large cup, because he was fighting the drink. He never even glanced at the woman he had married that afternoon, and said to his ex-wives, "I don't have to go to a psychiatrist. I know what's wrong with me. I was in love with my sister until I was thirty years old. The day I realized that I knew I could finally lick the bottle." He also said, "The time I knew I'd eventually have to give up the drink was the morning I woke up in Naples. I'd gone to a party in Chicago two and a half weeks before and I woke up in Naples in a first-class cabin full of flowers and empty whisky bottles and I didn't remember crossing the ocean—in fact, I didn't remember getting to the Dearborn Station."

When sober, he was gentle, witty and considerate and had the best manners of any man Jack had ever met. But when under the influence, he had been known to break up saloons, house parties, dramatic presentations, marriages, old friendships, political meetings. In later years, when, after months of abstinence, he felt a binge coming on, he hired a burly male nurse to accompany him and minimize the violence until he was too spent and sick to go on. Sometimes, the male nurse would be on duty two weeks on end. Carrington was of that old line of actors, disappearing even then, who behaved like actors, profligate, showily dressed, gallant, improvident, given to gestures. On the first day of the war in 1917, he had walked out of the theatre in which he was starring in New York, put a flower in the buttonhole of his expensive suit, and, swinging a cane, had strolled down to the nearest recruiting office to enlist as a private soldier. Born in a different era, brought up in other, less romantic schools, Jack nevertheless admired Carrington enormously, and when his own war came (it was in the middle of a picture), it took all of Delaney's arguments and the pleadings of his agent to keep Jack from following Carrington's example.

Once, on the set, a young actor had come up to Carrington and had asked him to tell him, in just a short sentence, what the secret was of being a good actor. Carrington had pretended to be thinking deeply, had rubbed the big, impressive nose judiciously and had answered, "Be delighted, my boy, be delighted."

On this wedding night, Carrington also spoke of the night of his first marriage to the bride. "It was an even fancier party than this," Carrington said to his ex-wives, as he sat between them, fastidiously sipping his coffee, "and I happened to pass behind a couch on which my new wife was sitting with an English earl whom I had met when I was playing in London, and she was saying, 'Of course, my dear, everyone knows Carrington is impotent.' " He chuckled good-naturedly, thinking of those distant, vernal festivities.

Jack spent most of the evening arguing. In fact, it seemed that ever since he had come to Hollywood two months before, he had spent almost every evening arguing. There were many things to argue about, of course, but for the most part what people argued about in the drawing rooms of Beverly Hills during that time was how good or bad the movies were and about the Spanish Civil War. "Making a good movie here," Jack said, out of the ripeness of his two months' experience as a featured player, "is a pure freak of luck. If anybody ever says an honest word in a movie it's the craziest kind of accident. Nobody must be offended—not the rich, not the poor, not labor, not capital, not the Jews, not the Gentiles, not mothers, not priests, not politicians, not businessmen, not the English, not the Germans, not the Turks, not anybody. The word above every studio gateway is COWARDICE, written in letters of fire. So nobody ever says a word of truth on any subject. Since I've come out here I've hardly met anybody over the age of twenty who hasn't been married at least twice and yet every picture that comes out is a poem in praise of monogamy. Just about everybody between the Pacific Ocean and the Los Angeles City Hall is chasing the dollar so hard they only have time to breathe on Sundays, and yet if you believed the movies, you'd be sure the only way to be happy is to live in a garret on twelve dollars a week. Ninety percent of the people here are so scared of Hitler they have nightmares about him every night of the year, and there hasn't been a whisper yet in any picture I've seen suggesting that he might be more dangerous than my Aunt Milly. There's more talk against Franco in Lucey's Bar during one lunchtime than there is in the trenches before Madrid and every time somebody announces he's going to make a picture about the Spanish Civil War, one letter from a follower of Father Coughlin stops it dead. Christ, this room is full of people who've spent most of their lives cheating and breaking laws and sleeping with other peoples' wives and they're all as fat and happy and respected as can be, and yet they keep making pictures in which crime never pays, in which the evildoer is always punished, in which a girl has to die or wind up in a life of shame if she as much as sleeps with her fiancé before she gets married. This is the first time in the history of any art that so many people, so much wealth, so much talent and machinery have been collected in one place to create a total disguise . . . the billion-dollar mask, the great big happy American smile . . ."

Standing in the middle of the room, dressed in a new dinner jacket made for him by a tailor to whom Delaney had introduced him, surrounded by handsome, tanned, perfumed, well-dressed people whose names were constantly in the newspaper, Jack rattled on happily, high on the unaccustomed wedding champagne, enjoying himself, orating, laying down the law, confident of himself and careless of consequences. He had a scornful feeling of superiority over the well-known people who were listening to him, some of them shamefacedly agreeing with him, others flushed and hating him. They were hungry for money, he felt, and would do anything necessary to gain it or hold onto it, while he, with no bank accounts, no stocks and bonds, no real-estate holdings or interests in oil companies, with only his youth and his talent at his disposal, believed that he didn't care a damn whether he was rich or poor. It was like being invincibly healthy and walking through a hospital ward for the incurably ill, the incurably ill who gluttonously kept feeding on the poison that was killing them. While he was talking, too, with the glass in his hand, and the good feel of the new suit on his shoulders, he was conscious of Carlotta Lee standing among the others, watching him with a hidden, tiny smile on her lips. The smile seemed to say that she had been judging him and had finally made up her mind this evening and that the judgment would please him. He had kissed her that afternoon—but only on the set, before a hundred actors, extras, grips, and he hadn't said more than a few words to her, outside the demands of the script, since he had started working on the picture, but he had decided that afternoon that he was in love with her and the smile, secret and inviting in the swirl of celebration, seemed to say, "Yes, of course."

It was the kind of evening that he had dreamed of for himself all through the awkwardness and hesitations of adolescence, and he was making the most of it. It was frivolous and garish and the arguments, at a time and in a place like that, were mere verbal exercises, and he knew after three or four evenings like this they would bore him forever more, but tonight he was making the most of it.

"Now, look here," said a man by the name of Bernstein, who had produced dozens of movies and who had been listening to Jack with a sullen pout on his heavy, sunburned face, "you're shooting a picture right now, with Delaney, aren't you?"

"Yes," Jack said, nodding at Delaney, who had come up to join the group.

"I suppose that's the big holy exception," Bernstein said, sneering. "I suppose that's a big fat work of Art."

"No," Jack said. "It's a piece of crap, like everything else."

There was a little hush and then Delaney laughed and everybody, with the exception of Bernstein, laughed with him. Delaney patted Jack on the shoulder. "The lad's only been out here two months," he said. "His vocabulary is still vigorous. He'll tone down."

"What the hell are you doing out here, if that's the way you feel?" Bernstein asked pugnaciously. "Why don't you go back to Broadway with the rest of the Communists?"

"I'm out here to make my pile, Mr. Bernstein," Jack said, taunting the man, enjoying his anger. "Then, in a year or two I'll buy a ranch and raise cows and orchids and retire from the public eye."

"A ranch," Mr. Bernstein said. "That's a new one. I'll wait to see your picture, young man. Maybe you'll be able to retire from the public eye sooner than you think." He stalked off, an outraged patriot of the magic and beautiful country created each day on the sound stages he loved and dominated.

"How old are you, Jack?" Delaney asked.

"Twenty-two."

"Good," Delaney said. "You can still talk the way you're talking. But get it all in now. Because at the age of twenty-three, it will be insufferable." With a grin, he went off, small, tough, knowing, to investigate the report that an English poet was drunk on crème de menthe in the kitchen and was making improper advances to the butler.

Carlotta was smiling more openly, the judgment in her long, green eyes clearer and clearer.

"I think this party is over the hill," Carlotta said. "I think it's time to take me home. Don't you?"

"Yes," Jack said.

And that was all he did that night. Take her home and leave her at her door. That night.

*

"I had a peculiar sense of honor. In those days."

Another night. They had been working on exteriors on the back lot and it was past eleven when they finished and once again Carlotta had asked Jack to drive her home, because her own car was in the garage getting a new grille put on it after a crash. She drove well, but too fast, and her car was constantly laid up, being repaired. They drove in silence, up the winding canyon road toward Carlotta's house. From time to time Carlotta's dog, a huge Belgian shepherd that she took with her almost everywhere, leaned forward from the back seat and licked the back of her neck and she pushed him away impatiently, saying "God damn it, Buster, control yourself." The dog would then sit back, hurt, his mouth open, panting, his tongue lolling, until he could contain his love no longer and would repeat the gesture.

Carlotta kept looking obliquely over at Jack as they drove, an expression composed of curiosity and amusement on her triangular, vivid pale face. Again and again since the night of the wedding, Jack had surprised that same look, disturbing, mocking, inviting, all at the same time, on Carlotta's face. For his own reasons, Jack had avoided, whenever he could, being alone with her or looking at her too closely, but the face, with its flooding vitality, its violent blond sensuality, its hint of malicious amusement, haunted his dreams and tormented his waking hours.

"You don't seem to have any trouble controlling yourself, do you?" Carlotta said. "Not like poor old slobbery, heart-on-his-tongue Buster here, at all."

177

"What do you mean by that?" Jack asked, although he knew what she meant well enough.

"Nothing," Carlotta said, laughing. "Nothing at all. What did you do back East—take a holy vow to be rude to movie stars?"

"If I've been rude," Jack said stiffly, "I'm sorry. Excuse me."

"You've been rude to everybody out here," Carlotta said carelessly, "and you're well loved for it. This is Masochism Alley out here. The harder they're hit, the better they like it. Don't change. It'll ruin your charm."

She had a strange way of talking. She had been brought up in Texas, one of seven children of an oil-rigger who had wandered all over the state like a gypsy with his brood, but there was no remnant of her native drawl in her speech. She had worked ferociously with speech teachers for two years and now when she spoke she sounded like a girl who had been to the best Eastern schools and who had consciously corrected all the more affected mannerisms of the language she had learned there. The voice itself was low and controlled and she made the men she knew uncomfortable and hesitant in her presence, as though she were ready at any moment to ridicule any stupidity or pretension. On the set she was concentrated and intelligent, selfish, ferocious in defending her interests, confident of her talent, merciless to fraud. Delaney had told Jack in the beginning, "I'll do my best to protect you from her, but you've got to watch out for yourself, too. She'll sweep you off the screen if you relax your guard for a minute."

Her body, which was justly famous, and which seemed lithe and soft and girlish, she kept hardened to an athlete's pitch, and she watched her food and drink like a heavyweight champion at a training table. She was twenty-six years old and when she wanted she could pass convincingly as eighteen. She read a great deal, without much plan or discrimination, as though making up for the lack of education in the oil-rigger's wake, and her mind was a grab bag of facts and quotations from the most surprising places. Fiercely intent on her career, she had never been married.

All these things, as they had been revealed to him in the past few weeks, had pushed Jack swiftly through the stages of admiration, desire, and finally, love. But he had said nothing yet.

Jack drove up to the sprawling white house set on the hillside and stopped the car. The dog began to whimper in back, eager to get out.

"Oh, Christ," Carlotta said.

"What's the matter?"

Carlotta indicated a Cadillac parked in her driveway. "I have a guest," she said. "You can't come in."

"Why not?" Jack asked.

"The guest would be jealous."

"Who is he?" Jack peered speculatively at the car. It was large, new, and rich, but in Hollywood that meant nothing. All it might mean was that somebody had scraped together a thousand dollars for the first down payment and was hoping for the best. He himself had an open Ford that he had bought second-hand.

"Who is he?" Carlotta asked incredulously. "Don't you know?"

"No."

"Are you kidding?"

"Am I supposed to know?"

Carlotta laughed and leaned over and kissed his forehead swiftly. "For ignorance," she said, "above and beyond the call of Hollywood." Then she told him the name of the owner of the Cadillac. It was Kutzer, the head of the studio, the man who had dubbed Jack, James Royal. "I thought everybody knew," Carlotta said carelessly. "It's been going on since two days before the Flood."

"Do you like him?" Jack asked.

"Stop whining, Buster," Carlotta said to the dog.

"Do you like him?" Jack repeated. Kutzer was at least forty, married, with two children. He had thinning hair and a small paunch, and was the object of fear and ridicule at the studio, like all other men in similar positions in Hollywood. Jack had never heard anyone say that he liked the man.

"Let's put it this way," Carlotta said. "I don't like him tonight."

"Well, give him my regards," Jack said flatly. "Good night."

Carlotta opened the car door, then closed it defiantly. "I don't want to say good night," she said. "I want a drink."

"I'm sure you'll be able to find a bottle in there," Jack said, indicating the house.

"I want a drink with you," Carlotta said. "Alone with you. And don't be so godamn twenty-two-year-old stuffy. Sit down and keep quiet, Buster." She settled against Jack's shoulder. "Do you know the way from here to your place, Jack?" she said.

Jack looked once more at the house, secret and dark with its drawn curtains, and at the shiny expensive car in the driveway. Then he started the Ford and turned it around swiftly and drove back down the winding canyon road.

Jack lived on the wrong side of Beverly Hills, below the trolley tracks, in a section of what were called patio apartments. The building was in the form of a hollow square, with an entrance through an archway and a big, fussy garden traversed by gravel walks.

As he stopped the car, he saw that the owner of a bungalow across the street was standing in front of his house in shirtsleeves and suspenders, gravely watering his lawn. It was hard to know what love of the earth or what detestation of his own fireside had driven his neighbor to this midnight ceremony.

They got out of the Ford and, with the dog sniffing before them, went through the arch into the central garden. There were lights on in some of the windows and from one of them came the strains of "Valencia" being played by a dance band on the radio. A damp fragrance of laurel and eucalyptus came up from the garden. Jack opened the door to his apartment and pulled the curtains so that when he put on the light his neighbors would not be able to see in. Before he could turn on the switch, Carlotta moved between him and the wall, and stood there, waiting, in the darkness. "Well, now," she said.

He put his arms around her and kissed her. As he held her he felt the dog sniffing inquisitively at his legs. He remembered their other kisses, on the set, under the lights and cameras and the eyes of the other actors and hairdressers and sound men and electricians. Well, at least we're reducing the audience, he thought cynically, it's down to one dog. The thought took the pleasure from the embrace.

As though she had guessed something of what he was thinking, Carlotta pushed away from him and touched the button on the wall. There was a whirring sound, but no light.

"What's that?" she asked, startled.

"You turned on the heat," he said. He switched on a lamp on the desk near the window and he saw, with surprise, that she still had her make-up on from the night's shooting. He had forgotten that they had both come directly from the studio. He looked at himself in a mirror. His face looked ageless, waxlike and unreal. When he turned away from the mirror, she had seated herself on the heavy, mission-style couch with her legs up. "You promised me a drink," she said.

He went into the kitchen and brought out a bottle of whisky and two glasses and a pitcher of water. Carlotta was looking around her with a grimace of displeasure, and he realized that he had forgotten how ugly and bare the rented, garishly furnished room actually was.

"When people first come out here," Carlotta said, "they always pick places like this to live in. I call them anti-homes." She accepted the glass and took a long swallow. "We both look ghastly," she said, touching her make-up. "Don't we, Buster?"

The dog was lying in the middle of the floor, watching her, and he wagged his tail, thumping it on the bare tile floor, on hearing his name.

"People're afraid to put down roots here," she said, speaking rapidly. It was the first time since he had been introduced to her that Jack felt that she had seemed nervous and ill-at-ease. "They have the feeling that the ground beneath all this bright green grass is unhealthy and that the swimming pools are poisoned." She waved her glass at the dark carved furniture, at the greenish stucco walls. "What this place needs is a woman's touch, as they say in the pitchers." She looked up at him uncertainly, inquisitively, her blond hair falling loosely over the shoulders of the sweater she was wearing. "There hasn't been a woman's touch at all, has there?"

"No," Jack said, sitting on the edge of the desk, facing her, being careful to keep his distance from her.

"So they tell me," she said, "so they tell me. They also tell me you're married. Is that true?"

"Yes," he said.

"They're catching 'em younger and younger these days," Carlotta said. She stretched out her legs on the couch, her toes touching in a little V. She rested her back against the high arm of the couch, cradling the drink in her two hands. "Where is she—your wife?"

"In New York."

"How is it she turned you loose like this?"

"She wouldn't come with me. She's working."

"At what?"

"She's in a play. She's an actress."

"Oh, God," Carlotta said, "will it never stop? Did you ask her to come out with you?"

"Yes," said Jack.

"And she wouldn't?"

"No."

"What's her name—I mean her stage name?"

"You never heard of her," Jack said. "Nobody ever heard of her. It's a tiny part."

"And even so, she wouldn't come . . . ?"

"No. She's very serious."

"Oh—is she good?"

"No," Jack said, "she's awful."

"Does she know that?"

Jack shook his head. "No," he said, "she thinks she's the American answer to Sarah Bernhardt."

Carlotta chuckled maliciously. "Have you told her?"

"Told her what?"

"That she's awful?"

"Yes," Jack said.

"What did she say to that?"

Jack grinned painfully. "She said that I was jealous of her talent, that I didn't have much of my own, that I didn't know what it was like to be devoted to my art, and that all I was good for was Hollywood, anyway."

"Happy days in the New York theatre," Carlotta said. She finished her drink and put it down on the floor beside her and the dog got up and came over and sniffed hopefully at it.

"How much longer," Carlotta asked, stretching back lazily on the couch, her arms above her head, "do you think your marriage is going to last?"

"Two days," Jack said.

"When did you decide that?"

"Tonight."

"Why?"

"You know why."

She stood up then and came over and stood in front of him, touching his shoulder lightly with her hand, the big, green eyes alive and somber in the mask of make-up. "I didn't come here only for a drink, you know," she said.

"I know. Come on, I'm going to take you home now."

She stepped back and looked at him, frowning, trying to understand. "You're the godamndest boy," she said.

"Listen to me," he said. "I'm going to take you home now and I'm going to fly to New York tomorrow and I'm going to tell my wife I'm in love with you and that I want a divorce and that I'm going to marry you as soon as I can."

Carlotta held his face in her hands, staring into his eyes, as if to make sure that he wasn't joking. "I'm a poor, simple, corrupt little girl who came to Hollywood at a tender age, Jack," she said, smiling crookedly. "I don't know if I can cope with all this purity . . ."

He kissed her, gently, putting a seal upon his words.

"And me," she said harshly. "What do I do while all this is going on?"

"You get the Cadillacs out of your driveway," Jack said. "Once and for all."

Carlotta moved back a step, touched her lips uncertainly. "Well," she whispered, "that sounds fair enough."

When they went out and got into the Ford with the dog, the man in the suspenders was still watering his midnight lawn. He stared at them from across the street, surprised, Jack was sure, that they had come out so soon.

*

"Tell me, how many times have you been married?"
　"Three times."
　"Good God."
　"That's it. Good God."
　"Is that normal in America?"
　"Not exactly."

"You're ruthless," Julia said, standing in the middle of the living room, with her legs apart, in the ingénue's pose, her face contorted and full of hatred. The apartment was on West Twelfth Street. It was in an old building with high ceilings and flaking walls and Julia had put up orange burlap curtains since he had been there last and had bought unpleasant-looking tubular furniture. In the next room, the child was crying, but nobody was paying any attention to him. "You keep saying how honestly you want to live your life," she said loudly. "Don't kid yourself. It isn't honesty. It's vanity and hardness of heart. You'll trample on anyone to get what you want. Your wife. Your child. Why couldn't you go out and have your affair in Hollywood with that old tart and keep quiet about it and come home to your wife like everybody else? Oh, no, not you. You even have to tell me in advance. Good God, what sort of a man are you? The Sir Galahad of the bedroom." Her voice was harsh and sarcastic, but even in her own home, fighting for what she considered her conjugal rights, she sounded like a bad actress in a bad play pretending to be harsh and sarcastic. At that moment, it was impossible to remember that he had ever thought he loved her, that he had thought she was beautiful, that they had ever lain warmly together in the same bed and stretched out their arms to each other in desire and affection.

"There's no use talking about it, Julia," he said, trying to keep his voice soothing and reasonable. "This is the only way I can do it. I'll take care of you and the baby and . . ."

"You don't have to take care of anybody," she said. She was weeping now and he was surprised that he felt no pity, only irritation, at the sound of that false, sobbing voice, at the sight of those young, almost authentically sorrowful tears. "I'm not going to give you a divorce," she wept. "I'm going to stay right here and I'll take care of the baby and when you come to your senses I'll be waiting for you. And I'll do better without you, too. You won't be here cutting away my confidence in myself, sneering at me, telling me I'm no good, that I'll never be any good. When you come back I'll be on the top, they'll be offering me every woman's part on Broadway . . . When you come back, I'll take care of you!"

Jack sighed. He didn't want to get into *that* again. She had the same stubbornness and drive as Carlotta, but because in Carlotta it was allied with talent, it made Carlotta admirable. Julia's ambition, her capacity for work, her faith in herself, only made her foolish.

"Julia," he said, unable to keep from uttering the warning, "if you had any sense, you'd quit. You'd quit before it was too late and you'd find a nice man and marry him and devote yourself to being a decent wife and mother."

"Get out," she screamed. "Get out of my house."

He went into the bedroom and looked down at his son, crying in his crib. I'll ask your forgiveness when you're a little older, he thought. Right now all he could feel was regret that the child had been born. He didn't kiss the wet little red face on the frilly pillow, and he left the apartment with relief. He was on the plane back to California two hours later.

"Volare, oh, oh . . . cantare, oh, oh, oh, oh. . . ."

Summer morning in the garden of the white house at the top of the winding canyon road. The table laid for breakfast under the striped umbrella. The mail neatly placed in two bundles beside the large glasses of orange juice, playscripts, scenarios, envelopes from the clipping service, letters, for Mr. James Royal and Miss Carlotta Lee, like the first act of a play, just after the curtain has risen, the actors waiting to come on, waiting just long enough for the applause for the pretty set to die down. The blue sky of California, in those days still free of smog, a brilliant backdrop for the grove of avocado trees with their formal shiny leaves and their heavy round fruit, like a child's drawing of an orchard. The smell of oranges and lemons in the ten-o'clock-in-the-morning sun.

Now the two of them were seated across from each other, Carlotta in slacks and a man's blue shirt, with the sleeves rolled up at the elbow, and Jack in sandals, slacks, and a soft wool sweater, facing each other across the flowers in the middle of the table, across the neatly piled correspondence from the unimportant, insignificant outside world.

Jack sat watching Carlotta open an envelope, her movements quick and precise, her skin glowing in the rosy light under the striped umbrella. She looked across at him. "What're you thinking?" she asked.

"I am thinking," he said, "of last night, and other nights and of how glorious you are and of how I am entwined, enlaced, captivated, enraptured, immersed, joyously sodden with sinful sex, and of how smart it was of you to get out of your father's oil camps and of how brilliant it was of me to get away from my father's prune-dryers."

Carlotta laughed. "Don't tell me," she said, "that that's spontaneous."

"Of course not," Jack said. "I composed it while shaving, as a kind of pre-breakfast plain-chant. Do you dislike it?"

"Go on," she said.

"Tomorrow morning," he said. "My powers of composition are exhausted for the day. Oh, murder, here's the godamn dog."

Buster came bounding in from his morning tour in the canyon brush. He danced around the table, barking in hysterical salute.

"Oh, shut up, Buster," Carlotta said and gave him a piece of honeyed toast to keep him quiet.

Buster had been the occasion of dispute when Jack had just moved in. "He's got to get out of the room," Jack had said, "while we're making love."

"He's very quiet," Carlotta had said.

"I don't care how quiet he is," Jack said. "He lies there, breathing and watching. I never can get over the feeling that he's either going to bite me in the ass or sell the story to the newspapers."

"He's a very discreet dog," Carlotta said. "He'll feel that we're unfriendly if we lock him out."

"I will wind up impotent," Jack said.

"In that case, out he goes. But he'll bark," Carlotta said.

"Let him bark."

Buster had barked for two nights, but had finally, glumly, given in. Now he lay just outside the door, breathing, as Jack put it.

"It's a beautiful day," Carlotta said, looking up at the cloudless sky. "You know what would be nice to do? Get in the car and go out to the beach and swim and have lunch out there, just us two, and . . ."

The telephone, which was on a long cord that ran from the house to the table, began to ring. "Your turn," Carlotta said, making a grimace.

Jack picked up the phone. "Hello," he said.

"Did you read the new stuff?" It was Delaney, as usual wasting no time on preliminaries.

"I read the new stuff," Jack said.

"Well?"

"It's terribly original, dear boy," Jack said, drawling.

"You bastard," Delaney said, without heat. "What the hell do you know? You never went past Freshman English. You have the literary taste of a butcher. You're a coarse athlete who doesn't know the difference between Henry James and Ladies' Night in a Turkish Bath. Your idea of the best movie ever made is *Rebecca of Sunnybrook Farm*. If your father hadn't been so godamn stingy he'd have sent you out for ten years to a course in remedial reading for backward children." Jack settled comfortably in his chair, smiling. "Have you withered to dust yet, you prune farmer?" Delaney asked.

"I am leaning back and drinking my orange juice in the presence of the most beautiful woman in the world," Jack said.

"Uninterrupted sex has robbed you of your powers of reason," Delaney said. "Tell that to the lady."

"I will do that very thing," Jack said, grinning.

"Tell me," Delaney said, "not that it makes the slightest bit of difference what a poor, illiterate actor thinks, but is it terribly original, or terribly, *terribly* original?"

"It wavers," Jack said amiably. "Sometimes it's one, sometimes it's the other."

"I am thinking an unmentionable thing about your mother," Delaney said. Then he sighed. "I'm afraid you're right, Jack. Meet me at noon and we'll drive down to the beach and have lunch and see if we can flog out some ideas to hand on to that pea-brain Myers for the rewrite."

"I shall be there," Jack said, and hung up. Carlotta was looking at him quizzically.

"No beach today," she said.

"Not with you," he said. "I'm going down with Delaney."

"If I were a real woman," Carlotta said, "I'd be jealous."

"If you were that kind of a real woman," Jack said, "I wouldn't be sitting here."

"You know," Carlotta said, "I think you're the first man Maurice Delaney has ever listened to in his whole life."

"I listen to *him*."

"He's used to *that*," she said.

"We'll go to the beach tomorrow," Jack said, "if it's a nice day."

"If it's a nice day and Delaney doesn't need you."

"If Delaney doesn't need me."

"Well," Carlotta said, biting into her toast, "it's a lucky thing I have my charities and my opium pipes for the long, lonely afternoons."

Jack chuckled and began to look through his mail. There was a letter from Julia. It was the first one since he had left her four months before. He nearly put it aside, to read in privacy, but he felt that that would be cowardly, so he opened it immediately.

"Dear Jack," he read, in the elegant, almost printlike, artificial handwriting, "I have been to see a lawyer and I will shortly file suit for divorce. I'm not asking for any money, as I have met a man

187

with whom I have fallen in love, and I am going to marry him as soon as I am free. I am arranging for custody of the child, of course. Since I don't want to sue in New York, where I would have to use adultery as the grounds for divorce, which would be unpleasant for the child when he grew old enough to ask questions, I am going to Reno. Naturally, I expect you to pay whatever expenses this will entail.

Julia."

Why does she keep saying, *the child?* Jack thought, irritated. I know his name. Then his irritation vanished as the meaning of the letter sunk in.

"Where do you want to get married?" he said to Carlotta, who was impatiently flipping through her own mail.

"What's that?" she asked.

He gave her the letter. She read it without expression. "Where did she learn to write letters?" Carlotta asked, when she had finished. "In business school?"

"Personally," Jack said, "I think it's the nicest letter I ever received in my whole life."

"You were right to leave her," Carlotta said. "She's an idiot."

"How can you tell from one letter?" Jack asked.

"Not asking for money," Carlotta said, biting on her toast. "She could have bled you white."

"Will you ask for money when we divorce?" Jack said, grinning.

"An arm and a leg," Carlotta said.

"In that case," Jack said, "I suppose we'd better stay married."

"I suppose," Carlotta said. She came over and kissed the top of his head, and ruffled his hair with her fingers.

"In California, I find," Jack said, "they have wonderful California mornings in the morning. Don't you find?"

"I find, too," she said. She kissed him again and went back to her place to finish her breakfast.

*

"What about that woman in the movie? . . . Weren't you married to her?"

"Yes."

"Did she please you?"
"Yes, she pleased me very much."

"It would never 'ave 'appened," the one-armed elevator boy was saying, in his cockney voice, "if I 'ad slept in me own bed, but my Aunt Penelope was visiting us and my mother pressed 'er to spend the night, so I went to my friend Alfred's, on the next street, and I bedded down there. Then, when the air raid started, I 'opped out of bed to open the window, and I 'eard the bloody whistle and the bomb 'it three houses down and the whole floor went up and down like a cat 'unching itself, and there was a big mirror on the wall and I saw it coming at me, slow-like, like slow motion in the flicks, turning end over end, and I watched it cut my arm off clean, right above the elbow . . ."

It was another poker game in the same hotel, and there was some new money, an Air Force lieutenant who had just come over from the States, young and excited and enjoying himself, with two easy missions behind him and feeling manly, gambling his flight pay recklessly. "I tell you," the lieutenant was saying, "there never was a leave like it. I don't believe I had my pants on twice in three days. I was up in Victorville in the desert, and before I took off for Los Angeles, a pal gave me a telephone number and told me to call it; the word was the lady put out, but promptly and forthwith and with the old aggressive Wild Blue Yonder spirit. So I called her and she said what's your name and I said, 'Lieutenant Dineen, ma'am," and she said, 'Lieutenant Dineen, present yourself at eighteen hundred hours,' and I presented myself, and she was a little old, maybe thirty, but stacked and artful, and she barely gave me time to finish my drink and we didn't look up from our work and call a halt for dinner until eleven-thirty. She was between pictures, she said, so she could spare the time, and we walked around this big white house on top of a canyon stark naked except for her wedding ring for three triumphant days, with this big police dog following us around getting an eyeful. I told her, 'Lady, if this is war, bring on the enemy.' And I earned the everlasting gratitude of a whole squadron of B-17's when I passed on the telephone number when I took off for overseas."

"Three kings," Jack said evenly. "It's my pot." He raked in his winnings. Seventy-two pounds. "She's more than thirty, Lieutenant," he said. "She's thirty-two."

A little after that, he went into the next room and made a telephone call and later that night he slept with another woman for the first time since he had married Carlotta. In his letters home he didn't mention the young lieutenant or the squadron of B-17's and when he wrote Carlotta that he loved her, he meant it and could say it with a whole heart. He had suffered too much from jealousy with Julia to be able to indulge in it himself, and he told himself that it was the war and that almost everything about a war was bound to be ugly and sad and complicated, marriage included.

But the last bonds of the chastity of his youth were loosed and he made love to all the eager girls who thronged London in that culminating season of the war. He made love to the beautiful ones with an extra thrill of aesthetic delight and to the plain ones with a touch of pity, but he made love to them all with hunger and pleasure and was much sought after when his change of attitude became known, although he refused to say to any one of them, however beautiful or dear or satisfactory she was, that he loved her. That, and only that, he reserved. And when the invasion came and he had to go off with the Signal Corps camera unit to which he had been assigned because he had been in the movies in civilian life, he left London with a huge sigh of regret, because there were still three or four hundred girls he hadn't slept with.

On his fifth mission, Jack heard, the young lieutenant's plane blew up over the Ruhr. No parachutes were seen.

*

Table stakes. You can only bet what you have in front of you . . .

The ward was quiet, the night light burned dimly over the door at the far end of the room, the maroon bathrobes hung in a neat line behind the beds, a man snored softly, another man turned uneasily and mumbled something that sounded like Savannah. Jack was awake. The pain was now solid and omnipresent. Large hammers seemed to be beating in rhythm within his head, in his throat, down the middle of his body, in the air around him. When he moved on the pillow, he had the feeling that his head was made out of thin transparent plastic and that it was being slowly and brutally inflated with a burning gas. He would have liked to scream, but he didn't scream. There were fifteen other men sleeping in the ward and he didn't want to wake them up. He waited. If it doesn't stop in five minutes, he thought, I am going to ring again. Two minutes later, he pressed the button.

It seemed to be two or three hours before the nurse came. He didn't recognize her. She was new in the ward, young and pretty and nervous about not doing things correctly.

"You've had your pill a long time ago, Lieutenant," she whispered. "Why don't you sleep, like a good boy?" She touched his pillow compassionately.

"I'm dying," he said.

"Now, now," said the nurse. "You mustn't give in to yourself like that." She touched the pillow again. Somehow, she must have gotten the impression that touching a pillow made her more nursely.

"I think you'd better call the doctor," Jack said, "and tell him I think I'm dying."

"The doctor saw you at eight o'clock, Lieutenant," the nurse said, trying to be patient, but sounding annoyed. "He said it was just a small inflammation and that he'd look at you again in the morning."

Now Jack realized that he knew the nurse. She had been in three times already that night, in answer to his calls, and he remembered that she had reminded him of a secretary in his father's office who always filed important papers in the wrong drawers. He seemed to be looking at her through a red mist, but now he remembered her, because he remembered that she had said the same thing all three times that night. It was a Saturday night and the hospital was only half staffed for the weekend and she was too new to want to take the responsibility of seeming to contradict the doctors. If the doctor had said at eight o'clock that the inflammation was nothing serious and would wait till morning that took on the authority of a direct order for the nurse. Besides, this ward was filled with men who were theoretically convalescing. They were not supposed to die, especially in the middle of the night, on her tour of duty.

So she patted the pillow one more time and went out.

Jack lay there for another minute, then moved slowly, using his one good hand to help him, and sat on the edge of the bed. But when he tried to stand up, his legs collapsed under him, and he fell, or rather diminished-floated, to the floor. He lay there, trying to think through the red mist. After a while he raised his good hand and tugged at the blankets of the bed next to him. "Wilson," he whispered. "Wilson."

He heard the stirring in the bed as Wilson awoke and looked for him. "Wilson," he whispered.

"Where the hell are you?" Wilson said. Then Wilson's head appeared over the edge of his bed, and a moment later, very carefully, because they were still picking bits of metal out of his legs below the knee, Wilson was on the floor next to him.

"Listen, Wilson," Jack said, "if I don't get to a doctor, I'm going to die."

Wilson was not like the nurse. For one thing, he had been in hospitals longer than she had, and he knew what could happen in them. He nodded and walked slowly toward the far end of the room, where there were two invalid's rolling chairs, and brought one back to where Jack was lying. It took ten minutes, with both of them sweating and their hands greasy, to get Jack into the chair. Then, barefooted and grunting with the effort of walking, Wilson pushed the chair in front of him, out of the room, into the long, empty corridor.

There was nobody to be seen, either in the corridor, or in any of the service rooms. Everybody was either off for the weekend or asleep or having coffee or taking care of crisis cases in other wings of the building.

"Do you know where you want to go?" Wilson asked, breathing heavily, leaning over the back of the chair. He was a Texan, with a slow drawl. His family owned a ranch near Amarillo, and you could tell, watching him as he lay on his bed staring down at his ruined legs, that he was wondering what it was going to be like when he tried to get on a horse again. His jeep had gone over a mine in Italy and everybody said that he was lucky to be alive at all.

"No," Jack said, trying to focus on the dimly lit, reddish, expanding and contracting tunnel. "Just find the nearest doctor."

Corridors went off at different angles from the one they were on, labyrinth-like, mysterious, cleverly planned. The hospital was newly built, and conceived with great ingenuity, but you had to know the key. After a while they both had the feeling that they could roll on forever, the rubber wheels of the chair hissing on the dark linoleum floor, roll on to the accompaniment of Wilson's painful barefooted shuffling and agonized breathing, past the miles of closed doors or deceptive lights from empty bays and washing rooms and deserted kitchens, roll on forever, unnoticed, lost, spiraling through the hushed, unpopulated hospital night.

Finally, there was a door with a frosted pane of glass and there was a light behind it. The light seemed tiny to Jack, far away, clear, and ringed in red. With a last, grunting push, Wilson sent the chair against the door and it opened. Sitting behind a desk facing the door was a man with colonel's eagles on the shoulders of his open shirt. He was small and gray and grizzled, hunched over papers on his desk, reading through steel-rimmed glasses.

Wilson sat down on the one chair near the desk, exhausted. "Colonel," he whispered, "Colonel . . ."

The Colonel didn't say anything. He looked quickly at Wilson, then came over to Jack and, with light, swift fingers, began to unwind the bandage from around his head. He examined the wound along the jaw for a few seconds, touching Jack gently. Then he whistled softly, under his breath, and went over to the telephone on his desk, dialed a number, and said, "This is Colonel Murphy. Prepare Operating Room Two. We're going to operate in twenty minutes."

The plastic balloon was now stretched to the utmost with its burning gas, but Jack smiled at the Colonel, because the Colonel had believed him. The Colonel believed, too, that he had been about to die. And now he was in the Colonel's hands and he wasn't going to die. And in the long run, that had finally been Jack's War Aim—not to die.

*

"She's more than thirty, Lieutenant. She's thirty-two."

"It would never 'ave 'appened if I 'ad slept in me own bed . . ."

"I don't know why they can't transfer you out to California," Carlotta was saying. "After all, they have hospitals there, too. I could see you all the time then. Virginia! Good Lord! How often can anyone get to Virginia? The only way I managed it this time was because I'm doing a personal appearance in Washington."

It was another season now. The war had been over for what

seemed like a long time. With the other men who were still in the hospital, Jack sensed that the civilians who came to visit them were impatient with them for being so stubborn, for clinging so long to a period that was finished and done with, like spoiled children who refuse to grow up and accept their adult responsibilities. Wilson had phrased it for them all after a visit from a relative. "Son," he had said, "we are messin' up the American premises. We all are just unwholesome debris that somebody imported from Europe by mistake." They were still taking chunks of metal out of his legs.

Jack and Carlotta were sitting under a tree on the hospital grounds. It was green and warm and pleasant, if you didn't mind the maroon bathrobes, and there was a view of distant bluish hills and it hadn't become too hot yet. Jack could walk all right now, and his jaw, although twisted and raw-looking, was more or less healed. There were still two operations on his jaw to be gone through, for what the doctors called cosmetic reasons—and he had just been told that the first operation was scheduled for the next morning. But he didn't say anything about it to Carlotta.

He didn't want to spoil the afternoon. Carlotta had only two hours to spend there and he didn't want to spoil them. She looked older, of course, and she was putting on too much weight, and she was sliding down the Hollywood hill, getting bad parts in bad pictures, and taking big cuts in salary, and complaining about the young girls coming up.

Jack saw the thickening of the throat, the deadish, overdyed color of the hair, the artificially pinched-in waist, the look of complaint in her eye and the sound of failure in her voice, and he remembered the voice of the young lieutenant in London saying that she was old, she was thirty, but she was stacked and artful. But he didn't say anything about any of these things, any more than he had said anything about the operation in the morning.

All he did was sit on the bench beside her, not even touching her, thinking, "I love you, I love you, I love you."

Stubbornly, he was sure that he hadn't been spared from death in the burning farmhouse, he hadn't survived the months of morphine and the hours on the operating tables and the journey in the invalid's chair with Wilson, to lose Carlotta or lose the heart of his feeling for her. He would return to the garden, to the heraldic leaves of the avocado orchard, with the fruit like a child's drawing, to the fragrance of the lemon and orange trees. In the new, forgiving, peaceful mornings of California, they would remake the pleasure they had created for each other.

"It's so unfair, your getting hit like this," Carlotta was saying. "Everybody else is home by now and nobody even *remembers* the war. It's not as though you were in the Infantry or anything like that, people expect you to get hit. But in the Signal Corps! What were you doing up so close?"

Jack smiled wearily. "Sleeping," he said. "The situation was somewhat confused."

"I can't stand seeing you like this, darling," Carlotta said, her voice trembling. "So thin, so tired, so—so acquiescent. I keep remembering how cocky you were, how arrogant . . ." She smiled tremulously. "So nice and impossible and telling everybody just what you thought of them."

"I promise," Jack said, "to be impossible again, when I get out of here."

"We had some good years, didn't we, Jack?" Carlotta said, and she seemed to be pleading for his assent, as though without his assent the years wouldn't have been real, wouldn't have been good, wouldn't have happened. "Five good years, before you went off to the godamn war."

"We'll have a lot more years," he said. "I guarantee."

"I don't know." She shook her head uncertainly. "Everything's so changed. Even the climate. The fog doesn't seem to burn off till noon most days, and I've never seen so much rain . . . I never seem to make the right decisions any more. I used to be so sure of myself . . . and I'm beginning to *look* so raddled . . ."

"You look beautiful," he said.

"Tell that to my public," she said bitterly. She hitched at her skirt, where it was bunching up at her waist. "I must lose weight," she said.

"Have you seen Maurice?" Jack asked. "How is he?"

"There's a rumor the studio's buying out his contract," Carlotta said. "His last two pictures've been bombs. Did he say anything about that when he was here?"

"No," Jack said. Delaney had visited him twice in the hospital, but their meetings had been uneasy and constrained. Early in the war Delaney had applied for a commission but he had been rejected, for a reason he had never disclosed to Jack, and the hospital full of wounded men had seemed to have a disturbing effect

195

upon him. He had spoken disjointedly, had avoided any mention of his work, had asked questions about Jack's war and then hadn't seemed to listen. Although he had come all the way from New York especially to see Jack, he had seemed hurried and absentminded all during his two visits and had appeared grateful when it was time for him to leave.

"You know what he had the nerve to suggest to me?" Carlotta said. "He told me I ought to move here close to the hospital so I could be available for you whenever you could see me. Those were the very words he used. Available. I told him that'd be the last thing in the world you'd want." Carlotta took out her compact and peered dissatisfiedly at her face. "I was right, wasn't I?"

"Of course," Jack said.

"Then I asked him for a job. He said for me to come back when I lost ten pounds and had been on the wagon for two months. Once you begin to go in that town," she said bitterly, "people think they can say anything that comes into their heads to you."

"How's Buster?" Jack asked, trying to change the subject, get Carlotta away from her grieving self-contemplation.

"He's dead," Carlotta said. She began to cry. "I didn't have the heart to write you. Somebody poisoned him. I tell you, California isn't what it used to be. It's filling up with the most horrible, vicious people . . ."

The fanged witness dead, Jack thought sadly, watching his wife dab at her eyes. Dead the wolflike voyeur, with his memories of the joyous flesh of better times.

"I'm sorry," he said, patting Carlotta's hand. "I was very fond of him." Now that the dog was dead, this was true.

"It's the one really near and dear thing I've lost in the war," Carlotta said, weeping.

Well, Jack thought, everybody must expect to lose *something* in a war. But he didn't say it. He wished he knew how to console his wife. He wished he could make her believe that when he returned, things would change, the climate would improve, California would no longer be full of horrible, vicious people, she would no longer be offered only bad parts in bad pictures, her salary would be restored, her confidence in herself re-established. But at that moment, Wilson came over in his maroon bathrobe to be introduced to his wardmate's famous and beautiful wife, and there was no time for comfort.

Drying her tears, Carlotta smiled at Wilson, in a very good imitation of the reckless, enticing smile she had brought with her to the Coast from Texas so many years before and which had had so much to do with her success. If Wilson saw that she had been crying, he no doubt thought that it was on account of Jack.

"Miss Lee," Wilson said politely, rocking on his destroyed legs, "I want to tell you that I have admired you since I was a young boy . . ." (Wilson was now twenty-four) ". . . and that I have always believed that you were the most desirable lady I had ever had the good fortune to set my eyes on."

"Well, now," Carlotta said, and once more she sounded the way she had when Jack first met her, gay and dangerous and sure of herself, "well, now, isn't that nice to hear?"

She didn't stay the full two hours. She left with a good half-hour to spare. She was afraid she'd miss the train to Washington, she said. She couldn't afford to be late these days. It wasn't like the good old days, she said, when she was riding high and could get away with anything.

That night, when the lights were out, after they had prepared him for the operation the next morning, Jack wept. It was the first time since he had been hit that the tears had come.

*

"In California, I find, they have wonderful California mornings in the morning. Don't you find?"

"Stay for lunch," Clara Delaney said. She was lying on a rubber mattress on the sand in front of the house, tanning herself. She was wearing a very brief bathing suit and she was almost completely black from the sun, and Jack was surprised, as he was each time he saw her in revealing clothes, by the firmness of her body and the robust beauty of its lines, under the harsh, disappointed, private secretary's face. "Maurice is out there someplace." She waved vaguely toward the ocean. "If he hasn't drowned. Is Carlotta with you?"

"No," Jack said, "she's not with me."

He climbed over the low wall that separated the Delaneys' patio from the beach and walked toward the water's edge. It was a weekday morning and the white curve of the Malibu beach, with its gaudy fringe of houses jammed one against the other, was almost deserted. The water was rough, and there was a wicked swell, and when the waves broke and spent their force, they receded with a choppy, dangerous green hiss and foamed into white water again as they met the next line of breakers coming in. Far out, Jack saw a speck. Delaney was swimming steadily, parallel with the shore, the dark speck rising and falling with the combers coming in to plume and break. Jack waved and after a while Delaney saw him and waved back and started in.

For a minute or two it looked as though Delaney wasn't going to make it. The tide pulled at him and he was caught just where the breakers were pounding down and his head disappeared again and again. Then he caught a wave and hurtled into the beach and stood up, the water sucking at his knees, a sturdy, brown figure, like an old lightweight, filled out a bit by time, but not too badly, amused by the attacks of the Pacific Ocean against him. He came out, smiling, his eyes slightly bloodshot from the salt water, and shook hands with Jack, his hand dripping, before he bent and picked up a huge white Turkish towel that was lying on the sand and vigorously scrubbed his thin red hair with it. Then he draped it around his body, like a toga.

"You should've come earlier," he said. "We could've swum together. The water's great."

"One day, Maurice," Jack said, "if you keep going that far out by yourself, they're going to find a drowned director somewhere along this coast."

Delaney grinned. "That'll be a laugh," he said, "for a lot of people, won't it? Want a cup of coffee?"

"I want to talk to you," Jack said. "I'm in trouble."

"Who isn't?" Delaney said. He glanced toward his house. "Is Clara out there yet on the patio?"

"Yes."

"Let's take a walk," Delaney said.

Side by side, walking on the hard sand just below the high-tide kelp, they paced along the beach. Thirty yards out, a line of pelicans skimmed along the inside edge of a wave, inches above the water.

"I'm thinking of throwing in my cards," Jack said, "and I want your advice."

"What cards?"

"Marriage cards," Jack said, watching the pelicans. "Career cards. The whole hand."

"Uh-huh." Delaney nodded. He stooped and picked up a stone and tossed it side-arm, like a shortstop, to scale along the shallows. When he did something like that you were surprised how young he seemed, how deft and vigorous all his movements were. "I was waiting for this," he said, without looking at Jack. "Carlotta's been giving you a rough time, hasn't she?"

"Yes," Jack said. "This morning she got in at eight o'clock."

"Did you ask her where she'd been?"

"No," Jack said. "But she insisted on telling me."

"Oh," Delaney said, "it's reached that stage."

"Yes."

"What do you say to her?"

"When I came back here, after the hospital," Jack said, "I told her I'd heard about her during the war and that I wasn't blaming her or judging her. What the hell, I was away more than five years. All I wanted, I said, was for us both to forget all that and start over again, and try to get back to the way we were . . ."

"The Innocent Warrior," Delaney said. "What did she say to that?"

"She said, fine, that's what she wanted, too. And for about two months, it *was* the way it had been. Anyway, *almost* the way it was. Then she began to duck out on parties, and disappear every afternoon . . . You know how dames operate out here. Then last night, she went the whole way and stayed out all night . . ."

"Does she want a divorce?"

"No. She says she still loves me." Jack smiled wearily. "And in a way, she does. The other men don't seem to mean anything much to her. At least, not individually. En masse, yes."

"Have you any idea about why she does all this?"

"I have my theories," Jack said. "Naturally." He shook his head painfully, forcing himself to talk, because he couldn't keep it to himself any longer. "It's so different from the way she was when I met her, when I married her, until I went away . . . You know, before she met me, she'd only been with one man, Kutzer. When I heard about him, I thought it was the typical Hollywood thing— the ambitious girl sleeping with the producer for the fat parts and the big publicity. But it wasn't like that at all, I found out. She was with him, and nobody else, for seven years. She loved him. With her, he wasn't the kind of hoodlum in tweeds he seemed to be to everybody else. With her he was kind and gentle and delicate, she says, and clever and honest. And I must say, when she told him she wanted to marry me, he behaved very well. He didn't threaten her or try to damage me—and at that time it would've been the easiest thing in the world for him to do me in—and he's been a good friend to both of us ever since. And with me—until I went overseas—she never looked at anybody else. Any more than I did. I'm sure of that."

"Yes," Delaney said. "That's true." He grinned sourly. "You were the most unnatural couple. So—what do you think happened?"

"First, she was lonely . . . She can't stand being alone. Then she began to feel that she was sliding . . . She had bad luck with two or three pictures and people began to pass her over and pick other girls for parts she thought she should have had. I don't have to tell you how ambitious she used to be. I can understand how it must have hurt her. And she began to get hipped on the subject of getting old. I think she began to look for reassurance in bed, once she'd lost it in front of the camera. Well, if that's what you're looking for, you never find it in any one bed. So you keep trying other beds, I guess."

Delaney nodded. He rubbed his head thoughtfully, pushing the frail reddish hair, matted with salt, so that it stood up erratically. "Well, Doctor," he said, "I think there's no need to take an x-ray. The diagnosis seems pretty clear. Now, how about you? What're *you* going to do?"

"I'm going to get out. I can't help her. All I can do if I stay is hate her. It's just about all used up," Jack said.

"I knew back in 1944 that one day you were going to come and tell me this," Delaney said. "I was at a party with your loving wife and she came over to me and she said, 'Maurice, I hear you're the best lay in town.'" Delaney laughed brutally. "It wasn't true, of course," he said, "but the implication was clear."

"I'm not going to ask you what happened after that," Jack said quietly.

"No," said Delaney. "Don't."

They stopped and looked out at the waves. The pelicans were coming back now, on their steady, unmoving wings, skimming a long green roller. "They obviously have some reason for doing that all day," Delaney said, with a gesture of his head for the pelicans, "but it's my opinion they're just showing off; they're saying, we don't look like anything much when we're sitting down, but we're pretty hot birds on the edge of a wave, all right. They're probably secret members of the Screen Actors Guild." He wrapped his towel more tightly around him. There was a wind coming down the beach from the north, and a high mist that made the sunlight pale and watery. "So—" Delaney said, "do you want to move down here and stay with us? This is a pretty good place for the summer and during the week there's practically nobody around and you can recuperate in peace. There's a guest room over the garage and you don't even have to see me if you don't want to."

"Thanks," Jack said, "but I think not. I think I'm going East for a while, and then maybe back to Europe."

"You got a picture to do in Europe?"

"No. I don't think I want to do pictures any more," Jack said slowly. "For one thing, I'll never get back to where I was before the war. Not with this face." He touched his jaw.

"There're still lots of parts. Like the one you read for me that you turned down last year. Maybe you won't get leads for a while, but . . ."

"I'm no good any more, Maurice," Jack said quietly. "You know that, don't you?"

"Well . . ."

"You know it," Jack insisted.

"Yes," Delaney said.

"You offered me that part out of friendship."

"In a way," Delaney said. "Yes."

"I'm not interested any more," Jack said. "Maybe it's the war. I don't know. It all seems like balls to me now. Being an actor doesn't seem like work for a grown man to me now. I guess the reason I feel that is that I never really *was* an actor. I just got into it by accident . . ." He shrugged. "I might as well get out the same way."

"What'll you do in Europe?"

"Well, I've been talking to a couple of people," Jack said, embarrassed, "about what the Quakers—the Friends—are doing there . . . refugees, rehabilitation, that sort of thing. I have a feeling in Europe this year it won't make much of a difference if a man's face is busted up a little here and there. Anyway, we spent so much time blowing the godamn place up, maybe it's a good thing to put in a couple of years trying to patch it together again. . . ."

Delaney laughed. "There's nothing like an unfaithful wife," he said, "to turn a man toward good works."

"Anyway," Jack said, "I'll decide when I'm in New York."

"How're you fixed for dough?" Delaney asked.

"I have my pension," Jack said. "A hundred and ninety bucks a month. And there'll be a salary attached to the job. And my agent made me buy some stocks and bonds before the war, when I was so rich I didn't know what to do with my money. They've almost tripled in value, he tells me. If I cash them in, I stand to get somewhere between a hundred and a hundred and twenty thousand . . . I won't starve."

"Ah, what a waste . . ." Delaney shook his head regretfully. "We were doing so good, you and me. We had it all wrapped up. It didn't seem as if our luck would ever run out. Only it wasn't just luck, either. We had a big secret. We didn't lie to each other and we knew how to work with each other. The godamn war," he said, with quiet bitterness. "All during the war I had a plan for us. I thought that when you came back we'd start an independent company together, you and me, and really show them how to make pictures. If you'd've come back in 1945, like everybody else, with a whole face, it'd've been a cinch, they'd have fallen over themselves to stuff the money in our hands . . ."

"Well," Jack said, "I didn't come back in 1945 with a whole face."

"And now," Delaney said, rubbing the side of his head reflectively, "I couldn't get the financing to do a three-minute short advertising condoms."

"That's only temporary, Maurice," Jack said, "and you know it. Plenty of people want you."

"Sure. Plenty of people want me. On their own terms. To do their own crap." He shrugged. "Ah, well," he said, lightly, "it'll change. It always does. And when it does, I'm going to come to you and grab you out of whatever you're doing and we'll make some pictures that'll knock the bastards dead." He grinned. "Just leave a forwarding address wherever you go, so that I won't waste any time looking for you."

"I'll leave a forwarding address," Jack said. It was hard to get the words out. Christ, he thought savagely, since the hospital I'm ready to cry at the drop of a hat.

"Meanwhile, if you need any dough . . ."

Jack shook his head, looking down at the sand.

"Well," Delaney said, "what do you want from me?"

"You got me out here," Jack said. "I want you to tell me it's time to go."

"Go," Delaney said harshly. "Go fast. I wish I could go with you. And don't wait. Pack and leave this afternoon. Get across the California border by midnight. Don't look back." His voice was bitter and strident, as though he felt responsible for what had happened to Jack and to the marvelous young girl Carlotta had been when he first saw her, as though Jack had crystallized for him all the fears and failures and betrayals he himself had suffered from, had witnessed, had inflicted, in this place. "Don't argue with her. Don't argue with anybody. Just go."

They didn't shake hands, and after a moment, Jack left Delaney standing there, senatorial and oracular in his towel-toga by the edge of the pounding sea. Jack went between two nearby houses to the road, where his car was parked, because he didn't want to have to say good-bye to Clara.

When he got home, Carlotta was out. He packed two bags hastily, and left a note, and started driving East by two o'clock that afternoon.

*

"You were right to leave her. She's an idiot."
  "How can you tell from one letter?"
  "Not asking for money. She could have bled you white."

"I have been talking to Miss Lee's lawyers," Mr. Garnett was saying, "and I'm afraid you're in trouble, Mr. Andrus." Mr. Garnett was a soft-spoken, balding man whose law firm didn't specialize in divorce cases. Jack had an irrational distaste for divorce lawyers, as for doctors who advertised that they specialized in venereal diseases. "She's asking for an enormous settlement. Her lawyers have been awarded an injunction tying up your bank account and all your assets, as of two days ago, on the grounds that you have no regular income against which alimony could be secured. Furthermore, they allege that you plan to leave the country, and your wife, as the plaintiff, must be protected."

203

"But it's ridiculous," Jack said. "I'm the one who's asking for the divorce." He hadn't claimed adultery because he hadn't wanted to drag the whole thing through the mud. He had envisioned a quiet, polite, undamaging divorce. "How can she expect to get anything from me?" he demanded.

"She's claiming misconduct, Mr. Andrus," Mr. Garnett said softly, "and I'm afraid she can make it stick."

"Good God," Jack said, "everybody in California knows she's been sleeping with everybody but the doorman at the studio."

"Can you prove that, Mr. Andrus?"

"I can't prove it, but everybody . . ."

"She can prove misconduct on your part, Mr. Andrus," said Mr. Garnett, looking respectably down at the papers on the desk in front of him. "Her lawyers inform me that they have had you followed while you were in New York and they have evidence."

"Oh, Christ," Jack said. He had met a Red Cross girl whom he had known in England, and more out of loneliness than anything else, he had stayed a few nights in her apartment. Without pleasure.

"Of course, Mr. Andrus," said Mr. Garnett, "you could hire detectives, too, to follow your wife, although I imagine that she will be very discreet until the case comes to trial. Still, it might pay to take the chance. I know a very good agency in California which has had excellent results in the past, and . . ."

"No," Jack said. He thought of the breakfast in the garden so long ago. No matter what, he couldn't set policemen on the trail of the woman who had sat across from him that morning. "No," he said thickly. "Forget it."

"There is one fortunate aspect to the situation," Mr. Garnett said. "She can't touch your pension. The government keeps that inviolate."

"Good old inviolate Uncle Sugar," Jack said, standing up.

"I'd like to have your instructions on this," Mr. Garnett said. "How do you want me to contest the case?"

"Don't contest it," Jack said. "I won't even be here. I'll be in Europe."

"I know the firm which is representing your wife," Mr. Garnett said. "They're quite—quite ruthless. It may be difficult to make any sort of compromise with them, unless you at least threaten to defend and file countercharges . . . And if your wife has been as . . . as indiscreet . . . in the past as you say, it may very well be possible, even now, to get testimony from hotel registers and maids and chauffeurs and similar witnesses."

"No," Jack said. "Nothing. Give her what she wants. Try to hold onto something for me, but if it doesn't work without all that, give."

"I'm terribly sorry, Mr. Andrus," Mr. Garnett said. He stood up to say good-bye. "Oh, one more thing. Your wife also claims the car you drove to New York and I believe she is arranging to have it impounded. Of course, I'll take the necessary countermeasures."

Jack laughed wildly. "Give her the car," he said. "I won't be able to afford the gas. Give the lady everything."

Saving the morning in the garden, he realized, as he walked out of the lawyer's office, was not going to be easy.

*

Sum up the night. In a little while dawn will break over the ruins and monuments and television aerials of Rome and it is time to make up the tally of memory. Forgotten voices have spoken, old songs have been heard, ghosts have coupled and parted, ancient wounds have opened and bled once more, the now and here of the Roman night has revealed itself to be a frail and dangerous platform on the crumbled columns of the past, the dead have made their brief appearance, fingers lifted in gnomic warning . . .

Out of all that gay, brave company . . .

Death.
The Presence was back in the room with him, breathing on the pillow beside him, patient, waiting. He felt under assault. The blows of the night had sapped him, the first church bells of morning were the final explosions under the walls. All his vitality, all the inner, thoughtless health that had pulled him through wounds and hospitals and failures and loss of love, seemed to be sliding away. With the fresh blood wet on his lip, he had the feeling that a voice had whispered in his ear, between sleeping and waking, "You will not leave Rome alive."

Veronica, he thought. Why isn't she here? Godamnit, why isn't she here? He closed his eyes tightly and remembered that full, enveloping body. He twisted miserably with desire. If she were here, he thought feverishly, it would all be different.

*

It is dawn in Rome and here and there the sound of a Vespa, hammering against the sienna walls, is heard, and the bells of various churches, among them Sant'Andrea della Valle, Santa Maria Sopra Minerva, Santissima Trinità dei Monti, San Lugi de' Francesi, Santa Maria della Pace, salute the new day, after the nightmare night.

Mass is being celebrated in the church of Santa Maria in Trastevere, for five old women in black shawls, rheumatically bowed over on the cold and drafty stone floor, listening to the sleepy young priest saying, Kyrie eleison, Kyrie eleison, Christe eleison, Kyrie eleison, Kyrie eleison, before going off to the day's work scrubbing floors in hospitals, office buildings, hotels. The market is being set up in the square near the Farnese Palace, flowers and artichokes from Sicily and the red oranges and the sogliole and the cefali and the triglie from the Mediterranean and the bricklike triangles of Parmesan cheese and the mortadella and salamis and the white, wet eggs of mozzarella piled on straw. The last, hilarious customers are coming up from the mulatto's basement night club on the Via Veneto, laughing loudly, speaking half a dozen languages, and starting their cars with a roar of motors on the bluish street. Jack's drunk, his knuckles a little swollen, sleeps uneasily now in his hotel room three streets away, fearing the onset of morning, even in his dreams preparing for the first two aspirin, the first Alka-Seltzers, the first Bloody Mary of the new day. The policemen on duty on the Via Botteghe Oscure, opposite the headquarters of the Communist party and the home of the Spanish Ambassador, lean against the wall out of the wind and wonder who is going to riot today and what heads will have to be clubbed, and the marine guard in front of the American Embassy waits for his relief, glad to be on the night watch, because the students don't demonstrate in front of the Embassy at night to show their disapproval of events in Egypt or Hungary or Algeria. Sleepily, the marine guard speculates on why it is that Italian students feel that they have to show their disapproval of upheavals in Africa and Central Europe by marching,

206

waving flags, in front of the American Embassy in Rome. The Tiber flows in its stone banks past the Castel Sant'Angelo and the Palace of Justice, flows under the stone bridges, a narrow, tamed stream to have flowed through all that history, on its way past Ostia toward the sea, past Ostia Antica, which has once been a thriving port of two hundred thousand souls, and is now only excavated ruins and a restored open theatre in the wintry green fields, spreading toward the black lava beaches.

The trucks rumble through the Piazza Colonna with the morning's newspapers, announcing scandal and crisis; the workmen begin putting up wooden stands for a parade on the avenue leading to the Colosseum, there is a smell of coffee from the all-night cafés, the last whores reluctantly leave the Piazza Barberini, where the fountain plays incessantly, the water cascading down the muscular shoulders and the upturned head and fishtail of the bronze figure of sea and earth.

And all over the city there is the stirring of women getting out of bed to buy bread, to make breakfast, to prepare children for school, there are the repressed, unheard groans of men stiffly pushing themselves into their clothes, sweaty from yesterday's underpaid labor, preparing for the starvation labor of today.

The clear, wintry Mediterranean dawn, pale green and cold rose, touches the white jerry-built walls of Parioli, built by Mussolini's millionaires and added to by Marshall Plan millionaires, touches the dome of the Vatican, the tops of the willows in the Borghese gardens, touches Garibaldi's bared head on the great statue in the janiculum with a peaceful, deceptive, hopeful light.

The Mediterranean light filters into the hotel room where Jack lies, hot-eyed, wakeful, caught in the drift of the past, remembering voices from another age. . . .

*

He looked at the leather traveling clock. Time to get up. He got out of bed and shaved. His face was haggard in the bright bathroom light and he cut himself under the chin and the cut didn't stop bleeding for a long time.

He dressed, feeling hazy and thick-fingered. He took Despière's envelope and put it into a dresser drawer under some shirts. He made sure to take his dark glasses, for disguise against Delaney's sharp examination.

When he started to go out, he saw an envelope under the salon door. He bent, feeling dizzy, to pick it up. There was no name on it, no address. It was of thin, flimsy paper, and he could feel that there was only a single sheet of paper in it. He opened it soddenly, knowing that it must be some new attack, some last foray by the night.

"Andrus," he read. It was written in red ink, a nervous, scrawled handwriting. "I came across a quotation that might interest you. It's from Pliny, arranged by Leonardo da Vinci, in his notebooks. Are you interested in natural history? Here it is . . .

" *'The great elephant has by nature qualities which are rarely found in man, namely honesty, prudence, a sense of justice, and of religious observance. Consequently, when the moon is new they go down to the rivers and there solemnly cleansing themselves bathe, and after having thus saluted the planet they return to the woods.*

" *'They fear shame and only pair at night and secretly, nor do they then rejoin the herd but first bathe in the river.'*

"Remember the elephant, Andrus, fear shame, cleanse yourself.
Bresach"

Jack stared dully at the thin sheet of red-scrawled paper. It had been Bresach prowling outside the door, he thought. He's crazy, he's capable of anything. Only a lunatic would come to a man's room at three o'clock in the morning to deliver a message like this.

He folded the letter neatly, and put it in his pocket. It took a great effort of will to open the door into the corridor.

Still, the days were bearable. It was the nights that one had to survive.

15

He waited in the restaurant until two thirty and ate his lunch and dawdled over his coffee, but Veronica didn't appear. He left the restaurant and went back to his hotel, but there was no message for him there. He was irritated with her and for a moment thought of forgetting her and going upstairs and trying to take a nap. He was exhausted from the night before and the session with Delaney in the dubbing room had been unpleasant and tiring. Delaney had nagged at him and been sardonic about the way he looked. "Christ," Delaney had said, "if you're going to stay up screwing all night, how can you expect to do your job right?"

He had cut Delaney short and had tried desperately to concentrate, but the effects of the night had been impossible to throw off. He knew that he needed sleep, but he knew he wouldn't be able to sleep unless he had tried to find Veronica.

He gave Guido the name of the hotel to which he had delivered Veronica the night before. Guido must have had a good lunch, because he was expansive and talkative, although Jack would have liked to be left in peace to doze in the back seat.

"France," Guido said, roaring down on a traffic light and slamming on the brakes two feet before he hit an old man with a brief case who was crossing the street. "France—that is the country." He spoke in French, their common bond. "They are blessed, the French. They have everything. All the riches in the soil, all the minerals, all the most beautiful women. And they are not crowded. That is their big blessing. They control the birth. It is not like here, like this senseless Italian incubator, where every day our women give birth to another twenty thousand unemployed. Why, in France, they even have to *import* workers." He shook his head at the unbelievable glory of this condition. "Imagine a country like that. The human being is king." He sighed loudly. "I should have stayed there. When my battalion moved out, I should have had the sense to desert and stay. Later on, I could have constituted myself prisoner and then become a citizen. The happiest months of my life I spent outside Toulon. My captain was a crook and he hired us out to a lady he was in love with who owned a vineyard and we worked on the vines for one whole spring and summer. The lady who owned the vineyard and whom our captain loved was an aristocrat. She told us, 'My poor children, you are going to lose the war and soon many of you will be dead, drink as much wine as you can now.' The wine of that coast is heavy and powerful and she understood when we had to sleep under the olive trees in the hot afternoons and she never told the captain. If it is absolutely necessary to work," Guido said authoritatively, "it is always best to work for an aristocrat."

Guido had told Jack that he was paid sixteen hundred lire a day, being paid only on the days he actually worked. That amounted to about two dollars and fifty cents a day, and he had three children to feed, but his shirt was always clean and ironed in the morning, he wore a neat tie, his shoes were shined, his hair brilliantly barbered.

He drove on the Italian theory. As soon as he got behind the wheel, he assumed that all other drivers were cowards and all pedestrians as agile as gazelles, so that he hurled the green Fiat with all the speed he could command at intersections and other cars, trusting that the other drivers would jam on their brakes in panic or veer off. He plunged down on all pedestrians, even one-legged men on crutches and old women leading babies, as though confident that they would somehow, miraculously, leap out of the way at the last moment. He had told Jack, proudly, that in all his years of driving, he had never as much as scratched the fender of a car. Like other absurd principles in Italy, Guido's seemed to work most of the time.

"When I read the newspapers," Guido went on, "and I read about the troubles that France is having, I am terribly sad. Especially in Algeria. I am sad for them and I am sad because in the Italian papers it is easy to see that the journalists are thinking, 'We have been kicked out of Africa, we have had our Mussolini, now it is your turn, your Mussolini is on his way. Now we will lecture you.'"

At the moment, Jack was sorry that Guido had ever learned to speak French.

"They cannot win in Algeria," Guido went on. With the job he had, with the long hours of waiting for his clients, he had ample opportunity to read all the newspapers and reflect upon the state of the world. "It is a guerrilla war, and to win a guerrilla war you must be prepared to use terror, to stamp out everything. The French use terror, of course, but they are too civilized to go all the way, so of course they will lose. Only the Germans and the Russians would be capable of not losing. But who would want to be a German or a Russian?"

"Do you belong to a political party?" Jack asked, interested, despite himself.

Guido laughed musically. "I work day and night," Guido said. "When could I have time to belong to a political party?"

"But you vote, don't you?"

"Of course," said Guido.

"What party do you vote for?"

"The Communist party," Guido said promptly. "Naturally. If you earn sixteen hundred lire a day, what party can you vote for?" The car was stopped at a traffic light and he turned to Jack. "No offense meant," he said politely. "Actually, it is a sign of my respect for you, Monsieur Andrus, my telling you. When other Americans ask me for whom I vote, I always say the Monarchists. The Americans seem to like that better. But you have lived in France, you understand Europe, even though you are a rich American. There is no reason I cannot tell you the truth."

He turned back to his driving. At the next light, he swung around again. "Of course, I am not a Communist," he said. "I only vote to show my contempt."

When they got to Veronica's hotel, Jack went into the lobby, half expecting to see the night porter still sitting facing the mirror, adoring himself. But there was a severe-looking old man with concierge's keys on the collar of his uniform who was behind the desk now. He spoke no English or French and all he kept saying when Jack gave him Veronica's name was, *"La signorina è partita."*

Jack's Italian was not up to finding out any more than that, but a German priest who came down the steps took pity on him and said he spoke some English and offered to act as translator.

"I understand," Jack said to the priest, "that Signorina Rienzi has left. Will you be good enough to ask if she has left a forwarding address?"

He watched the concierge shake his head when the priest translated the question.

"Ask him," Jack said, "what time she left?"

"Alle dieci," the concierge said.

"Ten o'clock," Jack said to the priest. "I understand." His throat was beginning to feel very dry. "Ask him if she left alone, or if there was a gentleman with her."

In heavy, Teutonic Italian, the priest translated. The concierge now seemed annoyed with the interrogation, and began to make notations on a series of cards on the desk. *"Sì,"* he said.

"Ask him if he knows what the gentleman looked like. Was it a young American with glasses, wearing a kind of khaki-colored overcoat?"

When the priest translated the question, the concierge glanced coldly at Jack. There was no doubt about what the concierge felt concerning aging foreigners who pursued young Italian virgins with such persistence. He spoke to the priest with a rising, cutting inflection in his voice.

"The concierge sayss he hass a multitude of osser ssinks to do besides taking desscriptions of vissitors to the *albergo,*" the priest said. The phone rang then and the concierge began to talk fretfully and at length to whoever was on the other end of the wire. Jack waited for a moment, then knew there was no satisfaction to be gained there. He thanked the priest, who beamed at him, to show that he was glad to be of service and that he held no ill-will against Jack for having won the war, and Jack went out to the little square

n front of the hotel, where Guido was polishing the Fiat's head-
ights with a rag.

Jack stayed in his room all afternoon, cursing himself for not
aaving extorted from Veronica the address of the friend with whom
she was supposed to be staying. There was no call from anybody all
afternoon, and by six o'clock, he was sure that something dreadful
had happened to her. He reread the insane note that Bresach had
slipped under the door during the night, and a shiver of apprehension chilled him. He found it ominous that Bresach was now avoid-
ng him. If I don't hear from her by tomorrow afternoon, he decided, I'm going to go to the police.

That night he was awakened again and again by the ringing of
elephone bells. But when he opened his eyes, the room was silent,
no bells were ringing.

In the morning he knew that he would have to find Bresach. But
the only people he could think of who knew where Bresach lived
were Veronica and Jean-Baptiste Despière. And Veronica was
gone and Despière was in Algeria, atrocity-hunting, address unknown. Before leaving for the studio, Jack went downstairs to the
obby and looked, without much hope, in the Rome telephone book.
There was no Bresach. He hadn't expected there would be.

The morning held a surprise for him. Without warning, he suddenly felt confident and easy, and he did very well with the scenes
he was dubbing.

"You have been touched by the spirit, boy," Delaney said, beaming. "You're fine. I told you all you needed was a good night's
leep, didn't I?"

"Yes," Jack said, "you told me."

That afternoon he went to the Embassy to see if anyone there
knew where Bresach lived or whether he had left his address there,
as Americans living in Rome for more than three months were supposed to do. But he didn't have much hope of that, either. Bresach
was not the sort of boy who would bother with the American Embassy.

When he was coming out of the Embassy he ran into Kern. Kern
was dressed in dark gray, and as usual, he had the air of a man who
aas just spoken on an equal basis with the head of a powerful state.
He stopped and smiled his slightly unpleasant smile at Jack. "I
aave been working on the case of your friend," he said.

"What's that?" Jack asked, confused. He had been thinking so concentratedly about Veronica that it was only with a wrench that he could make himself try to understand what Kern was talking about.

"Your friend Holt," Kern said. "He was in to see me and I told him I would take what steps I could."

"Oh, good," Jack said. "Thanks." He had forgotten all about Holt and his attempts to adopt a child. So much had happened since his conversation with Kern that it all seemed remote, blurred by time.

"I had been waiting for you to call me," Kern said, slowly and portentously nodding his yellowed head. "I thought we might get together for a drink."

"I've been meaning to," Jack said, wanting to get away. "But I've been terribly busy."

"I'm having some people in after dinner tonight, at my place," Kern said. "It might be interesting for you. All Italians. I don't imagine you know many Italians, do you?"

"Too many," Jack said, annoyed with the man for the smug offer of Italians, like a hunter who invites you to his house to dine off the pheasant he has just shot.

"I imagine you're joking," Kern said.

"Yes."

"I always make a point of centering as much of my social life as possible around the people of the country I'm stationed in," Kern said, making it sound like a rebuke to Jack and others like him who, Kern implied, frivolously wasted their time on mere Americans. "Even in the Middle East, where it was considerably more difficult, I kept to it. Would you like to come?"

"I'm afraid I can't tonight," Jack said.

"In any event . . ." Kern reached into his pocket, took out his wallet, and produced a card. "Here's my address. Try and make it if you can. We'll be there until quite late."

"Thanks," Jack said, pocketing the card. "I'll try. Well, so long I . . ."

"I found out a curious thing about your friend," Kern said. "I wonder if you knew."

"What's that?" Jack asked impatiently.

"He was a felon," Kern said. "He served time in prison. Did you know that?"

Jack hesitated, uncomfortable under the saffron, sardonic stare

The hell with it, he thought, he's not going to make me lie. "Yes," he said. "I knew it."

Kern nodded with a kind of mournful pleasure. "And yet you didn't think it necessary to tell me?" he said. "You were prepared to allow me to vouch for him to my Italian friends in this extremely delicate affair?"

"Oh, hell, Kern," Jack said impatiently, "he was in prison when he was twenty years old. It's all ancient history. He's a pillar of respectability now. How important is it?"

"You have a peculiar notion of what's important and what isn't important, Andrus," said Kern.

"Did Holt tell you himself?"

"No." Kern smiled with gloomy satisfaction. "I found out myself. In the course of my inquiries." He peered mistrustfully at Jack. "I wonder if there's any other pertinent information in your possession, Andrus, that I ought to have, before I go any deeper into this."

His wife's a dipsomaniac, Jack thought. That's pertinent. But I'll be godamned if I'll tell you. Find it out for yourself in the course of your inquiries, brother. "He's got a kind and generous heart," Jack said. "Is that pertinent?"

Kern sniffed. "Hardly," he said. He extended his hand. "Try and make it tonight, if you can. The view from my apartment is the best in Rome." He went gravely, ambassadorially, into the Embassy.

Jack hurried off, anxious to avoid meeting anyone else who might waste his time. He kept calling his hotel, asking if there were any messages for him, but there never were any messages, and finally the telephone operators, recognizing him, turned sullen when they heard his voice. He drank innumerable cups of coffee, sitting outside Doney's on the Via Veneto, although it was chilly and raw, because he hoped that Miss Henken, whom he had met there at the same time with Veronica, might appear and give him the information he was looking for. But Miss Henken didn't appear.

It was while he was sitting there, at the little table, sipping his ninth coffee of the afternoon, and feeling almost drunk from all the concentrated caffeine he had imbibed that he thought of Dr. Gildermeister.

"*At five o'clock every afternoon,*" he remembered Veronica's saying, "*he goes to his analyst.*" And, at another time, on the beach Fregene—"*Dr. Gildermeister. An Austrian from Innsbruck. 'I*

215

must warn you, young lady, Robert is a very finely balanced mech anism.' That was news. Hot from Innsbruck."

Jack jumped up and put a five-hundred-lire note for his coffee under a saucer on the table to keep it from blowing away. He went inside to the telephone booth and waited impatiently while a young man in a leather wind-jacket ruffled through the pages of the directory there, making notes of names and addresses in a greasy little black notebook. Uncharitably, Jack thought that he looked like a professional housebreaker making up a list of victims for his next year's haul. Finally the man in the windbreaker was through and Jack turned to the G's. It was true that in Europe you almost never could find anybody in the telephone directory of any city, but a doctor, even a psychoanalyst, must have his name and number and address available for the public. Jack was surprised to feel his hands shaking, and when he finally found the name, the print seemed to blur before his eyes in the bad light, and he had to lean way over, close to the page, to read Gildermeister, Dr. J. C., and an address on Via Monte Parioli, and the telephone number.

He started to dial the doctor's number, then stopped. He looked at his watch. It was three fifteen. Five o'clock, every afternoon Veronica had said. He hesitated, then decided to wait till five o'clock, so that he could talk to Bresach himself.

On his way back to his hotel, he was nearly run over by a man on a Vespa, who smiled gently and forgivingly at him as Jack leaped back onto the sidewalk. In Paris, the man almost certainly would have snarled, *"Sal con,"* at him, after a similar incident. There were advantages to being in Italy after all.

There was an air-mail letter waiting for him at the desk, from his son. He opened the letter as soon as he entered his rooms, and read it, standing next to the open window, with the sunlight streaming in on the typewritten pages.

"Father," the letter began, "I've just read the letter you wrote me from the airplane, and there's no sense in dissembling what I feel about it or trying to be polite about it.

"I detest it.

"What's more, I detest the whole way of life that makes it possible for a father to write a letter like that to his son."

Oh, Christ, Jack thought, not today! For a moment he contemplated crumpling the letter and throwing it away. Then he made himself read on.

"First of all—about Miss McCarthy. I assure you that if we

marry, we will make it stick. I do not need the advice of a cynical sensualist who has led a blatantly promiscuous life to guide me in matters of love. Don't think that because you've hardly ever bothered to see me that I am completely uninformed about you."

Jack grinned painfully as he read this. His mother has told him the facts of life, he thought. My life. If he only knew what it's really been like. Maybe I'll write him the truth—that it is not the promiscuousness I regret, but the occasions, all too many, of abstinence. See what the Puritan has to say about *that*.

"As for my so-called political activities," the letter went on, "you've obviously been coached on that subject by my mother, who is a hysterically nervous woman, a condition which I have no doubt you did your best to aggravate. She is married to a timid, third-rate man, whose mumblings would not be taken seriously by an intelligent ten-year-old child. As far as you're concerned, the position you hold, and which you seem so proud of, makes everything you say suspect. Your whole job, your salary, the soft life you lead in Paris with your frivolous wife, all depend upon your being a willing stooge for the system. Do the generals call for bigger bombs and bigger tests? You've got to say yes to them. Is the level of radioactivity rising dangerously throughout the world? You've got to pretend it is the propaganda of Communists and professional alarmists. Do most sane people think that giving atomic weapons to the Germans is like putting a loaded pistol in a criminal lunatic's hands? You've got to make believe you think the Germans are kindly, gentle folk whose reputation has been somehow blackened by a conspiracy of villains. I left Paris so abruptly last summer, because I didn't want to have to tell you these things. But now your letter has forced me to write what I feel.

"You advise me to be reticent. Like you, I suppose. Your reticence has been bought, and in your letter you suggest what price I might expect for mine. I tell you, if we all came as cheap as you, our reticence would bring us, very quickly, to a world of freaks and ruins.

"You write that the government is perfectly prepared and willing to hand out punishments to the men who oppose its policies. In saying that, I know you meant to get me to stop opposing those policies, even though I believe they are inhuman and suicidal. In reply, I'd use exactly the same argument to you to try to make you get out of the system, where every move you make, however insignificant and harmless it may be in itself, is a tacit vote of support and approval. You are not highly placed enough to oppose policy from within. All you can do is obey. If you think you are obeying sane and reasonable orders which will lead to a peaceful, healthy world, you are a fool, and I will have nothing to do with you. If you obey out of timidity and love of comfort, you are a coward, and I will have nothing to do with you. If you decide at any time to get out and come back to America, where it counts, and speak your mind, I will be most happy to treat you as my father.

Steven."

The sheets of air-mail paper were shaking in Jack's hands as he finished. He felt bruised and battered. This is what I started, he thought, the night I looked down into the crib on Twelfth Street and was sorry he had been born.

That is the end of my son, he thought, and crumpled the letter into a ball and threw it into the wastebasket and sat down on the edge of the desk, with his hands trembling.

There was no answer possible. The wall of arrogance, of hatred, finally revealed, was impossible to breach. The calm and reasonable arguments which could, with so much justice, be used to attack his son's position, would have no effect.

He remembered, with annoyance, his son's description of Hélène. Your frivolous wife. The idiot, he thought, she is gay, not frivolous. Even at twenty-two, a man should be able to tell the difference.

I should feel worse, Jack thought, looking down at the crumpled ball of paper in the wastebasket. A normal father would be in despair. He was angry and regretful, but no more. This afternoon it was more important to him to find a young girl whom he had met by chance on a street in Rome and who had disappeared than to come to grips with his estranged son. Maybe some other afternoon all this would change. Maybe some other afternoon he would feel he had to search out his son and give him his answer. But not this afternoon.

He went into the bedroom, picked up the script of Delaney's picture, and lay down on the bed to study the scenes he had to do the next day. At five o'clock, sharp, he called the number of Dr Gildermeister.

A man's voice answered, after three rings. *"Pronto,"* the man said.

"Signor Bresach, *per favore,"* Jack said.

The man talked for thirty seconds in Italian that even Jack could tell was marked by a heavy German accent.

"Do you speak English?" Jack asked.

"Yes."

"I would like to speak to Mr. Bresach, please."

"Not here," the man said impatiently.

"Is this Dr. Gildermeister?"

"This is Dr. Gildermeister. Who are you? What do you want?"

"This is a friend of Mr. Bresach's, Doctor," Jack said. He spoke quickly, because he had the impression that the man was on the verge of hanging up. "I understood that Mr. Bresach came to see you every day at five o'clock."

"Well, he is not here now," the man said testily. "He has not come for the last three days."

A small shrill of alarm rang somewhere in Jack's brain at this news. "Oh, I see," he said, trying to sound offhand. "That's too bad. It's about a job that's come up that I'm sure Mr. Bresach would be interested in."

"A job? What sort of a job?"

"A movie company is . . ." Jack began.

"I see, I see," the man said. "Well, he is not here."

"I wonder if you can tell me his telephone number," Jack said.

"He has no telephone."

"Could you let me have his address?" There was silence on the other end and Jack waited, tensely.

"Ah, why not?" the man said. He shouted the address, and Jack wrote it down. "And while you're at it," the man said furiously, "you might tell him it is absurd to skip three days. Absurd. That is no way for a sick man to behave. Tell him I am waiting for him, I am worried about him, and I expect to see him here tomorrow."

"I'll tell him. Thank you," Jack said, and hung up.

16

The address that Dr. Gildermeister had given Jack was that of
building on a narrow cobbled street without sidewalks not fro
the Palazzo Farnese. The building was dark with age, a cracke
fountain leaked in the courtyard, the windows along the wor
marble staircase were broken and there was a dank smell of wir
ter, like a cold river passing over stone, in the hallway. Chippe
plaster angels, darkened with soot, gave evidence that in the distar
past the inhabitants of the building had combined piety and wealtl
The heavy black wood doors on the landings looked like priso
entrances. Mingled with the smell of cats and winter there was th
peculiar sour cheese smell of Italian poverty.

Bresach lived on the fourth floor. Jack stood in front of th
heavy door, taking a little longer than was necessary to catch h
breath after the climb. Then he knocked on the door. While h
waited he heard children playing on the floor below and a radi

screeching out, " *'Volare, oh, oh! . . . Cantare . . . oh, oh, oh, oh!' "* loudly.

It was hard to imagine Veronica, with her shining long hair and her bright clothes, climbing these stairs and using her own key to enter the apartment behind the grimy door.

Jack knocked again. The door swung open, as though whoever was behind it had been waiting there silently, hoping that the knock would not be repeated and the door need not be opened. There was a man standing in the mouth of what seemed to be a dark tunnel, holding the door half-open. But it was not Bresach. The man was tall and a little stooped and he wore glasses and he was wearing a sweater and had a scholarly, gentle face and in-quisitive, weak eyes.

"Yes?" the man said.

From behind him, at the other end of the tunnel, which Jack now saw was an entrance hall that led, at right angles, into a room, there came the sound of typing, rapid and nervous.

"I'm looking for Robert Bresach," Jack said. "Is he in?" He moved a little closer, prepared to thrust his foot in the door if the man tried to close it.

But the man merely called back down the tunnel. "Robert, it's somebody looking for you." The man had an accent, not too strong, that was difficult to place at the moment.

The typing stopped. "Tell him to come in," Bresach's voice called out.

The man in the sweater smiled in a friendly manner and made a little, almost courtly bow as he opened the door wide and indicated to Jack that he should enter. The typing started up again as Jack went down the hall, which was hung with clothes, among them the khaki duffel coat. Jack turned into the room. It was small and ir-regular, but there were two long windows leading out onto a small balcony with an iron railing, and there was a jumbled view of ter-races, vines with their roots three stories in the air, washing, roof-tops, and the evening sky, filled by soft gray clouds, with patches of deepening blue, over the city of Rome. In front of one window there was a small table and Bresach was sitting at it, his back to the room, typing intently, by touch, bent over, peering at a pile of manuscript which he seemed to be copying or translating. He didn't turn around. He was smoking, and he had obviously been smoking a good deal, because the air of the room, with its closed windows, was hazy. There was one big bed, covered with an old piece of brocade, and a table in one corner on which stood a hot plate and a coffee pot. There were two or three wooden chairs, one of them broken, and a washbasin, and more clothes hung, neatly enough, on hooks along one wall. There were books on the floor. A large painting, done mostly in yellow and black, of a not quite recognizable animal, either in ecstasy or in terror, hung over the bed, and there was a cracked and gilded wooden crucifix about two feet high, leaning casually in a corner. The gilt was almost all flaked off the body of Christ and the limbs had a disconcerting uneven texture that realistically suggested flesh. There was no sign in the room that a woman had ever lived there.

There was only the one doorway, and the single room constituted the entire apartment. If a girl like Veronica were to come to live with you in a place like this, Jack thought, naturally you'd believe she loved you.

"Robert," said the soft, accented voice of the man in the sweater. He had followed Jack into the room.

Bresach finished a page, dragged it from the typewriter and put it down on top of a pile on the floor. Then he swung around. He looked gravely at Jack, squinting through his glasses. He needed a shave and there was a light, uneven stubble on his jaws and chin and he seemed tired and young and in trouble.

"Look who's here," he said flatly. "What's the matter—didn't you like my message?" He didn't stand up.

"I want to talk to you," Jack said.

"All right," Bresach said. "Talk." He took a cigarette from a crumpled pack and tossed the pack to the man in the sweater. He did not offer a cigarette to Jack.

"I think we'd better do it alone," Jack said, looking over at the man in the sweater, who was lighting his cigarette with extreme care, cupping his hands around the little wax match as though he were standing in a high wind.

"Max can hear anything you have to say," Bresach said. On his own ground he seemed sure of himself, offhand, sardonic. "I have nothing to hide from Max. Max, this is Mr. Andrus. I told you about him."

"Delighted," Max said. He made a half bow. "Robert has told me enormously about you." There was no irony or reproach in the man's voice.

"Max lives here," Bresach said. "He moved in when half a bed

222

fell unexpectedly vacant. You wouldn't want to chase a man out of his own house, would you, Andrus?"

"Robert," Max said, "I could easily go stand in the hall and smoke my cigarette while . . ."

"Stay where you are," Bresach said loudly. "Well"—he peered malevolently at Jack through his glasses—"how's flaming middle-age these days?"

Jack walked over to a chair near Bresach and sat down. "When you stop joking," he said, "I'll talk to you."

"Ever since Max moved in here," Bresach said, "the place has been ringing with childish laughter. Max is a Hungarian, and everybody knows that Hungarians are noted for their gaiety. We're saving up to buy him a violin, so we'll have it with music. He left all his violins in Budapest when the Russians brought up the tanks."

"Bresach," Jack said, "why've you stopped going to see Gildermeister the last three days?"

"Huh?" Bresach made a nervous, twitchy movement with his shoulders, and he stubbed the almost unsmoked cigarette out in an ashtray on the table. "What're you talking about?"

"I called the doctor," Jack said. "That's how I got your address. He's worried about you."

"He is?" Bresach said flatly. "Well, I'm worried about him. There aren't enough lunatics in Italy to keep a psychiatrist alive. I've promised him that when my godamn old man dies and leaves me his money I'll pay his passage to the States. Fifty dollars an hour I promised him. On Park Avenue."

"Why haven't you been to see him for three days?" Jack repeated, watching the boy closely.

"What the hell is it to you?" Bresach said. "Look—I'm busy. I'm translating a six-hundred-page book from the Italian and my Italian stinks. I promised it in four weeks. Leave me alone."

"Where's Veronica?" Jack asked softly. "What've you done with her?"

"Me?" Bresach said. "What're you talking about?"

"Where is she?" Jack stood up. He would have loved to take the grinning, sardonic boy by his skinny throat and strangle the truth out of him. At that moment he understood, for the first time, the passion of policemen who beat prisoners to obtain confessions.

"How do I know where she is?" Bresach said. "I haven't seen her since the day she walked out of here."

"Why did you stop seeing Gildermeister?"

"What the hell is it to you?" The nervous tic pulled at the corner of his mouth. "If you must know, I got tired of the old man. He was beginning to play God. I've had enough of that. I felt it was about time to give my poor old psyche a rest for a while." He jumped up suddenly and flung the window open. "Ah, it stinks in here," he said. "All this smoke." He peered out over the rooftops. "Try to find anybody in this city," he said bitterly. He turned on Jack. "If anything bad has happened to her," he said, "you're going to pay for it. I swear it. The next time you won't get away."

"Robert," Max said softly.

"I was trying to forget the whole godamn thing," Robert shouted at Jack. "I tried everything else, and now I was trying that. Now you come and start all over again. What do you want from me?"

Unless Bresach was the best actor in the world, Jack decided, he had had nothing to do with Veronica's disappearance. It was reassuring; it almost eliminated the possibility of violence; but Veronica was missing just the same. Now Jack's feeling of responsibility for the girl was mingled with irritation. If she weren't dead, she could have sent some sort of message. Unless . . . Unless what? Ex-lovers were not the only danger that young women risked in Rome, or anywhere. There were the melodramatic dangers to consider, like kidnapping and murder, and the prosaic dangers, like being run over by an automobile or suddenly falling ill. If Veronica were lying at this moment, unconscious, in a hospital, there would be no reason for the authorities to notify Jack or Bresach. Whatever had happened to her, Jack knew that he couldn't leave the city without finding her.

"I asked you a question," Bresach shouted. "What do you want from me?"

"I want you to help me find her," Jack said.

Bresach stared at him somberly. Then he laughed. The laugh sounded more like a strangled cough than a laugh. "Christ," he said, "that's a twist, isn't it? What makes you think I'd want to help you find her?"

"Because," Jack said, "if we don't find her, you'll lose all hope of ever getting her back."

The tic pulled erratically at Bresach's mouth. His eyes were cold and crazy as he stared at Jack. At that moment, Jack realized how close Bresach had come to using the knife on him the first night, how little it would take to drive Bresach to use it now.

224

"Okay," Bresach said hoarsely. "Okay, you miserable, reasonable bastard, I'll help you."

"Good," Jack said calmly. "Now—you know her friends. Let's start calling them."

Bresach sat down wearily. His energy seemed to come in sudden nervous spurts, in an irregular rhythm. "I've called them all," he said. "Ten times. They don't know where she is. Or if they do, they won't tell me."

"Anyway, we can try," Jack said. "How about her family? You told me they live in Florence and she visits them every weekend."

"Her mother and sister live in Florence," Bresach said. "With the sister's husband. But it isn't the weekend."

"Do you have her mother's telephone number?"

"Her mother doesn't have a telephone," Bresach said. "I never could call her."

"Well, we'll send a telegram," Jack said. "And after that we'll start making the telephone calls."

They went to a small hotel nearby to send the telegram. Max came along with them. Jack was grateful for his presence now, as a buffer between Bresach and himself. Bresach had put on his duffel coat over his shirt and Max, who didn't have an overcoat, had merely wound a red wool scarf around his throat and put on a fuzzy, faded green hat. The clerk behind the desk was busy with two Swiss tourists in black leather overcoats, and there was plenty of time to compose the telegram.

"If I sign it," Bresach said, "and Veronica's there or if they get in touch with her, they'll never answer me. They don't like me, anyway, even though they've never met me, because I'm a dirty heathen or because I have designs on Veronica or whatever, and they'll be delighted at a chance to baffle me. If you sign it . . ." He stared thoughtfully at Jack. "Do you think Veronica would have said anything to her family about you?"

"I doubt it," Jack said.

"No, girls don't go home and tell their God-loving mothers that they're sleeping with somebody else's husband. So if you signed it, just like that, they wouldn't know what you were talking about. Also, we don't want to get the family alarmed and running to the police, do we?" He grinned maliciously at Jack. "And have them asking, 'And just exactly what were your relations with the young lady, Mr. Andrus?' "

"We'll go to the police if we have to," Jack said. He thought for a moment. Then he took a telegraph blank from the desk and wrote, "A friend of your daughter, Jean-Baptiste Despière, has told me that she is interested in working for a travel bureau in Paris. The bureau with which I do business is looking for a young woman who can speak Italian, French and English. Could you wire me your daughter's address and telephone number so that I can get into contact with her." Then he signed his name and wrote the name of his hotel under it.

"I think this will do it," he said, handing the sheet to Bresach. "Better translate it."

Bresach read the message. "She speaks Spanish, too," he said.

"Put that in, too."

"Missing in four languages," Bresach said. He shook his head. The flippness and bravado were gone now and he seemed helpless and sad. He translated the message and gave it to the man behind the desk and refused to let Jack pay for it. "I'm more interested than you in finding her," he said stubbornly. "No matter what you say."

Jack and the Hungarian were standing at a little neon-lit, chrome bar with a huge gilded *espresso* machine. The telephone was at the back of the bar, and they could see Robert putting in one token after another and patiently dialing, patiently explaining, resignedly hanging up and starting all over again in his round of calls to Veronica's friends. Jack was drinking brandy and the Hungarian vermouth. Across from the bar there was an American pinball machine around which a group of young men were standing watching the players. The pinball machine made a grinding, gearlike noise and bells clanged when the ball hit the posts.

"He is a warm-hearted gentleman," Max said, indicating Robert. "It is not often that you find such sweetness of soul in a man so young. I have known him for over a year, since I first came here, and he has fed me and clothed me, and now he has taken me in. Even though we have to share the same bed. But he knew that I was living in the same room with four other people and I was sleeping on the floor. I must confess, he has made me revise my estimate completely of Americans."

"Be careful," Jack said, drinking his sweetish brandy. "Not all Americans are like that." Then he added, "Thank God."

"He is a boy who is born to sorrow," Max said softly. "So he is gentle with the sorrow of others. It is too bad about the girl. He loves her so much. Too much. That is no doubt why she left him. Even if one loves that much, one must hide some of it. For self-preservation. He wanted to own every minute of her life. That, one does not do. One must drink the wine of love, but one must leave a little in the glass, too."

Jack regarded the man with curiosity and respect. What Max had said seemed, at the moment, one of the sanest things he had heard on the subject of love in a long time. "Tell me," he said, "how does it happen that you speak English so well?"

Max smiled. "I am fifty years old," he said. "When I was a boy my family was rich. When you were rich in those days, you had an English nanny. And I went to school in England for two years, besides."

"Were you in Hungary during the war?" Jack asked curiously. It was a question he found himself asking all Europeans whose countries had been on the German side betwen 1940 and 1945.

"Which war?" Max asked.

"World War Two," said Jack. Somehow, it hadn't occurred to him that a Hungarian might call the few bloody days of the Budapest uprising a war.

"No," said Max. "I was not in Hungary for all of World War Two. I got out in 1943, when it was still possible to move around Europe a little. I got into Austria, and then, one night, I crossed the border into Switzerland secretly."

"Was it as easy as that?" Jack asked incredulously.

"Not quite. I bribed a railroad guard and he locked us in a baggage wagon."

"Us?" Jack said. "How many of you were there?"

"Seven," Max said simply. "My wife and my sister and her husband and their three children. I gave the guard at Buchs a bottle of cognac and half a package of cigarettes. That was all we had."

Seven lives, Jack thought, for a bottle of cognac and ten cigarettes. The price has gone up since then.

"The Swiss were admirable," Max said, defending Europe. He smiled wryly. "It is true that my firm still had some assets in the country and we could pay our way. They permitted me to choose our place of internment. I chose a ski resort. I became quite a good skier by the time the war was finished."

"Then you went back to Hungary?"

"Of course," Max said. "It was very hopeful there—for a while. We had two large factories—woolen factories—and I got them back.

227

For a time. Then, when the Communists took over, I stayed on as manager."

"How was it, working for the Communists?" Jack asked.

Max laughed softly. "Not so bad. In the beginning. Then they began to crack down. They would give us impossible norms to produce. In the beginning, you could argue with them. Then, later on, if you didn't meet the quota, you would be put in jail for sabotage. What most people did was say that the men under them were responsible for sabotage. Then those men would blame the men under them. And so on. Finally, it would get down to two or three men at the machines, who would be sent to jail. Then there would be peace for a month or two. Then the whole process would be repeated again."

"Oh, Christ," Jack said. He watched Bresach drop his tenth token into the telephone at the back of the bar. "How can people live like that?"

Max shrugged, swishing his vermouth thoughtfully around in his glass. "People live the way they can," he said. "After all, half the world is living like that now." He smiled apologetically. "I could not really do it," he said. "I could not send people to prison to keep out of prison myself. Perhaps it was all those years with the English nanny. I knew I had to get out. So when the Revolution broke out, I crossed the border. It is not so bad. I have always adored Italy."

Jack shook his head, thinking of the multiple exiles of the twentieth century, the borders crossed and recrossed under the guns, the modest, recurrent escapes. "Is your wife here in Rome with you, too?" he asked.

"No," Max said. "She died five years ago. In Hungary. I am quite alone."

"What do you think is going to happen in Hungary?" Jack asked.

"Nothing," said Max. "That is, it is going to get worse. And, eventually, of course, when they feel they are strong enough, the Russians are going to drop the bomb. On everybody."

"You don't see any other way out?"

Max smiled gently. "Do you?"

"I don't know," Jack said, thinking, Maybe Steve ought to come over here and talk to this man before he writes any more letters. "It is important to be optimistic."

"It is easier for Americans, perhaps. To be optimistic, I mean,"

Max said. "Of course, you had your chance and you missed it. Right after the war, *you* should have dropped the bomb."

"We couldn't have done that."

Max shrugged. "I suppose you must have had your reasons," he said. "Still, it was the only thing that could have saved you."

Bresach came back to the bar from the telephone booth. "Nobody has seen her," he said. "Now what?"

"Have a drink," Jack said. "You look as though you need it."

This time they all had brandy. It was past eight o'clock. Jack looked at the other two, the stooped, scholarly-looking, gentle-voiced man with the red wool scarf, adrift in Europe, and the exhausted, tortured boy. He felt tied to them, responsible to them. Suddenly it seemed terribly important to him that they should not leave each other. And, besides, he knew he had to stave off the inevitable hour when he would be alone in the night. "I have an idea," he said. "It's time to eat. Let me take you to dinner."

Max looked inquisitively at Bresach. "Why not?" Bresach said. "Why shouldn't you feed us? It's the least you can do. Take us to a good restaurant."

They had another brandy and then went off to dinner.

17

Bresach chose the restaurant. He had never been there before but he had heard Veronica speak of it once. Veronica had said she hadn't liked it and wouldn't go there again. On the assumption that if Veronica were still in Rome she would avoid the places where she had been with either Bresach or Jack, Bresach fixed on this one restaurant which he had heard her condemn.

She was not there.

It was a nondescript little *trattoria* and the food was no better and no worse than might be found in a hundred other *trattorie* of the city, and Jack had to agree with Bresach that Veronica must have had some ulterior reason for having kept Bresach away from it.

They had had two carafes of red wine and Bresach's face was flushed and he was talking all the time. Both he and Max, Jack noticed, devoured their food voraciously. Although it was warm in the restaurant, Bresach was still in his duffel coat, because he wasn't wearing a jacket.

"When I got out of the army," Bresach was saying, "I told my father to go to hell. I had a fifty-dollar-a-month pension and I met a man who was trying to make a documentary movie in New York and . . ."

"Why did they give you a pension?" Jack asked, puzzled. "What war were *you* in?"

"No war," Bresach said. "I'm not the stuff that heroes're made of. I got blown up in rehearsal. That's more my style. A mortar exploded in training and my knee nearly was torn off. They did a good job on it, though. I only limp when it rains. My father was furious. He wrote everybody. He felt the country wasn't showing him the proper respect, letting his son get blown up like that. He was even nice to me for two weeks. He gave me seventy-five dollars to take a vacation on Cape Cod. But I used most of it to pay a month's rent on a room on West Fourth Street, and then I broke the news to him that I wasn't going into his godamn business."

"What business is he in?" Jack asked.

"He makes paper cartons. He's the paper-carton king," Bresach said. "He regards paper cartons with a religious light in his eye. As far as he's concerned, the ability to make paper cartons is what distinguishes man from the beasts. When I told him I wouldn't go to work for him, it was like a bishop's son telling his father that he didn't believe in the existence of God. We had an all-night scene. He said I wanted to fiddle with the movies because I was too lazy to work and only wanted to hang around with cheap women and pansies. He told me he wouldn't ever give me a cent again and he'd cut me off in his will. My father's idea of a father goes back to the tribes of Israel. He and Mr. Barrett would've been the greatest buddies of all time. My mother sat around wringing her hands and weeping. Evenings in our house came right out of *Stella Dallas*. In the middle of his biggest speeches, I couldn't help busting out laughing. Every time I did that, he'd turn on my mother and yell, 'See what you've done?' Then my mother'd bawl all over again. I think my poor mother must hold the all-time record for female tears shed in America. What about *your* father?" he demanded. "What did *he* say when you told him you wanted to be an actor."

"He said, 'Be a good actor,' " Jack said.

"I told you, the last time I saw you," Bresach said bitterly, "you're a born lucky man. You even have a father like that."

"Had," Jack said. "He's dead now."

"Even more luck." Bresach poured himself some wine. The tablecloth in front of him was red with the wine he had spilled earlier in the evening.

"How did you happen to come to Italy?" Jack asked. He didn't want to talk about his father.

"Well, the man making the documentary picture went broke. Finally, I was doing everything, carrying cameras, hustling credit from the film-developing company, working in the cutting room. Twenty hours a day. Without pay. For a while I was eating on twenty cents a day. Then on nothing. I came down with pneumonia. My mother claimed my body from the authorities and took me home to nurse me. My father never came into my room. He was waiting for me to come to him and get on my knees and beg him to forgive me and tell him that I had seen the light, I would devote my life to paper cartons from then on. But while I was getting over the pneumonia I decided I had to come to Italy. The Italians were making the only pictures that wouldn't make an honest man vomit in the projection room. If you were serious about movies this was the only place you could come to learn. You know why the Italians have made the good pictures? Because they openly and unashamedly take pleasure in each other. They take pleasure in the whole Italian—in his vices and absurdities as well as in his virtues. They see the joke at the funeral, the corruption in the virgin, the holiness and the impiety at the same altar. When an American artist looks at a fellow-American his first reaction is a shudder of disgust. That's all right as far as it goes, but it's no basis for a whole art."

"What made you so sure you wanted to make pictures?" Jack asked curiously.

"The great art of the twentieth century," Bresach said portentously, "is going to come out of the movies. It's just made a beginning, the first stumbling steps." Bresach was waving his hands excitedly, obsessed with his vision. "All the beauty, all the tragedy and nerve of this century are finally going to be put on film, and every other art form is going to decay around it. The Shakespeare of this century is going to be a movie director. And he won't be working for just a few thousand people, locked into one language. He'll work for the whole world. He'll speak directly, without words, to the millions, and they'll understand him. Indians, Chinese, the Russian brute in Siberia, the fellagha, the peon, the coolie, the factory slave . . ." Bresach was talking almost incoherently now. "The lights'll dim in the smelliest little converted barn at the furthest end of the earth, and he'll go directly to every heart, he'll show them what it's like, what it is to be a man alive, black, brown, yellow, or white, what there is to hope for. He'll be their darling brother, their teacher, their creator, their entertainer, their love. Look at Chaplin. Who in our time has ever had a kingdom like the kingdom of Charlie Chaplin? I'm ambitious. I covet that kingdom." Bresach laughed hoarsely. "And naturally, we kicked him out, naturally we exiled him. For the whole world he represented the best thing that had come out of America in the twentieth century, so we couldn't bear it. We couldn't stand his light, malicious, brotherly, godlike laughter, so we cleansed ourselves of him. Do you know a man by the name of McGranery?"

Jack hesitated, trying to remember. "Yes," he said. "He was the Attorney General who signed the order that barred Chaplin from the United States."

"There!" Bresach crowed triumphantly, waving his arms, spilling more wine. "McGranery is immortal. If he hadn't done in Chaplin, his name would vanish like dogpiss on a hot rock. Now his fame rests secure. He showed the world what Americans are made of. McGranery, McGranery," he chanted crazily, "all hail McGranery, the immortal and ever-green memory of McGranery, in whose image we are made."

"Calm down," Jack said. "Everybody's watching you."

Bresach stared imperiously at the other diners in the room. There was a fat bald man with his fat wife, looking up over their *lasagne,* smiling tentatively, and a table with four middle-aged men who had stopped eating to regard Bresach with annoyed expressions on their faces. Bresach raised his hand in the Fascist salute. *"Il Duce!"* he said. "Trieste, Fiume. *Bella* Nizza."

Embarrassed, the other diners dropped their eyes and went back to their eating.

"Veronica used to complain, too, when I talked in restaurants," Bresach said. "She said I made so much noise, I must have Italian blood in me."

"Well, what's happened to you since you came here?" Jack asked. He wanted to keep Bresach off the subject of Veronica. But it wasn't only that—he was curious, too. Somehow, with the brandies and the wine and their joined quest for a missing girl, he felt involved more than ever with the boy, and interested in the events of his life, almost as if Bresach were a much younger brother who had been away for a long time, or a grown son.

"What's happened to me?" Bresach laughed bitterly. "Nothing. *Niente*. I've written a script. And I've gotten a couple of days' work as an extra in a picture about Nero, wearing a tin breastplate and helmet, and for two weeks I was permitted to run out for coffee and sandwiches for the second unit of a Hollywood company that was making a few exteriors in Venice."

"Did you learn anything?"

"I learned you have to have luck," Bresach said.

"Has anybody read what you've done on the script yet?" Jack asked.

"Yes. I have been highly praised." He laughed bitterly. "It is too good, they say, to do commercially."

"Let me read it," Jack said.

"Why?" Bresach demanded.

"Maybe I can help you."

"I do not accept money," Bresach said. "I am pure about my enemies."

"Oh, balls," Jack said. "First of all, I'm not your enemy. And second, I'm not going to give you any money."

"What, then?"

"Maybe I can get Delaney to read it. If he likes it maybe he'll take you on as an assistant," Jack said. "He's nearly finished with this picture, but there's still most of the cutting and dubbing and music to do. He's very good at all that. You could learn a lot from him. And he's almost certain to do another picture here soon." Even as he was talking, Jack was thinking that Delaney would profit more from the association than Bresach. Bresach's violence and naïve faith in the value of film might rekindle something in Delaney that had died down a long time ago.

"Delaney." Bresach made a face.

"Don't say another word," Jack said warningly. "Do you want me to talk to him or not?"

"Why're you doing this, Jack?" Bresach asked. "Out of what guilt?"

"Oh, hell," Jack said. "How many times do I have to tell you I don't feel the least bit guilty about you?"

"If I accept," Bresach said formally, "understand that the favor does not put me in your debt."

234

"I'm beginning to understand why your father was so exasperated," Jack said, "and why your mother cried."

Surprisingly, Bresach grinned, boyish, teasing, satisfied. "I'm beginning to get on your nerves," he said. "Good. Finally I'm going to get you to hate me. We are progressing."

Jack sighed. "Talk to him, Max," he said.

"Robert," Max said, "there is no law that says you must be absolutely impossible at all times."

"I want everything to be clear and well understood between us," Bresach said. "That's all. I don't want any murky passages."

"All right, I'll talk to Delaney about you," Jack said. "For what it's worth. Do you think you have talent?"

"I am a monster of talent," Bresach said gravely.

Jack laughed.

"That godamn laugh again," Bresach said.

"I'm sorry," Jack said. He had not meant to hurt the boy, but the laugh had escaped automatically. It was a gentle laugh, nostalgic even, as Jack recognized in Bresach the fierce certainty and immodesty of the untried, the young, the untested, the unwounded, the undiscovered.

"Actually," Jack said, "I'm laughing because I might have said the same thing, if anybody had asked me the same question, when I was your age."

"You crapped it away," Bresach said. "Why?"

"Be polite, Robert," Max said. "The gentleman means you no harm."

"Why?" Bresach said, disregarding Max.

"I'll write you a long letter," Jack said.

"What did you exchange it for?" Bresach said. "Your job in Paris?" He laughed harshly. "An organization of obsolete misfits pretending they can save the world with parades and belligerent statements to the newspapers, and falling into a profound, embarrassed hush whenever they hear the dirty laugh of reality outside the office door? What did you do, Jack, when the tanks came into Budapest? Where were you when the British fleet was at the mouth of the Suez Canal? What brilliant scheme did you come up with when the paratroopers tortured the fellagha in Algeria? What profound and illuminating criticisms do you make when Mr. Nasser incites everybody around him to murder everybody else around him? I know you. I know all of you . . ." Bresach said wildly.

235

"All you soft-assed, soft-voiced, soft-brained maneuverers, sitting out the twentieth century, making soft, polite little noises, whispering together at cocktail parties, to drown out the noise of atomic experiments, the ticking of bombs, the screams on the radio, the appeals for help of men who should be your friends and who are murdered between the third and fourth martini . . ."

"I do what I can," Jack said, not quite believing it, shaken, despite himself, by the violence of the boy's attack, and by the bitter echo, in his words, of the rebuke in Steve's letter. "What the hell—whatever I do, it's better than those idiotic pictures I was in."

"No," Bresach said loudly. "You were a good actor. You were honest. You weren't part of the brainless, optimistic conspiracy. If you weren't saving anybody else, at least you were saving yourself. You added to the population of the world one rescued soul. That's not to be sneered at. You shed *that* much light. Now what do you do? You spend your life spreading military darkness and political confusion. Tell me honestly, Jack, when you were twenty-two, when you made that first picture, would you have behaved the way you have here in Rome?"

"I slept with girls when I was twenty-two," Jack said, "if that's what you mean."

"You know damn well that isn't what I mean," Bresach said. "You're married now, aren't you?"

"You know I am."

"What do you tell your wife?" Bresach demanded. "Do you tell her you love her?"

"Knock off," Jack said. "Continue the lecture on politics."

"All right," Bresach went on, his tone reasonable and friendly. "You tell her you love her. But you make a mental reservation. Put it into figures. A reservation of ten percent? Twenty percent? What would you say? Two weeks in Rome in the year, maybe a couple of other weeks in London or Washington on affairs of state, with Veronicas always abundant—and that's going on the assumption that you're chaste in Paris, and I don't know why I should assume that . . ."

"You are being insulting, Robert," Max said.

"We are past insults, Jack and me," said Bresach. "We are at the point of murder. We are at the point where the truth is glaring in our eyes." He swung around again to face Jack. "What I'm saying is that your whole life is based on a system of hedging. So much commitment to love, but no total commitment, so much of a commitment in your work, but of course only an absolute idiot could commit himself there totally. The man of parts, in parts, the modern, disgraceful, useless, undependable, fragmented, vandalizing man. Is my language too strong?"

"Yes," said Jack. "But do keep going."

"On the subject of religion," Bresach said, "and what a subject that is to broach in the city of Rome. Are you a religious man?"

"No."

"Do you go to church?"

"Occasionally," Jack said.

"Ah," said Bresach, "of course. The civil servant. Ever since the Republicans got in, there has been a pious flood on Sunday mornings toward the higher brackets. Do you believe in God?"

"I have to skip that," Jack said. "Remember, I'm pressed for time. I have to leave for Paris in a few days."

"Nominally, what are you?" Bresach asked. "Protestant?"

"Lutheran," Jack said, "if anything."

Bresach nodded. "If anything. And your wife?"

Jack hesitated. "Catholic."

"And your children?"

"For the time being, they go to Mass."

"Aha," Bresach said with cold triumph. "For the time being they are the prey of superstition, of oppression, of bloody myths, of intolerance, ignorance, the worship of idols, all of which their father abhors. For the time being. You see, Max," Bresach glared at the Hungarian. "This man who has been picked from the whole teeming population of this earth to savage my life has not even the courage of his atheism, refuses even the small act of honor which would let him keep faith with his no-God. He is a slider and adjuster. Catch him by surprise and you will find him with his finger in the air, testing the wind. On some days he almost crosses himself. Worse, he permits his innocent and helpless children to cross themselves. He trims, he hesitates, he smiles at his own failings, he jokes about the gifts he has let slip through his fingers, he moves like an eel through the interstices of our society, he gets his salary by trading on everybody's fear that we're all going to be blown up tomorrow morning, he betrays his wife when he travels, he betrays himself when he breathes. Naturally women love him and fall at his feet, because he only gives himself partially, and what female can resist the partial man? He slides into bed as he sometimes slides into church, not quite believing in it, but liking the sound of the choir, the movements of the congregation, come, amen, the open thighs, amen, the douche bag, blessed be thy name, amen, married, unmarried, amen, amen!"

"Does he talk like this when he's sober?" Jack asked.

"Quite often," Max said.

"You must have some jolly evenings up at your place," Jack said.

"Don't joke," Bresach said harshly. "I'm attacking you. There will come a time when you will feel the blows, when you will weep with pain and remorse . . ." He ground some black pepper out of a big wooden mill onto the mozzarella cheese on the plate in front of him. "It's made out of buffalo milk," he said conversationally. "Did you know that?"

"No," Jack said.

"I always knew I wanted to live in a place where they milked buffaloes," Bresach said, taking a huge piece of cheese on his fork and stuffing it in his mouth. "In our country, we have got rid of the buffaloes and Charlie Chaplin. Up, McGranery."

"Don't start that again, Robert," Max said.

"So when I got better," Bresach said calmly, as though there had been no interruption in his story about himself and his family, "I blackmailed my mother into hocking a ring and giving me the money to come to Italy. I told her that if I hadn't gotten started in the movies in one year, I'd come back and make paper cartons for the rest of my life and honor my mother and father like a good boy. By the way, Andrus, what did your father do?"

"He had a small fruit-drying plant in California."

"God, the way people spend their lives," Bresach said. "Did he have a holy feeling about dried fruit?"

"No," Jack said. "It was just a way of earning a living. He didn't take business very seriously. As long as he made enough to support his family and buy the books he liked that was all he wanted."

"Was he American?"

"Yes."

"It was a lucky thing he died before McGranery got around to him."

"Robert," Max said warningly.

"I am learning everything I can about the man who is the most important man in the world to me," Bresach said, "John Andrus. Or James Royal. The double man. He is the two most important men in the world to me because he's robbed me of the thing that I wanted and needed more than anything else in my life. He is the Opponent, he is the Demon of Loss, he is the Destroying Element." Bresach was chanting crazily now, his eyes almost closed, the sweat streaming down his cheeks. "When I face him, I face my father, I face the paper-carton factory, I see a door closing in my face, I see my love vanishing down a thousand dark, unknown streets, I see my bed with a hunted man in it, not the warm girl who belongs there and who is gone. I look at him and I remember the day I tried to kill myself . . . It is vitally important to me that his father dried fruit in California. I must search out his last secret."

"You're dead drunk," Jack said.

"Even that is possible," Bresach said calmly. "But drunk or sober, you must learn about me, too. You are involved with me. We are the main elements in each other's lives. We are wound around each other like snakes in battle. You are a civilized man. What you do to me, you must do in full knowledge. At the end, no matter what happens, you must not be able to say to yourself, 'I didn't know. It was an accident.' " He drained his glass and poured himself another, full to the brim, the wine purplish and raw. His hands shook and the flaring throat of the carafe with the seal of the city of Rome on it, clinked nervously against the glass. "I am in despair," he said, "and you must know it."

"Robert," Max said softly, "it is late. It is time to go home."

"If Veronica isn't there," Bresach said, "I have no home. Without her I am zero, I am minus 273.1 degrees Centrigrade, where the protons stop their movement within the atom. Christ, who would have thought anything like this could happen in Rome? Veronica . . ." He took a deep breath. "Where is she?" he asked petulantly. "I need her. Maybe she's sitting at a table in a restaurant in the next block. It drives you crazy. We ought to be out roaming the streets sniffing for her perfume like bloodhounds. I lied to you the other night, Jack. I said there were ten thousand girls more beautiful than Veronica. It was a cheap, despicable, cowardly lie, and I said it because I wanted her so badly. I was begging for her. There is no girl more beautiful than Veronica." He put his hand into the pocket of his duffel coat and took out the knife and put it on the stained tablecloth between himself and Jack. "There it is, between us, you sonofabitch," he said, his voice choked.

"Robert," Max said softly. "That is no good. Put the knife away."

Bresach touched the knife, smiling crookedly at Jack. Then, surprisingly, he put the knife away. "It is the symbol of the unsheathed and upright penis," he said quietly, "in the dreams I dream. You see, I haven't wasted all my time with Dr. Gildermeister."

"The next time you see me," Jack said, "be careful. I may be carrying a gun."

"Will you?" Bresach nodded agreeably. "Yes, that would be the sensible thing to do, wouldn't it?" He stood up abruptly. "I'm leaving," he said, standing very erect and with extreme and self-conscious steadiness. "Pay the bill, Jack. I'll call you tomorrow about the date with Delaney."

He turned on his heel and walked rigidly out of the restaurant.

Max stood up, fumbling with his scarf. "It's late," he said. "Do not worry. I will bring you the script. Thank you for a most excellent dinner. Now, if you will excuse me . . ." He took his battered greenish hat off the hook and clamped it on his head and fled.

18

The sleeping pill. Lovely transparent plastic tube, soluble, jade-green in the bed-table light, loyally carrying its cargo, three grains of peace, across the perilous dark hours. To make the voyage from night to morning navigable for twentieth-century man. But in that sleep of drugs what dreams may . . . Further measures are necessary. The bottle. Haig, Dewar's, Black and White, Johnny Walker, reliable old friends, to be found at all good bars, in Rome or out of Rome. The steep, heavy-limbed midnight plunge into forgetfulness. Alcohol plus sodium-ethyl-methyl-butyl-barbiturate equals six hours of oblivion, and, after all, what's better than oblivion?

Sleep now, pay later.

Only for a moment, after the lights are extinguished, before the drug has put in its full claim on the exhausted, fretful body, is there the brief fingering of memory to be endured, a sense of loss, desire, guilt . . .

And in the morning, a wild, quick rush of dreams, with the telephone ringing, and the operator waiting to say, as instructed, *"Sono le sette,* Signor Andrus," to get you to the studio on time. And the Benzedrine to get over the sleeping pills and the Alka-Seltzer to get over the whisky and the black coffee for courage and to keep the hands from shaking too badly while shaving.

Sleep now. Pay later.

Sunday morning.

Jack came down into the lobby late. Bresach was waiting for him, looking skinny, pale, well-shaven, disdainful of the overdressed ladies who were passing through the lobby on their way to church. Jack looked at him with something close to hatred in his heart. Max had kept his promise. He had brought over the script that Bresach had written. And it was brilliant. It was about three Hungarian refugees and a young American student who lived in one room in Rome, given to them by a crazy old English spinster who had lived in Italy since she was a girl. Max's experiences had obviously gone into the writing of it. It was sad and funny and violent, and there was a grotesque and pathetic love story between one of the refugees and an American girl touring Europe with her mother, and the whole thing was done in the simplest and cleanest of terms, with a stunning directness of images and language and with a certainty and control that made it almost impossible to believe that it had been created by a young man who had had almost nothing to do with the making of movies before this.

Looking at Bresach across the lobby, and remembering the script, about which he had not yet spoken to the boy, Jack felt resentful and unfairly burdened by this new revelation of Bresach's resources. Now he was not only responsible, almost through no fault of his own, for Bresach's disaster with Veronica, but he was responsible for his excellence, his talent, his future.

It was with a sense of being trapped and suffocated that he watched Bresach cross the lobby toward him, malnourished, vulnerable, demanding, haunting.

"I am on time," Bresach said. It was an accusation.

"So I see," Jack said. He went over to the desk and dropped his key there. The porter handed him two envelopes. Jack opened the first one. It was a communication from the Italian Telegraph Service informing him that his telegram to Veronica's mother had not been delivered, because the recipient was not known at that address.

There's something for Sunday morning, Jack thought. To brighten the Roman Sabbath.

As he and Bresach walked out onto the street where Guido was waiting for them with the car, Jack handed the opened message to Bresach, without comment.

Bresach stopped and studied it, shaking his head. Jack opened the other envelope. It was a telegram. "Don't worry, dearest," it said, "Love, Veronica." It had been sent from Zurich, at ten thirty the night before. Jack read it twice, searching for a code, a hidden message. All this means, he thought, is that last night at ten thirty she was alive and in Zurich. As Bresach came up to him, Jack stuffed the telegram into his pocket.

"I can't make anything out of this," Bresach said, folding the communication from the telegraph company. "That's the address she gave me, all right."

"Did you ever send any other telegrams or letters there?" Jack asked.

"No," said Bresach. "It was only for emergencies. There were never any emergencies. Until now. How about the other one? Was that about anything?"

"No," Jack said.

They got into the car and sat back as Guido started down the sunny avenue, crowded, even this early, with its Sunday families.

Later on, Jack thought, maybe I'll show him the telegram. After I've had a chance to think about it. Zurich. Who goes to Zurich? Why does anyone go to Zurich?

Bresach hunched into his duffel coat in a corner, glowering out the window. They were passing a newly built church, its pale stone raw and incongruous amid the weathered walls on each side of it. Latecomers were hurrying up the steps for Mass, and Bresach regarded them as though they had insulted him. "That's what this town needs," he said. "More churches." He took off his glasses and wiped them on his necktie, violently, then put them back on again. "This is a waste of time," he said, "going to see Delaney. We're at opposite sides of an abyss."

"Why don't you wait and see?" Jack said.

"Did you give Delaney my script?"

"Yes."

"Has he read it?"

"I don't know."

"Have *you* read it?"

"Yes," Jack said. He waited for Bresach to ask him what he thought of it. But he only snuffled a little in his corner and said, childishly, "I don't know why I let you talk me into things."

"Do you want to get off here?" Jack asked, exasperated, knowing that it was only bad temper and rhetoric, that he could not let Bresach get off here or anywhere.

Bresach hesitated. "What the hell," he said. "I've come this far." He peered out at the street. "I thought you said Delaney lived opposite the Circus Maximus."

"He does," Jack said.

"This guy's going toward Parioli." Bresach gestured toward Guido, in the driver's seat.

"Calm down," Jack said. "You're not being kidnapped. Delaney's out there this morning. Taking riding lessons. It's the only time he could give you."

"Riding lessons?" Bresach snorted. "What's he going to do— gallop off to the Hundred Years' War?" He subsided into sullen silence for a moment. "Do you sleep at night?" he asked.

"Yes." Jack said nothing about the pills, the whisky.

"I don't," Bresach said gloomily. "I lie in bed and listen to Max's nightmares and wake him up when he gets to a border. I'm going to tell you something. If I don't hear from her this week I'm going to tell the police." He glared over at Jack, challenging him, waiting for argument.

"You don't have to go to the police," Jack said. "I heard from her."

"When?"

"This morning."

"Where is she?" Bresach was watching him narrowly, suspecting him.

"Zurich."

"What?"

"Zurich."

"I don't believe you," Bresach said.

Jack took out the telegram and handed it to Bresach. He read it, his lips tucked into a harsh, thin line, then crumpled it and put it in his pocket. "Dearest," he said.

"Have you any idea where she might be in Zurich?" Jack asked.

Bresach shook his head gloomily. "I don't have any idea where anybody might be anyplace." He took the crumpled telegram out of his pocket and flattened it out on his knee with great care and studied it. "Well, at least she's alive," he said. "Are you pleased?"

"Of course," Jack said. "Aren't you?"

"I'm not sure," said Bresach, staring down at the paper on his knee. "I fall in love once in my whole life, and it has to be someone like this." He tapped the telegram bitterly. "I had three months of happiness with her. What do you think—is that the limit? Is that the ration? And after that, limitless despair? Tell me, what about you? Supposing you never hear from her again? Supposing this telegram is the last word you ever get from her in your whole life— Zurich, escaped to Zurich—what happens to you? What do you do —just go back to Paris and live your nice bourgeois life with your wife and kids and forget about her?"

"I won't forget her," Jack said.

"Andrus," Bresach said, "do you know anything about love?"

"I know one or two things," Jack said. "I know it doesn't end with a telegram."

"What does it end with, then? I wish I knew. Do you know the story of the Spartan boy with the fox?" Bresach demanded.

"Yes."

"There's more to it than meets the eye," said Bresach. "It's an allegory, it's crammed with symbols, it's not what it seems to mean at all. The fox is love, and you have to hide it, and you don't bring it out on parade because you *can't* bring it out—it's locked inside you—and first it licks you playfully, and then it takes a little tentative nip, then it likes the taste—and then it begins to eat away in earnest—"

"Don't be so full of self-pity," Jack said. "That's one of the worst things about your generation."

"Screw my generation," Bresach said. "I don't belong to it and it doesn't belong to me. Me and the fox, that's what I belong to." Neatly, he folded the telegram, then threw it out the window. It swooped and twisted, leaflike and free on the windy, sunny avenue.

"Don't worry," Robert said, "dearest. There's a message for this year. Were you ever in Zurich?"

"Yes."

"Why?" Bresach asked.

"I was on my way skiing," Jack said.

"Skiing." Bresach grimaced. "You're too godamn healthy for my

245

taste. There are no exterior signs of rot. I can't stand people like that."

"Shut up."

"Did anyone ever tell you you look like a Roman emperor?" Bresach asked. "I mean, women who wanted to flatter you, or artistic drunks at parties?"

"No," Jack said.

"Well, you do. There're a thousand busts in stone and bronze all over Rome that look as though they were made in your family. The big, powerful nose, the thick, brutal neck, the fleshy jaws, the sensual, self-confident mouth, the look of blank command. 'All were skilled in religious discipline, expert in strategy, pitiless and rich.' " Bresach squinted behind his glasses, drawing on his memory with an obvious effort. "That's from Flaubert," he said. "He was describing the rulers of Carthage, but it will do for the emperors of Rome, and for you, too. With a face like yours," he said, "I'd be at least an army corps commander or the president of a steel company."

"Well, I'm not," Jack said. "I'm an under-secretary in an under-bureau."

"Maybe you're biding your time." Bresach grinned provocatively. "Maybe next year you'll blossom out and you'll have forty thousand men under your orders. You'll disappoint me if you don't, Jack. 'Expert in strategy, pitiless and rich . . .' " he repeated. "Do you think the American face is moving in your direction, Jack?"

"You're just as American as I am," Jack said. "Do you think the American face is moving in *your* direction?"

"No," Bresach said. "I'm a reject. I'm off the main line. If they could do it by law, they would revoke my citizenship. I'm tortured, short-sighted, and skeptical. I'm the stuff that exiles are made of."

"Bull."

Bresach grinned again. "There's something in what you say, Jack," he said. The car swerved violently, to avoid a Vespa that came charging out of a side street, carrying a young man and a girl, both of them leaning far over to make the curve. Bresach shouted in Italian at them, angrily.

"What did you say then?" Jack asked.

"I said, 'Why aren't you in church?' " Bresach said. He was still angry. He took out a crumpled pack of cigarettes and lit one for himself. For the first time, Jack noticed that Bresach's long fingers were yellowed from nicotine.

"Have you thought about what you want to tell Delaney?" Jack asked. He felt responsible for the interview and wanted it to go well, or at least decorously, and Bresach's mood now was disquieting. He had taken Bresach into the projection room with him the day before to see the film that was already assembled. He had watched Bresach while the film was being run, but Bresach for once had sat quiet and expressionless for an hour and a half and had left without venturing any opinion on what he had seen.

"Are you afraid of what I'll tell the great man?" Bresach demanded.

"No," Jack said. "I just want it to stay within the bounds of normal human intercourse."

"Don't worry. I'll be reasonable," Bresach said. "If it kills me. After all, I want the job."

"What are you going to tell him about the picture?" Jack asked, curiously.

"I don't know," said Bresach. "I haven't made my mind up yet." He threw his cigarette away. "How big a town is Zurich?" he asked.

"Three, four hundred thousand," Jack said. "Something like that."

"Everybody says the Swiss police are great at finding people," Bresach said. "They know in which bed everybody in Switzerland is sleeping each night. Is that true?"

"Approximately."

"I think I'll fly to Zurich tonight," Bresach said. "Catch her yodeling by the side of the lake. Will you lend me the money for the plane?"

"No," Jack said.

"You sound like my father," said Bresach. With that insult he slid down into his corner, his head turned, and spoke no more until they reached the riding academy.

Delaney was taking two-foot brush jumps on a big, nervous roan. The horse hadn't been nervous to begin with, but after fifteen minutes with Delaney, he was pulling at the bit, frothing, and backing and dancing sideways before each approach.

He has the same effect on actors, Jack thought sadly. Give him a quarter of an hour with any living thing and terror and mutiny raise their heads.

Jack and Bresach were leaning against the top rail of the fence that enclosed the big practice ring. Bresach had a slight, derisive smile on his face as he watched Delaney bump around on the roan. In contrast to the other riders, who were smartly dressed in whip-cord breeches and boots and English tweed jackets, Delaney was wearing a worn pair of blue jeans, a red flannel shirt without a tie, and ankle-high suede shoes. The riding master, a small, sixty-year-old Italian, his boots brilliant, his flaring jacket faultlessly pressed, the stock around his thin neck tight and without creases, stood in the center of the ring, calling out patiently in English, " 'eels down, Signor Delaney, 'eels *down!*" and, "Relax the grip on the reins, signore, if you please. Do not pull, if you please. The pressure always firm and even. Do not flap the 'eels. Do not confuse the animal, if you please."

Bresach chuckled at Jack's side. "Do not confuse the animal," he whispered.

Delaney went over the jump again and lost a stirrup and pulled wildly on the reins and the roan skittered off to his left. Delaney nearly fell off and Bresach chuckled again.

"For the moment, Signor Delaney," the riding master said, "maybe it is time to take a little rest. Let the animal breathe."

A groom took the roan's bridle and Delaney swung off, stiffly. "Next time," he said to the riding master, "I'll take that one." He pointed at a rail jump, three and a half feet high.

The riding master shook his head. "I do not think," he said, "that it is quite the . . ."

"I'll take that one." Delaney patted him on the shoulder and took off his gloves and came over to where Jack and Bresach were standing. He was grinning, enjoying himself, and he looked flushed and healthy from the exercise. He was sweating and vapor was rising from his forehead into the crisp, sunny air. Jack introduced him to Bresach, and Delaney said, shaking Bresach's hand, "I'm glad to see you. I haven't read your script yet, but Jack says you're a bright boy."

"Maurice," Jack said, "what in the world are you doing learning how to jump horses at your age?"

"That's exactly why," Delaney said. "My age. It's to keep from growing old. Each year I try to learn one new thing. To make up for the things I'm losing, the things I can't do as well any more. I figure I can go on improving as a rider until I'm sixty-five. The whole idea of being young is that you can feel yourself getting better and better at things. Am I right?" He looked at Bresach.

"I'm getting worse and worse at everything," Bresach said.

Delaney laughed good-naturedly. "At your age," he said, "you can afford to say things like that."

"What're you going to take up next year?" Jack asked. "Parachuting?"

"French," said Delaney. "I want to direct a picture in French before I'm sixty. They've got a couple of actors in Paris I want to get my hands on before I die."

There was a pretty dark girl in the ring now, on a tall, quiet bay. The girl didn't look more than sixteen, small, serious-faced, erect and light in the saddle. She started making a circuit of the jumps, and all three men watched as she seemed to lift the horse effortlessly over the obstacles, a rapt, intent expression on her face.

"Look at her face," Delaney said, his voice surprisingly harsh. "I want to feel like that before I'm through."

"You're liable to break your neck first," Jack said.

"I doubt it." Delaney watched the girl take the bay over a fence. At the moment when the horse cleared the top rail, its hind hooves bunched neatly high above the bar, Delaney made a little, clucking sound. Then he shook his head, dispelling some hopeless dream, and turned toward Bresach and Jack. "Jack," he said, "I spoke to an old friend of yours last night."

"Who was that?" Jack asked.

"Carlotta." Delaney let the name drop carelessly, but he was watching Jack with a glint of curiosity and amusement in his eye.

"That's a description of her," Jack said. "An old friend. Don't tell me she's in Rome."

"No," Delaney said. "She's in England."

"Sowing discord and alarm, no doubt," Jack said. "Did you tell her I was here?"

"Yes."

"What did she say?"

"She didn't say anything. She sighed," Delaney said. "Or anyway, it sounded like a sigh. It was a bad connection, it was hard to tell. She asked me if I thought she'd have fun in Rome."

"What did you say?"

"I said no." Delaney smiled at Bresach. "We're talking about one of Jack's many wives," he said.

"I know," Bresach said. "I've done my homework."

"On me, too?" Delaney asked.

"Of course."

"I've got some further information for you," Delaney said. "My wife moved out on me last night, too." He took out a big red handkerchief and wiped the cooling perspiration off his forehead.

"Is it serious?" Jack asked. It hadn't been serious in the past. Clara had moved out several times before, in protest against other of her husband's liaisons.

"I don't think so. She only went as far as the Grand." Delaney grinned. "You have no idea how peaceful an apartment in Rome can be if your wife is in a room at the Grand Hotel." He put the handkerchief back in the pocket of the soiled blue jeans. "Well, now," he said briskly to Bresach, "I understand you want to be a director."

"Yes," Bresach said.

"Why?" Delaney asked.

"I only make that speech drunk," Bresach said composedly. "I made it once already this week. To Andrus. Ask him."

Delaney eyed Bresach speculatively, like a fighter sizing up an opponent in the opening seconds of the first round. "You saw my picture, didn't you?" he said.

"I've seen a lot of your pictures," Bresach said.

"I mean the one I'm doing now."

"Yes," Bresach said.

"What do you think?"

Bresach hesitated, looking around him at the riders in the ring, the dark girl patting the bay's arched neck as she spoke quietly to the immaculate riding master, the groom standing at the roan's head, a seven-year-old boy in a velvet cap walking a short, closely coupled chestnut slowly around the edge of the ring. "Do you think this is a good place to talk about a movie?"

"It's a perfect place," Delaney said. "Nobody else understands English and there's a nice warm smell of horse manure in the air."

"Well," Bresach said. "What would you like—do you want me to flatter you or do you want me to tell the truth?"

Delaney grinned. "Flatter me first," he said, "and tell me the truth after. That's always a good system."

"Well," Bresach began, "nobody handles a camera better than you."

"That's okay," Delaney said, nodding. "For openers."

250

"Every shot you set up," Bresach continued, "is crammed with information."

"What do you mean by that?" Delaney was watching Bresach closely, skeptical but curious.

"What I mean is you're not interested only in the story and the characters in the foreground," Bresach went on rapidly, professorially, lecturing. "There's always something happening on different levels on the screen. You're always trying to tell us something about other people, the people in the background, at the same time, and making a comment on the scene, and telling us about the weather and the time of day or night, and working at the mood you want us to feel."

"Oh, you got that?" Delaney sounded surprised and pleased.

"Yes," Bresach said. "I got that. There aren't many directors who can do that consistently, but you're one of them. And you're graceful and ingenious at leading us with the camera from one story point to another, so that there's always a feeling of flow and connection in all your pictures. Of course, in this picture, as in all the pictures you've done in the last ten years, the feeling is phony . . ."

He stopped, waiting to see how Delaney would take this. Delaney was staring at the girl on the bay again, and all he did was nod and say, "Go on."

"It used to be real," Bresach said calmly, "in the beginning. Scenes slid one into the other because you felt they *had* to. Now, it's all skillful embroidery. On top. Under it, it's chaotic, accidental . . . Do you want to hear all this?"

"I'm charmed by it," Delaney said, flatly. "Keep going."

"I'll tell you how I feel about your old pictures," Bresach went on. "They gave me the feeling that they were made by a man who was obsessed by the idea of time running out, a man who had so much to say he had to cram everything in quick and under enormous pressure. Even some of the junky stories you picked . . ."

"And now?" Delaney said mildly. Jack was surprised to see that Delaney was smiling tolerantly.

"Now your pictures look and sound as if they were made by a vain and self-indulgent man, who'd throw away a whole character for an effect or for a gaudy scene," Bresach said. His voice sounded angry. It was as if in arranging the list of criticisms, their full criminality was suddenly revealed to him and offended him. If Jack had not read Bresach's script, he would have felt that what the boy was saying was impudent. But now Jack believed that Bresach was being just, and had earned the right to speak. And he was saying the things that Jack wanted to say, and would have been able to say to Delaney in the early, candid years of their friendship, and that Delaney would no longer accept from him. "For example," Bresach went on, "in this picture—you have that silly flashback to the war, just because you wanted to have the tear-jerker scene in the ruins between the hero and the little Italian boy. Sure, the scene is effective—the tears are jerked—but you stop the picture for fifteen minutes, for that one moment . . . The pressure's off. All that's left is the embroidery . . ."

Delaney nodded again, smiling faintly, squinting out at the other riders. Then he turned and pinched Bresach's cheek. "You're a cute little feller, aren't you, sonny?" he said. Then he strode out toward the riding master, shouting, "All right, *Commendatore,* I'm ready now. Let's go."

Jack and Bresach watched in silence for a moment. The blood mounted in Bresach's cheeks.

"He asked me, didn't he?" Bresach said harshly. "What did he expect me to say?"

"He asked you," Jack said, "and you told him. Bully for you."

Bresach put his hand up to his cheek. "I should've punched him in the nose."

"He'd've killed you," Jack said pleasantly.

"Well, there's no sense in hanging around now," Bresach said, "watching the cowboy. Let's get out of here."

"Don't be silly," Jack said. "You still want that job, don't you?"

"I have about as much chance of getting it as that horse there," Bresach said bitterly.

"Nonsense," Jack said, watching Delaney mount and pull the roan's head around to face the jump. "He's making up his mind right now. I know him. He's digesting what he thinks're the insults and figuring out just how you can be of use to him. Actually, the way you talked to him was the best thing you could've done."

"I was just beginning," Bresach said. "I have a dozen other . . ."

"All in good time," Jack said. "Don't push your luck."

Delaney was facing the jump now, twenty yards out. The roan was as nervous as ever, tossing his head and rolling his eyes and pulling against the bit. Delaney clucked to him and dug in his heels and the roan broke away with a leap that had Delaney rocking in the saddle. The roan approached the jump pulling to one side, and at the last moment, refused. Delaney went hurtling over the horse's head and landed with a hollow, collapsing noise on the other side of the fence. He lay still for a moment as Jack and the riding master and the groom ran to him. Before anyone reached him, he pushed himself up from the ground, stiffly, brushing the dirt off his face.

"I'm all right," he said. "Where's that godamn horse?"

"I think for today that is enough, Signor Delaney," the riding master said anxiously. "That is quite a shaking up."

"Crap," Delaney said. He strode over to where the groom was standing, calming the roan. The groom looked questioningly at the riding master as Delaney approached. The riding master shrugged and the groom gave Delaney a leg up. Delaney wrenched the horse's head around and went back to the starting point.

"He forgets," the riding master said nervously to Jack, "that he is no longer a young man."

They both stood next to the barrier as Delaney clucked to the horse, took him toward the jump in a confused gallop, and went over. There was a lot of daylight showing over the saddle, but this time Delaney stayed on. He rode the horse over to the riding master and swung off, dismounting with a debonair little leap into the soft loam of the ring.

"Very good, signore," the riding master said, gratefully taking the reins.

"It was lousy," Delaney said. He pulled out his handkerchief and wiped at the mud on his forehead, smearing it with sweat. "But I made it. Next Sunday I'll be great."

"What're you proving, Maurice?" Jack asked, as they started back toward Bresach.

"Me?" Delaney sounded surprised. "Nothing. I'm just out for the exercise and the fresh air." But he limped a little as he walked, and when he reached the fence he put out his hand shakily and held on for support. "Well, now, sonny," he said to Bresach, "I've been thinking over all the interesting things you told me. Under pressure, you said, didn't you?"

"Yes," said Bresach.

"Do you think you could help me put this picture under pressure, too? Cut out the embroidery?" Delaney sounded angry, almost as if he were on the verge of striking Bresach.

"Yes," Bresach said. "I could."

"Good. You have yourself a job. You start tomorrow morning."

Delaney brushed at the mud on the worn knees of the blue jeans. "Now, I'd like a beer. Come on . . ." He climbed over the fence and jumped down with an elaborate show of energy. Jack smiled at Bresach, but Bresach was watching Delaney sullenly, suspecting insults. As Jack crawled through the top two bars of the fence, Delaney stopped walking. He stood absolutely still, then turned slowly on his heels to face them. His lips were white. "Oh, Christ, Jack," he said in a voice that didn't sound at all like his voice. "Oh, Christ, it hurts."

Then he pitched face first into the gravel.

In the confusion of men running to the limp, muddy body lying on the gravel, and the babble of Italian and the rushing toward the car, with Jack holding Delaney under the shoulders and Delaney's head loose and bumping against his arms, one clear, precise thought came to Jack— This is what it has been about, he thought; Delaney's is the death that was announced to me.

19

They gave Delaney oxygen and anticoagulants, and called for a priest. When the car had driven to the modern white hospital, set on the hill among lawns and palm trees (California and Rome in a confusion of influences, echoes, borrowings), and while Delaney was being gently lifted onto the stretcher, the nun had asked Jack what the patient's religion was. Jack had hesitated, then said, "Catholic," for simplicity's sake. No matter what he had said, Jack was sure, with a name like Delaney, the nun wouldn't have taken any chances. The nun was a small, rosy-faced woman of about forty, brisk and competent, who spoke English with a slight touch of Irish brogue mingled with her soft Italian accent, as musical evidence of the influence of the Irish church in Rome.

First came the doctor, a self-assured, dapper man, who stayed behind the closed door a long time and who answered no questions when he came out. Then came the priest, young and pale and professorial, who prepared Delaney for eternity, everybody hoped, with no adverse effects on blood pressure or systolic beat. When the priest came out of Delaney's room, his expression was noncommittal, and Jack was sure that there had been no time for full confession. The priest's face, no matter how hardened he might have become in his calling to the sins of the world, would not have been so serene if Delaney had been strong enough to compose a complete list of his transgressions.

After the priest came the publicity man for the picture, magically called off a golf course, as if by some prodding of instinct, to ensure that Delaney's death—or survival—would be properly used for the advantage of the company in the newspapers, magazines, and over the radio circuits of the world. The publicity man was a big, heavy-set, youngish American, balding and with glasses, who set himself firmly in front of the white door at the end of the marble corridor, with a bulging brief case on the floor at his feet. In the brief case, Jack found out later, there were mimeographed copies of a biography of Delaney that the publicity man had prepared as soon as he was hired. Jack looked at the photographs and read the biography. The photographs had been taken ten years before. In them, Delaney looked young, eager and fierce. The biography only mentioned the last of his wives and none of his failures. Reading the mimeographed sheet, one would believe that Delaney's life had been a virtuous and triumphant parade, with success following success in an uninterrupted procession.

"How do you like it?" the publicity man asked as Jack read the release in the light from the window at the end of the corridor.

"When I die," Jack said, "remind me to hire you to write my obituary."

The publicity man laughed good-naturedly. "They don't pay me to rap them," he said. His name was Fogel. The breast pocket of his sports jacket was filled with cigars. From time to time he would take a cigar out to put to his lips. Then he would remember that he was in the presence of death and would soon be in the presence of the Press, and he would sadly put the cigar back into his pocket, preserving decorum.

Fogel talked briefly to Bresach, who stood next to the window, smoking cigarettes one after the other and staring down at the gardens. Then Fogel came over to Jack and said, in a whisper, "Get that kid out of here."

"Why?" Jack asked.

"I don't want the press to get to him," Fogel said. "He has the wrong attitude toward the hero." Fogel nodded toward the closed door. "And I'm sure he'll talk."

Jack recognized the correctness of Fogel's intuition. Bresach's account of what had happened that morning, with his interpretative remarks, certainly would not fit neatly with the mimeographed eulogy. So Jack went over to Bresach and told him that there was no need to hang around. Bresach nodded. He seemed subdued and a little stunned, youthfully unable to comprehend the sudden disasters that can fall upon aging flesh. "I can't believe it," Bresach said. "He was so full of piss and vinegar up on that horse. You'd think he was going to live forever. If you get to him, will you tell him I don't take back anything I said to him this morning, but I'm sorry I said it."

"Oh, hell, Bresach," Jack said, "it's Sunday. Give your precious integrity a day off. Go on home." He spoke harshly and with impatience. Now that Delaney was defenseless, he felt driven to protect him against all attack.

"Anyway," Bresach said, "I hope he gets better. You can tell him *that,* can't you?"

"I'll tell him, I'll tell him," Jack said.

Bresach took a last look at the white door, then walked slowly toward the elevator, as the first reporter, accompanied by a photographer, came hurrying down the corridor.

Jack started down toward the phone in the nurse's office in the middle of the floor, trying to look as if he had nothing to do with the Delaney case. He didn't want to have to fence with reporters and he didn't want his picture in the papers.

He called the Grand Hotel and asked for Clara Delaney. The phone rang a long time and he was just about to hang up when he heard Clara's voice, sounding shaky and low, in the earpiece.

"Clara," Jack said, "I'm at the Salvatore Mundi Hospital and . . ."

"I know," Clara said, in the same subdued, flat voice. "They called me. I know all about it."

"When are you coming over?" Jack asked. "Do you want me to pick you up at the hotel?"

"You don't have to bother, Jack," Clara said. "I'm not coming over."

And she hung up.

By eleven o'clock that night, only the doctor, the priest, and the nurses had gone through the blank white door of Delaney's room. Fogel had set up a kind of office for the newspapermen and photographers on the ground floor, but most of them had gone, after taking pictures of the doctor, of Jack, despite his protests, and of Tucino and Tasseti and Holt, who had arrived early in the afternoon and who remained, with Jack, in the corridor outside Delaney's room.

Jack didn't know why the others were keeping this vigil in the dark corridor, and if he had been asked about himself he would not have been able to reply coherently. Without formulating his reasons, even for himself, into words, he stayed within reach of Delaney's door because he felt that he was keeping his friend alive by his devotion. While he remained there, Delaney would not die. He was sure that as soon as he could, Delaney would make a signal to him, would instruct him, absolve him. He knew that he had to hold himself ready for the communication that he knew Delaney must be struggling to make. Until that communication was made, he could not leave.

The others might have felt that they were doing Delaney no good by their attendance, but no one suggested going. So they all stayed, for their own reasons, taking turns sitting on the two wooden chairs that the nurses had set out in front of the window at the end of the corridor.

The doctor had merely said that Delaney was doing as well as could be expected and could not see visitors at the moment. The doctor said all this in Italian for Tucino and Tasseti and in excellent English for Holt and Jack. The doctor had a habit of speaking in a whisper, which made his words seem freighted with hidden meanings and forced his listeners to lean toward him to catch what he was saying. By eleven o'clock at night Jack was unreasonably irritated with the doctor.

Tucino and Tasseti paced back and forth restlessly, their leather heels tapping importantly on the stone floor, as they talked in a hushed, excited hiss of sound throughout the evening. From time to time their voices rose and Jack had the feeling that they were engaged in a long argument that they had had many times before and which rose to regularly defined climaxes after every fifty lines.

Holt stood calmly at the window, a small, vague smile on his lips.

His sombrero was hung neatly on a radiator valve, a touch of Oklahoma, a breath of the plains, in the sick Roman night.

"I questioned the doctor carefully," Holt said, "and I have the feeling Maurice won't die. Naturally, the doctor won't make any promises. If he says a patient will live and then he dies, it would put him in an embarrassing position professionally, and I appreciate that. But quite a few of my friends have gone through the same thing. In the oil business. The strain . . . That's one of the reasons Mother insisted I arrange to take six months a year in Europe. If you enjoy being alive, there's no sense in working yourself into your grave, is there, Jack?"

"No," Jack said.

"I'm surprised about Maurice, though," Holt said, shaking his head, with the Stetson marks in a neat oval on his graying hair. "There's so much vitality there. He works hard, of course, but I don't think that's what did it. I have my theories, Jack . . ." He hesitated. "You don't mind if I speak frankly, do you?"

"Of course not."

"I know Maurice is an old friend of yours. He's a friend of mine, too, I like to think. I'm honored to be able to call him my friend," Holt said seriously. "What I'm about to say I say in the friendliest manner possible. I don't want you to think I'm talking behind a sick man's back or making a criticism. What I've observed about Maurice, Jack, is that he's abnormally ambitious. Am I right? Am I unfair in that deduction?"

"No," Jack said. "It's not unfair."

"He feels now that he's not living up to his ambition," Holt said. "That can affect a man's heart, can't it?"

"I would think so," said Jack.

Holt peered soberly out the window. It was raining lightly and the palm trees gleamed here and there in the black, windless drizzle. "Somehow," Holt said, "before I came here, it never occurred to me that it rained in Rome." He cleared his throat. "The other thing about Maurice—and again, I want you to bear it in mind that I don't mean it as a criticism—he doesn't lead a normal home life."

In the darkness of the corridor, Jack smiled at the gentleness with which the oil man judged his fellow man.

"If a man is disappointed in his ambition," Holt went on, staring down at the rain, "and he doesn't surrender, but keeps on fighting like Maurice—and mind you, I admire him for it—and if, at the same time, he's under a strain at home, if he doesn't find peace there—it's no wonder if at a certain moment between fifty and sixty he collapses. I'm lucky," he added irrelevantly. "After I met Mother I knew I would never look at another woman—in that particular way, I mean—again in my life. Maurice hasn't been lucky, has he, Jack?"

"He's looked at other women," Jack said. "If that's what you mean by being unlucky."

"Still," Holt said, "he won't die. I have a feeling about things like that. I've come into a room and seen a man who seems to be in perfect health, just gone through an insurance examination with flying colors and all that, and I've told Mother later, in the privacy of our own bedroom, 'We'll attend that feller's funeral before the year is out.' And I've rarely been wrong."

Look at me, Millionaire, Jack wanted to say. Look closely. What do you think about me? What will you tell Mother about me tonight in the privacy of your bedroom?

"I don't have that feeling about Maurice Delaney," Holt said, "and when I'm allowed to see him, I'm going to tell him so. What's more, I'm going to tell him that I have decided to go through with our deal. I'll finance him for three pictures in the next three years."

"That's very nice of you, Sam," Jack said, touched again, as he had been the first night he had met Holt, by the man's goodness.

"It's not nice," Holt said. "It's business. I'll make a damn good thing out of it. There'll be only one condition attached to it . . ." Holt stopped.

Jack waited curiously. One condition. What? That Delaney lead what Holt insisted upon calling a normal home life? That would be an interesting clause in a contract. It is furthermore agreed that the party of the second part have dinner with his wife each evening at eight o'clock for the duration of this contract.

"The condition is that I will sign the deal only if you consent to come in as the producer in charge," Holt said.

Tucino and Tasseti had come to a fiftieth line in their duologue and their voices resounded so loudly in the corridor that a sister poked her head out through a partly opened door and shushed them. Jack was grateful for the little disturbance. From this point on he did not want to say a word to Holt without weighing its effect carefully in advance.

"You're surprised, I imagine," Holt said, as the voices of Tucino and Tasseti diminished into an angry, low buzzing.

"Yes," Jack said, "I confess I am. After all, I never did anything like this before."

"No matter," Holt said. "You have had a great deal of experience, you're a man of intelligence. I'm sure you're a man of your word, and most important of all, you understand Maurice. If anyone can control him, you can. . . ."

"If anyone can control him." Jack smiled sourly.

"If no one can control him," Holt said, "maybe it would be better if he didn't come out of that door alive. Better for him," Holt added in his soft, drawling voice. He looked at Jack and chuckled at the expression on Jack's face. "You're surprised again, aren't you, Jack?" he said. "You wonder what an old hick like me knows about things like this. Listen, Jack, there're plenty of men who insist upon ruining themselves in the oil business, too. You get to know the signs. Anyway, it's not so magical . . ." He waved his hand. "I've been doing a little investigating. It's not as though Maurice took pains all his life to keep anything secret, is it?"

"No," Jack said.

"I've been doing some investigating about you, too, Jack." Holt's voice was dry, almost timid. "You don't mind, do you?"

"It's all according to what you found out," Jack said.

Holt chuckled again. "One thing I found out," he said, "is that I can afford to pay you a lot more than the government. I won't tell you what else I found out, except that it was all reassuring, it all jibed with the excellent impression you made on Mother and me."

"Let me ask *you* a question, Sam," Jack said. "What about him?" Jack nodded in the direction of Tucino, who was leaning now with his head against the wall while Tasseti whispered busily into his ear. "Where does he fit in?"

"He fits in all right," Holt said. "The company will be a joint Italo-American enterprise, and Tucino will have to find one-quarter of the money."

"Have you told him that you want me to be in on it?"

"I don't want you just to be in on it, Jack," said Holt. "I want you to run it. When the time is ripe, I'll tell Mr. Tucino."

"Do you think he'll stand for it?"

Holt chuckled. "There's nothing else he can do, Jack," he said. "He's on the verge of bankruptcy. It's not that I want you to take advantage of his position, Jack," Holt said, almost apologetically. "I admire his good qualities, as you know. I talked at considerable length about them the other night, didn't I? He's dynamic, he has quick ideas, he has a taste for what the public wants. But Italians do business in a different way from us, Jack. There are things that businessmen do to each other here, that are considered absolutely honorable, that would put a man in jail for five years back home. I'm going to be the president of this company. My name is going to be on it. You understand me, don't you, Jack?"

"Yes."

"It's not an easy job I'm offering you," Holt said. "You'll earn your money. You get twelve thousand five hundred a year now from the government. I'll give you thirty-five thousand a year for three years, with five percent of the profits."

"And at the end of the three years?"

Holt grinned. He touched the crown of the Stetson, hanging on the radiator valve. "We'll see, Jack, we'll see. I'm a businessman, not an old-age-pension scheme."

There was the tapping of solid heels, and Tucino came up to where Jack and Holt were standing in front of the window. "Listen, Jack," Tucino said, his glasses shining dimly in the subdued hospital corridor light, "I think maybe it's good idea you go to sleep now. You gotta lotta work to do tomorrow. Now we gotta move fast, finish the dubbing quickest possible, eh? Tell you the truth, Jack, Delaney is way over budget as is, already we're shooting three weeks over. I listen to what you been doing, I like it very much. Only very slow. I know it's not your fault . . ." He spread his hands to show how blameless he thought Jack was. "I know how slow the *Maestro* work. But now I take over, personally, on the set tomorrow. Now, without him, you finish up quick, eh, Jack, like a good boy, we get this whole picture in the can before Delaney comes outa hospital, eh?"

"I don't know, Mr. Tucino," Jack said. "If I rush through it and Delaney doesn't like it, when he gets out of the hospital, he's liable to want to do the whole thing all over again."

"Who knows when he come out of hospital?" Tucino said excitedly. "Who knows if he come out alive or dead? What am I supposed to do? Wait? Pay hundred and twenty people just to hang around because my director had to go horseback riding? By the time Delaney can say yes, no, or maybe, this picture is going to be playing in ten thousand theatres."

"Mr. Tucino," Holt said softly, the drawl a little slower than usual, "don't get excited."

262

"Mr. Holt," Tucino said, gripping Holt by both forearms, "I admire you. You're a gentleman. You got oil wells. You can afford to wait. I don't have no oil wells, Mr. Holt, I am in big rush."

The door to Delaney's room opened and the doctor came out. He looked fresh, remote. "Mister . . . ah . . . Andrus," he whispered.

"Yes?" said Jack.

"He insists upon talking to you," the doctor said. "I told him two minutes. No more. Please try not to excite him."

Jack looked around him doubtfully at the other men. "Any messages?" he asked.

There was a silence. Then Holt said, "Tell him he has nothing to worry about."

Jack went into the room and closed the door behind him.

There was a single, subdued light to one side of the bed, and a nurse was sitting in the shadows in the corner of the room. The light wasn't strong enough for Jack to see the expression on Delaney's face or the color of his skin. Under the covers, Delaney's body seemed childish and frail on the high hospital bed, and the sound of his breathing was harsh and irregular. He was terribly, pathetically small. The day of illness had already diminished him. He had a tube taped onto his cheek, branched into his nostrils, for the oxygen. When Jack came in and stood close to the bed, Delaney moved the fingers of his hand slightly in greeting. Jack had an impulse to take Delaney in his arms, cradle him, comfort him, beg his forgiveness.

"Sam Holt's out in the hall," Jack said. "He says there's nothing to worry about."

Delaney made a sound that Jack understood was meant to be a laugh.

"Jack," Delaney whispered, and his voice, too, seemed childish and frail, "two things. First—don't let Tucino touch the picture."

"Don't worry about the picture," Jack said.

"He's dying to get his hands on it," Delaney whispered. "There's still the last sequence to shoot. The one in the bar at the railroad station. It's the most important scene in the picture. He'll make it sound like *Aïda*. You have to help me, Jack. You can't let him do it."

"I'll do my best to stop him," Jack said, feeling helpless, and full of confused pity for Delaney because even now, living on oxygen and barely able to speak, his first thought was for his work. And what work! Jack knew the scene in the railroad-station bar. Delaney was right about it's being the most important sequence in the picture—but the picture itself was nothing, less than nothing. It was sad—absurd—that a man on the brink of death should be concerned with anything so inconsequential as ten minutes of celluloid. *Lord, I announce my coming. But first I must get certain actors onto their proper marks.*

"If I conk out," Delaney was saying, "I don't want the last thing I do murdered by that Italian."

"You're not going to conk out," Jack said.

Delaney turned his head slowly to one side, so that he could look directly up at Jack. "It's the godamndest thing, Jack," he whispered. "I'm not afraid. I don't know whether it's because I'm brave, or whether it's because I'm a damned fool, or whether I'm sure I'm going to live. I'll tell you something, Jack—until eleven o'clock this morning, I used to be scared shitless of dying. And now it's nothing."

There was a rustle in the corner where the nurse was sitting in the shadows.

"*Scusi,* Sister," Delaney said. "I have a dirty tongue."

"Signore," the nurse said coldly to Jack, "you are tiring the patient."

"Another minute, Sister," Delaney whispered, "another minute, please. He is my best friend. From when we were young."

"One minute more, that is all," said the cold, accented voice in the darkness.

"Listen, Jack, just listen," Delaney said rapidly, fighting time. "You've got to do it for me. You've got to take it over. Finish the picture for me. Jack, are you listening to me?"

"I'm listening," Jack said.

"What the hell," Delaney went on hurriedly, "you can do it. It's not as though it's all a mystery to you. You've been around long enough. If you tried, you'd be a better director than nine-tenths of the bastards with big names today. Whatever you do, it'll be better than Tucino. Shoot every angle. Take your time. Let them yell. Cover everything. Go slow on the cutting, on the dubbing. I don't want Tucino to have any prints made before I get out of this godamn hospital. *Scusi,* Sister. If Tucino yells, get Holt to shut him up. Holt's on my side. And he's tough. He can break Tucino in half if he wants to. And Tucino knows it. I'll be out of here in six weeks, Jack, the doctor's sure, and then I'll put it all together my-self . . ."

"Six weeks," Jack said, almost automatically.

"What'd you say, Jack?"

"Nothing."

"Get that kid. That kid today . . . what's his name . . . at the riding school . . ."

"Bresach."

"Get him to help you. Call him the dialogue director or your assistant or whatever. I read his script . . ."

"But you told him you hadn't," Jack said, remembering the morning.

Delaney smiled weakly against the pillow. "I wanted to sound him out first. The script's too damned good for a kid that age. I didn't want to praise him right from the beginning. There're tricks in every trade, Jack . . . I have a hunch about that kid. He's hot. He's got the movies in his blood. He'll come up with a lot of ideas. Use him . . ."

Use him, Jack thought. There's an order.

"Listen to him. Pick his brain," Delaney went on, gasping. "Maybe this is just what this picture needs. A fresh little sonofa-bitch like that. I have a hunch about him. That's the way I was at that age. Maybe this picture'll start me all over again. Jack, you promise . . . ?"

Six weeks, Jack thought. What will I tell Hélène? What Joe Morrison? What happens to my life?

"Jack," Delaney said, "you promise, don't you? I need you . . . Jack . . ."

"Of course," Jack said. Standing there, next to the high hospital bed, he knew that from the instant that Delaney had swept into the dressing room that night in 1937 in Philadelphia, this moment, this promise, this sacrifice, this despairing act of friendship, had been inevitable.

"You won't let me down, Jack," Delaney pleaded.

"No, I won't let you down," Jack said. "Now, I think you ought to try to sleep."

"In a minute, in a minute." Delaney grasped Jack's wrist. His fingers felt light, delicate, without force on Jack's skin. "One more thing . . ."

"Signore." The nurse rose in the shadows.

"Jack," Delaney said rapidly, his voice rasping, "go to Clara for me. She's got to come here, tell her, she's got to come here. Even for one minute. Just to walk into the room and kiss my forehead. Christ, she can do that, can't she? . . . What the hell is that to ask after all these years?"

"Signor Delaney"—the nurse came over to the bed, motioning with her head for Jack to go—"you must stop talking now."

Delaney's fingers closed more tightly on Jack's wrist. "And you have to go to Barzelli for me," he whispered. "Tell her she's got to stay away from here. If she comes, Clara won't come near me —tell her. You'll tell her, won't you, Jack?"

"Signore," the nurse said loudly, "I will call the doctor if you do not leave immediately."

"Yes, I'll tell her," Jack said. "Good night." He pulled his hand away from Delaney's grasp.

"She's got to understand," Delaney whispered. "Clara . . ." He turned his head away on the pillow. Jack went out of the room.

"Well?" Tucino asked. He was standing just outside the door, and Jack had the impression that he had been trying to listen, through the heavy, blank surface, to what Delaney had been saying in the room. "How is he?"

"Fine," Jack said. "Very confident." He felt dazed. His eyes were hurting him and he seemed to have difficulty in keeping objects in focus.

"I'm sure he's going to pull through," Holt said. He was holding his hat now, ready for departure.

"What did he say?" Tucino demanded. "Did he say anything about the picture?"

Jack hesitated, then decided against talking. For the moment. He was too tired, and he had errands to do first. Tucino would have to wait till morning. "He wasn't quite coherent," Jack said, thinking, Well, that isn't completely a lie. He picked up his coat, which was thrown across the back of one of the chairs. "I think we can all stand a little sleep," he said.

He managed to signal to Holt to hold back and the two Italians went down by themselves in the elevator, leaving Holt and Jack alone. Swiftly, Jack explained what Delaney had asked him to do.

"Don't worry about Tucino," Holt said. "I'll take care of him." He shook Jack's hand as he said good night.

Downstairs, Jack ran into Fogel, who was finally smoking one of his cigars.

"What a day," Fogel said, as they went out the glass doors into the wet night. "I'm going to get something to eat. Want to join me?"

"Thanks, I can't. I have some calls to make," Jack said. He peered through the darkness for Guido and the car. Headlights came on suddenly, and the car came up the driveway.

"Well, we did a good job down here," Fogel said, with satisfaction. "We were on the radio all day. All over the world. Delaney's never had as much publicity as this in his whole life. Too bad this had to happen on a Sunday. There're no evening papers. I bet we'd've made the front page in fifty cities. Ah, well, you can't have everything."

Jack got into the car, in front with Guido. He waved good night to Fogel, who was puffing deeply on his wet cigar, earning his money, happy in his profession, his only regret, in the middle of the century, that there were no evening newspapers on Sundays.

As Guido drove down the driveway, another car drew up to the entrance to the hospital. Two people got out. Jack was almost certain that one of the passengers was Stiles, and for a curious moment, he had the feeling that the woman with him was Carlotta. He shook his head, annoyed with his fantasies. This has been a rough day, he thought, I'm seeing things.

He sank back on the seat of the car, thinking, Six weeks . . .

"Monsieur Delaney is still alive?" Guido asked.

"Still alive," Jack said.

Guido sighed. "Poor man," he said.

"Oh, he'll be all right," Jack said.

"Never," said Guido. "I know these things. The heart. A man is never a whole man after it happens. Not if he lives another fifty years. Americans," he said. "They take things too hard. They can't wait. They must rush up to their graves and jump in with their two feet."

20

The staircase was dark and the wet night wind gusted in through the broken windowpanes, blowing out the matches that Jack lit to see where he was going. He had forgotten on what floor Bresach lived, and he had to light matches in front of every apartment on the upper floors to peer at the brass plates that gave the names of the occupants. He passed a couple embraced in the darkness on a landing and he was followed up a flight of steps by the soft laughter of the girl when he stumbled. When, panting and exhausted, he finally got to Bresach's door, he remembered it, though, and rang the bell impatiently, keeping his finger pressed against the button.

He heard footsteps approaching and took his finger off the button as Bresach threw the door open, a dark silhouette against a dim light high in the hallway ceiling.

Bresach didn't invite him in immediately. He stood there, in a torn sweater, a cigarette between his lips, staring suspiciously at Jack. "What is it now?" Bresach asked.

Jack pushed past him without answering and walked down the hallway toward the room at the end of it, from which there was a spill of light. Max was in bed, sitting up and reading, by the light of a small brass lamp, with his usual muffler wrapped around his neck against the cold. Even though he was in bed, he was wearing a sweater.

"Good evening, Mr. Andrus," Max said, putting his book down, and making a motion as though to get out of bed. "I'll be dressed in a . . ."

Jack waved at him impatiently. "Don't bother. I'm just going to stay a minute." He turned toward Bresach, who was leaning against the wall near the door, regarding him with a puzzled expression on his face.

"What's the matter, Jack?" Bresach said. "They throw you out of your hotel? We have plenty of room here, as you see . . ." He grinned malevolently, enjoying his poverty, Jack thought, feeling superior and holy because of it.

"Can you be at the studio tomorrow morning at nine?" Jack said.

"What for?" Bresach asked suspiciously.

"You've got a job."

"With whom?"

"With me," Jack said. "I'm finishing the picture for Delaney. You'll be my assistant."

Bresach looked sullen now, and walked restlessly back and forth in the small room. "What the hell do you know about directing?" he asked.

"Anything I don't know," Jack said sardonically, "you can tell me. That's the whole idea."

"What's this?" Bresach asked. "A joke? Is Delaney getting even with me for what I told him this morning?"

"It was love at first sight this morning," Jack said. "You reminded him of what he was like at your age. Insufferable."

Bresach grunted. "There's a lot more to the old bastard than I thought there was," he said.

"He told me to pick your brains," Jack said. "So, any ideas you have about acting or staging or cutting or anything, speak up."

"Don't worry," Bresach said. "I'll have plenty of ideas. Hey . . ." He came up close to Jack. "I thought you were supposed to go home in a couple of days."

"I was supposed to," Jack said, "but it turns out I'm not."

"Can you stand having me around, whispering into your ear day after day?" Bresach said.

"I'm not in this for my own amusement," Jack said. "I'm here to try to save Delaney's life." He did not tell Bresach that only by fulfilling every wish of Delaney's, every instruction, to the letter, did he feel that he was making amends for the years of neglect, for the friendship which he had selfishly allowed to lapse, for the ruin that he had done nothing to avert. "Well," he said, "I'm in a hurry. Are you going to be there at nine in the morning or not?"

Bresach rubbed his cheeks with his two hands, making a rasping, unshaven sound in the still room, as he decided. Max leaned over in bed and picked up the book he had been reading and turned down a corner of a page to mark his spot and put the book neatly on the floor. Jack saw the title. It was *The Possessed*. Max saw Jack glancing at the book. "It is not the language for Dostoevski," Max said, apologizing. "But it is good for my study of Italian."

"There's one thing I hate about this whole business," Bresach said.

"What's that?" Jack turned back to him.

"Finally you're going to think that I ought to be glad you came to Rome."

"I promise you that I will never think that you ought to be glad I came to Rome," Jack said wearily. "Make up your mind. I have to go."

"All right," Bresach said sullenly. "I'll be there."

"Good." Jack started out.

"Wait a minute," Bresach said. "I better have a script right now . . ."

Jack hadn't thought about that. He reflected for a moment. "You'd better get hold of Delaney's script. Here . . ." He took an old envelope from his pocket and wrote Hilda's address and telephone number on it. "This is his secretary. Call her and tell her I want you to have Delaney's script tonight. Then get a taxi and go and get it. She lives on the Via della Croce."

"No." Bresach was shaking his head. "I can't do it."

"What do you mean you can't do it?" Jack's voice rose in exasperation.

"I don't have the money for a taxi." Bresach leered at him, as if he had just told a good joke.

270

Jack took some bills out of his pocket and thrust them into Bresach's hand.

"I owe you three thousand lire," Bresach said. "I'll pay you back at the end of the week. When I'm rich and famous."

Jack turned and went out of the room without answering. The lovers were still on the landing. Jack could hear their heavy breathing all the way down to the ground floor.

"No," Clara was saying loudly, "I won't go to see him. I won't go near him. I don't care if he's dying." She was sitting on the edge of one of the twin beds in her room at the Grand. It was a small room, at the back of the hotel. Clara was living austerely, so that, in her bare room, she could think of her husband in the opulent, overfurnished apartment on the Circus Maximus and have one more reason for self-pity. Her skin was yellower than ever. Her hair was in curlers and she was wearing a long, pink woolen robe, like the robes young girls wear in college dormitories in magazine advertisements. She had kicked off her mules, and Jack could see the little flash of red from her painted toenails.

"And I don't believe he's dying," Clara went on, picking nervously at a curler above her forehead. "He's perfectly capable of doing it as a trick . . ."

"Now, Clara . . ." Jack protested.

"You don't know him the way I do. It's a way of bringing me to my knees. One more time." She stood up and went over to the bureau with a rustle of bare feet on the carpet. She opened a drawer and took out a half-empty bottle of Scotch which had been concealed under a pile of nightgowns. "Do you want a drink? I need one," she said defiantly.

"Thanks, Clara."

She went into the bathroom for glasses and water. She kept talking, her voice flat and complaining over the sound of the running water and the clink of glass. "That's another thing we can put to the credit of Mr. Maurice Delaney," she said, out of sight in the bathroom, her voice echoing off the old-fashioned marble walls. "He's turning me into a solitary drinker." There was silence for a moment, broken only by the sound of the water running from the tap. Then Clara began again, in another, harsher tone, "He can't kid me. He's not going to die. He has the resistance of a bull. Even

271

at his age—he can work twelve hours a day for eight months at a time and spend hours in bars talking to every bum he meets and visit women who live on the top floor of five-story buildings without elevators and . . ." She reappeared, carrying the two glasses half full of water, Medusa in curlers, playing barmaid, the scrubbed yellowish folds of her face set in implacable, vengeful lines. She poured the whisky carefully, not like a drinker, but like a house-wife. "Enough?" she said, holding up Jack's glass.

"Plenty," he said.

She gave him the glass and sat down again on the edge of the bed. She put her glass on the bedside table without tasting it. "This time," she said feverishly, "I'm going to teach him a lesson. He can't have me on any old terms. If he's going to have me, it's going to be on my own terms . . ."

"Clara," Jack said gently, "don't you think it would be wiser to wait to settle all this later, when he's better?"

"No," she said. "Because he won't settle it when he's better. The only time you ever get anything out of Maurice Delaney is when he's hurting and sorry for himself. You don't know him the way I do. Failure's the only thing that makes him human. Even before all this, if I wanted a new coat or an addition to the house or a trip to New York, I used to wait until he had a sore throat or a pain in his gut so he'd think he had cancer, or after he got panned in the newspapers. When he's feeling good he's got a heart of cement."

"He's going to be sick a long time," Jack said.

"Good," she said. "Maybe it's a blessing in disguise. Maybe now my fourteen years of hell will be over."

"What do you want, Clara?" Jack asked curiously. "A divorce?"

"I'll never divorce him," she said. She looked at her glass on the table beside her as though she had just remembered it, and took an old-maidish sip of the whisky. "Never as long as he lives."

"Why?"

"Because I love him," she said flatly.

"Love . . ." Jack shook his head wonderingly. Clara Delaney's concept of love seemed better suited for the basis of the regulations of a penal battalion than for a marriage.

"I see you shaking your head. Don't think I don't. What do you know about love?" Clara said contemptuously. "Every time a woman gets on your nerves for ten minutes you move on to the next one . . ."

272

"Now, Clara," Jack protested mildly, "that isn't exactly accurate."

"I know about you, I know about you," she said, accusing in him all that was easy and pleasurable and self-preserving in love. "You don't know anything, because you walk away from it every time it begins to hurt. I know," she said, her voice rising crazily, "and I'm the only one who does. You know what love is?" she demanded. "Love is endurance."

"I'm not going to argue with you," Jack said. "All I know is that Maurice asked to see only one person—you."

"Well, isn't that tender, isn't that melting?" she said. "Doesn't that come as a whopping surprise, after everything I've done for him?"

"What do you want from him, Clara?" Jack asked. "What do you want me to tell him?"

"You tell him that when I'm convinced that he's given up Barzelli—and all the other Barzellis—I'll take him back."

Jealousy is a form of faith, Jack thought. The true believers feel that the general infliction of pain is right and holy in the free exercise of their religion. He stood up. "Well," he said, "anything else you want me to say to him?"

"Say anything you want," Clara said flatly. "Tell him exactly what I said."

"I don't think you realize how sick he is, Clara," Jack said. "The doctor says he's to be kept as quiet as possible, he's to be spared any kind of excitement . . ."

"You hate me," Clara said, her pale, unpainted lips trembling. "Everybody hates me . . ."

"Don't be foolish, Clara." Jack reached out and tried to touch her hand reassuringly.

"Don't touch me." She pulled her hand back with exaggerated repugnance. "And don't lie to me. You hate me. You think I'm heartless, selfish . . . You think I'm willing to let him die. I'll tell you how heartless I am. If he dies, I'll kill myself. Remember my words. The happiest day of my life was the day he asked me to marry him. You know when he asked me to marry him? I was sitting in his outside office, typing, and he came in, looking as though somebody had just clubbed him over the head, all white, with a funny look on his face, as though he was trying to smile, as though he thought he was smiling, only he wasn't smiling . . . He'd just come from the front office and they'd told him they didn't want him any more. His contract still had two years to run and they'd offered to pay him off. Pay him off in full. Hundreds of thousands of dollars. But it was worth it to them, just to have him *not* make pictures for them. Can you imagine what that meant to a man like Maurice Delaney? He sat on the edge of my desk, telling me all this, pretending to himself he was smiling, pretending it didn't mean anything to him, and all of a sudden, without any leadup to it at all, he asked me to marry him. That day. I still called him Mr. Delaney. But he knew where he had to go for help. For help when he was in *real* trouble. Mr. Delaney. We flew down to Mexico and we were married that night. He doesn't have any of the money left, but he still has me. And he's going to have me till the day he dies. I'd jump off a cliff if he asked me to, and he knows it. There's nothing else in my life. No children, no work, no other men. Christ, I won't even go to a movie without him. But I won't go to see him. For his sake, as well as mine. We've got to get our lives straight once and for all. He's got to stop dividing himself up, throwing himself away, making a fool of himself in everybody's eyes, doting on whores, buying them diamond bracelets, don't think I don't know about that, along with everything else, even when it takes the last penny out of the bank . . . If he's ever going to be saved it's got to be now. After this, it'll be too late, I'll never have the chance again . . ."

She was weeping now, ugly, huge sobs shaking her narrow shoulders in the girlish pink robe, her head down, her hands clutching each other in her lap, her bare feet, with the frivolously painted toes, moving in a kind of aimless shivering dance, hanging down from the bed. "If you want to hate me," she whispered, "go right ahead. Hate me. Let everybody hate me."

"Nobody hates you, Clara," Jack said softly, moved and embarrassed by her outbreak. He touched her shoulder. This time she didn't pull away. "I wish I could help," he said.

"Nobody can help," she said. "Nobody but him. Go away now, please."

Jack hesitated a moment, then started toward the door.

"Don't worry," Clara said tonelessly, gripping her glass in her two hands, "he's too mean to die."

Jack went out. He was certain that as soon as the door was closed behind him, Clara would go into the bathroom and pour her drink into the basin and then put the whisky bottle back in the bureau drawer, under the nightgowns, to be left there until she received her next visitor.

Barzelli lived out on the Via Appia Antica. There was very little traffic and Guido drove swiftly past the dark tombs and the ruined aqueduct, fitfully suspended in the watery reflection of the headlights. In the sunlight, the crumbling masonry bore witness to the pride, the industry, the cleverness of Guido's ancestors. At night, like this, in the winter rain, they brought to mind only images of ruin, dissolution, and the emptiness of human vanity. The arches had carried water to a city that had deserved to fall; the tombs commemorated kings who did not deserve to be remembered.

Guido drove into the graveled driveway of a spreading, two-story flat-roofed house, set in a sloping garden. He had obviously been there many times before. All the curtains were drawn, but there was a light on by the side of the door.

"I won't be long," Jack said hopefully. He had a twinge of guilt about keeping Guido from his bed and his family. What's Delaney's heart to Guido, Jack thought, that Guido's Sunday with his wife and three children should be spoiled because of it?

He rang the bell. From within, faintly, there came the sound of jazz being played. A butler in a starched white jacket opened the door.

"Miss Barzelli, please," Jack said.

The butler nodded and took Jack's coat and laid it on a huge gilt and brocade chair, one of a pair that flanked the doorway in the wide marble hallway. Now the music was louder. A phonograph was playing Cole Porter, a woman's voice was singing, "It's too damned hot . . ."

The butler led the way toward a pair of high closed doors, carved and painted white, touched, too, with gilt. Barzelli likes the look of gold, Jack thought, she wants everyone to know how far she's come from the village in Catania where she was born. The butler didn't ask Jack's name. He threw the doors open without ceremony and waved Jack in. He seemed used to having men he had never seen before appear late at night and ask, in any language, to see the lady of the house.

Barzelli was dancing in the middle of the room with a tall curly-haired young man in shirtsleeves. She was wearing tight green slacks and a black blouse with a low oval neckline and she was dancing in her bare feet on the veined marble floor. Lounging in the room were two other young men, in dark suits. One of them was lying stretched out on a long woolly white couch, his feet, in their narrow pointed black shoes, comfortably crossed on the fluffy cushions. A glass of whisky rested on his breastbone. The men hardly looked at Jack when he entered—one incurious, heavy-lidded glance of dark, long-lashed eyes, opaque with drink, and then they languidly turned their heads again to watch Barzelli and her partner as they danced. They were not the same young men whom Jack had noticed at the bar of his hotel and later at the night club, but they were of the same type. Ordinary riflemen of the Roman legion, Jack thought, easily obtainable to fill in for casualties at the nearest replacement depot. There were no other women in the room. Even before a word was said, Jack had the feeling that everybody there, with the exception of Barzelli, had been drinking all Sunday.

Barzelli saw Jack over her partner's shoulder. She smiled at him and made a little slow gesture with her long fingers to welcome him, but she didn't stop dancing. "The drinks are in the corner, mister," she said.

Jack stood at the doorway, watching her. He felt uncomfortable, like a trespasser lured by mistake to watch a spectacle he had no wish to see. If there had been another woman besides Barzelli in the room he'd have been more at ease. This way, it was almost as if he'd blundered into a place where some obscure and unpleasant rite was being conducted, a rite that had been performed many times in the past, a rainy Sunday, Roman, Appian rite, perverse and disturbing, celebrating boredom, satiety, sensuality, parasitism, luxury.

The priestess danced, barefooted, in her ceremonial green and black, moving her tightly encased lovely hips in slow, obscene movements to the chant from the phonograph. Her hair loosened and swung in a dark mass over her bare full shoulders, from which the collar of her blouse had slipped. A distant, dreamlike smile was fixed on the soft, wide lips as she swayed, half leading, half led, close to her partner, whose silk shirt was stained with sweat. Jack had the feeling that they had been dancing like this, tranced, connected, mechanical, bored, titillated, for hours. The dark young men in their dark suits, acolytes, priests, worshippers, past and future participants, watched, bemused, making ritual slow trips to the bar to pour the accustomed libations. The light was garish and hard. A neon strip ran all around the room two feet below the high ceiling, behind a carved molding. There were roses everywhere, in tall glass vases, many of them faded and losing their petals. Three huge portraits of the lady of the house, by three differ-

nt artists, were the only paintings on the dark blue walls. One of
he paintings was a nude, Barzelli stretched out, with her arms
bove her head, on a red rug.

The temple was disorderly, as though its servants were under-
aid or carelessly regulated, but all appointments were there for
very occasion. The place of sacrifice was no doubt the long white
ouch, but the young man lying there with the highball glass on
is breastbone was certainly not the chosen victim. An habitué of
he sanctum, he made familiar use of the holy objects. The true
ictim, Jack felt, was lying behind a blank white door in a shadowed
oom, breathing oxygen through a tube taped onto his cheek.

The music came to a stop. The mechanical arm of the phonograph lifted slowly and fell into place on its rest as the turntable
ushed into stillness. The dancers stood for a moment, arms on
ach other's shoulders, hanging loose. They swayed gently, too
veary or too inert to break away. Then Barzelli said something
n Italian and her partner laughed, briefly, and went over to the
lass table, piled with bottles, in the corner of the room, that
erved as a bar. Barzelli brushed her hair back with one hand, with
 quick movement, and approached Jack. She stopped close to him,
miling at him, without friendliness, her hand on her hip, in a pose
hat betrayed her early years in the village in Catania. "You do not
rink?" she said.

"Not for the moment," Jack said.

"I suppose you have come to tell me something about poor Mau-
ice." Her tone was challenging, hostile.

"More or less," Jack said.

"Jumping horses!" She snorted derisively. "He has no actors to
lominate on Sunday, so he uses animals." She eyed Jack, smiling
oldly, waiting for him to answer. "You do not think so?"

"I hadn't thought about it," Jack said.

"Well," Barzelli said impatiently, "what is it? What secret terrible
nessage are you bringing?"

Jack looked around him. The dark, drunken eyes of the young
nen were on them, incurious but attentive. "Can we talk alone?"
e said.

Barzelli shrugged. "If you want," she said. She turned and walked
oward a closed door at the other end of the room. Jack followed.
3arzelli opened the door and they went into the dining room, a long
are room with an iron-and-glass table and spindly gilt chairs. An-
ther portrait of Barzelli, this time in a black dress and black hat,

hung over the sideboard, and an elaborate glass chandelier shed harsh white light over the table. Jack closed the door behind him Barzelli sat down at the head of the table, her elbows on the table top, her hands supporting her chin. Jack saw that she wasn't wearing anything under her blouse, and her full breasts, which had contributed, as much as anything else, to her success, were clearly visible against the thin stuff of her blouse.

"Sit," she said, indicating a chair on her right.

Jack sat down carefully. The chair looked so frail that he was afraid it would break under him.

"So," Barzelli said, "what does the poor man want? He was supposed to have lunch with me today. I waited and waited. I was furious. Luckily, some friends dropped in . . ." With a twitch of her shoulder she indicated the room from which they had just come "So the food was not wasted."

They've been drinking since one o'clock, this afternoon, Jack thought. No wonder their eyes look like that.

"That Mr. Fogel finally called me at five o'clock," Barzelli said angrily. "It hadn't occurred to anyone before that that maybe the star of the picture should be told the director was dying. It is an unimportant little detail."

"I'm sorry," Jack said. "I should have done it."

"It makes no difference." Barzelli shrugged. "Mr. Fogel said he probably would not die, anyway." She reached over in a long stretching, fluent movement and picked a dried fig out of a glass basket of fruit in the middle of the table. She tore it in half with her strong, even teeth, and chewed loudly. "What am I supposed to do?" she asked indifferently. "Do we shoot tomorrow?"

"Report to the studio for your regular call," Jack said. "Didn't they tell you?"

"My poor dear man," Barzelli said, "you do not understand the Italian movie business. Chaos. Maybe in three weeks they will straighten things out. So—I am to be on the set tomorrow?"

"Yes."

"Is that what you came to tell me?" she asked, chewing loudly "All this long trip so late at night?"

"No," Jack said. "I . . ."

"Who is going to finish the picture?" Barzelli said. "Tucino? I warn you, if he goes near the camera, I walk off and I stay off . . ."

"It won't be Tucino," Jack said, surprised and grateful at this unexpected ally.

"Who, then?" Barzelli asked suspiciously.

"I'm not sure," said Jack. He had decided this was not the time to have it out with Barzelli, alone with her, in her own home. He had the feeling he would need help with her when she found out he was taking over. "It will be settled sometime tonight."

"It had better be settled to my satisfaction," Barzelli said. "Tell them that."

"I'll tell them."

"Then what?" Barzelli said. "What are you here to say?"

Jack took a long breath. What was he here to say? I bring a message from the depths of marriage; help rescue my friend where he drowns in fourteen years of love and hatred; understand the bitter, octopal twinings of a man and woman who have spent a good portion of their lives devouring each other, strangling each other, rising and diving in the treacherous element, surfacing into the air, plunging below, always terribly clasped, supporting, hurting, caressing each other. What was he there to say to this glittering, impervious woman with her shining white teeth, her glowing skin, her superb, victorious body, her perfect health, her cunning, self-adoring brain, her retinue of beautiful young drunkards on the other side of the door? What was he there to say? Learn pity in a moment, become human before midnight, weep one small tear for the suffering of a poor, foolish, desperate soul. He could say some of this, or all of this, to any other of the men and women he had met since he had come to Rome, to Bresach, to Max, to Veronica, to Holt and his wife, to Despière, to Tasseti, even, and hope to have some portion of it strike a sympathetic chord somewhere within them. But with Barzelli . . . He stared at her. She was leaning forward, displaying the smooth sweep of her breasts, chewing evenly on her dried fig, regarding him impassively, waiting, ready to reject any claims on her. Anybody but Barzelli, he thought. But he had to say something. Delaney, lying behind the blank white door, had the right to expect him to say *some*thing . . . The instructions, to the letter . . .

"Clara Delaney," he began flatly, "refuses to go visit Maurice in the hospital."

"Good," Barzelli said. "He can die in peace if he has to."

"No," Jack said. "It's the one thing he wants, that he thinks he must have."

"Did he say that?" Barzelli asked, harshly.

"Yes."

"Imagine that. That dry washrag of a woman." She shook her head in wonder. Then she shrugged. "Well, even the worst atheists call for the priest when they think they're going to die. So—Signora Delaney won't go to the hospital. *Tragedia*. How does that concern me?"

"Delaney asked me to ask you please not to visit him in the hospital," Jack said, clumsily. "He says if his wife hears you've visited him, she'll never come to his room . . ."

For a moment, a look of puzzlement, incredulity, spread over Barzelli's face. Then she put her head back and laughed aloud. Her laugh was merry and deep and innocent. At that moment, Jack hated her and had an overpowering impulse to lean over and kiss, the gentlest and hungriest of kisses, the smooth, powerful throat, where it swept up from her bare shoulders. Deliberately, he sat farther back in his chair, averting his eyes. Abruptly, Barzelli stopped laughing. *"Mamma mia,"* she said. "American women! They belong in museums! Imagine that! And what do you do after you leave me, Mr. Andrus?" she asked, biting the words off. "Do you go to every one of the fifty women that Maurice Delaney has slept with since he was married and request them, for the sake of Mrs. Delaney, not to visit the great man in the hospital?" She jumped up and strode back and forth, like a prowling animal in a cage, her bare feet padding on the marble floor with a surprisingly hard, calloused noise. "For your information, Mr. Andrus," she said angrily, "and for Mr. Delaney's information, too, let me tell you that I have no intention of visiting him in the hospital. I hate sick men. I avoid them. They disgust me. Tell that to Mr. and Mrs. Delaney. Tell that to the lovebirds."

Jack stood up, getting ready to leave. Every time he changed his position abruptly, he felt dizzy and a haze seemed to obscure his vision. Now the sight of Barzelli prowling back and forth, barefooted and furious against the background of neon-lighted portraits, all considerably out of focus, was intolerable to him. He longed to be alone in the car with Guido, driving quietly through the dark night back to his own room.

"One more thing you can tell her," Barzelli was saying, her lips curled back in a grimace of scorn. "Her husband has not made love to me. Not ever. He has slept in the same bed with me, but he has not made love to me. Is that sufficiently clear? Should I write it out in Italian? You can have it translated by the clerk in your hotel. *He has not made love to me*. It may be of interest to her. It is of no

terest to me. American men, too," she said. "Maybe they belong
museums, too!"

Suddenly she regained control of herself. She stood absolutely
ill, leaning over the back of a chair, staring coldly at Jack. "It is
no consequence," she said. "Why not be calm? Tell Maurice I
ould like him to get well. Why not?" She shrugged. "It does me no
arm. Now, it is really very late and we are all going to have an
npleasant day tomorrow, we must sleep." She indicated a door
at led into the hallway. "You do not have to go through the young
en again. I see that they disturb you."

21

Keep out of the bedrooms of your friends, Jack thought, as he s[...]
beside Guido, on the road back to Rome past the tombs; or eve[...]
out of the living rooms of the friends of your friends—there a[...]
unpleasant mysteries hidden in such places.

He closed his eyes and dozed and awoke in the swiftly movi[...]
car only as it swept up the hill toward the Quirinal. The figures [...]
the two horse tamers at the heads of their enormous stone stee[...]
loomed in the dark square. The sentries stood with their machi[...]
pistols in front of the president's palace.

"Nothing more tonight, Guido," Jack said as they drove up und[...]
the *portico* of his hotel, a few minutes later. "But I'm afraid I[...]
need you in the morning at about eight fifteen. I'm sorry for t[...]
day . . ."

"No need to be sorry, monsieur," Guido said. "When disast[...]
strikes, one expects to lose a little sleep."

Jack looked across at the grave, handsome face, and thought h[...]

atient and capable and resilient the man was, how gentle and
understanding. He has lessons to teach all of us whose errands he
has run this Sunday, Jack thought. Hard-working, graceful, sweet-
tempered and enduring, Guido seemed, at that moment, to repre-
sent the deepest values, the permanent, marvelous, ever-replen-
ished gifts of his race. It was one of the blackest marks against
Guido's country, Jack felt, that it could find nothing better for him
to do than to drive the spoiled, invading children of the twentieth
century around the city of Rome. I must do something for him,
Jack thought, I must do something enormous.

"Tell me, Guido," Jack said, "if you had some money, what
would you do?"

"Some money?" Guido asked, politely puzzled. "How much
money?"

"A great deal," Jack said.

Guido thought for a moment. "I would take my wife and my
three children to Toulon for a week," he said, "and visit the vineyard and the lady for whom I worked during the war."

Two hundred, two hundred and fifty dollars, Jack calculated.
Hardly more. In Guido's calculation, a great deal of money. Well,
Jack decided, I'm going to give it to him. When they pay me. My
tribute to Italy.

He sighed. He was tired and it took an effort to get out of the
car. "Good night, Guido," he said. "See you in the morning." Let
the gift come as a surprise.

"Good night, monsieur," Guido said. "Sleep well."

He drove off.

The concierge had three messages for him. They all said the
same thing. Call Operator 382 in Paris. Parigi, the hotel operator
had written. The first one had come in at noon, the last one only a
half-hour ago. Jack looked at his watch. It was only ten minutes
past one. So much had happened that day that it seemed impossible
that it was only ten minutes past one. He suddenly realized that he
was very hungry and he ordered a bottle of beer and some cheese
and bread to be sent up to his room. As he waited for the elevator,
crushing the three bits of paper in his hand, he remembered the
morning, with Bresach waiting for him in the lobby, and Veronica's telegram, *"Don't worry, dearest . . ."* Fifteen hours ago.
Another era, when people could write, Don't worry, dearest. Zurich,
he remembered. How were the heart cases in Zurich tonight, how
did the Swiss stand on the subject of the fidelity of Delaney to his

wife, what was the opinion, in that neutral country, of Barzelli and her three drunkards?

The telephone was ringing as he unlocked the door to his apartment. Jack switched on the light and went over to the desk and said, "Hello, hello . . ."

"You don't have to snap my head off," a woman's voice said with a little laugh.

"Who's this?" Jack asked, although he knew.

"You know who it is, Jack."

"Carlotta," Jack said flatly. He hadn't spoken to her since the morning in California, and had only communicated with her through lawyers, and it had been nearly ten years, but he knew. "I thought I saw you when I was leaving the hospital."

"You don't sound overjoyed to hear my voice," she said.

"Carlotta," he said, "I've had a hard day and I'm tired and there are several calls I have to make . . ."

"I'm down on the third floor," she said, "with Stiles and a bottle of champagne. Why don't you join us?"

"Tell Stiles he'd better go home and go to sleep," Jack said. "He's called for nine o'clock in the morning. And, while you're at it, you can tell him to lay off the champagne."

"I'll tell him all those things," Carlotta said. "I'll tell him we want to be alone. I'm sure he'll understand."

"I'm not coming down," Jack said.

"That's not very friendly, Jack," she said.

"I don't feel very friendly."

"After all these years." Now she was playing, mockingly, at being hurt. "I've forgotten any grudges I might have held against you . . ."

"Grudges . . ." Jack began to cut in. Then he stopped. He wasn't going to argue with Carlotta. Not tonight. "What the hell are you doing in Rome, anyway?"

"I was in London, having lunch," Carlotta said, "and I heard the news over the radio."

"What news?" Jack asked confusedly.

"About Maurice. I got the first plane I could. After all, he's one of the oldest friends I have in the world. And the radio sounded so ominous . . . as though he . . ." She interrupted herself. "They wouldn't let me in to see him at the hospital and all they told me was that he was doing as well as could be expected . . . Jack . . ." Her voice sank. "Is he dying?"

"Probably not."

"Have you seen him?"

"Yes. For a minute."

"What was he like?"

Jack hesitated. What was he like? He was like Maurice Delaney, that was what he was like. Once more he was worrying about a silly movie and a silly woman, more or less as usual, except that this time he was doing it flat on his back in a hospital bed, taking oxygen. "His spirit was high," Jack said. That much was approximately the truth. "He said he wasn't afraid of dying."

"Oh, poor Maurice. Do you think they'll let you see him tomorrow?"

"I imagine so."

"Will you tell him I'm here, Jack?"

"Yes."

"And will you tell him I'll stay here until he's better and that I want to see him?"

"Yes."

"You sound terribly impatient with me, Jack," Carlotta said reproachfully.

"I'm trying to reach Paris."

"After that, don't you want to come down here? Just for a minute . . . I'm so . . . so . . . *curious* about you." She laughed.

"I'm sorry, Carlotta. Not tonight."

"Jack, will you answer one question for me?"

"What's that?"

"Do you hate me?"

Jack sighed. After Clara and Barzelli, it was easy to hate the entire female sex. "No," he said flatly, "I don't hate you, Carlotta. Good night."

"Good night," she said.

He hung up the phone, and sat hunched over it on the desk, with his overcoat on, staring at it. Carlotta. Along with everything else, Carlotta.

Then the phone rang again. He let it ring three times, sitting with his hand on it, then picked it up. It was Paris, asking if this was Mr. John Andrus, and then he heard his wife's voice, against a background of music and other voices.

"Jack, Jack, can you hear me?" Hélène was saying, her voice faraway and indistinct, muffled by distance and the pulsating sound of something that sounded like a guitar. "Are you all right, Jack? I read it, in the papers this morning—isn't it awful—and I've been trying to call you all day. Can you hear me, Jack?"

"Barely," Jack said. He had the feeling that there was something puzzling in what she had said, but he was too tired to figure it out. "What's that noise behind you?"

"I'm at Bert and Vivian's," Hélène said. "It's a party. They have a Russian gypsy here. She's playing a balalaika and singing. Can you hear me?"

"Well enough," Jack said. Unreasonably, he was annoyed with her for talking to him from a place where her voice was nearly drowned out by a balalaika and a gypsy.

"I've been worrying about you all day, *chéri*," Hélène was saying. "I'm sure it must be horrible for you."

You couldn't have been worrying too much, Jack was tempted to say, if you're still out at one thirty in the morning, with all those drunks around you. Then he was ashamed of himself for thinking it, and didn't say it. After all, what was Hélène supposed to do? She had never met Delaney, and she hardly could be expected to sit mournfully by the telephone because, a thousand miles away, he had been brought down by illness. Now the noise of the party swelled and Jack couldn't make out what his wife was saying. There was just the timbre of her voice, hurried, affectionate, and a little heightened by drink. He listened, dazed with fatigue, vaguely comforted by the tone of love and the feeling that finally, in this long day, there was someone who was interested in helping *him,* rather than demanding something from him. There was a knock on his door and he shouted "Come in," and the waiter entered with his beer and cheese.

"What's that?" Hélène said. For the moment the line was absolutely clear and the singing behind her and the other voices had hushed and he could hear her as though she were talking in the next room.

"It's the waiter with some bread and cheese," Jack said. "I haven't eaten all day." He motioned to the waiter to put the tray down on the desk next to the telephone.

"Oh, Jack, that's just what I was afraid of," Hélène said. "You're not taking care of yourself. Don't you want me to get on the plane tomorrow and come down there?"

Jack hesitated, watching the waiter open the bottle of beer. He fumbled in his pocket and tossed two hundred lire on the tray for the waiter who bowed ceremoniously to him in thanks.

"Jack," Hélène said, "did you hear me?"

"Yes, I heard you," Jack said.

"Wouldn't it be nice if I came down?"

The idea of having Hélène by his side for the next few days, staving off Carlotta, acting as a buffer against Bresach and Clara, being there to talk over the problems presented by Holt's offer, was suddenly marvelously attractive.

"Well," he started to say, "I think . . ."

There was a burst of laughter over the phone, from the guests at Bert and Vivian's, and the balalaika and the gypsy voice came loudly over the wire. Now that's too much, Jack thought, giving in irritably to his nerves. If she wanted so damned much to talk to me, she could have at least found a quiet room to call from. Perversely, he remembered her complaining at the airport that he hadn't made love to her for two weeks and accusing him of being eager to leave. The claims, ambushes, demands, entrapments, of women. The music on the wire was infuriating him. He felt himself trembling. He knew he didn't want his wife in this room. He felt cold, unconnected, grateful for the distance between them. Whatever love he was capable of in his exhaustion and worry, he was saving for Delaney. At that moment, he felt, if Hélène pressed him, he might say that he never wanted to see her again.

"What were you saying, *chéri?*" Hélène said. "This damned noise."

"Nothing," he said.

"When do you think you'll be coming home?"

Now, he thought. The explosion. "Things are all balled up here," he said. "I may not get out for another six weeks."

"Six weeks?" She sounded incredulous.

"I'll write it all in a letter," he said.

"But what about Joe Morrison? What about your job?"

"I'll write him a letter, too."

"He won't let you do anything like this . . ."

"He'll just have to," Jack said. "Listen, this call is costing a fortune . . ."

"I don't understand. What's happened to you? Don't hang up," she said hurriedly. Then away from the receiver, "Please, boys, less noise, I'm talking to Rome." Then again to him, "Jack, are you all right? You're not making any sense. Are you drunk? You can't stay away six weeks . . ."

Then he realized what had puzzled him in the beginning of her conversation. "Hélène," he broke in, "what do you mean you read it in the paper this morning? Delaney had his attack at eleven o'clock . . ."

"Delaney?" Hélène said. "Who said anything about Delaney? This damned connection . . ."

"Hélène," Jack said, "speak slowly and clearly. What did you read in the paper this morning?"

"Jean-Baptiste," she said. "He was killed yesterday. In Algeria. In an ambush. Didn't you know? Didn't you read the newspapers this morning . . . ?"

"No," Jack said. "Now, listen. I'm going to hang up now. I'll call you tomorrow . . ."

"Jack," Hélène said desperately, "wait a minute. I have to talk to you. I can't. . . ."

He hung up. He couldn't get a sound out of his constricted and aching throat. He sat looking at the telephone for a long time. He wanted to weep. If he could weep, the intolerable pain in his throat and behind his eyes would be eased. But no tears came. All he could do was sit hunched over on the desk and stare at the telephone. The telephone went slowly and rhythmically in and out of focus.

Then he remembered the envelope that Jean-Baptiste had given him the night of the Holts' cocktail party, when he had gone off to his little war. The envelope was in a bureau drawer in the bedroom, under a pile of shirts. For a moment, Jack debated with himself whether or not to let it go till morning. His eyes were heavy, his bones ached, he wanted to drop, fully clothed, onto his bed and sleep. Sitting there, he wasn't sure that he could find the energy even to move into the bedroom. But he made himself stand up and go get the envelope. When he came back into the living room, he held the envelope in his hands for a long time before he tore it open.

"Dear Dottore," the letter began, in spiky French script. "You must not be surprised. In a murderous world it is normal to be murdered. If you are reading this, it is because I am dead. I expect it, this time. I do not know why. A feeling of bad luck, maybe. I have had the feeling of bad luck several times before, and nothing has happened to me, and perhaps this time it will be the same and I will reappear in Rome and ask you for the envelope and you will never know about my feeling of bad luck, and we will

288

celebrate my return together, as usual. Only this time, the feeling is stronger—

"*Eh, bien,* the worst is over. Now to business. You will see, included in the envelope, aside from this letter to you, quite a few manuscript pages. The manuscript is the article on your friend Delaney. It is unfinished. If you glance through it, you will see that I have said some harsh things about him. Living, I would not mind having it published. But dead, I would prefer to have it destroyed. I would not like my last words to be harmful and critical. I have already been given a big advance on this piece from the magazine and if they found what I have written they would undoubtedly have it finished in the office and publish it. The money is spent, but a dead man has the right to be slightly dishonorable. So read it or do not read it, as you like, and then destroy it. You can even go so far as to tell your friend Delaney that I admired him. This is even partly the truth.

"Finally, if I am killed in this little miserable war in Algeria, I will be very sorry. It is all shit on both sides, and one should not be asked to die in it.

"I am sorry to burden you with this, my dear Jack, but in running down my list of friends, before writing this letter, I have come to the conclusion that everybody else whom I could trust is already dead.

"Be assured (as we polite French put it at the end of our letters), my dear *Dottore,* of my sentiments devoted and distinguished.

Jean-Baptiste"

The last two lines were written in English, as though Despière had been loath to end a letter like this on a serious note. Self-mocking and ironic, skeptical of pompousness and lofty notions, Despière had signed off his life in his accustomed style.

Delaney, Jack thought, Despière. In the same day. I was warned, and now it is happening. *Jamais deux sans trois.* French proverb. Never two without a third. The night is not over. It has been prolonged by one death.

Jack made a neat pile of the manuscript pages and put them on the desk. He couldn't bring himself to read it. Not now.

He went into the bedroom. The bed had been turned down for the night by the maid many hours before, the reversed sheet making a crisp triangle of white in the light of the bed-table lamp, reminding him of hospitals. He was too tired to undress. He took off his shoes with an effort, feeling stiff and sore, and turned off the lamp. But sleep would not come. Memories of Despière crowded in on him.

"*. . . and we will celebrate my return together, as usual.*"

There had been the return from Indochina, where Despière had nearly been killed, ingloriously, in a jeep accident. Despière had telephoned as soon as he reached his hotel and he and Jack and Hélène and the American mannequin Despière had been more or less living with at the time had gone out to dinner and to several bars and night clubs, drinking champagne all the time, toasting the driver of the jeep and the driver of the truck that had hit it, and various other people, as their names came up, so that they had all been quite drunk by two o'clock in the morning. Despière, who still was suffering from the aftereffects of concussion and whose head was bound up in a huge bandage that looked like a crooked turban had insisted upon doing a wild triumphant dance in the middle of the floor, with Hélène, even though, from time to time, Hélène had to hold onto him to keep him from slipping to the floor.

"You ought to stop him," Jack had said to Despière's girl. "He's going to feel like hell in the morning."

The girl shook her head. "Nothing'll stop him tonight," she said. "I tried to stop him from drinking this evening, before we met you, and I told him he'd suffer tomorrow. All he did was laugh and say, 'Of course I will. But I must celebrate that I am alive. I am ready to pay for the joy in the morning.' "

The mannequin was married to someone else now, and living in New York, and Jack was sure that when she read about Despière in the papers at breakfast, she would remember the night club and Despière in his turban of bandage dancing crookedly and triumphantly to celebrate the fact that he was alive and saying, "I am ready to pay for the joy in the morning."

I was warned that one would die, Jack thought, lying in the dark room, *perhaps I should have warned him as he left the cocktail party. But I thought that it was I who was being warned—about myself.*

He lay still, trying, with his eyes shut, to make himself realize that there would never be again the ring on the telephone, the amused voice, saying, *"Dottore,"* or *"Monsieur le Ministre,* I am once more in town. I am afraid it will be necessary to have a drink immediately."

290

And then, later, I thought it was Delaney. But we are both alive. Only Jean-Baptiste . . .

Only Jean-Baptiste . . . Naturally, Jack thought, it had to be him. How could I have ever missed it? The most integral of Europeans, with his gift of languages, his drifting across borders, his history of having fought in so many different lands, in France, in Russia, in Germany, Africa . . . With his intelligent, pessimistic appraisal of what Europe had come to, mixed with his hard French gaiety and mocking clarity of vision. The professional spectator of the age's violence. Finally, the spectator must be sucked in, must become an actor. Despière had long ago used up his spectator's allowance of time and luck. The age could not continue to permit him to go on indefinitely . . . The atrocity editor, he had called himself. There was no final way of remaining on the edge of atrocities, removed from them . . . In the long run, the editor looks down at his desk and sees that the story that has been placed there that day is his own.

Now he was afraid to sleep. His blood drummed in his ears and the muscles of his neck felt rigid, as though they were straining, independently of him, to pull his head from the pillows. He sat up and turned on the light, then got off the bed and went back into the living room.

A window had swung open and the wind had blown the pages of Despière's manuscript off the desk. There were sheets of paper scattered all over the floor, giving an impression of lunatic disorder to the room. Wearily, he shambled over the flowered rug, bumping into the furniture, bending over and retrieving each sheet. They were not numbered, and now they were in a jumble, a maze of loose paragraphs typed on an old machine with a bad ribbon that made for wavy lines and sudden dark blotches on some letters. It was written in French and Despière had crossed out some things and added a great many others in ink, to complete the confusion. Jack read at random.

"Americans," he read, "artists included, differ from Europeans in that they believe in the continuing upward curve, rather than in a rhythmic beat of accomplishment . . ."

God, Jack thought, dead or alive that sentence would have to be rewritten to get past an editor.

"That is," Jack read, "an American, starting at any given point, believes that his career must go from success to success. In the American artist, of any kind, it is the equivalent of the optimistic businessman's creed of the continually expanding economy. The intermittent failure, the cadenced rise and fall of the level of a man's work, which is accepted and understood by the European artist, is fiercely rejected as a normal picture of the process of creation. A dip is not a dip to an American artist, it is a descent into an abyss, an offense against his native *moeurs* and his compatriots' most dearly held beliefs. In America, the normal incidence of failure, either real or imagined, private or public, which must be expected in such a chancy and elusive endeavor as writing novels or putting on plays or directing motion pictures is regarded, even by the artist himself, as evidence of guilt, as self-betrayal. The look of disaster which we see in the eyes of American artists, their sense of being outside the approval of the American culture, is not there by accident. They cannot keep on their countrymen's continually mounting curve, and they take to spectacular and desperate innovations, or to drink or to commerce because of it. In quite a few cases, they have taken to suicide. Some artists, being of stronger stuff, merely keep up a violent pretense that they have never failed. These artists will contend that their public has failed and their critics—never themselves. Maurice Delaney, who twenty years ago, made two or three of the best pictures of that time, is one of these . . ."

Jack put the pages on the desk, with an ashtray to hold them in place. The dead, he thought, are attacking the dying in Rome tonight. I'll read it through some other time, he thought, when all our wounds are cured.

He went into the bedroom. This time he undressed. He lay down carefully, hoping by the slowness of his movements, to keep his blood from drumming in his ears. It worked. He closed his eyes and slept.

He thought he heard a telephone ringing in his sleep, but when he woke up, the room was silent. His nose was bleeding, not much, but steadily, and he went into the bathroom for a towel and went back to sleep with the towel bunched up under his nose and over his mouth, so that, dozing uneasily, he had the impression of drowning. He had only one dream that he remembered in the morning, and it was a brief and inconsequential one. In the dream the telephone rang again and a voice said, "Zurich is calling, Zurich is calling." There was music over the wire and then a woman's voice, light and clear, said, *"Jamais deux sans trois."*

22

"So," Delaney said, "tell me all about everything. How did it go?"

It was eight thirty in the evening. Delaney still had the oxygen tube strapped to his cheek, and he was lying in the same position as the night before, and once more the nurse was sitting in the shadows in the corner of the room. But Delaney's voice sounded stronger, and his color, as far as Jack could see in the lamplight, was almost restored. Delaney said that he felt fine, that he had no pain, and that if it weren't for the doctor, he would get up and go home. There was a good chance that he was lying, out of pride, but there was no doubt that, for the time being at least, he was much improved. His first words were not about his wife, or about Barzelli, but about the movie.

"What was it like on the set today?" he asked. "Don't skip any of the details."

"It went okay," Jack said. "Better than anyone had a right

to expect." Actually, Jack had been grateful for the tension and confusion of a movie set and the necessity of concentrating on the problems of actors and soundmen and electricians. It had kept him from thinking about Despière all day. Now that the day was over, he found that he was beginning to accept the fact of Despière's death. He had decided not to say anything about it to Delaney. There was no telling how Delaney, in his present state, would react to the news. "I found I knew a lot more about directing than I thought I did," he said.

"I told you," Delaney said. "Nine out of ten directors don't know *anything*. How about the kid—Bresach—is he panning out?"

"He's very useful," Jack said.

"I knew it," Delaney said, with satisfaction. "I had a hunch about that kid."

The truth was that Bresach had been a good deal more than useful. While Jack had worked with the cameraman setting up the lights and the camera movements, Bresach had rehearsed the actors, especially Barzelli and Stiles. When the time had come to put the scene on film, the results of his work had been electrifying. Barzelli, who had started the day with the worst grace possible, had played her scene with more feeling than she had shown at any other point in the picture. But it was Stiles who had been the most surprising. Somehow, whispering to the actor in a corner of the set, Bresach had coaxed Stiles into new depths, and Stiles had played with a credibility and sense of pathos that had started a spate of surprised whispers from everybody else on the set. And it hadn't only been a lucky accident. Jack had allowed Bresach to work with the actors all day, while he purposely fussed longer than was necessary with the mechanics of shooting, and by the end of the day the actors and Tucino, himself, were saying that Bresach was better than Delaney ever was. But there was no need to tell the sick man that. It probably wasn't completely true, either. Bresach wasn't better than Delaney ever had been—he was merely better than Delaney ever would be again. But that was no news to break in a hospital room. All the violence of emotion, the rawness of manner and instability of mood that Jack had come to associate with Bresach had seemed to vanish the moment he was confronted with actors. In their place there was patience, and a searching, almost tender interest, that the actors had responded to immediately. Where Bresach had learned what he knew about directing for the camera, Jack had no idea. Perhaps he had been born with it. Per-

294

haps, in the twentieth century, a new gene had been added to the human collection—the movie gene.

. "Aside from everything else," Jack said, "he pulled a miracle this afternoon."

"What kind of miracle?"

"The hardest kind," Jack said. "He got Stiles to stop drinking at lunch."

"What?" Delaney turned his head in surprise. "How did he do that?"

"Very simply," Jack said. "He saw Stiles pour himself a glass of wine in the studio restaurant and he went over, without a word, and knocked the glass out of his hand."

Delaney made a sound of disbelief. "With everybody watching?"

"With two hundred people watching."

"Did Stiles hit him?" Delaney asked. Stiles was well known as a brawler. He was a big, powerful man, who was that curiosity, a drunk who picked fights and then won them.

"No, he didn't hit him," Jack said. "He went pale, then he laughed a little, and asked the waitress for a glass of water."

"God damn it," Delaney said. "And I had to miss it." He moved painfully in the bed. "Listen, Jack—there's something I have to talk to you about. Holt sent me a note this morning. About talking to you about coming in with us as executive producer . . ."

"Take it easy," Jack said. "All this can wait . . ."

"Now I can tell you, Jack," Delaney said, ignoring the interruption. "I planted the idea when we started talking about setting up a company. That's the real reason I asked you to come to Rome. So Holt could get to know you. It worked out just the way I hoped it would. He's crazy about you . . . Remember, Jack, back in California, I told you one day we'd work together again, I told you to leave a forwarding address . . ."

"Yes," Jack said, "I remember." He didn't want to talk about it now. Not in a sickroom, not with this feverish, distraught man, not this week. "Take it easy, Maurice, there's plenty of time . . ."

Delaney lifted his head from the pillow and stared at Jack. "You're going to take the job, aren't you?" he asked.

"I'm thinking about it," Jack said.

"Thinking about it?" Delaney said harshly. "What the hell is there to think about? You'll make at least three times the dough you're making now—just to begin with. You won't have the crappy government on your back all the time. You'll have the chance of winding up a rich man. You'll be a hundred times freer, your own boss. You're the only man I've ever been able to work with and not despise at the end. That's true, Jack. You know it's true. Holt won't interfere at all. We can make just the kind of pictures we want . . ."

We, Jack thought. Is there a *we* here? There is the kind of pictures you want, and there is the kind of pictures *I* want—if I want *any* kind of pictures, and that still has to be decided.

"It's the chance of a lifetime, Jack," Delaney was pleading now, his voice hoarser than it had been, and trembling a little. "It's what I've been waiting for since I was a kid . . ."

"I know," Jack said. "I didn't say I wasn't going to do it. I just said I was thinking."

"Look, Jack," Delaney said, speaking rapidly, "I know just what I want to do. Bresach's script. I've been thinking about it ever since I read it. It can be beautiful. You read it. Don't *you* think it can be beautiful?"

"Yes," Jack said.

"We'll buy it from him. We'll work with him on it. It's rough now, but I've got a thousand ideas on it already. Give it the old Delaney touch. It could be the best picture I ever made. Christ, I wish I could get out of here tomorrow. It's just the kind of thing that's right for me. Even Clara said so. I sent it over to her to read, even though she was sore at me. That's the last word I got from her, the night before this happened. 'This is for you,' " she said. I haven't been as excited about anything for twenty years . . ."

"Don't talk so much," Jack said, wondering why the nurse, in her corner, let Maurice go on like that. "I promised the doctor I'd do all the talking."

"Screw the doctor," Delaney said. "I told Clara some of the ideas I had for changes. You can ask her what they are, you'll see what I'll do with it . . ."

"Has she been here yet?" Jack asked. "Clara?"

Delaney grunted. "No." Suddenly, now that they were no longer talking about Bresach's script, he was calm again. "Did you talk to her?"

"I talked to her. Or rather, she talked to me."

"Anything new?"

Jack shook his head. "The usual," he said. "When she's sure

you're through with Barzelli—and all the other Barzellis—she'll come back."

"The hell with her," Delaney said. "Let her stay away, if that's the way she feels about it." Having lived through the night and the day, and confident now of his survival, Delaney was falling back more and more to his normal tone. "Marriage," he said gloomily. "She knew what she was getting. What the hell, she'd been my secretary for five years before we got married. The beauties of my character couldn't have come as a complete surprise to her." He twisted restlessly. "Did you go to Barzelli?"

"Yes."

"What did she say?"

"Don't worry," Jack said, carefully. "She won't come to visit you."

"Did she understand?" Delaney demanded. "Did you make her understand?"

"I think so," Jack said.

"She's a marvelous woman. You don't know how marvelous she is."

"I have to tell you one thing she told me," Jack said, speaking now not for Delaney, but for his own sake, his own enlightenment.

"What's that?" Delaney sounded wary.

"She said you never made love to her."

"Is that what she said?"

"Yes. She said I could tell that to Clara if I wanted to."

"Did you tell it to Clara?"

"No. Do you want me to?"

Delaney put up his hand in a weary, defensive gesture. Then he let his hand drop limply on the blanket. He shook his head against the pillow and closed his eyes and lay there without moving, the sound of his breathing through the tube the only noise in the still room. The nurse sat quietly in her corner. Jack had the feeling that she was dozing, not making the effort to understand the snatches of conversation that drifted over to her. The watcher at so many sick-beds, so many deathbeds, she had heard all confessions, all conversations. Her curiosity was now confined only to such things as pulse and temperature. The doctor had said that Jack could stay for fifteen minutes. He still had six or seven minutes to go. Before his time was up, the nurse would not interfere, no matter what she heard or understood or half understood.

"It's true," Delaney said. "I didn't make love to her. I held her in my arms naked, night after night, but I didn't make love to her. I never did anything like that before with any woman." His voice was low and tired. His eyes were still closed. "I don't know why that's all I did. Maybe I wanted it to be completely different with her than with anyone else . . . When I held her in my arms, it made me feel the way I felt when I was a young man. She renewed me, she made me flower . . . I would leave her at three, four in the morning, and I'd drive back home, and somehow, I'd feel I was beginning all over again, like when I was a kid in New York, as though nothing could stop me. As though by denying myself my pleasure, I made myself a better man. As though I was really, finally, beginning to get the idea of love . . ." Now he opened his eyes and turned his head to stare at Jack. The eyes were bright and glittering in the haggard, unshaven face. "The one woman I wanted in my whole life that I could have had and I didn't take, and she made me flower. Go understand that. Go understand anything. Go make my wife understand that . . ."

The Irish Antaeus, Jack thought, falling back nightly on the shapely Italian earth. Who am I to crush the illusions of renewal of a sick and burnt-out man? If he feels his wounds cured, is it the business of a friend to say he still sees blood, more blood than before?

"Those flowers came from Carlotta," Delaney said abruptly, as though he regretted the confidences he had revealed and hoped Jack would forget them. He indicated a huge bunch of red roses in a glass vase. "She was here last night, but they wouldn't let her in. She sent me a note. She asked me if I need anything." He laughed briefly, bitterly. "If you see her, tell her, yes, I need something— a new heart. Have you spoken to her?"

"Only for a minute," Jack said. "On the phone."

"Imagine her flying from England," Delaney said. "Of all the women I've known . . . Ah, God, what a tangle. You know what I've been lying here thinking all day, Jack . . . I'd like to see everybody I've loved or hurt or used or befriended or hated and explain myself to them. Explain why I did what I did, explain how they hurt me, or how they helped me. Disentangle myself . . ."

"You'd need a cop in the room to handle the traffic," Jack said, purposely making light of the idea. It certainly couldn't help prop up Delaney's morale to lie in bed like that totting up final accounts.

"Most people think I'm a sonofabitch," Delaney said flatly.

"All my life, it's been the same. Even as a kid. And all my life I've pretended I didn't mind. Pretended . . ."

"I'll put out a circular," Jack said. "Maurice Delaney is not a sonofabitch. It'll save a lot of time."

"About women, for example . . ." Delaney went on, ignoring Jack's flippancy. "When I was a kid I was ugly and I never got the girls I wanted. Or any girls, for that matter. Then I got to be a big shot, and all of a sudden it turned out I wasn't ugly at all, I was witty and charming and so irresistible it was Standing Room Only for months in advance." He chuckled drily. "If I didn't look in the mirror, I could damn near make myself believe I was six feet tall and beautiful as a picture. So I made up for lost time. I guess I was making up for the girls I didn't get when I was young and ugly. I guess I was always afraid that one day the dream'd be over and some woman would look at me and laugh and say, 'Why I know you, you're that little ugly runt, Maurice Delaney, from the South Side in Chicago.' There was once a girl out on the Coast who tried to kill herself on account of me—because I left her. They saved her all right, but not by much, and when I heard the news, the first thought I had wasn't, Thank God she's alive, it was, How do you like that, there's a woman who thinks I'm worth dying for. I'll tell you something—for one second, until civilization set in—I was pleased. Well, I suppose the people who say I'm a sonofabitch aren't far wrong . . ." He sighed. "I guess I'm getting tired . . ." he said, his voice trailing off. "I'd better sleep. Thanks for coming . . . Don't let me down, Jack. We can knock them dead, you and me. Be a good lad, leave a forwarding address . . ." He closed his eyes, allowing his weakness, in the evening hush of the great hospital, to take possession of him.

Jack stood up and nodded to the nurse, immobile in her corner, and went quietly out of the room.

There were newspapers all over the salon, five or six French newspapers and the Mediterranean edition of the New York *Herald Tribune*. Despière was on the front page of the French papers and on the second page of the *Tribune*. The story was brief, routine, and pointless, and Jack had read it and reread it again and again. Despière had gone out on a patrol, there had been an ambush, a grenade had been thrown. All the papers had his age

wrong, for some reason. Thirty-two, the papers said. His only surviving relative, the newspapers said, was a sister in Bayonne. He
was going to be buried, with military honors, in Algiers, the next
day. Despière had liked soldiers, and had considered them childish, and the idea of a military funeral would have amused him.

Jack collected all the newspapers and stuffed them into the
wastebasket, so that he wouldn't read the story over and over
again. The manuscript of Despière's article on Delaney was still on
the desk, under the ashtray. Jack opened the desk drawer and put
the manuscript in it. Despière had written that he wanted it destroyed, but Jack couldn't bring himself to do it—yet.

He picked up the shooting script of the picture and tried to concentrate on it. There was to be no work on the set the next day,
because it was a holiday of some kind. For once, Jack was grateful
for the abundance of holidays in Catholic Europe. It took some of
the pressure off and made it possible for him to prepare more thor-
oughly. But the mimeographed words ran into a meaningless blur
under his eyes, and a list of names pounded in a weary, repetitive
rhythm through his head—Delaney, Despière, Veronica, Hélène,
Carlotta, Barzelli, Clara, Bresach, Delaney, Despière, Veronica,
Hélène, Carlotta, Barzelli, Clara, Bresach . . .

It is like a run on a bank, he thought. All the demands for payment come in at once. Panic. The attack is from all sides. No event
is single or simple or clear or uninvolved with any other event. He
made himself study the script on the desk in front of him. That
was one of the things that was false about the script. Event followed event in a reasonable and logical order. That was the thing
that was false about all movies, all novels, all stories. They were
orderly and therefore untrue.

The telephone rang, but it was a wrong number, a drunken
American voice asking for Marylou MacClain, and refusing to believe that Marylou MacClain was not there.

The telephone reminded him that he had promised to write to
Hélène, explaining what was happening. He had sent her a telegram in the morning, but it had been brief and, he was sure, from
her point of view, unsatisfactory. He got out some air-mail paper
and started writing rapidly, trying (falsely) to put into comprehensible order the reasons why he had to stay in Rome. He had just
written, All my love, Jack, when there was a knock on the door.
Jack put the letter face down on the desk and went over and
opened the door.

Bresach was standing there, bareheaded, hunched into his stiff coat, two scripts bulking under his arm. He came into the room without a word, threw the scripts onto the couch, and sank into an easy chair, his legs sprawled in front of him, his hands in his pockets. He looked exhausted and exhilarated. Jack closed the door and stood watching him. Bresach grunted, wearily.

"Can I have a drink?" he said.

"That's a good idea," Jack said. He poured drinks for both of them. He was surprised at the feeling of pleasure he had at seeing Bresach.

Bresach drank thirstily. He glanced at the newspapers stuffed into the wastebasket. "The poor bastard," he said. "Despière. After going through so many wars . . ."

"If you keep at it long enough," Jack said, carefully, not wishing to give vent to his emotions, "there's always one war that'll get you."

"Algeria!" Bresach snorted. "I don't know whom I pity more, Despière or the poor tortured fellagha who threw the grenade. I never liked Despière. In fact, I should've hated him. If it wasn't for him, you'd never've met Veronica. But this . . ." He made a grimace. *"La gloire . . ."*

"You didn't really know him," Jack said.

"The French give me a pain in the ass," Bresach said.

"Do you know what he wrote about Algeria, just before he was killed?" Jack asked. "He wrote that it was all shit on both sides."

"I said the French give me a pain in the ass," Bresach said. "I didn't say they weren't intelligent."

"Drop it," Jack said curtly. "I don't want to talk about it."

Bresach noticed the tension in his voice. "Sorry," he said. "What the hell—people get killed. Tomorrow they'll drop the bomb on you and me and my bowlegged Aunt Sally. If I had tears to spare, I'd shed one or two for the Frenchman. But I'm all cried-out. I wake myself up during the night, crying, reaching out in the bed for Veronica. I weep for the living. Old-fashioned, romantic poem." He said it savagely. "I am full of self-loathing," he said. "There will come a day when I will no longer forgive myself for not having committed suicide. Ah, Christ . . ." He took a long gulp of his whisky. "I didn't come here to talk about that. I've been thinking about the picture. Are you interested in hearing what I've been thinking about the picture?"

"Yes."

"We can never make it great," Bresach said, "but we can make it non-vomitous."

Jack laughed. Bresach looked at him suspiciously. "What the hell are you laughing about?" he asked.

"Nothing."

The phone rang. "God damn it," Bresach said, "can't you tell them downstairs not to call you?"

It was Holt on the phone. "Jack," said the soft, drawling, flat voice, "I'm going out to see Maurice at the hospital. They told me I could see him for two minutes, and I wanted to let you know what I'm going to tell him. I'm going to tell him how wonderfully you and that boy have taken over and how grateful we all are to you both . . ."

"Thanks, Sam," Jack said, touched again by the unexpected gentleness and grace of Holt's manners. "Bresach is here with me, working, and I'll tell him what you said."

"I want you to know," Holt went on, "that if there's anything you need, anything at all, don't hesitate to ask."

"Don't worry, Sam," Jack said. "We'll ask."

"Well?" Bresach demanded, after Jack hung up. "What did he want?"

"He wanted to pin a medal on both of us and he did," Jack said. "Now, what have you got to say about the picture?"

"All in due time," Bresach said. "But I have to eat first. I've been throwing up all day and I'm bleary from hunger. Have you eaten yet?"

With surprise, Jack realized that he had forgotten to eat dinner. It was ten thirty. "No," he said.

"I'll treat you," Bresach said. He finished his drink and stood up. "Now that I'm going to be a big famous movie director," he said sardonically, "I must learn to start picking up checks. And I couldn't think of a better check to start on than yours."

Bresach insisted upon going to Pasetto's for dinner. He had never been there before, but he had heard that it was the best and probably one of the most expensive restaurants in Rome. "I have to worry about my position now," he said, grinning, as they got into the taxi in front of the hotel. "I can't afford to be seen in just any old joint."

It turned out that Holt had taken him off to one side during the day and had given him an envelope with a hundred thousand lire in it. For incidental expenses, Holt had said tactfully.

"What he doesn't know," Bresach said, "is that I have only two incidental expenses—food and rent."

When they sat down at a table in the crowded restaurant, Bresach looked around him critically, and said, "Have you noticed that when Romans want to make a place luxurious, they inevitably revert to the décor of the public bath?"

He was also critical of the clientele of the restaurant. "Italians," he said, scanning the other tables with a cold eye, "are the most beautiful people in the world—until they get rich."

"Be careful," Jack said. "Now you're started there's a good chance you may be rich some day."

"Never," Bresach said. "I've already decided what I'll do if I ever have any money. I'll squander it. I'll keep myself in lean and white-fanged poverty. Nobody ever did any good work with a fat bank account behind him."

"Do you really believe that?" Jack asked.

Bresach grinned. "Partially," he said.

Now Max came into the restaurant, chafing his hands and looking frozen and humbly out of place as he went down the center aisle between the diners searching for Bresach. He had on the same rough jacket he always wore, and the inevitable wool scarf. Bresach waved to him and he made his way among the waiters toward their table.

"You don't mind if Max eats with us, do you?" Bresach said. "This is a ceremonial feast—the breaking of the long fast—and it wouldn't be right if he wasn't here."

"It's up to you," Jack said.

Max smiled shyly and shook both their hands before sitting down. "Did you see that display of food at the entrance from the bar?" he said, wonderingly. "Do people eat like that every day?"

"From now on, Max," Bresach said, "you will eat like that every day. You will get fat and disgusting."

"I sincerely hope so," Max said. "I am by nature a glutton."

Bresach insisted upon doing the ordering for all of them, frowning at the menu while the headwaiter hovered over them. "I'm disappointed," he said, "I thought everything would be more expensive."

He ordered oysters, with white wine, and *fettucini* with fresh gray truffles scraped over them and pheasant cooked with grapes, and a bottle of Barolo. "You see," he said to Jack, "I put my economic theories immediately into action."

But when the food came, he only toyed with it, praising it, but eating very little of it. Max wolfed everything down with open pleasure. In the middle of the dinner, Bresach stood up. "Excuse me," he said abruptly. "I'll be right back."

He strode purposefully toward the men's room.

"He's going to throw up again," Max said, shaking his head worriedly. "He started last night after you came with the news and he's been doing it all day. He told me, when he was a boy in school, every time there was an examination, he would do the same thing."

"There was an examination today all right," Jack said. "And he got damn good marks. He looked like the calmest man in Rome all day."

"I told you before," Max said, "he is an extraordinary boy. He has fantastic powers of control over himself." He paused. "Most of the time." He shrugged. "Until I met Robert I always thought Americans had nerves of steel."

When Bresach came back he was very pale and sweat dewed his forehead in little drops, but he ordered coffee and French brandy and large cigars for all of them. "Tonight," he said, "we skimp on nothing. Wasn't it Bismarck who said a man shouldn't die until he has smoked one hundred thousand good cigars? I still have a few to go."

He leaned back against the upholstered banquette, the cigar seeming much too large for the thin, drawn, boyish face. "I am doing my best," he said, "to look gross and self-satisfied, so the waiter will be polite the next time I come. Now, Jack," he said, "to business. How far are you willing to go to make this picture of Delaney's respectable?"

"Pretty far," Jack said. "If it came out well, it'd do Delaney a lot more good than all that oxygen he's taking."

"Exactly," Bresach said. "Would you be willing to ask Holt and Tucino to give us an extra week's shooting with Stiles and Barzelli?"

"It'd cost an awful lot of money," Jack said cautiously, "and they're way over schedule as it is . . . There'd have to be some powerfully convincing reasons. What're you thinking of?"

"One thing I'm thinking of is having Stiles dub himself," Bresach said. "After what he showed today . . . Look, Jack, I think

I can talk honestly to you. You're afflicted with many faults, but vanity doesn't seem to be one of them . . ."

"Cut the flowers," Jack said. "What's on your mind?"

"This evening," Bresach said, "I listened to all the scenes you dubbed for Stiles, Jack. It's not bad, but it's not good enough. I'm not trying to offend you," he added quickly. "You understand that, don't you?"

"I understand," Jack said. "I'm not offended."

"You're not an actor any more," Bresach went on. "You're an intelligent, hard-working man with a good voice who always seems to be on the verge of being an actor and never quite moves over the line. Fair enough?"

"Fair enough," Jack said.

"And even if you were an actor, you're not Stiles. You're better than Stiles, of course, in what Stiles has done up to now—but that's because he's been so awful. Delaney froze the poor drunken bastard so badly, he never got a word out straight."

"What you propose we do?"

"I propose we unfreeze him," Bresach said calmly, blowing out a huge cloud of cigar smoke. "De-alcoholize him and unfreeze him in one operation."

"How do you think we're going to be able to do that?" Jack asked.

"I read Sugarman's script tonight," Bresach said, seeming to ignore Jack's question. He touched the bound scripts that were lying on the chair beside him. "I got Hilda to dig it up for me. I wanted to see what the story was like before Delaney walked all over it. I thought maybe I could find a little scene or two that could help Stiles . . ."

"Well, what did you find?"

"Corruption, naturally," Bresach said. "That's what I found. In Sugarman's script it's the man's story, but Delaney fell in love with Barzelli and switched it all around. Only the story won't stand it. So we have all those dreary scenes with Barzelli at the center of them, doing nothing, just combing her hair or looking soulfully out of the window or getting undressed and showing her pretty legs, killing the picture. And all Delaney could think of for Stiles to do was sleepwalk through the picture like a melancholy St. Bernard, yearning, saying, 'I love you. I am sad. I love you . . .' " Bresach made a sound of disgust. "I found a lot more than a little scene in Sugarman's script. He had the man drunk half the time and making fun of himself and saying the opposite of what he meant and treating the girl horribly and hating her a good deal more than he loved her. It's a good part and Stiles can play it marvelously."

"If he stays sober. Maybe," Jack said.

"Did you know that for the first two weeks of shooting Stiles didn't take a drink?"

"No, I didn't know that," Jack said.

"Well, he didn't. Then he saw what Delaney was doing to him and he gave up," Bresach said. "Well, if he did it the first two weeks, he can do it the last two. If he's convinced that he's going to get something out of it."

"How are we going to convince him?"

"By putting in as many of the old scenes as possible—or shooting wild lines and close-ups and fitting them in wherever we can. And even the scenes that we can't change, we can redub with Barzelli and Stiles, but with a completely different adjustment. Drunken, self-mocking, bitter . . . And wherever we can't get away from the old lines and they're just too awful to be borne, we can have music or the noise of trains or any godamn thing in the background, so that the worst of it'll be drowned out. We'll prove to Stiles that we mean what we say, that we're working for him, working to keep him in the movie business, that we're trusting him and that we think he can do it . . ."

Even as he listened, keeping his face blank and noncommittal, Jack felt himself being caught up by the boy's eagerness, his astuteness, his nervous, almost intuitive sense of what was wrong with the picture and how it could be made right, his fierce desire to do their work well. Suddenly, Jack felt exhilarated, tireless, happily swept up in a flood of ideas for improving the picture. The last time he had felt anything like that, he realized, had been in the old days before the war, when he and Delaney had sat up night after night, arguing, roaring, laughing, excited, as they worked together. "All right," he said, indicating the two scripts lying on the chair, "show me what you think we can do."

Bresach put the two scripts on the table with shaking hands. "We start . . ." He stood up. "Excuse me. I have to throw up again."

He hurried through the restaurant toward the men's room.

"Poor boy," Max said sorrowfully. "All this good food."

When Bresach came back, he was pallid, but calmer. He sat down next to Jack, and they started going through the two scripts, page by page. It was past one o'clock when they had finished, and the lights in the other parts of the restaurant had been dimmed and their waiter was standing against a post, sleeping on his feet.

"All right," Jack said, "I'll ask Holt for more time. Right now." He went to the telephone and called Sam Holt's number. The telephone was answered promptly, and it was Holt's voice, lively and pleasant, which said, "Hello?"

Jack explained swiftly what he and Bresach had been doing and about the extra week's shooting.

"Do you guarantee that it'll be worth it?" Holt asked.

"In something like this," Jack said, "nobody can guarantee anything. All I can say is I *think* it's worth it."

"That's good enough for me, Jack," said Holt. "You've got your extra week. Don't hang up. I have some more news for you. I went to see Maurice tonight, and he said he'd read a new script by this boy, Bresach, and that it's very good and that he wants to do it as his next picture when he gets out of the hospital. Have you read it, Jack?"

"Yes," Jack said.

"Do you agree that it's worth doing?"

"It's very much worth doing."

"Good," Holt said. "You tell the boy I want to see him sometime tomorrow in my office to arrange the terms. I'll be there all day. Will you tell him that?"

"Yes," Jack said. "Good night, Sam." He went back to the table, which was littered with cigar ashes and bits of paper now. Max and Bresach had got the waiter to bring them one last brandy.

"It's okay," Jack said. "Holt's giving us the week."

"Why not?" Bresach said carelessly. "It's only money." He stood up. "Max, let's get the hell to sleep."

"One more thing," Jack said. "He wants you to come to his office sometime tomorrow. Delaney's told him he wants to buy your script and do it, and Holt wants to make the deal with you."

"Robert," Max said excitedly. "Did you hear that?"

"I heard it," Bresach said. "Deathbed Studios, the new colossus of the Industry."

"You're going to make the deal, aren't you?" Max asked.

Bresach drained the last of his brandy. "Possibly," he said. He looked speculatively at Jack. "Did Delaney talk to you about this?"

"A little."

"What did he say?"

Jack was sorry Bresach had posed the question, but made himself give an honest report. "He said that with some changes he had in mind it could be the best thing he ever made."

"He intends to make some changes?"

"He said he had a thousand ideas," Jack said. "Give it the old Delaney touch."

"Oh, Christ," Bresach said. "And he wants to direct it himself?"

"Yes."

"Even so," Max said, "it's too big a chance to let slide, Robert."

Bresach pushed his empty brandy glass along the tablecloth, like a man making a move in chess. "Andrus," he said, "have you anything to say on the subject?"

"Not at the moment."

Bresach nodded. "Not at the moment," he said. He started walking. "Let's get out of here. We've still got a lot of work to do tomorrow. Come to my place. There's no telephone to bother us. I don't like your place for working. It has a persistent stink of treachery in it."

Jack ignored the jibe. "I'll be there at twelve. We both can use a morning's sleep."

In silence, they went past the sleepy-eyed waiter out onto the street. It was cold and a wind was blowing, and Max said, old-maidishly, to Bresach, "Button up your coat."

"Well," Bresach said, taking a deep breath, "it hasn't been a bad night's work." He rubbed his eyes wearily. "I'll tell you something about yourself, Jack. I'm sorry you're as smart as you are and as decent as you are. It is becoming more and more impossible to detest you." He grinned, gaunt and hollow-eyed in the cold light from the street lamps. "If you hear from Veronica," he said, "tell her to come visit the set sometime. See me in all my tinsel glory. Maybe that's what I need to stop me from throwing up. The face of love."

23

The telephone rang, as usual, at seven in the morning, to wake him up. Dazedly, he got out of bed and prepared to shave. It was only while he was putting the lather on his face that he remembered that he was not going to the studio that morning. He stared blearily at his reflection in the mirror, the lather making him look bearded, like a disreputable old man, broken and disfigured by a lifetime of dissipation. He washed the lather off and dried his face and looked at himself again. Now he didn't seem like an old man any more, but his face was disagreeably webbed under his eyes and unhealthily pale. Annoyed with himself for not having remembered to cancel the operator's call the night before, he got back into bed. He made himself stay under the covers for an hour, but he couldn't sleep, and he finally got up and called for his breakfast.

He didn't open the newspapers that the waiter brought in with him, in case there was anything in them about the funeral of Despière. The less he thought about Despière today and in the days to come, the better for the control of his nerves. As he drank his coffee, it occurred to him that he had nearly four hours to wait before his appointment with Bresach. He thought of the other guests of the hotel, breakfasting, like him, at this hour in their rooms, and preparing to set out and enjoy the wonders of the city. This morning, he thought, for a few hours, I, too, will be a tourist. It may be the last chance I get. He went over to the desk and got the old 1928 Baedeker and propped it on the table in front of him as he sipped his coffee and ate his sugared roll.

The idea of touring Rome, even for a morning, by the aid of a guidebook that had been published in 1928 was a pleasant one. In the stiff, proper prose, the city of thirty years ago seemed more orderly, more leisurely, more substantial than the city of today. In that city nothing very bad could happen to you. The only real danger in 1928, it seemed, was that you might overtip the natives.

He read at random. Under Churches and Learned Institutions, there was a paragraph headed Guide-Lecturers (English or English-speaking) *Prof. L. Reynaud,* Via Flavia 6; *Signora P. Canali,* Via Vittorio Veneto 146; *Mr. T. B. Englefield,* Via Cesare Beccaria 94; *Miss Grace Wonnacott,* Via dei Gracchi 134. . . .

That's what I need, he thought, in this city—a guide-lecturer (English or English-speaking) to explain it all. What would *Signora P. Canali* have to say, across the thirty years, about her compatriots Veronica Rienzi and Barzelli and Tucino, how would *Miss Grace Wonnacott,* that English lady of Via dei Gracchi 134, describe that complex descendant of Irish immigrants, Maurice Delaney?

Lead me among the monuments, *Mr. T. B. Englefield,* show me the stones where love and ambition are buried, take me to the very spots where the rape, the crucifixion took place, where the last cries were uttered, where rose the shouts of triumph, where the kings marched before their assassins, where the gladiators amused the multitudes. I have friends who amuse the multitudes, and in not too different a way, and who also pay an extreme price when they lose.

Idly, Jack turned the page.

PLAN OF VISIT

2nd day. Walk from *Sant'Onofrio* through the *Passeggiata Margherita* to *San Pietro in Montorio* and there await the sunset . . .

And there await the sunset.

How peaceful, Jack thought, sipping his coffee, to await the sunset in 1928 at San Pietro in Montorio.

The telephone rang. It had a tinny, impatient sound, as though the operator hadn't slept well the night before and was irritated with the world this morning. Jack leaned over and picked up the phone.

It was Carlotta. "I'm sorry to call you so early," she said, speaking quickly, crowding the words in, "but I wanted to get hold of you before you went out. They haven't let me in to see Maurice yet and I wondered . . ."

"He's all right," Jack said. "He got your roses."

"Jack," she said, "don't be so short with me. Please. I want to see you. It's ridiculous, both of us in the same hotel, after so many years . . . Will you take me to lunch?"

"I can't," he said. "I have an appointment at noon."

"What're you doing until then?"

"Sightseeing."

"Where?"

"The Sistine Chapel." It was the first thing that came into his head.

"Isn't that remarkable," Carlotta said. "That's just where I'm going this morning."

"When did you decide that?"

"Two seconds ago." She laughed. Her laughter was composed and friendly. "May I come along with you?"

Why not, Jack thought. Everything else has happened to me in Rome, I might as well visit the Sistine Chapel with my ex-wife. "I'll be down in the lobby in fifteen minutes," he said. "Can you be ready?"

"Of course," she said. "You remember how fast I dress."

Remember, Jack thought, as he hung up. Women use that word as a club.

He went into the bathroom, and for the second time that morning, put the old man's disguise of lather on his face.

She was in the lobby when he came out of the elevator. She was talking to another woman and she didn't see him for a moment and he had an opportunity to study her and observe what the years had done to her. She had put on weight and the old, flickering sharpness of her face was gone. Her beauty had diminished, but without leaving signs of bitterness in the process. By some magic of time, the jittery neurotic she had been when he had last seen her had been transformed into a robust and sunny matron. As he looked at her, conversing brightly with the other woman, it occurred to Jack that if he were asked to describe her now he would use the old-fashioned phrase, a comely woman.

Her hair, which had gone through the usual spectrum of Hollywood colors, now seemed a faded and natural blonde, and she filled, a little too completely, with an outmoded generosity of flesh, her smart dark gray suit. Looking at the smiling, firm-skinned, full face and the over-womanly body, Jack remembered the choice that a Frenchwoman had once told him ladies over thirty-five had to make —between the face and the derrière. Either you dieted and exercised, the woman had said, and kept your behind slender and allowed your face to grow haggard and lined, or you opted for your face and let your behind spread. Carlotta had clearly opted for her face. Wisely, Jack thought.

When he came up to her, the fuss of introductions to the other woman, a Princess Miranello, who had a long upper lip and prominent gums and a Back Bay accent, made the meeting conventional and without embarrassment.

"I'll meet you at one o'clock for lunch," Carlotta said to the other woman.

"Well," the princess said, making what Jack imagined she thought was an arch face in his direction, "if you have a better offer . . ."

"I have no better offers," Carlotta said. "See you at one." She put her hand lightly on Jack's arm and they started out of the hotel together.

"Who's the princess?" Jack asked.

"Maggie Fahnstock, of Boston. She's an old friend of mine. She knows all about you. She thinks it's awfully moving, our meeting each other like this in Rome, after so long . . ." Carlotta's tone was light and amused. "Are you awfully moved?"

"Awfully," Jack said. He saw Guido waiting beside the Fiat across the street and waved to him. Guido jumped into the car and started to turn against the traffic toward the hotel.

"She's seen you before," Carlotta said. "In a restaurant the other night, with two men. She examined you carefully. She said you looked like a happy man."

"Good old Maggie," Jack said. "That sterling judge of character."

"She also thought you looked very handsome," Carlotta said,

without coquetry. "She said you looked as though you'd be good for another twenty years. She asked me why I left you."

"What did you say to that?"

"I told her that I didn't leave you," Carlotta said. "You left me."

"It's amazing," Jack said, "how many different opinions eye-witnesses can have of the same accident."

Guido drove up to the door and Jack helped Carlotta into the car, before getting in himself.

"Cinecittà?" Guido asked.

"San Pietro," Jack said.

Guido looked up into the rear-view mirror, to make sure that Jack was not joking. Then, reassured, he put the car into gear and swung out into the street.

On the way to the Vatican, Carlotta talked about herself. She talked in a chatty, friendly way, as though Jack were an old acquaintance, and no more than that, with whom she could gossip freely and inconsequentially. She had married Kutzer, the head of the studio, she told Jack, a year after her divorce from Jack had become final. Jack nodded. He had read about it and had debated with himself about sending a cablegram. He had not sent the cablegram.

Kutzer had divorced his wife, settling close to a million dollars on her, and married Carlotta. "I was at the bottom," she said, but flatly, without emotion. "I was in despair about you. The only parts I could get were degrading and my reputation was so bad that even in Hollywood the only parties I could get invited to were for drunks and fairies and dope addicts." She laughed lightly, without regret or self-criticism, like a woman speaking of some innocent failing she remembered from her childhood. "He was the most faithful man I ever met," Carlotta said. "I was his girl for seven years and then he waited nearly another ten years for me to finish with you—and in all the time I was with you he never as much as held my hand or talked to me about anything but work, when I was on the lot—and then one day he called me and said it was absurd for me to ruin myself the way I was doing and that he wanted to marry me. I had a terrible hangover that morning and I would've done anything to be left alone so I said yes. And it turned out that he gave me the happiest years of my life until he died. You knew about that, didn't you?"

"Yes," Jack said. He had read in the newspapers two or three years before that Kutzer had dropped dead walking up the stairs to his office one evening after dinner. Taciturn, brutal, intelligent, rich, faithful, overworked. A thousand people had turned out for his funeral, most of them glad that he was dead. The happiest years of Carlotta's life . . .

"People have different periods of their life when they are made to be happy," Carlotta was saying. "Some people between twenty and thirty. Others between thirty and forty. Others never, I suppose. I found out that I was made to be happy after forty."

"Lucky you," Jack said.

"How about you?" she asked. "What's your best period?"

The best period. It would have been easy to say. Starting the night of the dog and the Cadillac in the driveway, going through the mornings in the California garden and the calls from Delaney, that different, whole, exuberant Delaney, and ending with the war. But he didn't say it. It was gone and no good would come of dwelling on it. "I haven't figured it out yet," he said.

"Are you surprised I said I was in despair when we broke up?" Carlotta asked.

"Mildly."

"What did you think I was?"

"Well," Jack said, "if I had to put it in a word, the word would be rapacious."

Carlotta looked away from him, out the window. "That's not such a nice word, is it?"

"No," Jack said, "it's not."

"I didn't want you to go away," Carlotta said, turning back to him, looking at him gravely, "and the lawyers suggested that if I made it cost you too much, you might reconsider, you wouldn't act hastily . . ."

"In love," Jack said, "it's always wise to consult a lawyer."

"Don't make fun of me, Jack," she said. "You told me over the phone you didn't hate me."

"I didn't say anything about not hating your lawyer, though. It's a funny thing, I don't seem to remember—even when you knew I wasn't coming back, that you cabled me saying it was all a trick, you were returning my money . . ."

"I wanted to punish you," she said. "And by then I was in too deep. And I was worried about money. I never saved any, and I was on the way down. A man can always take care of himself."

314

"I took care of myself magnificently," Jack said. "Some years I even manage to buy two suits a year."

"I had to have the security," Carlotta said, and for a moment her voice was sullen and complaining and made Jack remember the day at the hospital in Virginia. "The way things were going then, in two more years I would've been a whore," she said. "Oh, not one of those on a street-corner or in a house, but a whore just the same." She smiled brutally. "Your stocks and bonds saved me from that. Did Wall Street ever do a better turn than that? You ought to be delighted you managed to save me."

"I am," Jack said, flatly. "That's what I am—delighted."

"I don't need money any more," Carlotta said. "Kutzer saw to that. So if you're ever in trouble, you know where to come—for a loan."

Jack laughed.

"Have it your own way," she said, shrugging. "Don't come to me. Listen, Jack, you're not going to hurt me. I told you—this is my time to be happy."

"I am well known," Jack said, "as a man who likes all his wives to be happy."

"You're antagonistic, Jack," she said. "I'd hoped it would be different. I had hoped that when we met we'd be friends. After all, after so many years . . ."

Jack said nothing.

"You don't like the word friends," she said.

"I neither like it nor dislike it."

"It won't hurt me," Carlotta said. "I can't be hurt any more. But until you learn to think of me as a friend, you will never be completely happy."

"If you've gone in for Christian Science," Jack said, "this is a queer place for it. St. Peter's is staring us in the face."

"Whatever you think of me," she said, "I'm glad I got this chance of seeing you. To ask you to forgive me . . ."

"Where do I begin?" Jack said brutally.

". . . for that day in the hospital in Virginia," Carlotta said, ignoring his question. "It's haunted me. It was the worst performance of my life. I came there to assuage you, to promise you that everything would be all right when you got out, to tell you I loved you, and then, when I saw you, I felt so guilty I couldn't say a word I'd prepared. I let myself be a selfish, stupid, whining bitch. I knew what I was doing and somehow I couldn't stop it. I cried all the way back to Washington in the train."

"It was a short ride," Jack said, unmoved.

The car stopped and they got out and Jack told Guido, in French, to wait for them, they probably wouldn't be too long.

"On this stone, I shall build my church," Jack said, as he and Carlotta went across the colonnaded piazza, and alongside the cathedral toward the chapel.

"In the book," Jack said, touching the Baedeker, "it says the best light for viewing the chapel is in the morning." He squinted up critically through the wintry grayness. "Maybe they mean a morning in June. We go everywhere at the wrong time, don't we?"

He had been there twice before, on other visits, but each time the place had been crowded and the effect of the paintings had been diluted by his consciousness of the sightseers shuffling and whispering about him. This morning, there were very few people there, two men in black sitting silently on the benches along the side and a student or two moving quietly from time to time across the bare floor. Now the full impact of the room hit him. The effect was not like the effect that any other work of art had had on him. It was like peering down into the deep crater of a volcano, momentarily quiet, but secretly dangerous, unpredictable, explosive, beneath its calm surface.

The effect was not religious, either. Actually, he decided, it was antireligious. He could believe in Michelangelo after looking at the ceiling of the chapel, but he could not believe in God.

Flesh, the paintings announced, flesh. Man is flesh, God is flesh, man makes man, man makes God, all mysteries are equal, the sibyls and the prophets are equally right, equally wrong, believe in any one of them at your peril. On the scroll of the Delphic sibyl, if only your eyes were keen enough to make it out, is the same message that covers the pages of Zacharias' book—"I am guessing."

And on the wall behind the altar, the bodies of the aged athletes writhing in the Last Judgment, below the shadowy figure of Christ high under the vault, repeated a similar message. The saved souls on the right hand of Christ were indistinguishable by any marks of merit or holiness from the damned souls being dragged down to hell on Christ's left hand. Salvation was the caprice of the usher who made out the seating plan on the last day.

316

The painting made him remember another painting—Titian? Tiepolo?—that he had seen once in Milan. It was called La Fortuna, if he remembered correctly, Chance, Luck, Fate, and it was of a beautiful woman striding along, with her left breast bare. From the nipple of the bare breast spouted a stream of milk which was being drunk by a group of happy, smiling men, the lucky ones of life. Charming and ludicrous and arbitrary nourishment. But to the right of the beautiful woman, there was a group of men in agony, who were being driven along, scourged by a whip that the woman held in her right hand. The unlucky ones. The ones who came in at the wrong time or who had bought the wrong ticket and who got the dry right teat and the whip. Equally arbitrary. Put *that* up in your church, Jack thought. It makes just as much sense. Call it the First and Last and Only Important Judgment, and pile the altar in front of it with votive offerings.

Looking at Michelangelo's huge dark painting, Jack was reminded, more than anything else, of photographs he had seen, just after the war, of thousands of naked women being paraded before SS doctors in the German concentration camps. The doctors examined the women briefly, decided within ten seconds whether the women were useful for work or for whatever other purposes the Germans used women like that, and made a sign. The women he had saved were put into one line and lived that day. The women he put into the other line were sent to the furnace. Maybe, thought Jack, staring at the smoky whirl of bodies behind the altar, God is an SS doctor, and Michelangelo had advance information.

He thought of Despière, born and baptized a Catholic in Bayonne and being buried as a Catholic this morning in Africa, and the idea of Despière, or Despière's soul, being subject, this morning or on any morning, to this inaccurate and grotesque selection, was intolerable to him.

"I've had enough," Jack said to Carlotta. "I'll wait for you outside."

She had stood next to him silently, staring up through her glasses at the ceiling. Her face looked grave and puzzled. "I've had enough, too," she said. "I'll come with you." She took off her glasses and put them in her bag and they walked across the bare floor and out together without any further words.

The sky was overcast when they came out and the piazza was gray and melancholy in the flat light. They stood in front of the fountain and stared back at the huge bulk of St. Peter's.

"I had a curious feeling in there," Carlotta said. "I had the feeling that Michelangelo didn't really believe in God."

Jack looked at her sharply. Momentarily, he wondered if he had spoken in the chapel without realizing it.

"What's the matter?" Carlotta asked. "Why are you looking at me like that?"

"Because that's what I was thinking in there, myself," Jack said.

"Married people," Carlotta said. "After a certain number of years they begin to think the same thoughts at the same time. It's the final fidelity."

"We're not married."

"Sorry," Carlotta said. "I forgot." For a moment, uneasy, they both stared at the cathedral. "How many people who helped build this church," she said, "do you think *really* believed?"

"Probably most of them," Jack said. "The age of faith . . ."

"I don't know," Carlotta said. "It's hard to tell from their work. For example—in there—those scenes from the Bible. The Botticelli of Moses kneeling before the burning bush. But Botticelli also painted Venus rising from the foam. What did he believe? The miracle of the burning bush or the miracle of the birth of Venus from the sea? Why one more than the other? What do *you* believe?"

"When we were married," he said, "what did you think I believed?"

"Oh, I supposed you thought there was a God, of some kind—"

"Maybe I still do," Jack said reflectively. "There is a God. Yes, I believe that. But I don't think He has any interest in us. Or at any rate, not the interest that any religion says He has. That is, it does not affect Him whether we murder our fellow man or honor our father and mother or covet our neighbor's wife. I can't feel that self-important. If there is a God, maybe He's a scientist and this world is one of His laboratories, in which He practices vivisection and observes the results of chemical experiments. Why not? We are cut apart living, we are poisoned, we die by the million, like monkeys in laboratories." He spoke savagely, allowing the bitterness he felt over Despière's useless death to flood through him. "The monkey who dies because he is used as a control and is not inoculated against a disease certainly is not more of a sinner than the monkey who has been protected and merely has a low fever for a couple of days. Maybe we're God's monkeys and we suffer and die for His information. And the guilt we feel from time to time when we break what we consider His laws may be just another interesting

318

virus He's managed to isolate and control. And faith may be just a side effect or symptom of the guilt virus, like the hives people get who can't tolerate penicillin."

Carlotta was frowning. "I don't like to hear you talk like that," she said. "It's too gloomy."

"Actually, it's not as gloomy as Christianity," Jack said. "After all, you believe in vivisection, don't you?"

"I'm not so sure."

"Of course you do. If one child in the world is saved by the death of a million monkeys, you feel it's a fair bargain, don't you?"

"I suppose I do," Carlotta said reluctantly.

"Well, isn't that a more cheerful thing to believe than that we're going to be consigned to eternal punishment for characteristics over which we have no control and which are built into the human animal, just like his eyes and ears and his five senses? At least, this way, we can hope that there is some Purpose behind it all, that somewhere in the universe some profit will accrue because of our sufferings. Until now, we've been able to believe that the experiments of scientists had a useful, constructive object. Now, of course, what with the hydrogen bomb and germ warfare and all the rest of it, we're not so sure. A scientist today is suspect. And with good reason. After all, if you judge by the harm it's done to humanity, a good-sized segment of the scientific community should be locked away as criminally insane. But we can still hope that God is a pre-1940 scientist, Whose hand perhaps has slipped a little, but Whose intentions are still reasonable. Only God's reasons of course must not be confused with our reasons—any more than the experimenter's reasons must be confused with the monkey's, cut open on his table."

Carlotta shivered inside her light cloth coat. "I hate talk like that," she said. "Let's go back to the car."

Jack took her arm and they started walking toward where the car was parked. "Did you feel all this all the time?" Carlotta asked. "Even when I knew you?"

"No," Jack said. "I think only in the last week or so. Since I came to Rome. I've moved into a new department of my life. Some curious things have happened to me in the past two weeks."

"If I were you," she said, "I'd stay away from this city from now on."

"Maybe I will," he said. "Maybe I will."

Before they got to the car, where Guido, alert and polite, was standing, with the door open, Carlotta turned and took a last look at St. Peter's. "So many churches," she said, "all over the world, and all for nothing, for a lie, a dream . . . What a waste."

Jack shook his head. "It's not a waste," he said.

"But you just said . . ."

"I know what I just said. But still, it's not a waste. Even if that was the only thing to show for it—" Jack gestured toward the mass of the church. "Even if the only thing that had ever come out of the whole process was what Michelangelo did in there, it would be worth it. And, of course, there's infinitely more than that. Not only the substantial things, the stones, the statues, the windows, the paintings—but the comfort it has given on this earth to the faithful . . ."

"The faithful," Carlotta said. "Trapped by a lie."

"Not trapped," Jack said. "Ennobled. I envy them, I envy every true believer with all my heart."

"Then why don't you believe?" Carlotta asked. "Can't you stand a little comfort yourself?"

"Why don't I believe?" Jack shrugged. "Have faith, they say. It's like saying, Be beautiful. I would like to be beautiful, too . . ."

They stood for a moment more, looking across the bare, stone sweep of the piazza. A wind had sprung up, cold and cutting, and some nuns who were hurrying toward the cathedral steps seemed to be floating across the pavement on their billowing habits.

"It's going to rain," Jack said. "I'm sorry we came. It's the wrong morning. Let's go back to Rome."

In the car, returning to their hotel, they were silent most of the way. Carlotta sat in one corner, her face thoughtful and grave, not looking at Jack. After a few minutes she spoke. "Do you know why I never talked to you before about religion?" she said. "Because religion is mixed up in my mind with death. And I can't bear to think about death. Do you think about death much?"

"During the war, I did—a great deal," Jack said. "And recently, since I came to Rome."

Carlotta took off her gloves. She looked down at her bare hands and slowly caressed one with the other. "This flesh," she said softly, and Jack knew what she meant by the gesture and why she had said the words. She reached out her left hand and took his and clung to it. "Jack, will you take me out to dinner tonight, please? I don't want to be alone tonight."

"I don't think that would be a good idea," Jack said, as gently as possible. He could have told her he was busy, but he wanted to let her know that he was refusing her as a deliberate choice.

She withdrew her hand abruptly. "Sorry," she said. She put her gloves on again, smoothing the wrinkles elaborately.

How many times, Jack thought, have I watched this woman perform this plain, everyday, vain, appealing, feminine act. How many voyages, great and small, happy and unhappy, have been introduced by that dry, leaflike little womanly noise.

"Jack . . ." she began, then stopped.

"Yes?"

"Do you know why I really came to Rome?"

"If you're going to say that you really came to see me," Jack said, "I'm not going to believe you."

"No, I wasn't going to say that. I came to see Maurice Delaney. As I told you." She made an impatient movement with her shoulders. "If they'll ever let me into his room. Do you know why I came to see Maurice?" She waited for a moment, but Jack didn't say anything. "I came to see him because of all the men I ever let make love to me, he gave me the most pleasure. And I thought, now, if he was dying, he would like to hear that."

"I'm sure he would," Jack said drily.

"You know how important love was to me . . . Sex, if you prefer that word . . ."

"Was?"

"Was. I found out that it was the most important thing. The center of my life. So if a man gives you . . ."

"I don't need any diagrams," Jack said.

"You're not angry that I told you that, are you?"

"No," Jack said. It was almost true.

"Now," she said, "I somehow have the feeling that I can say anything to you, tell you everything."

"Our divorce," Jack said lightly, not wishing to have her say anything more, "has not been in vain."

"Like me, Jack," she whispered. Her head was down into her collar and her voice was thin and plaintive. "Please like me."

He was silent.

"We'll see each other again, won't we?" she said. "Before I leave Rome."

"Of course," he said, lying.

24

In the small, cluttered room on the fourth floor Bresach and Jack worked all afternoon, organizing, page by page, the changes, additions, and cuts that they had blocked out for Delaney's picture the night before in the restaurant. They worked swiftly and efficiently together, understanding each other with a minimum of words, and collaborating with each other, at least for this afternoon, as though they had done at least a dozen jobs together before this. Hilda, Delaney's secretary, whom Jack had enlisted to help them, had been taking it all down in shorthand, and by six o'clock, when fatigue made them call a halt, she had a huge sheaf of notes that she took home with her to transcribe.

After she had gone, Jack accepted a cup of coffee that Max, in silent, anxious attendance, had prepared. Jack sipped the coffee gratefully, leaning back in his chair and thinking pleasurably of the work they had accomplished that day. "Maybe I'm delirious or suffering from shock," he said, "but I think this is finally going to be a wonderful picture."

Bresach, also drinking coffee, out of one of the two cups in the apartment, grunted. "Control yourself, Andrus. Beware of the euphoria of the depths."

"It's not euphoria," Jack said. "I'm being as cold-blooded as I know how to be. I repeat—I think we're going to have a wonderful picture."

"Non-vomitous," Bresach said. "That's as far as I'll go."

Jack put down his cup and stood up and stretched. "All right. Wonderful and non-vomitous."

"How do you think Delaney will take it?" Bresach asked.

"He will thank us for saving his life."

"You don't think you're being naïve?"

"I'll tell you what I think," Jack said. "If he was up and around, he'd probably object to a lot of things we're doing. Not all, but a lot. But this way, he'll get to see the whole thing, already done. Whatever you may think about him, he's no fool, and even if he wants to recut it somewhat or add one or two of the old things, he'll recognize that it's been improved."

"Well," Bresach said, shrugging, "you know the man better than I do."

"Yes, I do," Jack said. "Shall we keep going tonight? I can be back here by about nine o'clock."

"Oh." There was a curious little silence, and Bresach and Max exchanged glances.

"What's the matter?" Jack asked.

"Nothing's the matter," said Bresach. "It's just that Holt invited me to dinner. He told me to ask you to come, too. Max, too. I think he feels guilty if he doesn't pay for dinner for at least twenty people a night."

"When did you see Holt?" Jack asked. He had avoided talking about Holt's proposed deal to Bresach and had been grateful that Bresach hadn't mentioned it. He would have to make a stand sooner or later, but he wanted it to be as late as possible, when the other problems had been solved.

"I went there this morning," Bresach said. "To his office."

"What did he say?"

"He made a very generous offer," Max said quickly.

"He's a very generous man," Jack said. "What did he say?"

"More or less the same thing he told you last night," Bresach said. "X number of dollars for the story and a weekly salary to work with Delaney when he gets out of the hospital and can get around to preparing the script and shooting it."

"X number of dollars," Max said. He waved his hands agitatedly. "Why don't you tell him? Fifteen thousand dollars! It's a fortune."

"You forget, Max," Bresach said, smiling with a touch of malice at his friend, "that I'm the son of a rich father and I despise money."

"I don't care how rich your father is," Max shouted. "You don't have enough money to eat three meals a day, and you know it."

"Take it easy, Max, take it easy." Bresach patted Max's shoulder soothingly. "Nobody says I'm turning the money down."

"What did you tell Holt?" Jack asked.

"I told him I wanted to talk to you first," Bresach said. "I told him I trusted you. Not with girls . . ." He grinned sourly. "But with something like this. He said you were coming in with him and Delaney as producer . . ."

"That isn't definite yet," Jack said.

"Last night," Bresach said, "you said you didn't want to comment at the moment. How about this moment?"

Jack walked over to the window and stood with his back to the room, looking out at the dark roofs of the buildings across the court and the lighted windows of kitchens in which women were preparing dinner. He thought of Delaney, lying in his hospital room, planning, even now, how he was going to make the picture of Bresach's script. He remembered Delaney's excitement and hope for the project and he remembered how much he owed Delaney. But he knew the time had come to decide how much he owed the boy, too. With all his violence, and all his talent, Bresach was vulnerable and could be easily damaged. Easily crushed, perhaps. If this first venture went wrong, if Delaney appropriated it, corrupted it, overlaid it with the tricks and curlicues and sure-fire melodrama and sentimentality that had disfigured his work in the last ten years, there was no telling what the effects would be on Bresach. Aside from what it would do to the story itself, which was delicately and unsentimentally composed, and which would fall apart if it were done wrongly. A third allegiance. To a hundred or so sheets of badly typed paper. And Sam Holt— What did he owe Sam Holt?

324

"Mr. Andrus," he heard Max begin to speak.

"Sssh," Bresach said. "Let the man think."

Irrelevantly, the youthful voice made him remember his own son, and the letter in the airplane and the letter from Chicago. He stared out across the court into the lighted windows, feeling the chill of youthful eyes upon him, Bresach's, Steven's, his own, when he was their age, Delaney's, at the time when Delaney had come for the first time into the dressing room in Philadelphia. Two whole generations of young men, he thought, sons and fathers intermingled, are waiting for me to betray them.

Let the man think . . .

If a question like this had been placed before that young Delaney who had entered Jack's life that night, how would he have answered it? Jack smiled a little to himself, remembering the violence of Delaney's harangue about poor Myers' play and the stricken expression on the producer's face before he fled the room. Well, Jack thought, in honor of my friend, in gratitude for what he has taught me . . .

He turned back toward Bresach and Max. "You'd be a fool to let anyone else touch it," he said. "Especially Delaney. Now I have to go to the hospital, and after that I have to go back to my hotel to shave and dress. When you find out what restaurant Sam Holt is taking you to, call and leave a message. I'll join you later."

He was conscious of Max's sad, reproachful glance as he picked up his coat and left the apartment.

Delaney was sitting up in bed and eating his dinner when Jack came into the room. He had been shaved and his complexion was ruddy and he was having a glass of red wine with his meal. He waved his fork when he saw Jack. The equipment for the oxygen was nowhere in sight. He looked as sound as he had at the airport when he had come to meet Jack, and his voice had its old throaty power when he said, "Should I ring for dinner for you, too? It's a hell of a restaurant."

He had awakened that morning feeling good, he told Jack. It was as simple as that. He had secretly walked around the room when the nurse was out, and his legs weren't wobbly and there were no pangs in his chest. "If it wasn't for the godamn cardiogram," he said, "I'd have packed my bag and been out of here by noon. Do you think that cardiogram could be all screwed up?"

"No," Jack said.

"It's possible," Delaney said, almost as though he thought that if he convinced Jack, he could leap out of bed. "Don't neglect the possibility. Doctors've been wrong before, you know. And Italians with machinery . . ."

"Italians are better with machinery than anybody in the world," Jack said.

"Well, anyway," Delaney said, grumbling like a little boy, "I'm going to go to the john by myself. I don't care how they scream. They're through slipping me their bedpans." He drank some of his wine. "This is damn good wine. I tell you, Italians know how to run a hospital." He held the wine up in front of his face and frowned, as it brought something back to his mind. "Remember what that poor bastard Despière said about Italian wine?"

"Yes."

"Don't be tactful," Delaney said. "I read the papers this morning." He finished the wine. "I told him he was going to get his fool head blown off. You know, I have the feeling he expected it, and he didn't care one way or another . . ."

"He cared," Jack said.

"Then what did he keep going for?"

"Maybe he needed the money."

Delaney made a face. "I suppose if you're going to get killed you might as well get paid for it." He started on a plate of vanilla ice cream. He ate with gusto, noisily stuffing a dry biscuit into his mouth along with the ice cream. "Italian ice cream—best in the world. Girls, ice cream, and fast cars—what more does a country need? I should have come here when I was twenty-five. With a whole godamn heart. If he had to be killed, maybe it's just as well he did it now, before he finished that piece on me." Delaney grinned. "The Frenchman didn't like me. Oh, no, my boy, the Frenchman couldn't stand my guts. When he looked at me and he didn't know I was watching, it was like a big sign on his face, 'I think Maurice Delaney is Sonofabitch Number One.' In French. Do you know how to translate it into French?"

"Not literally," Jack said. He wanted to steer Delaney away from this subject. Uneasily, he tried to remember where he had hidden the manuscript of Despière's article.

"Marvelous ice cream," Delaney said, putting down his spoon.

326

He rang for the nurse, and leaned back comfortably against the pillows propped against the tilted back of the bed. "This has been a refreshing day," he said. "They even plugged in a phone this afternoon." He waved to indicate the instrument on the table next to the bed. "The doctor's allowing me two calls a day. I only made one and they still owe me one. I looked at that phone for an hour before I made up my mind who I wanted to call first. Clara or Barzelli. I was going to toss a coin, only I didn't have a coin on me." He smiled, making fun of himself. "Then I decided, what the hell, I'm an old man with a bum heart, why kid myself, why not make peace in the family. It only took three minutes of talk and the battle was won. Clara's coming over in an hour. They're putting up a cot in here and she's going to sleep here, give the nurse a night off. She'd be here now, but she promised she'd have dinner with Hilda. In the long run, you can't escape the clutch of women, Jack. But a man has to try." He sighed contentedly. "I feel so good I could smoke a cigar. And I hate cigars."

As Delaney rattled on, enjoying his reborn sense of vitality, Jack felt reassured about what he had come to say. Delaney might not like it, but he would be able to take it.

A little round sister, who sounded starched as she moved, came in to take the tray. "Signore," she said to Delaney, "a lady has telephoned, a Signora Lee. She inquires to know if she is permitted to come to pay a visit. I have promised to call her back at her hotel."

"Tell her she is not permitted. Tell her I am dying a long, slow, agonizing death and I am in a coma most of the time and I do not recognize anybody."

"Signore," the sister said disapprovingly. "It is not a matter to be joked. I will merely say that for the time being it is not permitted." She went out with the tray.

"Carlotta," Delaney grumbled. "That's all I need. Have you seen her?"

"Yes."

"What's she like?"

"Fat."

Delaney laughed. "The plump, loaded widow. Kutzer left her a pile." He shook his head. "God, how people turn out."

"She told me why she wants to see you," Jack said.

"Why?"

"You gave her more pleasure in bed than any man she's ever had anything to do with," Jack said, "and she thought it would be a fitting thing to tell you before you died."

Delaney laughed brutally. "Well," he said, "everybody likes to have a reason for a pilgrimage to Rome. The bitch. To say a thing like that—even to an ex-husband."

"No, she's not a bitch," Jack said. "It's just that she's obsessed by the subject. Or at least she was. Now, I think she's only obsessed by the memory of the subject."

"You know how it happened?" Delaney demanded.

"No."

"Do you want to know?"

"If you want to tell me."

"Ah, why the hell not," Delaney said. "It's so long ago, and it's the one thing I ever hid from you, and it made me feel like a bastard for years. It was during the war," Delaney said. "You were overseas, and I took her out to lunch to bawl her out because it was common gossip that she was spreading herself all over town. I told her that she ought to be ashamed of herself and what a remarkable guy you were and that she was going to regret it and that she was ruining her life, and she looked at me across the table, and she said, 'I'm not going to stop. And since I'm not going to stop, why don't you get in on some of the fun along with the other boys?' " Delaney sighed and smoothed out some of the creases in the top sheet with the palm of his hand. "My curse, for a long time," he said, "was that when it was offered to me I couldn't refuse it. I told myself I wasn't doing anything to you. I knew that when you got back you'd break it off with her sooner or later, no matter what I did or didn't do. So we got up from the table and drove out to a motel in the Valley and praised the afternoon. It only lasted a few weeks. I felt like too much of a heel. Outside of my work, I have very few principles, and it's never occurred to me that I am universally loved for the sweetness of my character, but sleeping with my best friend's wife while he was off getting shot up in a war never did make me particularly proud of myself. Even if I was just one of a long parade. So I put a term to my black villainy." He drawled the sentence mockingly. "Ah—it's a load off my mind. I've always wanted to tell you and now the deed's done. You angry?"

"No," Jack said. "And I wasn't angry then. It's not important. And it wasn't important then."

328

"Not to anybody but me," Delaney said softly.

The room was silent for a moment, and Jack wondered if Delaney was dropping off to sleep. Delaney had moved the shade on the lamp so that it shone away from him and Jack could only make out Delaney's face dimly, in the shadows against the pillows.

"Maurice . . ." Jack said, tentatively.

"Yes?"

"Are you going to sleep?"

"Hell, no. Why?"

"Because there's something we have to talk about."

"I'm listening," Delaney said.

"It's about that script of Bresach's. I don't think you ought to do it."

Delaney sat up in surprise. "I thought you said you liked it?"

"I like it very much," Jack said. "But I think it's too much of a job for you right now . . ."

"In six weeks, I'll be out of here. The doctor says . . ."

"You'll kill yourself if you start working again after six weeks," Jack said.

"Kill, kill . . ." Delaney said irritably. "I'm getting tired of people prophesying my death. If I want a drink, if I screw a girl, if I walk to the bathroom, if I read a script . . ."

"Come on, Maurice," Jack said gently. "You know it's not the same thing."

"I know, I know." Delaney sighed. "How long do you think I ought to knock off?"

"A year."

"A year! What happens to the script? What happens to you? What happens to Holt?" Delaney's voice was taking on a querulous, sick man's tone. "In a year, everything can slide away from you. I might just as well be dead as try to wait a year. What do I do for a year? Knit? Ever since I started, as a kid, I haven't taken a vacation for more than two weeks. I'll go out of my mind."

"I didn't say you had to take a complete vacation," Jack said. "I just said you shouldn't get on the set and direct, because that's man-killing . . ."

"Who'll do it, then? Hilda? The Angel Gabriel?"

Jack took a deep breath. "Bresach."

Delaney sat up sharply, his head suddenly in the light. He stared at Jack. "Are you kidding?"

"No."

"He's only twenty-four years old."

"Twenty-five," Jack said. "He's old enough to write it, he'll be old enough to direct it."

"Where do I come in, then?" Delaney asked. "Where do you come in?"

"Holt wants to set up a company to do three pictures, doesn't he?"

"Yes."

"Well," Jack said, speaking quickly but calmly, trying to keep a tone of argument out of his voice, "this can be the first picture. You can help produce it. He'll need plenty of help. You'll be invaluable to him. And at the same time, you won't be killing yourself day after day on the set. And while you're recovering, you can search around for the other two stories and start preparing them, and when you're well enough, a year from now, you can start shooting them . . ."

"Where're *you* during all this?" Delaney demanded.

"I hope I'm back in Paris," Jack said, "with my wife and family, quietly doing my job. You don't need me."

"I need you," Delaney said harshly. "You don't know how badly I need you. Where the hell do you think I'd've been these last few days without you?"

"You can find someone else."

"Name him," Delaney said.

"Well, not at this moment, but . . ."

"Not at this moment," Delaney said. "And not tomorrow, and not in a month or a year from now. I've told you before, and I'll tell you again—you're the only man I've ever been able to work with for any length of time without an explosion. Do I sound selfish?"

"Yes."

"Well, I meant to," Delaney said. "But I'm selfish for you, too. I want to get you out of that narrow, little obscure rut of yours pushing a pen for the government in Paris . . ."

"Maybe I'm happy in what you call my narrow, little obscure rut," Jack said, trying to keep his voice from rising in anger. "Or maybe I don't think it's such a rut . . . maybe I think I'm doing an important job and doing it well."

"You didn't look like a happy man the day you got off the plane," Delaney said. "Were you?"

"What difference does that make?"

"Were you?"

"No," Jack admitted. "It happened I was at a low period."

"What did I tell you?" Delaney said triumphantly. "I saw the signs, I saw the signs. You were wallowing in bureaucratic melancholy, you were feeling useless and half-dead. Why, even in the short time you've been here, you've come to life, you seem ten years younger. Listen, Jack, you're no boy any more—you probably only have one more big move left to you in your whole life. Don't miss it, don't miss it . . ."

"I'll think it over," Jack said wearily. "I'll write you from Paris."

"The hell with it," Delaney said. "If you won't come in, tell Holt and Bresach the whole thing's off . . ."

"You bastard," Jack said.

"Nobody ever pretended I wasn't a bastard," Delaney said smugly. "Well, partner?"

Jack sighed, then smiled. "Okay, partner."

"Call your wife and tell her to rush to Berlitz and start taking Italian lessons immediately," Delaney said. "A new and glorious life is opening for her. I wish I had a bottle here. To celebrate."

"If we had a bottle here," Jack said, "I'd probably hit you over the head with it."

"Save it for the next board meeting," Delaney said briskly. "So, partner, you think Bresach can do it?"

"Yes."

"It's an idea, it's an idea . . ." Delaney said. "What the hell, if anybody'd ever given me a chance when I was twenty-five, I'd've dazzled them. And it wouldn't be as if the kid was out in the blue, all on his own. We'd be on tap every day . . . What sort of kid is he, Jack? Can we work with him? Do you like him?"

"We can work with him," Jack said.

"You don't like him," Delaney said.

Jack sighed. "I don't know," he said. "I've never been as confused about anybody in my whole life." Maybe I love him, Jack thought, maybe I'm looking for someone to take the place of my son Steven, because I just found out my son hates me, maybe I'm afraid he'll kill himself. "You got some time on your hands?" Jack said. "I'll tell you a long story."

"I have all night," Delaney said. He chuckled a little sadly. "I have all year, lad. Tell me a story."

"Once upon a time," Jack said, "a man came down to Rome to lend a helping hand to an old pal for two weeks . . ."

"I love the beginning of the story," Delaney said, settling comfortably into his pillows. "Go on."

Then Jack began to go over the two weeks, trying to get it all in, leave out nothing, the drunk on the steps, the bloody nose, the emotion on seeing himself on the screen, so many years later, in *The Stolen Midnight,* the dream of bulls, the premonition of death, the concourse of dead friends, the meeting with Veronica, the love-making, the crazy visit of Bresach with the knife, the disappearance of Veronica and his involvement with the boy because of the necessity of finding out what had happened to her, his fascination with Bresach and pity for him, his admiration for the violence and purity of his ambition, mingled with his fear that just that violence and purity would shatter him.

Delaney listened without a word, immobile in the bed, with the slanting light of the lamp cutting a sharp diagonal line above his head against the wall and ceiling.

"My feeling about him is all mixed up," Jack said. "I couldn't put it in a word. He entertains me. I enjoy him. I have hope for him, in the way I would like to have hope for my son, and I feel guilty about him because I was the instrument for hurting him, the way I feel guilty about having hurt my son. I worry about him, because there is something terribly fragile about him, and finally, and I suppose absolutely irrationally, I feel responsible for him."

Jack lapsed into silence. Delaney was lying back, his body motionless under the covers, his hands clasped across the chest. After a while, he spoke, his voice rueful and humorous. "God, what a two weeks," he said. "No wonder you seem so much more alive. You have no idea how much I envy you . . . You don't think the boy'll be tempted to use his knife on me one of these days, do you?" He laughed.

"No," Jack said. "I think that's behind him."

"Tell me, Jack," Delaney said, his voice low and gentle, as he spoke from the pillows, without moving his head, "if I'd been completely well, if this thing hadn't happened to me—" He tapped his chest. "What would you have advised the boy to do?"

"What do you mean?" Jack asked, although he knew what Delaney meant.

"Would you have told him to let me do his script?" Delaney said. "Or would you have told him to hold onto it and do it himself? Of course, it's just a theoretical question." There was a touch of irony in the way Delaney spoke the last sentence.

"No," Jack said. "It's not theoretical. Because he asked me, this evening, just before I came here."

"And what did you say, Jack?" Still the light, friendly tone of irony. "Did you consider a long time?"

"Yes," Jack said. "I thought about you . . ."

"The poor, old, infirm pal, lying in the hospital, plucking piteously at the coverlets with his nervous, wan fingers . . ."

"No," Jack said soberly. "I thought of you the night I met you when you raised such honest hell in the dressing room in Philadelphia."

"And you told the kid to keep it out of my hands?" Delaney said flatly.

"Yes," Jack said.

Delaney tapped his chest again in an unconscious small gesture. "Well, I asked you and you told me." He chuckled. "There's nothing like honesty in a partnership, is there, Jack?"

"What would you have done if you were in my place?"

Delaney waited a moment before answering. "The same thing," he said, "the same thing . . ." He grinned painfully. "If I was that age again and back in Philadelphia. Now? Today?" He shook his head. "I don't know. I'm a long way from Philadelphia. Who knows what filthy, corrupt thing I'd've said? You see, Jack—I wasn't lying before when I said I needed you." He sat up, his face coming abruptly into the light. There was a curious, soft smile on his lips, the sort of smile to be seen on the lips of old men as they watch children at play. "Thanks for coming, Jack," he said. "Now, for Christ's sake, go out and get some dinner. You're going to need all your strength."

Jack stood up. He hadn't kept track of the time and he hadn't realized it was so late. He would have liked to be able to tell Delaney how close he felt to him, how the gap of the years between them had been finally bridged by what they had said to each other that evening. But he had never been overt with Delaney and he could not be overt now.

"Jack," Delaney said, as Jack stood with his hand on the doorknob, "you said you had hope for the kid . . ."

"Yes."

"How about the old man, Jack?" Delaney said softly, "Me. Have you got hope for him?"

"Yes," Jack said. "A great deal."

Delaney nodded gravely. "Good night, partner," he said. "Drink three martinis for me."

· He was sitting up straight in the bed, smiling and healthy-looking, when Jack went out.

25

He was bubblingly cheerful as he drove back to the hotel. He felt a holiday desire to mark the occasion. The fears and hesitations of the last few days seemed remote and without foundation, now that the decision was finally made. He felt relieved that the event had proved he had underrated Delaney's honesty and sense of justice, and he was grateful that his friend had lived up to an earlier estimate of his qualities. Mingled with all this was a sense of self-satisfaction. He had been called on for help, and he had come through. Although matters had swiftly become more complex than anyone had contemplated, and more dangerous, as Jack thought of Delaney now, he regarded him as a rescued man. And the rescue was Jack's doing. It was very seldom, throughout his whole life, that Jack had been satisfied with himself, so this moment had an added dividend of originality to it.

Physically, he was fresh, and agreeably conscious of his hunger.

He looked forward to the three martinis he was going to drink in Delaney's honor and the dinner with Bresach and Holt. The sorrow over Despière's death was as keen as ever, but it was pushed back in his consciousness by the optimism and excitement that came with the realization that he was making a new start in life. The risks he was running—the security he was giving up by leaving the government service, the pension he was forfeiting, the danger that none of the three pictures would ever be any good and that he would be left jobless and a failure as he approached fifty, only served, at that moment, to enhance his sense of youthful well-being. Risks lightly taken, dangers gaily run, were part of being young. Maybe the best part.

It is not difficult for Rome to seem the fairest city in the world in which to live, and that evening Jack was convinced it was exactly that. He decided to get Hélène down as soon as possible and start her looking for a house for the family. A house out in the Campagna, close enough to the city for daily visits, he decided, with a garden. Olive trees, vines (the warm, Biblical dream that haunts northerners), the sound of the children speaking Italian to the gardeners and maids, the easy access to the beaches in the hot weather. It would be nice to be rich again, too, after the long years of not being rich at all, not to have to worry about whether or not they could afford a new car, new clothes, a holiday . . . The independence and informality of his new job, where he would be more or less his own boss, able to speak on equal terms with anyone, promised an exhilarating change, after the years of being weighed down by the bulk of the governmental pyramid, the years of worrying whether some word he had said, some paper he had prepared, would unwittingly give aid to the Russians or incur some higher-up's displeasure. There are more third-rate people among politicians and civil-servants and generals, he decided, with what he considered was newborn clarity, than among the people who make movies, and it is more difficult to avoid them and to keep yourself out of their power.

He sat erect on the front seat next to Guido, looking out happily at the city of Rome, its streets still busy under the street lamps, and even the blare of the car radio, playing *"Volare, cantare,"* could not dampen his spirits. He didn't even ask Guido to turn the radio off.

When he got to the hotel, he told Guido he was going to bathe and change his clothes and would be down in fifteen minutes. He was whistling under his breath as he strode into the lobby, thinking of the bath that awaited him and the fresh clothes as fitting elements of the rites of purification and renewal before the next episode in his life.

As he came near the desk, he stopped.

Veronica was standing there.

Her head was down and she didn't see him because she was scribbling a note on a piece of the hotel stationery.

Even with his first glance, he saw that she seemed very different from his memory of her. She was wearing a pale beaver coat that was obviously new, and her hair was combed upward and she was wearing a hat. She looked older than the girl to whom Despière had introduced him, less showy, but much more carefully groomed. After a moment, Jack walked up to the desk and stood next to Veronica, who did not look up from her writing. "Six fifty-four, please," he said.

At the sound of his voice, Veronica stopped writing. She stared down at the piece of paper in front of her, then crumpled it and put it in an ashtray on the desk. Only then did she turn to face Jack. "It was for you," she said. "This note. There's no need now, is there?"

"No," Jack said. He took the key from the man behind the desk. "Do you want to come upstairs with me?"

"No," Veronica said. "Not with you." She was speaking in quick whispers, without looking directly at him, so that, from a little distance, it would hardly seem that they were talking to each other. "I'll follow you. I'll take the back elevator. In two minutes."

"What's going on here?" Jack asked. "You don't have to talk to me at all, if you don't want to."

"I must not be seen with you," she said. "I am married now. I must be careful. I am going to leave here now and walk around the block once."

"Oh, God," Jack said. "Do you remember the number of my room?"

"I remember, I remember," she said, and walked swiftly toward the door. Jack watched her, for a moment. Married or not married, her way of walking had not changed.

*

The knock on the door came promptly, and she came into the room with a little smile, at home, familiar, swinging her new fur coat, touching her smartly arranged hair. She looked around her casually, standing in the middle of the room. "Nothing much has changed here, has it?" She said. "Are you glad to see me?"

"I don't know," Jack said. "I haven't sorted out my feelings yet. At the moment, I'm exasperated. Do you want to take your coat off?"

"I'm terribly sorry. I can't," Veronica said, her voice that of a polite, false guest at a cocktail party. "I only have a minute. I have to meet my husband at the Hassler. He had a late appointment, or I wouldn't have been able to pass by at all. You shouldn't say that you're exasperated." She made a small, unpleasant pout. "You'll make me sorry I came to see you."

"Oh, Christ," Jack said.

"Did you miss me?" she asked.

"Sit down."

She shook her head. "No," she said.

"Well, then, *I'll* sit down," Jack said. He dropped back onto the couch and put his feet up on the low coffee table in front of it. Veronica stood in the middle of the room, facing him, her coat thrown back in a position that he remembered. He also remembered the V of lipstick on the bathroom mirror and the first afternoon they had made love and the night on the beach at Fregene, and he felt shaken and unsure of himself and resentful of her husband, whoever he might be.

"I was afraid I wasn't going to be able to see you at all," Veronica said. "We only arrived this morning. And we're flying to Athens tomorrow. On our honeymoon. It was my idea, stopping off for a day. I had to see you," she said. She licked the corner of her mouth nervously. "I felt I owed you an explanation."

"I think the best place to explain anything is in there." Jack gestured with his head toward the bedroom. "Take off that godamn coat." He knew it sounded brutal, and he wanted to be brutal.

"If you're going to talk like that," she said, "I'm going to have to leave right now."

"All right," he said, "I won't talk like anything. Explain."

"Although," she said, smiling, "I *am* glad you still want me. I was afraid by now you'd have forgotten me."

"I am not glad I still want you," he said. "And if you're going to tease me, you can get out right now."

"You're not as nice as you were two weeks ago," she said sulkily. "Not at all as nice."

"That's true. Every two weeks I take a turn for the worse."

She looked at her watch nervously. It was a new watch, set in diamonds, and Jack didn't remember having seen it on her wrist before. Naturally, he thought, if she's just come from Switzerland.

"Well," she said, "actually it's silly for me to stand like this." She sat down in the easy chair at the end of the couch farthest from Jack. She crossed her legs with a noise of silk, and once more Jack felt himself swept, almost angrily, by the wave of generalized and impersonal lust that the sight of those rosy and perfect legs and those pointed Roman shoes had given rise to in him when he had first met her.

"I can bear everything about you," he said, "but your presence."

"What?" Veronica asked puzzledly. "What did you say?"

"Never mind."

"It sounded insulting."

"In a way perhaps it was," he said. He made certain that he sat absolutely still.

"I wanted everything to be clear and clean between us," Veronica said, with her hint of a pout. "That's why I came here. But if you're going to say mean things . . ."

"All right," he said. "I won't say mean things. Didn't you say something about being married? Give me a clear and clean description of your marriage."

"I'm not ashamed of anything I've done," Veronica said petulantly, like a schoolgirl caught coming in through a hallway window after hours. "I did what I had to do to save myself."

"Whom are you married to?" Jack asked. "Do I know the gentleman?"

"No, you don't," she said. "And I won't tell you his name."

"Does he know me?"

"No."

"Does he know anything about me?"

"Of course not," she said calmly, recrossing her legs. "And he's not going to."

"I see you're well launched on a happy marriage," Jack said.

"You can say anything you want," she said. "Your cynicism can't affect me."

"Who is he?"

"He's thirty-one years old," she said. "Very nice-looking. He's Swiss. He comes from one of the best families in Zurich. I've known him for nearly two years. He wanted to marry me from the beginning, but he couldn't . . ."

"Why not—was he married?" Jack said. "What did he do, poison his wife last week?"

"No, he wasn't married," Veronica said. She sounded childishly triumphant at having scored this point. "He's never been married. But he couldn't marry me until he was thirty-one."

"What is that?" Jack asked. "An old Swiss law?"

"Don't make fun of me, Jack," Veronica said in a low voice. "Please. I've had such a bad two weeks . . ."

"You're not the only one," he said. Then he was sorry for his tone, and spoke more gently. "I won't interrupt any more," he said. "Tell it any way you want."

"It's all so complicated," Veronica said. "We met here in Rome when he came into the agency to ask about flying to Munich. His family owns a big insurance company and they do business all over the world. I'm going to travel with him wherever he goes. He's promised me. At least until we have children. Finally, I'm going to get out of Italy." The tone of victory, of an almost hopeless desire at last fulfilled, resounded in her voice. "But he couldn't marry me before. On account of his family. His father's dead, but he has an awful mother and three stuffy uncles and they wouldn't have approved of his getting married to me. After all—a little Italian girl with no money who worked in a travel agency and a Catholic besides. And by the terms of his father's will, until he was thirty-one, his mother and his oldest uncle could have cut him off almost without a penny if they disapproved of him. And they would have, too. You don't know those big Swiss families. They wanted him to marry someone else, a girl from another big Zurich family, and he had to make believe he was on the verge of proposing to her. . . . We had to hide the fact that we even knew each other. We only saw each other on weekends, in Florence, secretly, in a hotel . . ."

"Oh," Jack said, "that's the mother you went to visit in Florence."

"What do you know about that?" she asked suspiciously.

"Bresach," Jack said. "He told me."

"How did he happen to tell you that?"

"We've become very chummy," Jack said. "On the days he's not threatening to murder me."

"Well," Veronica said defensively, "I had to tell Robert *something*. I couldn't tell him I was going to meet my fiancé every weekend, could I?"

"No," Jack said. "Of course not. Incidentally, just for my own information—where *is* your mother?"

"She lives with a sister in Milan."

"No wonder the telegram came back," Jack said.

"You mean you tried to send me a telegram?" Veronica sounded surprised.

"Bresach and me. Not to you. To your mother."

"Why in the world would you want to do that?"

"We were foolish," Jack said. "We were curious about whether you were alive or dead."

"I wanted to call you . . ." Her voice had lost its self-assurance now, and was wavery, threatened with sobs. "But I was afraid if I heard your voice I'd change my mind. And it was all so much in a hurry . . . Georg had arranged everything with the mayor of a little town outside Zurich. I'd already sent all my papers to him weeks before, before I ever met you . . . And then, that night, you couldn't get into the hotel with me and you were so cool and superior when we were on the beach together . . ."

"You mean," Jack said, keeping his voice reasonable, "that if I had made love to you that night, you wouldn't have gotten married . . . ?"

"Maybe," she said, fighting back the tears. "Who knows? Remember, I told you I wanted to come to work in Paris and you made it plain . . . ?"

"I remember," Jack said, cutting her off. He tried to smile gently and absolvingly at her, but he had no idea how the expression came out.

"You didn't want me," she said harshly, no trace of tears now. "Or you only wanted me for a few minutes at a time, at your convenience. And Robert wanted to devour me. And the others—all the others I haven't told you about. Men don't take me out just to amuse themselves or entertain me—they want to tear me apart—"

Jack nodded. "Yes," he said. "I see what you mean. But it's your own fault."

"Whosever fault," she said bitterly, "I'm the one who suffers. And each time it was getting worse. I lied to you. I'm not as young as I said I was. I'm twenty-seven. I went upstairs in that hotel and I sat in my room alone and I thought, If this is what love is like, I don't want love, I can't handle it. I'm too romantic not to be married. I give too much. That's right, smile if you want to. But it's the truth, and I realized it that night. And the next morning I was on the plane for Zurich. Finally, I was protecting myself, I was behaving sensibly. Is there anything wrong in that? You don't know what it's like, being a girl alone in this town—hardly earning enough to pay the rent and buy stockings—going from man to man—with everything depending upon accidents—whom I met, whom I had dinner with, whom I made love with—if I hadn't walked past the table at the moment you happened to be sitting with Jean-Baptiste . . ." She stopped, panting. All her composure was gone. Her face was tortured and the fashionable bright little hat over it seemed incongruous and pitiful. "I read about it the morning I got married. I cried at the wedding, and Georg made fun of me, but I wasn't crying because I was a bride. I was crying because I kept remembering the first time we were together and you said you thought I was Jean-Baptiste's girl and I said I wasn't, I was your girl . . ." She stood up. Her lips were trembling. "I can't cry. I can't go meet my husband with my eyes red. Poor Jean-Baptiste. He was so gay that afternoon, so sly . . . And I said, 'There's a bad man there, mixed up with a very good man.' Nobody knew what was going to happen. To any of us. I've got to go. I must go." She moved her head and her arms, erratically, as though freeing them from restraining bonds. "Say good-bye to me."

Jack stood up slowly, trying to control his face, trying not to show to her how much she was moving him. One soft word, he thought, one kiss, and she won't leave. She won't ever leave. He was frightened by the fierceness of his desire to keep her there, keep her from leaving. In the time that she had been gone, his desire for her had grown secretly within him, unknown to him. Now her presence was like a brilliant light suddenly switched on, revealing it to him, nakedly, with harsh precision. "Good-bye," he said, his voice flat and toneless. He held out his hand.

Her face was pale and hurt and childish. "Not like that," she said, whimpering. "Not like ice."

"Your husband is waiting for you at the Hassler," he said, with purposeful cruelty. "Have a good time in Athens."

342

"I don't care about my husband," she said. "I don't care if I never see Athens. I want us to say good-bye like human beings . . ." The tears were close to the surface. "With generosity."

She moved toward him. He stood there, motionless, abstracted, as though he were viewing the scene from a great distance. She put her arms around him and kissed him. He kept his eyes open, unblinking. He kept his body rigid, unresponsive, as he felt her lips on his. The remembered taste. The remembered softness. He stood there, still, wanting to put his arms around her, hold her, thinking, Why not? Why not? The beginning of a new life. Why not begin it with something I want this much? I will count to ten, he thought crazily, and then I will tell her I love her (later, we will discover the truth), that she must not go. A new life. This was the day of the beginning of the new life. He made himself count. He reached six, dizzied, assaulted.

Then she broke away from him.

"It's hopeless," she said quietly. "I'm a fool."

He stood where he was for a long time after she had left the room.

The telephone rang. He let it ring again and again before he answered it. It was Bresach. "We're eating dinner at the Hosteria dell'Orso," Bresach said. "It's a party. Tucino, Barzelli, the Holts. We're drinking champagne. I think they're launching me. Are you coming?"

"In a while," Jack said. "Don't wait for me to start. I still haven't cleaned up."

"What the hell have you been doing all this time?"

"Nothing," Jack said, thinking, He never did catch us together. "Arranging things. Saying good-bye to a friend."

"Are you all right?" Bresach said. "You sound awful queer."

"I'm fine," Jack said. "I'll be over right away."

He hung up. He waited at the phone, waited for it to ring again, or for the door to open. But the phone didn't ring and the door didn't open and after a few minutes he went into the bathroom with the two basins and the mirror on which the loving, coquettish V had been scrawled in lipstick. Methodically he shaved and bathed, before putting on fresh linen and a newly pressed dark suit. Then he went out, looking like any other polite American tourist, on the town for a night in Rome.

26

He had the three martinis. Then three more. Then champagne with dinner. And more champagne when they went upstairs to the night club. It was a way of making the night bearable, after the unbearable scene with Veronica. The liquor didn't make him drunk. It gave everything around him a crystalline clarity. He sat with a fixed, small smile on his face, in his dark, American suit, regarding the people at the table with him and the dancers on the floor, their edges sharp, their movements unambiguous.

Everybody at the table was happy, for various reasons, and many toasts were drunk and many bottles emptied. Bertha Holt was happy because she had found a woman from Naples with six children who was going to give birth in two weeks to a seventh, which she was willing to give up for adoption to the Holts because even six mouths were more than enough for her and her husband to feed.

Sam Holt was happy because his wife was happy and because

Delaney had called him from the hospital and had told him about the agreement he had come to with Jack, and new continents of legal tax evasion were opening before him.

Tucino was happy because he had read Bresach's script and because Holt had said they could go ahead with forming the company and now it looked as though Tucino would certainly avoid bankruptcy for at least another three years. Tucino, although shrewd, was an optimist, so he liked the beginnings of things better than the middles or ends of things, and he was beaming behind his glasses all night and calling Bresach, "Our young genius" and raising his glass to the fortunes they all would make in their new and perfect association.

Tasseti wasn't there, but Jack was sure that he must be happy that night because for once he didn't have to listen to Tucino.

Barzelli was happy because she had had a day's vacation and had used it to sleep, so that she looked rested and beautiful and she was sure that every man in the room wanted her. Give or take a man or two, this was probably true. She sat next to Bresach and talked earnestly to him, between toasts.

Max was happy because Bresach was there and they both had had enough to eat.

Bresach was happy because he was drunk, and he hadn't overheard what Veronica had told Jack earlier in the evening. If he hadn't been drunk, there would have been many other reasons, all perfectly valid, for his being happy that night.

Jack looked at them all, in the new, crystalline light which the martinis and the champagne were shedding on them, and was glad that they were happy, and pitied them for the short duration of their joy, because on this night everybody's past was known to him, and all futures were revealed. He was neither happy nor unhappy. He was coldly and accurately balanced, like the machines that are made to trace the orbits of protons in the unimaginable distances of the atom. The martinis and the champagne spread their winter starlight on his soul, too, and he looked with electronic detachment on what was revealed there. Frozen and static in that cold, bodiless glare, he saw himself in Veronica's arms, caught between saying Stay and Go, forced to say one or the other and knowing that sorrow waited whichever word was spoken. Too sane and responsible to seize the pleasure whose denial was crippling him, too sensual to be able to congratulate himself on escaping from the web of lies and betrayals that was the corollary of claiming that pleasure, he was that interesting example of modern life, a man who lived in a permanent condition of being torn asunder.

As a result of many careful observations, conducted under a good light, with the most precise equipment, we are now happy to be able to present the whole picture of John Andrus, briefly notorious as James Royal. He is responsible, honorable, useful to his friends, and when forced to betray anyone, makes certain that the betrayed party is himself. Further details in our next bulletin.

Thinking these thoughts, sitting politely at the night-club table, Jack chuckled, the pleased chuckle of a scientist whose experiments have checked against theory. Now, he thought, looking around him, I can focus on the others.

The essential thing here, he thought, as his eye roamed the table, is a man called Delaney. For this last brief time, he is still the element in which we move, the force that binds us together. The champagne, for the last time, is for him. Without him, we would not be here, in these positions, but the next time we are assembled, it will no longer be because of him. Youth will be served, whole hearts will be served, money will be served, love will be served. Bresach will have taken his step toward the center of the system.

It is like a wake, Jack thought. Delaney's friends are gathered to drink to his disappearance, in a place where he was known and respected and where the absent man spent his happiest hours. A man who would seem to be Delaney would reappear, of course, but so different in quality and power that it would only be out of politeness and convenience that he would be called by the same name. Remembering Delaney and Barzelli together on that other night, Jack looked to see if Barzelli's hand was under the table, on Bresach's thigh. But it wasn't. The replacement was not yet total.

Thirty years from now, Jack thought, regarding Bresach and remembering Delaney at the same table, with success and failure behind him, how will Bresach look at these midnight ceremonies, what women will he be whispering to, and what will thirty years of money and work and disappointment make him say to them?

"Remember the man in the hospital, my dear young friend," Jack said, speaking slowly and distinctly. Bresach looked at him puzzled, across the delicious Catanian vista of Barzelli's bosom tastefully displayed that night under pink lace. Jack raised his hand gravely, in warning, greeting, and friendship, in love and farewell, as fathers raise their hands to the captains who are their sons and who are parting, with the music playing, for distant wars.

346

"What the hell has come over you tonight, Jack?" Bresach asked. Jack noted that his voice was thicker than usual, and shook his head, remembering how many of his friends and lovers had been lost in alcohol, that glittering, deceptive sea.

"Wine, nerves, ambition, women and overwork," Jack said cryptically. He turned his small, night-club-clear smile on Mrs. Holt, because Mrs. Holt, floating above the table in tulle like something Marc Chagall would have painted if he had been born in Oklahoma and lived in Rome, was saying, "I do so want you to meet Mrs. Lusaldi, Jack. She is the lady who has been kind enough to promise us her son. She knows it's going to be a son this time. She has four boys and two girls, and she's never guessed wrong. She was up at our house this evening and I wish you could have seen her. She is as wide as a piano, with beautiful dark skin, and she sat there with a shawl over her head, and I declare, all that I could think was that a fertility goddess had descended upon our *palazzo.*"

Careful, Bertha Holt, Jack wanted to say, careful. What would the ladies in Oklahoma City think if they heard you use language like that? Would they let their daughters come to Rome?

"What I've always liked about Italians," Mrs. Holt said dreamily, floating wispily above the rumbas and the church domes of the Roman night, "is they always have such beautiful teeth. Teeth are so important. Don't you agree, Jack?"

Jack agreed that teeth were important and then Tucino gallantly asked her to dance, because of the occasion, and she said, "Oh, that is too kind," and stood up and drifted into his arms and followed him with a demure, drunken smile on her face, like a kitten whose cream has been mischievously laced with brandy.

Light-footed, frail, and unfertile, she went through the figures of the dance in those robust Italian arms, and Jack watched her with pity because she was committed to the belief that a son, anybody's son, would bring her happiness.

To pity Tucino required a godlike act of compassion, because you could only pity him generically, as a representative of an attractive but doomed species, the race of gamblers, those optimists who cannot hold themselves back from doubling their bets, going from one dizzying win to another, until the final loss. Sometime before you are sixty, Jack thought, watching Tucino as he maneuvered Bertha Holt among the dancers, there will come an evening when you will not be able to buy a dinner in this place.

Max was perhaps the most to be pitied, because he was at the climax of one exile and was at the beginning of another. He would never be as close to Bresach again. Bresach had shared his bed, because there had only been the one bed; he had shared his hunger, because he had been living on crusts; and in that Spartan sharing he had restored Max's shaken faith in man's goodness and love. Now there would be many beds, and daily feasting would quickly become routine and unnoticed. Brotherhood would become charity, and charity is just one condition of exile, as persecution is another. Exulting in Bresach's triumph tonight, Max, because he was wise, knew that each new triumph would move Bresach further from him.

Pitying Barzelli was an aesthetic exercise, impersonal and pure, because all that was pitiable about her was that she would grow older and her beauty would be destroyed by time. If it could be said that one could pity a lovely, uninhabited building that the years would inevitably bring down into dust, then it could be said that Barzelli could be pitied.

Sam Holt was a different matter. As he watched his wife dance, his eyes fond, pleased at the sight of her pleasure, his destiny was painfully clear. His happiness was moored in his wife and that anchorage was hazardous and exposed.

As if he were conscious of Jack considering him, Holt turned his head and smiled at him. "It's quite a night," he said. "Isn't it?"

"Quite a night."

"I can't tell you how glad I am that you're coming in with us," Holt said. "It gives me a great feeling of confidence. We needed a man like you. Solid, responsible, tactful."

For my tombstone, Jack thought. Here lies, in desperation, A Responsible Man.

"I've been thinking," Holt said. "Remember I talked to you about my brother-in-law, Bertha's kid brother—I told you I wanted to put him on the payroll as an assistant producer, for tax reasons . . . ?"

"Yes," Jack said. "I remember."

"Well," Holt said, "I've reconsidered. I'm not going to do it. I'm not going to burden you with him. Not that you wouldn't like him," Holt said with hurried loyalty. "He's a good boy. But, after all, this isn't his line of thing . . ." He smiled wryly. "I'll take care of him some other way. The same old way. The Bureau of Internal Revenue way. Help pay for some of those rockets going to the moon." Holt sighed resignedly, as, for the hundredth time, involuntarily, and feeling a little ashamed of himself for the calculation, he computed what that good boy, Bertha's brother, aged forty-five, was going to cost him for the rest of his life. Then his face brightened. "This is a nice celebration, isn't it?" He looked benignly across the table at Bresach, who was chuckling at something that Barzelli was whispering into his ear. "I bet that boy is going to remember this night for a long time. Ah—it's a shame Maurice can't be here with us tonight."

The wake, Jack thought. He's here, all right. The spirit moves among the champagne glasses. Only the corpse is absent.

"It's been quite a day all around," Holt said. "I suppose Mother told you about the Italian lady who has kindly offered to allow us to adopt her child when it . . ." He cast around for a modest description of the event. "When it . . . uh . . . arrives."

"Yes," Jack said, "she told me. Congratulations."

"We can have it immediately," Holt said. "That way Mother can really feel that it is all hers. She's going to go out shopping tomorrow morning for baby clothes and a baby carriage. It will make a great change in her life, don't you think?" There was a note of pleading in his voice.

"Without a doubt," Jack said.

"For the better," Holt said, hastily, fearful of leaving the suggestion of an alternative in Jack's mind.

"Of course," Jack said.

"I am going to write to various educators in the United States about the boy," Holt said. "Taking a chance that it will be a boy . . ." He laughed slyly. "I would like him to go to the best schools. Groton or Andover, or one of those. I understand you can't apply too early. I want him to feel that he has all the advantages . . ."

Then, past Holt's shoulder, Jack saw Veronica. She was making her way around the edge of the floor, behind the headwaiter, who was leading her to a table on the other side of the room. There was a tall blond young man bulking beside her, holding her by the elbow.

Of course, Jack thought agonizedly, I should have expected it. Where else would honeymooners go if they had only one night in Rome? Sit in a dark corner, Jack prayed. Sit where no one can recognize you. He looked down the table at Bresach. Bresach was turned toward Barzelli now, speaking intently.

Veronica and the blond man sat down at a small table. It was just around the corner of the room. Jack sighed with relief. But then he saw Veronica's profile appear out from the edge of the wall, softly lit by one of the projectors. He realized that she had leaned forward, just enough to be seen from Jack's side of the room. Then the dancers swept across his line of vision and he couldn't see her for the moment.

"In the years to come," Holt was saying, still on the subject of the education of his son, who had not yet been born to the dark Neapolitan lady, "whether we Americans like it or not, we're going to be called upon to lead the world—or our half or quarter of the world." He was very earnest and he put his hand on Jack's wrist in emphasis, the big, rough, capable hand formed by years of labor and not yet softened by wealth. "What we have to do is to try to keep the world—recognizable. It's going to change, sure, but it's up to us to make the changes recognizable in the terms of what we've had and liked up to now. And we'll never do it by fighting for it. One more war and this world won't be recognizable to our dear God Who created it. We'll have to do it by work and example and persuasion. It's a funny thing," he said, shaking his head, "we're a nation of lawyers and yet we can't persuade a single foreigner to piss downwind unless we bribe him or threaten him with the hydrogen bomb. But that doesn't mean we should stop persuading. No, sir," he said with emphasis. "All it means is we have to learn to persuade a damn sight better. And if a man is well educated and he behaves like a gentleman, he can be much more persuasive, more useful. I am no gentleman myself, I grew like a weed, as the saying goes, so I can say these things without offense . . . And if the boy happens to come from this . . . uh . . . robust common stock, and he is European by blood, and if, as we intend, he does not break his ties with his own country . . . Well," he said diffidently, "maybe Mother and me, we'll have contributed something valuable . . ."

"Excuse me," Jack said. He had seen the man who was with Veronica come out from behind the wall, on his way past the bar toward the men's room. "I've just seen a friend," Jack said, standing up. He knew that Holt must be hurt by what must have seemed to him Jack's rudeness, but there was no time to lose. "Excuse me for a minute, please. I must say hello."

As unobtrusively as possible, Jack went along the edge of the dance floor, in the direction of the bar. Bresach didn't even look up as Jack passed him. Then Jack, with the dancers between him and

350

the Holt table, made his way back to where Veronica was sitting, alone, with a glass of champagne before her, and the bottle in a bucket of ice on a stand within reach. She was wearing a dress of cream brocade that left her shoulders bare and she had pulled her hair into a knot to one side. The whole effect was of sophistication and cool beauty that made her seem almost a stranger to Jack. Whatever anguish she had suffered earlier in the evening had been carefully erased from the cool, lovely face she was presenting to the world and her husband now.

"Veronica," Jack said in a low voice, as he came up to the table, "what the hell are you doing here?"

She looked up, startled. "Oh, Jack," she said. She glanced worriedly past him at the doorway through which her husband had gone. "Please. My husband will be back in a minute. I can't talk to you now."

"You've got to get out of here," Jack said. "Right now."

"Now, Jack," she said, "please don't start anything. You've hurt me enough tonight. I don't want to have to introduce you to my husband. We've been with some of his friends until now, and it's been bad enough, trying to answer their questions about people I know in Rome . . ."

"Listen to me," Jack said harshly, grasping her hand. "Bresach's over there. On the other side of the room."

"I don't believe you," Veronica said, nervously eyeing the doorway. "Robert never came to a place like this in his life."

"Well, he came tonight," Jack said. "I'm telling you this for your own good." Now he regretted the martinis and the champagne. He was not saying what he wanted to say. He didn't want to talk to her about Bresach. He wanted to talk to her about himself. He would have liked to be able to say, "Now let us go back to the moment this evening in the hotel when you kissed me and I counted to six and you said, 'Like human beings. With generosity!'" He had a sudden distasteful vision of himself as an onlooker and intermediary, the observer of others' passions, the agent of their hatreds and desires, the recipient of their confessions, the channel of their communications, but never the actor, never the giver, never wholly involved, always ready to break off. *Involved,* he remembered from the night with the Morrisons, *involved,* he remembered from the accusation of his wife.

"What am I going to do?" Veronica said. Her voice was low but almost hysterical. "I told my husband I wanted to go dancing. He didn't even want to come. And we haven't been here ten minutes. We have a whole bottle of champagne, and . . ."

She stopped. A little dry sound like a sob escaped from her. Her husband was coming through the door and making his way through the dancers. He came up to the table and stood there, smiling politely at Jack, waiting for Veronica to introduce him. Tucino and Bertha Holt danced by slowly.

"Yes?" Veronica's husband said, a little uncertainly, because Veronica hadn't said anything yet. He was a tall, wide-shouldered blond man, young and sharply handsome, with probing, careful blue eyes. "Veronica?" He looked steadily at Jack, the question mark at the end of his wife's name very marked.

"Oh," she said, breathily, "I'm sorry, Georg. I . . . This is Mr. Andrus. A . . . a friend of mine. He came over to congratulate me. My husband, Georg Strooker . . ."

"How do you?" Strooker said. He had a heavy voice and, for those three words, at least, no accent. He put out his hand. Jack shook it. The hand was hard and powerful.

"I . . . I hope you and Veronica will be very happy," Jack said. He felt confused. He had drunk too much that night, and too much had happened.

"Thank you very much," Strooker said formally. "I am sure we shall be." Now the accent of Zurich was detectable, but not comically. There was nothing light or comic about this large, hard young man with the sharp blond face and the glacial blue eyes. Strength through Joy Department, Jack thought, Swiss Division. Strooker did not sit down, nor did he ask Jack to sit down.

"I . . . I sent Mr. Andrus an announcement," Veronica said, too loudly. "From Zurich. He's . . ." She stopped, and Jack saw her eyes widen and her mouth tighten as she looked past him.

"Well, now," said Bresach's voice at Jack's shoulder. "Look who's here. With a new hair-do. Welcome to the Eternal City."

"Robert," Veronica said. She was trying to look sprightly and matter-of-fact, but even in saying Robert's name a note of desperation trembled in her voice. "I never expected to see you in a place like this."

"Great changes have taken place," Robert said, keeping his eyes fixed on Veronica, "since I saw you last . . ."

"Veronica," Strooker said, "will you introduce me to the gentleman, please."

"Yes, of course," Veronica said hastily. "I'm so sorry. I haven't come back to earth yet." She laughed falsely. "This is my husband, Robert, Georg Strooker . . ."

"Enchanted Georg, old man," Bresach said, without turning, still staring down at Veronica. "How was the wedding? Fun?"

Then Jack knew that Bresach was not going to let anyone off from anything. "Come on now," he whispered and took Bresach's arm. "Don't be a fool."

Bresach shook his arm loose, roughly. Strooker was watching him coldly, puzzled, suspicious, unpleasant.

"What I think," Bresach said, still staring at Veronica, "is that we all ought to be invited to drink to the health of the bride and groom." With a sudden movement, he reached past Jack and picked the champagne bottle out of the ice bucket. He stood with it in front of him, cradling it against his shirt front, not heeding the damp spot that was spreading on his shirt from the wet bottle. "I now dub thee Cuckold Premier," he said loudly and slowly. He raised the bottle high in the air above him and solemnly tilted it and poured the wine onto his head. It foamed in his hair and ran down into his collar. All this time he kept staring unblinkingly, his face expressionless, at Veronica.

"Stop that," Jack said sharply, getting ready to leap between Bresach and Strooker if Strooker made a move. But for the moment Strooker was too surprised to say or do anything. He just stood where he was, regarding Bresach doubtfully, trying to decide whether Bresach was a harmless drunk or somebody who would have to be dealt with harshly in a moment or two.

"Now, friend," Bresach said, turning to Strooker, "we must not omit you from the ceremony." Before Jack could make a move to stop him, he had raised the bottle once more and was pouring champagne over Strooker's neatly brushed blond hair.

"Robert!" Veronica screamed.

"I hereby dub thee Cuckold the Second," Bresach was saying. For a moment nobody moved. The music and the dancing had stopped, and the room had fallen into a deep hush. People all over the room sat still, expectant, watching Bresach and Strooker. Strooker himself appeared bemused, disbelieving, as he stood there looking mildly at Bresach, for a second or two seeming to be a willing participant in the ceremony. Then he moved so quickly that there was no time to save Bresach. Strooker's hand snapped up, slashing at Bresach's arm. The champagne bottle hurtled through the air and broke with an explosive noise on the dance floor. Then Strooker slapped Bresach twice, with a sharp, cracking noise, across the face. Bresach's glasses splintered and blood appeared immediately around his eyes. He made no gesture to defend himself. He merely stood there, grave and immobile, as though the whole scene were rehearsed and inevitable. Jack grabbed him around the shoulders and started to pull him away, but Strooker came after Bresach, punching him in the face. As Jack struggled clumsily in the narrow space between the tables to get Bresach out of harm's way and at the same time ward off Strooker's blows, Max magically appeared between the two men, grabbing at Strooker's arms. Strooker, who was by far the larger man, pulled one arm free and hit Max in the mouth. Max fell back against another table, which kept him from sinking to the floor. But the distraction had been enough. Waiters sprang upon Strooker and held him, making placating Italian noises. Holt and Tucino came up and led Max and Bresach away, while Jack stood in front of Strooker, prepared to fight him off if he broke away from the restraining arms and tried to go for Bresach again. The band had started to play loudly again and Veronica was weeping with her head down on the table.

Strooker suddenly stopped struggling. He said something in German, but the waiter didn't understand him. "All right," he said in English, "now let me go."

Warily, the waiters stepped back. Strooker was pale and his hair was soaked with champagne, but he went around the table and sat next to Veronica, without looking at her. He stared coldly out at the roomful of people who were watching him. His hand was bleeding from Bresach's broken glasses, but he paid no attention to the blood staining the wine-soaked tablecloth. "I believe we will need another bottle of champagne," he said to the headwaiter, who was standing nervously over him. Jack couldn't help but admire him at that moment.

"I'm terribly sorry," Jack said to Strooker, "about my friend. I imagine he's had a little too much to drink tonight."

"Yes," the man said flatly, "I imagine he had." Then he turned to Veronica. "Sit up," he said, without expression. "Do not be a child."

Slowly, her eyes stained with tears, she sat erect. "Please . . ." she whispered.

"Sit up," Strooker said evenly, staring out across the room, beginning her lifelong punishment.

354

There was nothing more to be said or done at that table, and Jack turned and went across the dance floor, conscious of all the eyes watching him.

*

Jack said he would take Bresach and Max home in a taxi. He had washed the blood off Bresach's face in the men's room of the night club and had made sure that no bits of glass had cut into his eyes. Bresach submitted to everything that was done to him with the tranced, passionless expression of a sleepwalker. He didn't say a word to Jack and he didn't say good-night to the Holts and Tucino and Barzelli, who were waiting on the street in front of the club to see if Bresach was all right before going home.

"It's too bad, it's too bad," Holt said worriedly. He was holding his wife's arm protectively, as though the fight in the night club had reminded him all over again how violent the world was and how frail and vulnerable was his wife. "What a way to end an evening like this." He shook his head sadly. "It's hardly the sort of thing you'd expect in a place like this. In Rome—in the best place in Rome. In America, of course, you expect it, it doesn't come as a surprise . . ."

"Oh, it's not so terrible," Barzelli said. She seemed ironically amused by the incident. "He's a young man. Young men fight. He'll be all right in the morning. All he needs is a new pair of glasses."

As Jack was bundling Bresach and Max into the cab he heard Tucino complaining, "One night Tasseti doesn't come, and this happens. Just when you need him. If Tasseti was here, I assure you nobody would have hit a guest of mine and got away with it."

"Why do you say guest of yours?" Barzelli asked. "Mr. Holt paid the bill."

"I was speaking in a wider sense," Tucino said, with dignity, as he walked toward his car.

In the taxi, the only sound for a while was Max sucking on his lip, which had been cut. Then Max said, "I didn't like that man's face. He looked like a commissar. That girl has my complete pity, having to live with a man like that."

He went back to sucking his cut lip.

All the way home, Bresach sat in the corner, his head against the window, weeping silently. There was nothing to be said, no comfort that he would accept, and the other two men held their peace and kept their heads averted as the taxi rattled through the narrow streets of the sleeping city.

When the taxi stopped, Max said to Jack, "You do not have to come up. I will take care of him. Come on, Robert," he said to the boy, with infinite gentleness.

Jack watched the two of them disappear into the dark, vaulted doorway, then told the driver of the cab to take him to his hotel. On the way, it occurred to him that Veronica and her husband were probably still at the night club, finishing their champagne, the man with the face of the commissar, as Max had put it, stonily continuing the punishment he had begun when he had told Veronica, "Sit up. Do not be a child."

Last chance, last chance, Jack thought. Tomorrow she will be in Athens and it will all be over.

For a moment, he hesitated. He even leaned forward to speak to the driver. He sat there, poised on the edge of the seat, uncomfortable, insecure, as the taxi took a corner fast. Then he sat back, thinking, No, let the poor girl rest in her insured Swiss bed.

Five minutes later he was at the door of his hotel.

27

There were two messages waiting for him at the hotel—both of them from Clara Delaney, both of them requesting Mr. Andrus to call Mrs. Delaney at the hospital, no matter what hour he got in.

On the way up to his room in the elevator, he kept staring at the messages, scrawled almost illegibly by the night operator of the hotel. *At the hospital, at the hospital,* he read over and over again. The wake, he thought guiltily. It amused me this night to pretend we were attending Delaney's wake.

Jack hurried down the silent, carpeted corridor toward his door. He unlocked it, leaving the key in the lock, and went directly to the telephone on the desk in the salon. The maid had left a single lamp on, next to the telephone, and the instrument gleamed in the tight cone of light in the shadowy room.

It took a long time to reach Clara Delaney at the hospital. The nurse on duty at the desk at the switchboard at first refused to call Delaney's room at that hour and only went to speak to Clara after a heated argument.

Jack looked at his watch. It was two thirty-five. While waiting, he thought of Sam Holt saying, "In Rome—in the best place in Rome," and the blood around Robert Bresach's eyes after Veronica's husband had broken his glasses.

Finally, there was a series of clicks on the phone, and Clara's voice, saying, "Hello."

"Clara," Jack said, "what is it? Has anything happened?"

"Who is this?" Clara asked. She sounded irritated and sleepy.

"Jack. You left a message for me to call. I just got in, and . . ."

"Oh," Clara said flatly. "Jack."

"Is Maurice all right?"

"About the same," Clara said. There was a curious dull tone in her voice, a lack of resonance, that made whatever she said sound hostile.

"I'm glad you finally decided to go and see him, Clara," Jack said, thinking, It's just like Clara—when she finally condescends to visit her invalid husband, she makes sure to destroy his night's sleep. "I'm sure it's the right thing to do." Now that he knew that Maurice hadn't taken a turn for the worse, Jack was sorry he had called. Whatever Clara had to say to him could be better said and more easily endured in the morning. "Look, Clara," he said, "it's awfully late. I'll be coming by the hospital tomorrow night as usual, and . . ."

"No you won't."

"What did you say, Clara?"

"I said you won't be coming by the hospital tomorrow," Clara said. "I won't let you into Maurice's room."

"What the hell are you talking about?"

"Maurice's friends are permitted to come and visit him," Clara said. "You're no friend."

Jack sighed. "Clara," he said, "obviously, whatever you have to say is very unpleasant, and it's too late now to be unpleasant. I'll speak to you in the morning . . ."

"You'll never speak to me again, " she said loudly. "Don't think I don't know what you've been doing to poor Maurice, while he's been lying helpless on his deathbed. He's told me everything."

"What have I been doing to poor Maurice?" Jack asked. He knew it would be better to hang up immediately and take his chances on

358

reaching Delaney directly in the morning, but he couldn't help being curious about this new attack of Clara's.

"Betraying him," Clara said harshly, her voice whistling in the telephone. "After everything he's done for you . . ."

"Now, Clara," Jack said evenly, "try to talk reasonably, like a woman in full possession of her senses. Just how am I betraying Maurice?"

"Don't patronize me," Clara said shrilly. "I'm through with all that. We had it all out tonight, Maurice and I, and we decided that from now on he's going to listen to me, he's going to let me take care of him. He realizes that all his life he's been too wild and thoughtless and trusting, and he's paying for it. Now," she said triumphantly, "if anybody wants anything from Maurice Delaney, they have to come to me first."

The born jailor, Jack thought, has finally reached the apex of her profession, she has been given the key to the jail. "I don't want anything from Maurice," Jack said, "and I don't want anything from you. But I'll come over right now and straighten this out."

"Don't bother," Clara said. "You won't get in. I'm at the door. From now on he's not going to waste his time and affection on people who stab him in the back . . ."

"All right, Clara," Jack said quietly, "I think that's enough for tonight. I'll try to figure this out in the morning. I'm going to bed now." He prepared to hang up.

"I know everything," she shouted, and Jack wondered how many patients the mad, dry voice was rousing into pain and anxiety in the sleeping hospital. "And now Maurice knows everything. Everything about his good friend, John Andrus, that he picked up out of the gutter when he was a dime-a-dozen actor in New York without a penny to his name. Don't think I don't know what's been going on behind his back. Don't think I don't have my sources of information. Hilda calls me three times a day, and I spoke to Sam Holt myself just ten minutes ago. You can't hide anything from me . . ."

Maybe, Jack thought, if Maurice is lucky, he will die before dawn and never have to listen to his wife's voice again.

"I'm not trying to hide anything, Clara," Jack said, keeping his voice low and calm in the hope that his example would have a soothing effect on her. He knew that she was in the same room as Maurice and he wondered what listening to that mad, wailing, night-time voice, with its burden of misery and hatred, was doing to the sick man.

"Do you deny that you tried to put Maurice on the shelf for a year?" Clara shouted, as loud as ever.

"I tried to convince him to save his life," Jack said. "I don't deny that."

"Save his life!" she screamed. "Don't you worry about his life! He'll outlive you and me." There was no testimony, medical or otherwise, Jack realized, that would ever make Clara believe that the vital, energetic man she had married was not immortal. In a crazy way it was a tribute to Delaney and a tribute to the power of her love for him. "You tried to get him out of the way for a year," she went on, "while you and that boy took over. You knew how much that boy's script meant to Maurice. You knew how he loved it. You knew it would put him right back on top again if he did it, so you schemed to take it away from him. And you took advantage of him while he was lying helpless to get him to agree. And you even had the gall to tell Maurice to his face that you told the boy not to let Maurice do it. Because you thought he was too weak to fight back. Do you deny that?"

"I don't want to talk to you any more, Clara," Jack said. "I don't think you're sane enough to listen to reason."

"Oh, I'm sane all right," she said wildly. "And that's just why you tried to hide all this from me. Because you didn't want to get found out. And it's not enough that you're trying to ruin Maurice's future—don't think I don't know how you and that crazy boy are plotting to change everything he's done on the picture, all the beautiful, subtle things, to spoil everything. This is Maurice's last chance, you sonofabitch, and you're trying to kill it, deliberately kill it, and you have the courage to come to his sickroom and pretend to be worried about him, pretend you're his friend, send him flowers."

I've got to hear her out, Jack thought, holding the receiver away from his ear. Let her get it all out, and then talk to Maurice . . .

"And I know why you're doing it, don't think I don't!" She ranted on. "You're jealous of him. You've always been jealous. Because he's successful and that's iron in your soul, his success. And because he slept with that whore of a wife of yours and you've never forgiven him . . ."

Jack heard Delaney's voice, at a distance, "Clara," Delaney said, "for Christ's sake, shut up."

"I'll shut up when I'm good and ready," Clara said, in full flood.

Then, again to Jack, "Don't think you're going to be able to squirm out of this. Maurice has already spoken to Holt. You're off the picture and that crazy boy, too. Tucino's taking over tomorrow morning and he's finishing it up, and you can go back where you belong, with the other clerks . . ."

"I want to talk to Maurice, please," Jack said.

"You'll never talk to him again as long as you live," she said.

"Oh, Christ—" It was Delaney's voice. "Give me the phone."

For a moment, there was only the sound of Clara's harsh breathing, then Delaney's voice came over the line, weary, toneless. "What do you want to say to me, Jack?" he asked.

"Is it true that you told Holt you wanted Tucino to finish the picture?" Jack asked.

"Yes."

"Listen carefully, Maurice," Jack said. "It's not for me I'm saying this, it's for you. I'm going to get Holt to keep Tucino away and let Bresach and me finish the picture for you. It hasn't got a chance any other way . . ."

Delaney sighed. "Jack," he said flatly, "if I hear you're anywhere near that set tomorrow I'm going to get out of bed and come down and get behind the camera myself."

"Maurice," Jack said, "this may be the last chance I get to talk to you—maybe the last chance *anybody'll* get to talk to you—so you'll have to listen to the truth for once. You've ruined yourself out of vanity, Maurice, and you're completing the ruin tonight. And your wife serves your vanity, because she *wants* you in ruins. Because then you come to her, because when you're sore and hurting, you're all hers. She told me that herself the third night I was in Rome, Maurice. You're a man teetering on the edge of a cliff, and everybody knows it. Everybody but you, Maurice. I've done everything I can to pull you back—there's still a chance you can be saved— There's still a lot to be saved. You proved it when I talked to you this evening in the hospital. Don't throw it away . . ."

"You finished?" Delaney said.

Jack sighed. "Yeah," he said, "I'm finished."

"Get out of town, Jack," Delaney whispered. "Fast."

Slowly, Jack put the telephone down. There was a little mechanical click and then the room was silent.

Lost, he thought. And I thought tonight I had rescued him. Jack remembered his self-satisfaction that evening and shook his head sadly. There was one more thing to be done. He picked up the phone again and asked for Holt's number. He'll be awake, Jack thought. Tonight everybody is awake.

"Sam," he said, when he heard Holt's voice, "I suppose you know why I'm calling."

"Yes," Holt said. "Mrs. Delaney did me the honor of telephoning me fifteen minutes ago."

"I guess that winds it all up then," Jack said.

"Not necessarily," Holt said. "I'd like to respect Maurice's wishes as much as possible, Jack, but there're many other people involved and a great deal of money. If you'll agree, we'll continue just as we are now, with you as director, and hope that Maurice finally will listen to reason."

"No, Sam," Jack said. "He won't listen to reason and I won't continue. He got me down here and he's given the signal to go. And I'm going."

"I understand," Holt said. "I'm terribly sorry. Is there anything I can do for you?"

"I'm going to get the first plane out of here I can," Jack said. "Will you get hold of Bresach and explain it all to him?"

"Of course, Jack."

"If you ever come through Paris, look me up, Sam. I'll take you and Bertha to dinner."

"I certainly will," Holt said. "You can depend on that. What time is your plane?"

"I think there's one around one o'clock I can get on."

"I'll have your check at your hotel during the morning," Holt said.

Jack laughed ruefully. "You're not getting much for your money, are you, Sam?"

"I'm in the oil business," Holt said. "I'm used to gambling. And losing."

"Are you going to go on with the deal with Delaney and Tucino?" Jack asked, curiously.

There was a long pause on the line. "I honestly don't believe so, Jack," Holt said. "I guess I'll stick to the oil business. I seem to be able to handle it better."

"Uh-huh," Jack said. "Well—take care of my friend Delaney for me, Sam."

"I'm afraid there's not much I can do there," Sam said quietly. "Or anybody. Good night, Jack."

"Good night." Jack put down the phone.

Finito, he thought. In my best Italian.

He looked around the empty room, dark except for the cone of light from the desk lamp, shining on the telephone. It was cheerless and cold, falsely luxurious, a place for travelers, for loneliness and lost hopes. A bottle of Scotch, half-filled, stood on a table near the door, with an opened bottle of soda and some glasses. Jack poured himself a shot with a little of the soda. The soda was flat, but it didn't make any difference. He sipped at the drink, standing up, still wearing his coat with the collar turned up.

Friendships end, he thought, love dies. With a mechanical click.

He didn't feel like going to sleep. Still holding the glass, he went into the bedroom and put on the light and got out his two bags and began to pack. Pack it all away, he thought, pack up the city. He threw the 1928 Baedeker (*and there await the sunset*) into the bottom of the bag which he had once gripped to use as a weapon against Bresach's knife. Then he tossed in Catullus (*Look, where the youths are coming . . .*) and rifled the drawers of the bureau and carelessly piled shirts in on top of the books. He noticed dark wet drops on the shirts and realized his nose was bleeding, not much, but bleeding. He held a handkerchief up to his face and drank some more and continued packing.

Pack it all up.

In this room, in the middle hours of the night, death had touched him, had fingered him over, had whispered a dubious warning, had counted over for him lost friends, suicides, the fallen in battle, those who had died of disappointment or injustice or debauchery or merely because it had been their time to die. Carrington, Despière, Davies, the men who had played poker while London was burning, Myers, Kutzer—that mortal assembly, answering, "Here," to the cry of memory, "Here," from the graves in California and Africa and France.

He drank some more and pushed the bloody handkerchief against his face and laid the three suits into the ingenious, patented, useless American valise, like three ghosts in the Roman night, and thought of the dreams he had dreamt in this bed, of the girl he had loved there, of the knife and the crumpled sheet, of the moment when, for a second or two which he never would be able to forget or deny to himself, he had cherished the idea of dying.

He had not died in Rome. Delaney had come close, and perhaps would come closer. Despière had died, although outside the city. Despière, whose soul had recognized the city as he had come through the Flaminia Gate for the first time, and who had always been ready to celebrate and pay for his joy in the morning.

Drink and bleed and pack it up.

Where was the gypsy singing tonight? What was his wife, that pleasurable woman, as Despière had once put it, doing at this very moment?

He thought of women lying in their beds this night. His wife, secure, he thought, in her love for him, but with her own secrets, sleeping neatly, who would welcome him home and say, as she did each time he had been away, "Did you enjoy yourself, *chéri?*" What if he asked her, "Did you enjoy yourself, *chérie?*" and she answered him truly. Would he be able to bear that?

Veronica, in her marriage bed, that full, ecstatic body, newlywed passion, after whatever cunning explanations she had devised to allay her husband's suspicions. The cuckold's champagne dry now on that well-brushed Alpine head.

"Oh, God," he said bitterly and went into the salon and poured himself another drink.

Bertha Holt, ladylike, soaked in alcohol, under her husband's faithful, loving eye, happily dreaming of baby carriages, nurses, bibs, diapers, waiting for rich Italian loins to produce the infant who was to save her and give a meaning to her life.

Clara Delaney, demented on a cot in the dark hospital room, in full fierce possession of the ruins around her, dissolving what was left of her husband in the acid of her love.

Barzelli, whose image floated through the dreams of countless men each night throughout the world, asleep, remorseless, casual, powerful, amused, in her gilt Appian palace, handling love and money and fame with the rough hard-headedness of a peasant woman handling a brood of noisy, beautiful children.

Carlotta, who had somehow learned to conquer herself, who had found that she was meant to be happy after forty, who had lived for love or sex, or whatever combination of the two she could grasp in her hunger, and who had emerged into tranquillity, against all odds . . . Alone, who had not wanted to be alone . . .

The lines of love, webbing the night, leading where? To Bresach with the blood around his eyes, to Despière, dead for a salary, to Holt and the burden of his wife's bottle, on the hunt for other men's children, to Delaney, caught in the cage of his wife's jealousy, cut off from his friends, cut off from the woman in whose arms he had lain in joy and innocence, and who had, by his report, made him flower through the long nights of the Italian winter. The lines of love, leading in Jack's case, to his divided life, three wives, triple anguish, doubt, disappointment, anger, hatred, routine. "You know, you haven't made love to me for more than two weeks." The soft, accusing voice at the airport. (*Why didn't she shut the gypsy up?*)

The clutch of women. Delaney's words.

Agony everywhere.

What was the anodyne? Work, ambition . . . ? Holt had worked, Maurice Delaney was still ambitious. And as far as the worth of what they had accomplished—who was there to say that in some eternal scale of values, the two or three good movies that Delaney had made when he was young did not more than balance Holt's thousand oil wells? In the silent, totalizing hours of the night of man, was Holt assuaged by the thought of his oil, was Delaney cured by the memory of two or three beautiful hours of film he had created in another age?

Despière, dead in Africa, had been ambitious in his own way, had worked, had fought. That specialist and almost-survivor of wars, who could only say, much later, as he moved up for the last time, to the sound of the guns, "It is all shit on both sides."

Death, death, the voices had whispered to him. The song the sirens sing in Rome, making oblivion alluring, nothingness a delight. Tied to no mast, his ears not stoppered by wax, he had listened, had reached out his hand in the direction of the music.

It was incredible that it had happened to him. Not for that healthy and responsible man, John Andrus, the sly look at the open sixth-story window, at the full bottle of sleeping pills. Not for him the envy of the dead who had, one way or another, solved their problems, who no longer had to measure themselves daily against what they had been when they were young, no longer had to test themselves at each move, with every decision, for decline and compromise.

Only it had been for him.

In the past two weeks, something had happened to him that had never happened before—he had begun to long to die.

There had been many reasons for it—the wanton blow on the steps of the hotel as he arrived, to tell him that he had been singled out of all the men in Rome that night for punishment or warning ("That's what they sang when the *Doria* went down" and ladylike laughter in the taxicab), the flow of blood, the stained jacket (Whose was it—the murderer's or his victim's?)—the bull hanging above the doorway—the boy with the knife—the dream of the bald men in aprons dismembering his own body in the forest—the German priests frustrating his love, making his love disappear—the names of the dead in the movie theatre and that slender boy who had been himself and for all intents and purposes was also dead—(*"Eh, bien,"* Despière had written, himself racked by premonitions, "the worst is over. You must not be surprised. In a murderous world it is normal to be murdered.")—Delaney toppling into the gravel at the riding ring, unrescued, unrescuable . . . The right and left hand of Christ at the Last Judgment. The Companions of the Right Teat under Fortune's whip. The First and Last and Only Important Judgment.

Jack shook his head. Don't inquire further. There were many reasons, but whatever they were, now he was standing alone in a city of tombs and memorials, in a cold, dark room which belonged to no one and welcomed no one, and it was after midnight and long before dawn, and he was struggling with the feeling that perhaps it would have been better if he had never been dragged out of the burning building, if Wilson, in the wild flight down the hospital corridors with the wheelchair, had never found the colonel's office.

He turned on the light of the chandelier and poured himself another drink and went over to the mirror hanging on the wall and coldly examined himself. God's monkey, strapped onto the universal vivisection table. The mirror is the knife.

He became aware of a curious sound. It was low and hoarse and animal-like, rising and falling, the lament of a beast in agony. It was coming from the street, and Jack moved away from the mirror and pulled back the curtains and stepped out onto the little balcony. He looked down. A bareheaded man was standing with his coat open and his arms flung up, in the middle of the dark, empty street, shouting, the same words over and over, to the sky, to the dark, shuttered windows, to the blind walls of the city of Rome. Near him, two prostitutes had stopped to watch him. At first Jack couldn't make out what the man was saying, or even what language he was using. Then he heard, in English, the words thickened by drink and terror, "Oh, God, I'm all alone. Oh, God, isn't there anyone to help me? Oh, my God . . ."

One of the prostitutes laughed. Her laughter floated up, pure and girlish, in the slot between the buildings.

For a moment, looking at the solitary American figure with the arms upflung and the coat flapping in the wind, Jack was sure that it was the drunk who had hit him the first night in Rome. Then the man put his arms down, and, moaning incoherently, staggered along the middle of the street until he reached a lamppost. In the light, Jack could see more clearly. It was not his man.

"Oh, God," the man lamented, wailing, staggering now onto the sidewalk and against the dark walls of a building, "Oh, God, I'm all alone. . . . Won't anyone help me?"

Then he stopped moving for a second or two. He ran his fingers through his hair, took a deep breath, looked around him slyly. Then he buttoned his coat briskly and, head back, with his arms swinging at his sides like a soldier on parade, walked quickly to the corner and disappeared.

Jack blinked. The whole thing had happened so quickly, had been so bizarre and fleeting, that it was hard to believe that it hadn't been an apparition, a waking dream. For a moment longer, Jack stared at the corner around which the man had disappeared, wondering if he still heard on the restless night wind that shifted the curtains uneasily behind him, the echo of the lamenting voice, calling, "Alone . . . alone . . ."

The prostitute laughed again, then the two women hurried away.

He went back into the room, closing the window behind him. He paced around the carpeted room, glass in hand.

The night was harsh and dangerous. Cries of agony were uttered in the streets. The room had too many mirrors and was saddened by a regiment of memories. The gilt hotel clock ticked too loudly over the doorway and made intolerable suggestions. The drunk's, "Alone," was a presence in the room, a judgment, a threat.

Jack knew he could not spend this night in these cold rooms. Suddenly he remembered the sound of the woman's laughter from the street. Now, irrationally, he was sure that he recognized her, that it was the German with the red shoes. He started to go toward the door. That's the way to end it all up, he thought, end up Rome in the arms of the German whore. Why not? To this bitter voyage put a bitter end. At least he would not spend the rest of the night alone.

Then he stopped. The word. It had been used once before that night. "—that whore of a wife—" Clara's demented voice.

Even better, Jack thought, vengefully. Why leave the building? We have a whore in the family.

He went to the phone. "Miss Carlotta Lee, please," he said, cunningly sounding like a reasonable and responsible man, so as to keep his reputation unclouded at the telephone switchboard. He looked at the clock. Ten minutes past three. Here's a test of a divorce, he thought, waking an ex-wife at ten after three in the morning.

"Yes?" Carlotta said. Her voice was drowsy.

"Carlotta," Jack said, "it's ten minutes past three. May I come and see you?"

There was silence for a moment. Then she said, "The number is three twenty-four. The door will be open."

But then there was no revenge at all. It wasn't that way at all.

They lay side by side in the dark on the wide bed. The room was small, enclosed, the warm air fragrant with perfumes he thought he had forgotten and which now swept him back to rooms which he had left long ago.

They had made love gravely, like people who had sworn to fulfill a solemn commandment. They had made love slowly, lingeringly. They had made love tenderly, as though each of them were conscious of a precious secret fragility in themselves and in each other that had to be protected. They had made love obsessively, as though the years had built up in them a riotous hunger that no single act of love could ever possibly assuage. They had made love with the comfort and knowledgeableness of familiars and the delight and shock of a first confrontal. They were at home and in a foreign land, lovers and strangers, ecstatic and matter-of-fact. Finally, they had made love with joy and forgiveness and long, absolving pleasure in each other.

She lay in the crook of his arm. Gently, he touched her. The skin was wonderfully soft. Flesh, he remembered from the afternoon in the chapel, flesh.

She sighed drowsily, happily. We are content in our flesh, he thought, we are blessed in our flesh, we are merry and holy in our flesh, we celebrate in our flesh. We accept the knowledge and certainty of death in our flesh, we are ready to pay with our flesh for the joy of the night in the light of the morning.

God's monkey, he thought. But a fair proportion of God's experiments deal with love, pleasure, understanding. If there is a bargain here, it is not an unreasonable one.

They fear shame, he remembered, *and only pair at night and secretly, nor do they then rejoin the herd but first bathe in the river*

. . . Tonight, he thought, amused, we have paired at night and secretly, nor are we rejoining the herd. We are approaching the high level of conduct of the elephant. *Consequently,* he remembered, *when the moon is new they go down to the rivers and there solemnly bathe, and after having thus saluted the planet they return to the woods . . .*

The moon is new tonight, he thought, my river is the Tiber.

He moved his hand to her breast, then down along her ribs and hips. Her body was no longer the magnificent young woman's body of the California mornings. The lines had thickened, the contours were much fuller, she would always look too heavy, a little ungraceful, in fashionable clothes, and he knew that she would never regard herself in the mirror without a twinge of regret for her lost beauty. But that abundant, practiced body had this night given him an intensity of pleasure, a sense of completion, that he had never felt before.

"It isn't like making love," he whispered into her ear, "it's like taking in the harvest."

She chuckled. "There is a Spanish saying," she said. "Men pretend otherwise, but they really like fat women, sweet wines, and the music of Tschaikovsky."

They laughed together, under the bedsheet. The laughter was sensual, the healthy laughter of old friends, good lovers, forgivers, enjoyers. It dispelled ghosts, took the pain out of memory, threw a reasonable human light on fears and premonitions.

"Fat woman," he said, stroking her shoulder comfortably.

"I knew this had to happen," she said. "Somehow, sometime."

"Yes," he said. Now that it had happened, it seemed inevitable to him, too.

"We couldn't let the hatred stand," she said.

They lay quietly for a while. "You're leaving tomorrow?" she asked.

"Yes."

"Are you going to make love to your wife tomorrow?"

"Yes."

"Will you think of me?"

"No. I will think of my wife." At that moment he knew that he desired his wife more than he had ever desired her before, and knew that he would take her into his arms with love and delight, and that he would cherish her. What had begun in his mind as an act of vengeance, Carlotta, in her lavish womanhood, had turned into an act of compassion and forgiveness. Forgiving her had finally brought down the wall that Jack had erected between him and love, between him and the belief in love, the wall that he had started building the night when London was on fire and the young pilot had said, "She was a little old, maybe thirty, but stacked and artful."

He kissed her gently. He didn't tell Carlotta what he was thinking, but she was moved by the gentleness of the kiss and smiled at him. "Are you pleased this happened?"

"Yes," he said. "I have more reasons to be grateful to you than you know."

"I'm glad," she said. Then, after a pause, "Are we ever going to make love again, you and I?"

"I suppose so," he said. It is no longer necessary, he thought. But he didn't tell her that. Instead, he said, "Some time. Some town."

She chuckled softly, a little sadly. "Some time," she whispered. "Some town."

In the morning, he shopped for gifts for his wife and children, using the ten-thousand-lire note the Boston lady had thrust on him as she bundled the drunk into the taxicab. He walked lightly down the busy sunlit streets of Rome, examining the shining display windows. Although he hadn't slept more than an hour during the night, he was clear-eyed and untired, and he enjoyed taking a long time among the scarves and sweaters of the woman's shop and among the puppets and model automobiles of the toy counters. He had Holt's check in his pocket and he felt rich, as one should in Rome, and bought extravagant presents.

He cashed two hundred and fifty dollars in travelers' checks at his hotel and put the lire in an envelope to give to Guido at the airport. The grateful sacrifice to the gods of the locality, he thought, gumming the envelope. He called no one during the morning, not Carlotta or Delaney or Holt or Veronica or Bresach. It all ended last night, he told himself.

His plane was due to leave at one and Guido drove him out along the Naples road in silence. Guido looked sedate and sorrowful in the brilliant noon sunlight. Jack felt that Guido liked him and was sorry that the two weeks were over. He will think of me kindly, Jack thought, when he arrives in Toulon to visit the woman in whose vineyard he worked during the war.

At the entrance to the airport, he gave Guido the envelope and asked him not to open it until he got back to Rome. Guido nodded gravely, his dark eyes emotional, and they shook hands. Jack waited outside the terminal until he saw Guido spurt away back toward Rome. Then he followed the porter with his bags into the building. He had his bags weighed and his ticket validated and was just about to go through the door marked *Dogana,* when he saw Bresach hurrying through the entrance. Bresach wasn't wearing glasses and his eye sockets were a grievous mess of ugly little cuts and he peered short-sightedly around until he saw Jack. He hurried over.

"I wanted to say good-bye," he said, without preliminary. "Holt told me you were leaving. Among other things."

"How's it going at the studio?" Jack asked.

Bresach laughed sourly. "Chaos. Everybody's yelling at everybody else. There're meetings everywhere. Even in the men's rooms. Stiles is drinking again. Tucino is roaring. He fired me twice this morning. Nobody has shot a foot of film. I have a feeling they won't finish this picture until next Christmas. Ah—the hell with it." He shrugged. "I have something for you." He reached into the pocket of his coat and took out the clasp knife, closed. "Here, take this," he said. He sounded bitter and unhappy.

Jack took the knife. He hefted it once and slid it into his topcoat pocket.

"I should've used it," Bresach said, his face twitching. "On someone. Maybe on myself."

"Don't be a fool," Jack said tolerantly.

"I should've killed her last night," Bresach said. "Veronica. Nobody should be allowed to go unpunished for the things she's done to me. To a man who loved her the way I did . . . Instead," he said, "I pulled that idiotic gag with the champagne . . ."

Jack smiled. "Actually," he said, "it was kind of funny. And maybe it was good for the marriage. It started it off on a realistic basis."

"And then I let myself be led off like a baby," Bresach said with bitter self-loathing. "Two weeks ago, a week ago, I'd have stayed there and fought, even if they'd killed me . . . And that's the worst thing. You know why I let Max take me away?"

"Why?"

"Because even as I was standing there, even as that bastard was hitting me, I was thinking, 'If I fight, they'll give me to the police, they'll lock me up, maybe they'll kick me out of Italy, I'll never get a chance to finish the picture, do my own . . .' "

"Well," Jack said, "that might be true."

"I've turned cozy, I've turned careful," Bresach said, his face pale and tortured and the raw little scars looking redder than ever against the white skin. "One little whiff of success, one tiny puff, and look what it's done to me. A month from now I'll laugh at the whole thing. Just like everybody else. And it turned out it was all for nothing. It serves me right. I deserved it. In five years what sort of man will I be? What the hell is going to happen to me?"

"You'll survive," Jack said. "Just like everybody else."

"Jack . . ." Bresach sounded hesitant, uncomfortable. "If I ever need you again—will you help me?"

Jack looked thoughtfully at the boy, standing there in the ruins of his hopes, near-sighted and in despair, with the ugly little wounds around his eyes. He had a surprising desire to cry. "Sure," he said. "Call me. I'm easy to find." He tried to smile at him.

"In the meanwhile," Bresach said, "have you got any advice for me?"

Jack ran his fingers through his hair, taking time, trying to find the one word that would help. Then he remembered Carrington, that marvelous man, and what he had told the young actor who had come to him and asked for advice on how to be a good actor.

"Be delighted," Jack said. He touched the boy's shoulder with his hand, then went through the door into customs, leaving Bresach standing there alone.

Fifteen minutes later, the plane took off. It rose above the green of the race track, banked across the winding river, with its reflection of small, fleeing white clouds. Jack was at the window. He bent over for a last look. Below him, under the mild Mediterranean sky, the lovely city, busy and golden, glittered in the sun.

The plane straightened in its course. Jack leaned back in his chair, and unhooked the safety belt as the plane climbed north toward the Alps.

Well, he thought, I have saluted the planet.

ABOUT THE AUTHOR

Novelist, short-story writer and dramatist, IRWIN SHAW was born in New York City in 1913 and received his education in the public-school system of Brooklyn and at Brooklyn College, where he played on the varsity football team.

His first professional writing was for daytime serials for the radio. In 1936 his famous anti-war play, *Bury the Dead,* was produced; this was followed by another play, *The Gentle People,* which was produced in 1939. His short stories have appeared in *The New Yorker, Colliers* and other national magazines. He has written many plays for the screen. During World War II, he saw service in Africa, England, France and Germany, first as a private and later as a warrant officer. His widely acclaimed first novel, *The Young Lions,* was published in 1948, and in 1950 a collection of his short stories was issued under the title of *Mixed Company. The Troubled Air,* his second novel, published in 1951, examined the American conscience in mid-century. His most recent novel, *Lucy Crown* (1956) dealt with the emotional crisis of a woman past her youth and the consequences to herself, her husband and her son. A book of short stories, *Tip on a Dead Jockey,* was published in 1957.

From his home in the Swiss Alps he travels frequently to London, Rome, Paris, the Basque coast of France, and his native country.